LAST Strand

AN ELEMENTAL ASSASSIN BOOK

JENNIFER ESTEP

Last Strand

Copyright © 2021 by Jennifer Estep

Print book ISBN: 978-1-950076-06-2
eBook ISBN: 978-1-950076-05-5

Cover Art © 2021 by Tony Mauro
Interior Formatting by Author E.M.S.

Fonts: *CCAltogether Ooky* and *CCAltogether Ooky Capitals* by Active Images, used under Standard License; *Times New Roman* by Monotype Typography, used under Desktop License; *Trajan Pro* by Carol Twombly/Adobe Systems Inc., used under EULA.

Published in the United States of America

Last Strand

AN ELEMENTAL ASSASSIN BOOK

JENNIFER ESTEP

To all the fans of the Elemental Assassin series who wanted more stories, this one is for you.

To my mom and my grandma—for everything.

To myself—for doing things my way.

❈ 1 ❈

"I've always wanted to rob a bank."

Finnegan Lane, my foster brother, made that pronouncement in an exceptionally bold, gleeful tone. A wide grin stretched across his tan, handsome face, and a conspiratorial gleam brightened his green eyes, further indicating his interest in committing a serious felony.

"But you work at a bank," I pointed out. "Why would you ever want to rob one?"

"Plotting an elaborate heist. Liberating trays of diamonds, stacks of gold bars, and piles of cash from a supposedly impenetrable vault right out from under the noses of our enemies. Executing a complicated, convoluted plan that goes completely off the rails but somehow still works out at the very last second." Finn's grin widened, and he rubbed his hands together in anticipation. "C'mon, Gin. This is the stuff that *dreams* are made of."

I snorted. "I think you need some different dreams. You know, ones that are a lot less dangerous and illegal."

"And ruin all the fun? Absolutely *not*." He winked at me.

"Besides, we all know that Dangerous and Illegal is my middle name."

"And here I thought it was Alexander," I drawled.

Finn ignored my teasing and checked his reflection in the rearview mirror, making sure that his walnut-brown hair was still perfectly, artfully in place. Then he straightened his green tie and smoothed his silvery suit jacket, both of which were also still perfectly, artfully in place. Apparently, looking good was another key component of my foster brother's bank-robbing fantasy.

Someone deliberately cleared his throat, and Finn and I both glanced over our shoulders at Owen Grayson, my significant other. With his blue-black hair, violet eyes, and tan skin, Owen was just as handsome as Finn was, albeit in a rougher, less polished way, especially given his slightly crooked nose and the thin white scar that slashed across his chin.

Still, my heart always skipped a beat at the sight of him, and my gaze roamed over the navy jacket that stretched across his broad shoulders before following the line of his gray tie down his chest. Mmm-mmm-mmm. Perhaps I'd been hanging around Finn too long, but few things appealed to me more than Owen Grayson in a snazzy suit. Or perhaps I just liked his buttoned-up look because I knew about all the hard, defined muscles that lay underneath the fine fabric, sort of like knowing what was hidden beneath the wrapping paper on a Christmas present. Well, unwrapping Owen out of one of his many suits was *always* a treat for me.

"Um, I hate to point out the obvious, Finn, but you've actually been in a bank robbery before," Owen rumbled.

Finn kept his grin fixed on his face, but his jaw clenched, as though he were grinding his teeth to hold the happy expression in place.

Several months ago, Deirdre Shaw, Finn's long-lost mother, had swanned back into Ashland, chock-full of fake apologies and hidden agendas. Supposedly, Deirdre had wanted to make up for lost time, but she'd really been plotting to rob First Trust, the bank where Finn worked. Thanks to me, Deirdre's heist had gone sideways, but not before she had revealed her true, duplicitous nature and had brutally tortured her own son with her elemental Ice magic.

Finn's longing to finally get to know his mother had been far more precious than any diamonds, gold bars, or cash in the First Trust vault, and Deirdre's cold, cruel, calculated betrayal had utterly destroyed that longing—along with a good chunk of Finn's heart. Perhaps even worse, he'd had to kill his mother to stop her from killing me, something that still filled my own heart with guilt and grief.

Owen's gaze flicked back and forth between Finn and me. He grimaced, realizing that he'd hit about a dozen different nerves. "Sorry. I wasn't thinking. I didn't mean…" His deep voice trailed off, and he grimaced again. "Sorry."

Finn waved his hand, indicating that all was forgiven, but his grin had vanished, and his eyes had dimmed. My heart squeezed tight at his obvious pain—pain that I was partially responsible for, even if Finn claimed otherwise.

Someone else deliberately cleared his throat, breaking the awkward silence. "I don't know why we're talking about robbing a bank. Technically, we have every right to be here. Well, Gin does."

Silvio Sanchez, my personal assistant, spoke up from his position beside Owen in the backseat. Silvio was about twenty years older than us thirtysomethings, and his gray hair and eyes gleamed in the morning sunlight filtering in through the windows, as did his bronze skin. My assistant was also dressed in a suit, although his was a dark, subdued gray, compared to Finn's lighter, brighter, silvery threads. Still, Silvio looked just as polished as my brother and my significant other did.

"After all, the account was left to Gin," Silvio continued, pointing out facts the way he so often did. "So she has every right to access the funds. *If* she ever decides to get out of the car."

He raised his eyebrows at me in a silent, chiding question. I sighed, faced forward, and looked out through the windshield again.

The four of us were sitting in Finn's silver Aston Martin, which was parked on the third level of a garage down the street from the Bellum Bank. Normally, going to a bank would be no big deal, but the people flowing in and out of the doors were far more dangerous and devious than your usual bankers and customers.

That was the problem.

The Bellum Bank was no ordinary financial institution. Instead of being a place for regular folks to cash checks and apply for mortgages, the Bellum Bank catered to Ashland's underworld. Even criminals needed somewhere to deposit their money, as well as store their other ill-gotten goods, and the Bellum Bank was a one-stop shop for shady financial transactions, money laundering, and more.

And now I had an account there.

Well, technically, it wasn't *my* account but rather one that had been left to me by Fletcher Lane, Finn's dad and my foster father and assassin mentor. I had no idea how much money was actually in the account. All I knew was that Fletcher had wanted me to use the funds to destroy my uncle, Mason Mitchell—something that I was eager to do.

After months of investigating, I had finally discovered that my dear uncle Mason was the head of the Circle, a secret society that was responsible for much of the crime and corruption in Ashland, as well as so much misery, heartache, and pain in my own life.

Among his many, many crimes, Mason had tortured his own twin brother, my biological father, Tristan Mitchell, to death for daring to question his leadership of the Circle. Then, several years later, Mason had ordered Fire elemental Mab Monroe to murder my mother, Eira Snow, and my older sister, Annabella. Mab had tried to murder me too, along with my younger sister, Detective Bria Coolidge, although we'd both managed to escape the Fire elemental's wrath.

A couple of weeks ago, Mason had finally crept out of the shadows he'd been hiding in for so long. My uncle had dropped all sorts of nasty familial bombshells on me—including the fact that Fletcher used to work for him. That revelation had done the most damage to my heart, and I was still struggling to make peace with all the horrible things my beloved mentor had done on Mason's orders.

But Fletcher had eventually gotten out from under Mason's thumb, and he'd stolen a good chunk of the Circle's money—money that Mason desperately wanted back. Despite my uncle's best efforts, I was the one who'd found Fletcher's black ledger, which had been hidden away for years. And now, here I was, sitting outside the bank where the money was supposedly being kept.

Only one problem: I was too afraid to go inside and actually *get* said money.

I might be Gin Blanco, the assassin the Spider, the supposed queen of the Ashland underworld, but I'd been on so many wild-goose chases over the past few months, with clues that only led to more clues, that part of me didn't want to go inside the bank and have to solve yet another mystery Fletcher had left from beyond his grave.

I couldn't bear being disappointed again.

Not now, when I finally knew who Mason was. When I was *this close* to taking my revenge on him. When I was within a stone's throw of killing the bastard for all the terrible things he'd done, for robbing Bria and me of the normal, happy life we should have had with our father, mother, and sister. That we *would* have had, if not for Uncle Mason's twisted need for power and control.

"Silvio's right." Finn cut into my dark thoughts. "Are we going to sit here all day, or are we actually going to go inside and get our loot?"

His green eyes brightened, and he rubbed his hands together again, as though his fingers were itching with excitement at the thought of how much money might be in Fletcher's mystery account.

"Gin's loot," Silvio corrected in a mild tone.

"What good is loot if you don't share it with the people you love?" Finn quipped right back to my assistant.

Owen snorted. "Why do I think that's your not-so-subtle way of asking Gin for the biggest share of the money?"

Finn grinned again. "Well, I'm not saying that Gin loves me the most, but I *do* have the advantage of having known her the longest. That's got to count for something, especially when it comes to loot. Right, Sis?" He started batting his eyelashes at me, like a debutante flirting with a potentially rich husband at a cotillion.

"Oh, please," I replied. "You only call me *Sis* when you want something."

He kept batting his eyelashes. "I have never been shy when it comes to money. Besides, don't I deserve a little *something-something* for helping you investigate the Circle these past few months? Don't we all? Especially after we rescued you from Mason's creepy cemetery. Why, he would have crushed you like a bug with those broken tombstones if we hadn't driven him and his men away."

This time, I was the one who grimaced. Even though my wounds were healed, sharp stings still pricked my skin, and my entire body ached with remembered pain. Mason had used his Stone magic to explode tombstone after tombstone and pelt me with the resulting rubble, torturing me just like he had my father all those years ago. My uncle would have literally Stoned me to death if my friends hadn't shown up to help me—and if my nemesis hadn't risked his life to save mine.

"I think what Finn is trying to say is that it was *our pleasure* to come to your rescue for a change, Gin, instead of you saving us like you have so many times before." Silvio shot my brother a pointed look.

"Oh, yeah, sure," Finn replied in a breezy tone. "That too. But I'm mostly thinking about the money."

His grin widened, and he rubbed his hands together for a third time. A welcome laugh bubbled up in my chest and tumbled past my lips. I could always count on my brother to lighten even my darkest mood—and distract me from my painful memories.

"All right," I said, giving in to the inevitable. "Let's go see what Fletcher had in the bank."

Finn *whoop-whooped!* and opened the driver's door. I smiled and opened my own door.

The four of us got out of the car, went over to the low stone wall that cordoned off this level of the garage from the open air beyond, and stared down at the street below.

It was just after nine o'clock, and people were trudging along the sidewalks, veering off into office buildings to go to work. Still more folks were sitting in cars, waiting for red lights to turn green so they could head to their own buildings and work. I looked past the foot and vehicle traffic and stared at the Bellum Bank, which dominated this part of downtown.

The bank was housed in an enormous five-story building that featured wide gray stone steps, classic Greek columns, and intricate carvings. Instead of being set back from the street, the Bellum Bank was unusual in that it was in the center of things, with both foot and vehicle traffic flowing all the way around it. A broad street led up to the front of the building before curving into a large roundabout. From there, cars could go either right or left, veering around the bank, or circle the roundabout and head back in the direction they'd come from.

A white marble statue, shaped like a woman with a bucket dangling from one hand and her other fist raised high in victory, stood in the middle of the grassy park in the center of the roundabout. Marisol Patton was famous for sounding the alarm and starting a bucket brigade that had stopped a fire from raging through downtown Ashland in the early 1900s.

Marisol was one of several historic statues in this part of downtown, and my mother, Eira, used to bring Annabella, Bria, and me here in the summer to eat ice cream and play in the grass in the statue's shadow. My heart twinged at the happy memory, but I shoved it away. I needed to be sharp and focused right now, not dull and melancholy about the past.

Silvio glanced down at the tablet in his hands. My trusty assistant never went anywhere without his electronics. "Everything is the same as before on the traffic cameras that Bria helped me access through the police department's website. People and vehicles moving around like normal. Nothing unusual, and no sign of any bad guys." He paused. "Well, other than the ones going into the bank, but I suppose that can't be helped."

No, it couldn't, which was one of the many problems with our potential "bank robbery," as Finn had dubbed it. As soon as I stepped into the bank, someone was bound to recognize me. Criminals loved to gossip as much as everyone else did, and it wouldn't be too long before news that Gin Blanco had visited the Bellum Bank got back to Mason. My uncle was smart enough to put two and two together and realize that Fletcher had hidden the Circle's money at the bank. And then Mason would come for that money—and for me too.

Of course, I'd thought about wearing a disguise, but knowing how paranoid Fletcher was, the old man had probably set up the account so that only I could access it, and I didn't want to risk not being able to get the money. No, I needed to go in as myself, transfer the funds to my own account at First Trust, and get out as quickly as possible.

"Let's do this," I said. "Silvio, stay here in the garage and monitor the traffic cameras. Owen, take the car and park it out on the street, just in case we have to leave in a hurry. Finn will go into the bank with me."

Finn tossed Owen the car keys, then moved off to talk to Silvio, who was still swiping through screens on his tablet.

Owen laid his hand on my arm. "Are you okay? You've been quiet ever since we got here."

Sometimes I hated that Owen knew me so well and could tell when something was wrong. Still, his concern touched me, the way it always did. "Just worried, I guess."

"About what?"

I gestured out toward the bank. "If this is really it, the jackpot at the end of the rainbow. Or just another step in a seemingly endless climb to topple Mason off his lofty perch."

Sometimes I felt like I'd been investigating the Circle for years instead of months. And every time I thought I'd finally learned all of the evil group's secrets, some new horror popped up and knocked me right back down on my ass again. Not for the first time, I wondered if I was trapped in a never-ending cycle of futility, like Sisyphus doomed to push a boulder up a hill for all eternity.

"I'm just...tired," I continued. "I want to know that all of this, everything we've suffered, all the bad guys we've faced down, hasn't been for nothing. That we destroyed the Circle and made things better for everyone in Ashland. That eventually, Mason will get the horrible death he so richly deserves. And that all the secrets and lies will finally *end*."

Understanding sparked in Owen's violet eyes, and he stepped closer, gently squeezing my arm, before sliding his hand down and threading his fingers through mine. "Well, no matter what happens, we'll face it together, just like we always do. Okay?"

I nodded, lifted my head, and pressed my lips to his. The kiss was quick, soft, reassuring, but it still made heat simmer in my veins, as did Owen's rich, metallic scent and the warm strength of his body mingling with my own. I swayed into him, resting my cheek on his shoulder, and he circled his arm around my waist, pulling me even closer.

"Less canoodling, more looting," Finn called out.

Owen chuckled. Me too. We held on to each other a moment longer, then broke apart.

"Be careful," Owen whispered.

"You too," I whispered back.

I forced myself to smile at him, then turned away and jerked my head at Finn, who fell in step beside me. Together, we headed for the stairs.

My face was calm, my stride smooth, but dread churned in my gut like a chainsaw. Despite Owen's reassurances, I was still deeply worried about what Finn and I would find inside the bank—and if I would be frustrated and disappointed in my quest for revenge yet again.

F inn and I made it down to the street. My phone beeped, and I pulled it out of my pocket and checked the message from Silvio.

You're still clear. ☺

I glanced up. Silvio was hovering in the shadows on the parking garage's third level. I flashed him a thumbs-up, and then Finn and I walked down the block, cut through the roundabout park, crossed the street, and trudged up the front steps of the Bellum Bank.

Up close, the historic building was even more impressive. The stone gleamed like a gray pearl in the morning sunlight, while the Greek columns spiraled up three stories like oversize candy canes. Eagles with olive branches clutched in their talons were carved into the centers of the columns on the left side of the wide, shallow steps, their heads turned to look at the eagles clutching arrows that adorned the columns on the right side.

Silvio had told me that *bellum* was the Latin word for war and that the carvings were supposed to represent a balance between peace and war. I wondered which one I would find inside the bank. My gaze locked onto the arrows.

I was betting on war—I always did.

A giant guard dressed in a black uniform with a matching brimmed hat was standing outside the bank's glass doors, as though this were a legitimate financial institution and not a depository for blood money. Then again, I supposed that I couldn't cast stones, given how much money I had made from killing people over the years. The seven-foot-tall giant eyed Finn and me, his hand resting on the gun holstered to his black leather belt, but he let us push through the doors.

Glossy gray marble walls. Tall, wide windows. Brass chandeliers with old-fashioned bare bulbs. Wooden desks and chairs scattered here and there so that bankers could conduct business with various folks. People in business suits scurrying around. Others in more casual clothes standing in line and checking their phones.

At first glance, the Bellum Bank was eerily similar to First Trust and all the other banks in Ashland. But the longer I looked around, the more I noticed the differences.

More than a dozen giant guards wearing black uniforms, hats, and guns lined the walls, studying everyone who stepped inside the building, as well as keeping an eye on the folks who were waiting to be helped at the freestanding desks in the middle of the lobby.

The security cameras mounted to the ceiling constantly swiveled around, and I was willing to bet that a team of guards was sitting in a room somewhere deeper in the building, analyzing the feed, maybe even running a facial-recognition program to see exactly who was entering the bank.

There were no metal detectors, though. Of course not. Many of Ashland's criminals, including me, would never willingly give up their weapons. Still, the plethora of guards was more than enough to make even the most reckless, hotheaded underworld boss think twice about trying something stupid.

The tellers were stationed behind a long counter that was encased in bulletproof glass, and customers were required to put their checks, cash, and more into narrow metal drawers, so that the tellers could safely slide the contents over to their side of the counter. Behind the tellers, an enormous eagle was carved into the back wall, although this one clutched only arrows in its talons, and its beak was open wide, as though it were about to scream out a warning the second anything bad happened.

Even more striking than the guards, cameras, and bulletproof glass was what the building itself whispered to me. Over time, people's thoughts and especially their emotions sink into whatever stone is around them. As a Stone elemental, I can hear all those emotional vibrations, from the smallest bit of angry gravel to the largest, heaviest slab of sleepy concrete. The bank's gray marble walls hummed with a dark, deadly chorus, reflecting the ill intentions of all the criminals who had strolled through the lobby, as well as the murderous deeds those criminals had committed in order to get the money and goods they had deposited here.

I'd been right. I had most definitely found war—or at least the preparations for it. Disturbing chorus aside, this wasn't a bank so much as it was a fortress. No wonder Fletcher had stashed the Circle's money here. Even Mason Mitchell and his seemingly endless supply of giant goons would have a hard time busting in here.

"It's a good thing we don't actually have to rob the bank," I murmured. "We'd never make it through the lobby, much less to whatever storage units they have in the back."

"Oh, I'm sure we could find a way. We always do." Finn

eyed one of the female guards along the wall, who gave him a suspicious stare in return. "It would just be really loud and messy and potentially fatal for everyone involved."

He was probably right about that.

I glanced around again. "I suppose we should go stand in one of the teller lines—"

A metal door embedded in the back wall buzzed open, drawing my attention, and a woman stepped through the space and headed toward Finn and me. She was about my age, early thirties, and dressed in a money-green pantsuit that brought out her shoulder-length black hair, dark brown eyes, and golden skin. Dark green eye shadow and plum lipstick highlighted her attractive features, and she strode toward us with all the smooth confidence of a fashion model strutting along a runway.

The woman stopped in front of us. Without her black stilettos, she would have been shorter than me, although the heels put her right at my eye level. Her only jewelry, if you could even call it that, was an old-fashioned silverstone skeleton key that dangled from the long matching chain hanging around her neck.

But the most interesting thing about the woman was her Fire magic. Even though she wasn't using her power, wasn't trying to conjure up any sort of flame, intense heat still blasted off her strong, toned body in steady waves, as though I was standing next to a blazing furnace.

"Hello, Ms. Blanco," she purred in a soft, dulcet voice. "I'm Drusilla Yang, the senior vice president. Welcome to the Bellum Bank."

She held out her hand, which I politely shook, even though I had to hide a grimace as the invisible waves of her Fire magic washed over my skin. Fire was the exact opposite of my own Ice magic, and Drusilla's power screeched up against mine like a discordant song. She released my fingers, and I had to resist the urge to look down and see if they were smoldering.

I also had to resist the urge to let loose a string of curses. I'd been hoping to slip into one of the teller lines, state my business, transfer Fletcher's money into my own account, and slip back out again, but of course, my luck could never be that good.

Not only was Drusilla Yang the senior vice president, but she was also the daughter of Charles Yang, the Fire elemental who owned the bank. According to what Finn had told me, Drusilla was Charles's right hand, and she practically ran the bank these days, since her father was semiretired.

Drusilla's appearance had caused quite a stir, and everyone in the lobby was staring at us, from the people sitting at the desks to the folks waiting in line to the guards standing along the walls. Every second that ticked by and every curious gaze exponentially increased the chance Mason would hear that I'd been here, but I couldn't ignore, snub, or scurry away from Drusilla Yang, not in her own bank. All I could hope for now was that Mason would assume I had some other business here besides retrieving the money Fletcher had stolen from him.

"And what am I, Dru? Chopped liver?" Finn interjected.

Drusilla gave him a cool look that was decidedly at odds with the Fire magic still rippling off her body. "Chopped liver would be far more palatable than you, Lane. Especially since you have a nasty habit of stealing my clients."

I might not have had any dealings with the Bellum Bank, but Finn certainly had. Despite catering to criminals, the bank also dealt with all the other ones in Ashland, including First Trust. On the ride over here, Finn had said that he and Drusilla were friendly rivals, but Drusilla's glacial glare indicated that he'd seriously overestimated the *friendly* part of their relationship.

A grin spread across Finn's face. My brother never backed down from an insult or a challenge. "Just like you have a nasty habit of stealing *my* clients, Dru. I'd say that makes us even."

"Mmm." She made a noncommittal sound, but her continued ice-queen routine didn't faze Finn, who kept right on grinning at her.

Drusilla rolled her eyes, a common reaction when dealing with the incorrigible, exasperating Finnegan Lane. Then she waved her hand. "Follow me, please. My father would very much like to meet the infamous Gin Blanco."

She wasn't speaking any louder than normal, but her voice carried, and I could have sworn that the marble walls took great delight in making my name echo through the lobby.

Gin Blanco, Gin Blanco, Gin Blanco…

People were still staring at us, and now even more interest filled their faces. I had to hold back another string of curses. Nothing would be low-profile about my meeting Charles Yang. In fact, this sort of tête-à-tête would garner large, unwanted interest from the Ashland underworld. This just kept getting worse and worse.

Drusilla was only doing her job, but she might as well have held a flashing red neon sign up over my head that read, *Hey, Mason! Gin is here, and so is your money!*

Drusilla spun around on her stilettos and strode away, once again moving with smooth grace and confidence. Along the wall, a couple of guards stepped forward, their hands on their guns. One of them jerked his head in Drusilla's direction, his meaning crystal clear: follow his boss, or he would make us follow his boss.

I would have liked to tell the giant where he could shove his silent threat, but the Yangs ran things here, so I stayed quiet. Besides, I had to follow Drusilla's lead if I wanted any chance of getting my hands on the Circle's money.

I glanced at Finn, who nodded. He knew the dangers as well as I did, but the potential reward was worth the risk. So together, we fell in step behind Drusilla Yang and headed deeper into the bank.

Drusilla strode over to the door set into the back wall that she had come through earlier. The guard posted there reached out and opened the door, and she sailed through to the other side. Finn and I followed her.

The door opened up into a long hallway, with glass-fronted offices set into the walls and corridors branching off in different directions. Compared to the hustle and bustle of the lobby, this section of the bank was eerily quiet, and only a few people were sitting at desks inside the offices, murmuring into phones and typing on keyboards. This was where the real, more serious, profitable—and criminal—business was conducted.

Drusilla strolled through a couple of corridors before stopping outside a large door. Curiously enough, instead of being made of wood or metal, the door was covered with a slick, shiny mirror that threw our own reflections back at us. Drusilla stepped off to the side and entered a code in the keypad embedded in the wall. Finn, of course, took the opportunity to make sure his hair and tie were perfectly in place, even though he'd just checked them a few minutes ago in the car.

I eyed my own reflection. Given our trip to the bank, I'd shed my usual comfortable T-shirt and jeans for a subdued black pantsuit, in hopes of blending in with the rest of the business types. I might be gussied up like a banker, but I was still armed like an assassin. The suit jacket hid the two silverstone knives tucked up my sleeves, as well as the one nestled in the small of my back. Two more knives rested in the sides of my fashionable but functional black boots. The Spider never went anywhere without her weapons, especially not a place as dangerous as this one.

Like Drusilla, I was also wearing a silverstone chain around my neck, only mine featured a pendant—a circle surrounded by eight thin rays. My spider rune, the symbol for patience. A silverstone ring, also stamped with my spider rune, glinted on my right index finger, and both the ring and the pendant were filled with my Ice magic.

The same spider rune was also branded into my palms, although the scars had faded to a pale silver over the years. A parting gift of torture from Mab Monroe, back from when she'd tried to murder me when I was thirteen, when I was still the innocent Genevieve Snow.

I'd pulled my dark brown hair back into a sleek ponytail, but I wasn't wearing any makeup. No amount of liner, shadow, and mascara would hide the worry and wariness in my wintry gray eyes. Not today. Not *any* day Mason Mitchell was still alive and plotting against me.

Despite my gnawing worry, I kept my face blank, not giving any hint of my inner turmoil. I was pretty sure this was a one-way mirror and that whoever was sitting on the other side was studying every little thing about me, trying to find any potential weakness. And I could not afford to be seen as weak—not here.

The keypad beeped, and the mirrored door buzzed open. Drusilla swung it outward, then gestured for Finn and me to step inside. "My father is waiting for you."

I glanced at Finn, who nodded again, and we strode forward.

The mirrored door led into a surprisingly minimalist office. The walls and floor were the same blank gray marble as the rest of the building, and no paintings or rugs brightened or softened their hard, slick surfaces. Two gray metal chairs perched in front of a chrome desk that featured a laptop, monitor, keyboard, mouse, and landline phone. The only decoration, if you could even call it that, was a one-dollar bill encased in thick glass that was centered on the front edge of the desk, facing out toward the chairs.

Once I determined that there were no guards or other immediate threats in the office, my gaze locked onto the man sitting behind the desk. He looked to be in his sixties, with short black hair generously peppered with silver, dark brown eyes, and golden skin. The resemblance between the man and Drusilla was obvious, and he was as handsome as she was pretty.

"This is my father, Charles Yang, the CEO of the bank," Drusilla said, pride rippling through her voice.

Charles got to his feet, buttoned his navy suit jacket, and held out his hand to me. A benign smile creased his face. "Ms. Blanco. It's a pleasure to finally make your acquaintance. Your reputation precedes you."

"As does yours, Mr. Yang," I replied, reaching out to shake his hand.

His Fire magic washed over me the second his fingers closed around mine.

For the second time in the last five minutes, I hid a grimace. Charles wasn't quite as strong as Drusilla was, but he was still a formidable elemental, and the invisible waves of his magic scorched my skin, just like his daughter's had in the lobby earlier.

According to what Finn had told me, the Fire magic that

ran in the Yang family was one of the reasons Charles and his bank had flourished for so many years, despite dealing with the worst of the worst in Ashland. Charles and Drusilla might play the part of bankers, the same way I played the part of a restaurant owner, but rumor had it they dealt with their enemies the same way I dealt with mine: quickly, brutally, permanently.

Seeing the Yangs up close, and especially feeling their magic, was more than enough to convince me the rumors were true and that I needed to proceed with caution.

Charles released my hand, dropped down into his seat, and gestured for Finn and me to take the chairs in front of the desk. We did so, and Drusilla moved to stand beside her father.

I glanced back over my shoulder. The office door had silently swung shut behind us, revealing that it was covered with a one-way mirror that let me see out into the hallway beyond. A neat trick and a good way to size up potential clients—and enemies—before they entered the office. My respect for and wariness of the Yangs increased tenfold.

Charles gestured over at a metal beverage cart. "Bottled water? Juice? Coffee?"

Finn perked up. "I could always go for a coffee. Chicory, if you have it—"

I not-so-discreetly shoved my elbow into his side, making his request cut off into a loud, undignified grunt. We were here for business, not beverages. The quicker we accessed Fletcher's account, transferred the money, and got out of here, the better off we would be.

Finn shot me a sour look, but he sat back in his chair. I focused on Charles again, forcing myself to smile as though nothing was wrong and I couldn't still feel his and Drusilla's Fire magic rippling through the air like a forest fire about to rage this way and burn me alive.

Charles leaned back in his own chair. "What can I do for you, Ms. Blanco? I'm quite surprised to be hosting you in my establishment. I thought Stuart Mosley took care of all your banking needs." Interest filled his face. "Perhaps you need something Mr. Mosley is unwilling to provide? Something a bit more…off the books than what Stuart usually handles? Our regulations are far looser and much more profitable than what First Trust offers."

Finn stiffened. He didn't like the digs at Mosley, his mentor who owned First Trust. Mosley was my friend too, but I wasn't here to defend his honor.

"You're right. Stuart Mosley does handle all of my banking needs," I replied. "But Mosley and Mallory Parker are currently honeymooning in Snowline Ridge, and I don't want to disturb them."

A few weeks ago, Mosley and Mallory had gotten married at the Five Oaks Country Club, and I'd been honored to take part in the lovely event as a bridesmaid. The actual wedding ceremony had gone off without a hitch, although Emery Slater, Mason's henchwoman, had crashed the following reception with several goons.

I had whipped out my knives and killed a couple of the giants, but Emery had forced me to leave the reception to keep her from murdering the innocent guests. Mosley and Mallory had forgiven me for ruining their big day, but I hadn't forgiven myself, and the wedding crashing was yet another reason I despised both Emery and Mason.

Charles's dark eyes narrowed in speculation, as did Drusilla's. According to Finn, the two of them had been at the wedding and the reception, although I didn't remember seeing them. The Yangs obviously weren't buying my story about not disturbing Mosley, but I didn't bother to elaborate. They probably wouldn't believe a word I said anyway. I certainly wouldn't have, if our positions had been reversed.

"So what can I do for you?" Charles repeated, sinking back a little deeper into his cushioned chair. If nothing else, I had piqued his curiosity.

Once again, I was painfully aware of all the people who'd seen me in the lobby—underworld bosses and minions who were no doubt already texting about my visit. Every second I delayed was another second Mason had to dispatch his men here, so I decided to get right down to business.

"I want to access an account that belonged to my foster father, Fletcher Lane. He left it to me upon his death." That was more or less the truth, although I didn't offer any more details. The less the Yangs knew about Fletcher's account, the safer Finn and I would be.

Finn pulled a small manila envelope out of his suit jacket pocket and slid it across the desk. "Fletcher Lane was my biological father. I have a copy of his will and death certificate, along with the account number. I can provide other documentation, if needed."

"That won't be necessary," Charles murmured. "I remember Mr. Lane and his instructions very clearly."

Instructions? Curiosity filled me, but Charles didn't offer any more details. Instead, he reached out, snagged the envelope, and pulled out the papers inside. He didn't even glance at the will or the death certificate. Instead, he grabbed the sheet with the account number and held it up where both he and Drusilla could see it. They frowned at each other.

"I'm afraid there's been some mistake," Charles said, looking at me again.

My heart plummeted with disappointment. I knew it—I just *knew* it. This was yet another wild-goose-chase-slash-treasure-hunt that Fletcher had orchestrated to protect the stolen Circle money, along with his many, many secrets—

"This isn't a traditional checking or savings account. It's the number to one of our private vaults," Charles continued.

I couldn't stop myself from blinking in surprise. "Private vault?"

He nodded. "Yes. In addition to traditional accounts, we also offer storage facilities for our clients who have…larger items that can't be so easily liquidated into cash."

I could hear what he wasn't saying, that the Bellum Bank was a depository for criminals to squirrel away gold, jewels, artwork, and other items that were either too hot to immediately fence or too unique and memorable to ever dispose of. At least, not without attracting the unwanted attention of other criminals—people who had probably had that same gold, jewels, and artwork stolen from them in the first place. So what was in Fletcher's vault? What had he wanted hidden from prying eyes?

I glanced at Finn, who shrugged. He had no idea what his dad might have stored here either.

"You're absolutely certain it's a vault and not an account?" Finn asked.

Drusilla crossed her arms over her chest and stared down her nose at him. "I think we know our own business."

Finn arched an eyebrow at her sarcastic tone. He opened his mouth to snipe back, but I elbowed him in the side again, making another loud, undignified grunt tumble out of his lips.

"Can we see the vault?" I asked. "Right now?"

Charles's eyebrows lifted. "Are you in some sort of rush, Ms. Blanco?"

Tick-tick-tick. By this point, I could almost hear the seconds slipping by, like a clock in my mind counting down the time until Emery Slater and her giants burst into the office and made me take them to Fletcher's vault. And the other, more cynical, suspicious, and paranoid part of me couldn't help but wonder if Mason *already* knew about Fletcher's vault. If my uncle had already made a deal with the Yangs, and this meeting was a stall tactic by Charles and Drusilla, a way for them to delay me until Mason could arrive.

"You know how it is. Things to do, people to kill." I gave him a thin smile, then purposefully tugged my sleeves, as though I were adjusting them.

Charles's gaze dropped to my arms, and he tensed, as though he were expecting me to palm the knives he knew I had hidden up my sleeves, lunge across the desk, and stab him. Beside him, Drusilla tensed as well, and her Fire magic flared in her eyes, making them burn like dark bronze stars. She was more than ready to blast me with her power should I attack her father.

I quit fussing with my sleeves and sat back in my chair, that thin smile still fixed on my face, as though nothing was wrong. Finn kept his gaze on the Yangs, although he subtly dropped his arm to his side, ready to reach around and grab the gun hidden under his jacket in the small of his back.

Charles stared at me a few more seconds, then jerked his head at his daughter. "Drusilla, please escort Ms. Blanco to her vault."

Instead of replying, even more magic flared in Drusilla's eyes, and her fingers twitched, as though she was thinking about roasting me with her Fire power for daring to threaten her father. I admired her protective urge, but I didn't have time to wheel and deal and mess around, so I reached for my own magic. Then I started drumming my fingers on the chair arm, letting tiny bits of elemental Ice fly out every time one of my fingertips struck the metal.

A piece of Ice hit the dollar bill encased in glass on the front of Charles's desk. *Tink.* That one soft sound reverberated through the air, booming as loud as a gunshot in the quiet office.

"Drusilla," Charles repeated, a clear command in his voice.

Her lips pressed into a flat, unhappy line, but the magic dimmed in her eyes. "Of course, Father."

She jerked her head. "Follow me." She muttered the words like they were a vile curse.

Finn and I both stood up, as did Charles. I respectfully tipped my head to him.

"Mr. Yang, so nice to meet you," I said in a pleasant tone. "I look forward to engaging your services again in the future."

He nodded, but the faint smile on his lips didn't even come close to reaching his cold eyes. He didn't like my threats either. I stared at him a moment longer, then turned and followed Drusilla out of the office.

I might have gotten what I'd wanted, but I wondered if the cost had been worth it—and if I'd just made two dangerous new enemies.

✲ 3 ✲

rusilla led us out of the office, and the mirrored door automatically swung shut and locked behind Finn and me.

The space between my shoulder blades itched, but I resisted the urge to glance back. The only thing I would be able to see would be my own reflection in the mirror and not Charles in his office, murmuring into a phone and ordering his guards to make sure we never left his bank alive. I shoved my paranoia away. I didn't think I had threatened the Fire elemental harshly enough for him to take that drastic step—yet.

Then again, the Spider wasn't exactly known for her ability to make friends, just more danger for myself.

"This way," Drusilla muttered.

Despite her obvious hostility, Finn and I had no choice but to follow her. Drusilla strode from one corridor to the next, moving deeper and deeper into the building. We passed a few guards stationed at various intersections, and the men and women all nodded respectfully to Drusilla, while eyeing Finn and me with suspicion. The security cameras mounted to the ceiling also swiveled around to track our movements. I wondered if Charles Yang was watching the live feed on the monitor in his office. Probably.

Drusilla finally stopped in front of an elevator, which was covered by a thick iron grate that stretched from the floor all the way up to the ceiling. She nodded at the guard posted there, then grabbed the silverstone skeleton key on the long chain around her neck and inserted it into a slot in the wall, right where the elevator's call button should be. Drusilla turned the key, and a faint *ding* sounded, along with the creak and grind of the elevator slowly rising.

A few seconds later, another *ding* sounded, and the iron grate rattled back, revealing an enormous old-fashioned freight elevator. The space was easily big enough to accommodate whatever loot you might have stolen from your enemies. Bricks of cash, pallets of framed paintings, maybe even a sports car or a small boat.

Drusilla gestured for us to step inside the elevator with her, then inserted her skeleton key into a slot in a metal panel. She turned the key, and the iron grate slid shut. Next, she punched a button marked *VL*, which I assumed stood for *Vault Level*. The elevator slowly descended, the metal car creaking ominously.

"How old is this thing?" Finn asked.

"Older than you are," Drusilla replied in a snide voice. "More mature too."

Finn stuck his tongue out at her, proving her point. Drusilla sighed and looked upward, as if asking some higher power for the patience to deal with my brother instead of simply roasting him alive with her Fire magic. Finn was taking this *friendly rivals* thing to a whole new level of childish hostility. Well, that, and he just enjoyed acting like a big kid.

We rode the rest of the way in tense silence. The elevator coasted to a stop, and the grate rattled back, revealing two giant guards standing in a gray marble corridor. Off to the right, an *Exit* sign glowed a bright neon red over a metal door that I assumed led to some emergency stairs. A keypad was embedded in the wall there, indicating that you had to have a code to open the door and access the stairs.

Drusilla stepped out of the elevator and flashed her skeleton key at the guards, who nodded respectfully. "This way," she said, setting off down the corridor.

The two giants fell in step behind her, leaving Finn and me to bring up the rear.

Drusilla rounded the corner, moving from that initial plain, featureless corridor into one that was covered with mirrors. The smooth, shiny glass panels were trimmed with thick seams of silver and took up large sections of the walls. At first, I didn't understand why they were down here, but then I realized that the panels were spaced an equal distance apart and that each one had a keypad embedded in the wall beside it.

Not mirrors. Doors, just like the one outside Charles Yang's office.

"What is this? A carnival fun house?" Finn muttered in a low voice that only I could hear.

I eyed my reflections, each new version of me looking more worried than the last. Our footsteps tapped out a low, ominous beat, like drums in a movie signaling that something bad was about to happen, and the walls hummed as though the stones were constantly sharing dark, dangerous, hushed secrets with one another.

"There's definitely nothing fun about this," I murmured back to Finn.

He shuddered, and we walked on.

Drusilla led us through a maze of mirrored corridors, turning right and left in no apparent pattern. As we walked along, I noticed two sets of colored arrows embedded in the floor—red ones on the right side of the hallway and green ones on the left side—although I had no idea what they were for.

Finally, Drusilla stopped in front of a particularly large mirror at the very end of this corridor. Once again, she inserted her skeleton key into a slot embedded in the wall. She turned the key three times, and three corresponding *clicks* sounded.

Drusilla removed her key and let it and the attached silverstone chain drop back down against her chest. Then she gestured at the keypad on the wall. "This is Fletcher Lane's vault. We employ a two-step verification process, much like that for a safety-deposit box in a regular bank. I used my key, and now you two will have to enter the correct code on the keypad. You have three tries to enter the correct code. If you do not, then the vault will go into lockdown, and you will not be able to access the contents until my father says otherwise."

"So you and your father can access the vaults anytime you want to? How handy for you," I drawled.

"No, we cannot access the vaults anytime we want to," Drusilla snapped back. "Our vaults are absolutely secure. If a vault goes into lockdown because of a forgotten password or the like, then it is drilled open. In cases of disputes between two or more parties, my father makes the final determination of who owns the vault in question. Those are just some of our security protocols to prevent unauthorized users from accessing vaults and valuables that don't belong to them."

Her icy tone made it clear that she thought we were unauthorized users. She might be right about that.

I glanced at Finn, who was chewing on his bottom lip, worry filling his face. The same worry gnawed at my heart. Fletcher hadn't mentioned any code in his letter to me.

"There are no security cameras down here, no cell service either, so you can access your vault in absolute privacy," Drusilla continued.

I pulled my phone out of my pocket and glanced at the screen. No signal, which meant that Silvio couldn't text me updates about what was happening outside the bank—and any potential enemies who might be heading my way. Not good, but I'd come this far, and I wasn't leaving without at least *trying* to open Fletcher's vault, so I slid my phone back into my pocket.

"When you're done, follow the green arrows on the floor to the elevator, and the guards will see that you get back up to the lobby level," Drusilla said.

She gave us another cool look, then whirled around and strode away. The two giants eyed Finn and me, their hands on their guns as they backed away. For the first time, I realized that they weren't here to watch over the vaults and their contents. No, the giants were guarding Drusilla, probably to keep us from forcing her to open this vault and all the others, even though she claimed she couldn't do that. Smart.

Drusilla reached the end of the hallway and disappeared around the corner. The giants followed her, and the eerie echoes of their footsteps faded away.

Finn and I both waited a minute to make sure they were gone. Then my brother threw his hands up in frustration.

"A code? Really, Dad?" he muttered, as though Fletcher could hear him from wherever the old man was in the great beyond.

I sighed, not any happier about this than Finn was, then bent down and studied the keypad. It was a regular ten-digit keypad, and I couldn't tell what, if any, numbers had ever been punched on it.

I straightened up. "Could the code have something to do with the account number, the vault number, that Fletcher wrote down in Mason's black ledger?"

Finn shook his head. "Nope. There were no extra digits in the number. Its only purpose was to lead us here, to the Bellum Bank and this vault. Besides, Dad was smarter than that. He would never have made the code the same as the vault number. That would have been way too obvious."

"Unless Fletcher thought doing the obvious thing would be really clever in this case," I pointed out. "Should I try it?"

"Might as well," Finn muttered. "Maybe we'll get lucky."

I entered the number. A sharp, warning *beep* immediately sounded, and one of the three lights on the top of the keypad winked over to red. Frustration filled me. No luck for us. Shocker.

"Well, you're right. It's definitely not the vault number," I said, trying to put a positive spin on things.

Finn shot me a sour look.

"Do you have any other ideas what the code might be?" I asked.

"Dad's birthday, your birthday, my birthday. It might even be Deirdre's birthday, if Dad was feeling particularly ironic. It could be anything." My brother shrugged. "But he left the ledger for *you* to find, Gin, so I'm guessing the code has something to do with you and the Circle."

"What about spelling out *The Circle* with numbers?" I suggested. "Fletcher did steal their money, after all. Or whatever might be behind Door Number One here."

Finn shrugged again. "That's as good a guess as any."

I entered those numbers and held my breath, hoping, hoping, hoping it was the right code—

Beep. The second light on the keypad bloomed a bright, bloody red. I bit back a curse. Only one chance left.

Finn threw up his hands in frustration again and started pacing. The mirrors fronting the other vaults caught his quick, angry movements and reflected them back on one another in an endless series of fast-moving Finns. Staring down the long, wide corridor at the mirrors made my head spin and my stomach lurch, so I dropped my gaze to the floor to steady myself.

I was just about to lift my head and tell Finn that we should keep working on the code when I spotted something stuck to the wall at the bottom corner of the mirror that fronted Fletcher's vault. For a moment, I thought it was some trick of the lights and reflections, but I stepped to the side, and the object didn't move, unlike Finn, who was still pacing. What was that?

Curious, I crouched down to get a better look. I wasn't imagining things. Something *was* stuck to the wall.

A pink pig sticker.

I blinked a few times, but the shape didn't change. A pink pig sticker about the size of a dime was clinging to the wall, a tiny speck of defiant color among all the slick gray marble and shiny silver mirrors. I traced my finger over the sticker, which was worn and faded, as though it had been stuck in this spot for quite some time. Why would that be down here? Unless...

My heart lifted, and I shot to my feet and whirled back around to the keypad.

"Gin?" Finn asked, stopping his pacing. "What are you doing? We only have one chance left. Don't you want to talk about it some more before you try another code?"

I ignored him. With a trembling hand, I carefully punched in the numbers that would spell out two distinct yet familiar words: *Pork Pit*. Then I let out a tense breath and hit the *Enter* button before I could change my mind.

Beep.

Another angry little noise rang out, and the third light on top of the keypad winked to red. My heart dropped like a brick thrown out a window. I was wrong, and now we'd have to go back to Charles Yang and beg, grovel, plead, and probably bribe him to let us into Fletcher's vault—

Beep-beep-beep.

Three more noises rang out, and one by one, all the red lights slowly winked to green. A moment later, three more *clicks* sounded, and the mirrored door buzzed open.

"You did it!" Finn whispered, his eyes wide with shock. "You guessed the code! You opened the vault!"

I stood there, heart hammering, staring at the little sliver of space that indicated the vault was open. I didn't know how long I would have stayed frozen in place if Finn hadn't spoken up.

"What are you waiting for? Open it!" he said in an eager voice.

His words snapped me out of my stupefied shock, and I lunged forward. My heart was still hammering against my ribs, and my hands were trembling and sweaty, but I grabbed the edge of the mirror and swung the heavy door back to reveal…

A treasure trove.

That was the only way to describe it. Black metal shelves lined the vault's three marble walls, stretching from the floor all the way up to the low ceiling, while a single lonely chair perched in front of a black metal table in the center. The furniture was nothing special, but every available inch of the shelves was covered with cash and valuables.

Fat, shrink-wrapped bricks of fifty- and hundred-dollar bills were stacked up on the shelves to my right, while rolls of tens and twenties bound with blue and pink rubber bands were piled up on the shelves to my left, and loose, haphazard stacks of five- and one-dollar bills covered the shelves along the back wall. Dozens and dozens of large gray canvas bags were also situated on the shelves and clustered on the floor around the table, their lumpy shapes making them look like soldiers who were guarding the money. Three more bags were perched on the tabletop itself. One of those bags was partially open, revealing a mountain of bright, shiny, pristine quarters that looked like they had never even been touched.

But the money was only the start of the treasure. Gold bars also squatted on the shelves, along with white velvet trays covered with diamond rings, pearl necklaces, and ruby bracelets. I even spotted a sapphire-encrusted tiara gleaming on one tray, next to several open boxes containing gold and silver watches.

Oh, yes. Some sort of cash, coins, or gems covered every single surface, and the combined currency turned the inside of the vault a dull, washed-out green, which was only broken up by the sparkling jewelry and the sly glints of the quarters, dimes, and other coins peeking out of the tops of the open bags.

"A room full of money," Finn whispered in a low, reverent tone. "I feel like Scrooge McDuck. This—this is straight out of my *dreams.*"

As if in a trance, Finn slowly stepped inside the vault. I followed him, my gaze still darting around and around, trying to take in everything at once. Even among all the many, many secrets Fletcher had kept from me, this one was a doozy.

"How…how much money do you think is in here?" I asked the question in a normal tone, although the stacks of cash soaked up the sound of my voice.

In an instant, Finn shook off his wonder, and a calculating look filled his face. "Well, it's hard to say, exactly. The right side looks to be mostly fifties and hundreds, but the smaller bills drastically lower the value, especially all those fives and ones I see on the back shelves. And of course, the gold bars, jewelry, and watches are only worth what someone is willing to give you for them, especially if they're stolen goods. Which, knowing Dad, they probably are."

"But?"

"But…if we just count the money right now, and every shrink-wrapped brick is at least ten thousand dollars, and every roll of tens and twenties is at least five thousand…" His voice trailed off, and his eyes narrowed a little more, as he did the math in his head. "Rough guess? I'd say at least ten million dollars."

Normally, ten million dollars was nothing to sneeze at, but Finn's guesstimate made me frown. From the way Mason had described things, Fletcher had stolen an enormous, crippling amount of money from the Circle coffers—enough money to prompt my uncle to threaten to kill everyone I loved if I didn't find it for him. Surely, my friends' lives were worth more than a mere ten million dollars.

Finn wandered over to the table in the center of the vault. He stopped, as though something had caught his eye, then stepped around behind the table. He snorted out a laugh. "Hey. Come look at this."

I went around the table. Out of sight of the vault door, a small, silver-framed painting was leaning up against the gray canvas bags of coins. The image was of a woman in a light gray dress who was perched on a large, flat gray rock and staring out over a field of grayish wildflowers. A gray stone castle lurked in the background, along with some dark gray mountain peaks, while a few thin white clouds dotted the silvery sky. The only real pop of color was the closed book on the woman's lap, which was a bright blood red against her pale dress.

A bolt of recognition shot through me. The painting was called *A Lady's Reverie in Gray*—and it was a fake.

Memories flooded my mind of the last time I had seen the real painting. I'd come across the genuine artwork on an assassin job I'd done with Fletcher years ago, and I knew exactly where the real painting was, even to this day. So why had the old man left this fake in here? Why keep a forgery in a vault full of valuables? It didn't make any sense.

Finn bumped me with his shoulder, jarring me out of my thoughts. "Forget the pretty picture. I was talking about this."

He pointed down at the tabletop, where someone had used several coins to spell out a single word: *Gin*.

"Fletcher," I whispered, knowing this was his handiwork.

My heart warmed and wrenched at the same time, and I bent down and took a closer look. Not only had Fletcher spelled out *Gin*, but he'd also turned the dot over the *i* into a crude spider rune made up of coins. I placed my hand on the table, right beside the *G*, which was made of shiny silver quarters.

I pictured Fletcher sitting at the table, softly whistling while he painstakingly arranged the coins to leave me one final message, one last strand in this complicated treasure-hunt web he'd created. The image made me smile, despite the sadness flooding my heart.

"Why do you think Fletcher spelled out my name?" I asked. "It's such an odd thing to do."

"No idea," Finn replied. "Maybe he got bored when he was working or relaxing or counting the money or whatever he did in here. It's not like he used hundred-dollar bills to spell out your name. Now, *that* would have been impressive."

I gave him a sour look, but Finn grinned back at me.

Seeing my name spelled out both jarred and puzzled me, and I couldn't look away from it. So I pulled my phone out of my pocket, leaned down, and snapped several photos of the *Gin* coins, zooming in on a few of them. Then I straightened up, turned around, and snapped photos of the rest of the vault, getting some wide-angle shots of the money on the shelves, as well as some closer views showing the different denominations. I also took a few pictures of the gold bars, jewelry, and watches, along with several of the fake *Reverie in Gray* painting.

Finn dipped his hand into one of the open bags on the table and let the pennies inside trickle through his fingers. The bright, gleaming coins *tink-tink-tinked* together like wind chimes. He grinned at me again, although I didn't return the happy expression.

"What's wrong?" he asked. "You did it. You finally found the money that Dad stole from Mason."

I shook my head. "It doesn't seem like...*enough*."

He stopped messing with the coins. "What do you mean?"

"Mason put a lot of time, effort, and manpower into kidnapping Bria, threatening me, and crashing Mosley and Mallory's wedding." I gestured at the shelves around us. "All that for ten million dollars? I just assumed Fletcher had stolen a lot more money than that from the Circle."

"Ten million dollars isn't exactly pocket change," Finn pointed out. "And Dad stole this money years ago. It would have been worth a lot more back then. Plus, we don't know how much of it he paid back to Mason. Maybe this is all that's left."

"I know that, but Mason could have stayed hidden in the shadows and bribed, threatened, or intimidated that much money out of someone. Like Damian Rivera. He was a Circle member, and he could have easily loaned Mason ten million dollars out of his own personal fortune. Or think about those jewels Deirdre stashed away at the Bullet Pointe theme park. Why, those gems were probably worth more than all the cash in this vault."

Damian, Deirdre, and their respective goons were just some of the many folks I'd tangled with since I'd started investigating the Circle, and each subsequent fight for my life had taken a little bit more out of me than the battle before. No wonder I was so tired. Near-death experiences tended to wear a person down, even an assassin like me.

Finn tipped his head, acknowledging my points. "Maybe Mason did squeeze some money out of Damian Rivera at some point. We definitely know that he tried to recover the jewels, because we almost got killed in the process. Maybe the jewels Deirdre had squirreled away were separate from the money Dad stole from the Circle."

Finn wandered over to the right side of the vault, grabbed a brick of cash from one of the shelves, and tore off part of the plastic wrap. Then he plucked a bill off the stack and waved it at me like a flag. "I certainly wish there were a lot more bricks of hundreds in here. And don't even get me started on the bags of coins."

"What's wrong with the coins?"

He let out a disgusted snort. "The bags of coins, especially the pennies, are far too big, heavy, and awkward to lug around for the actual monetary amounts they represent. They're a waste of space. I have no idea why Dad brought them here, or all those fives and ones. Maybe he was being petty and paying Mason's monthly tithe in pennies, quarters, and small bills."

After Fletcher had stolen the Circle's money, he'd instigated a sort of reverse-blackmail scheme. Instead of paying someone to keep a secret, Fletcher had returned some of the stolen funds a little bit at a time to keep Mason from coming after him. At least, that was my theory, and all these bags of coins made me think that Finn was right too. Fletcher probably had forced Mason to count out his blood money, down to the very last penny.

"Either way," Finn continued, walking back over to me, "we'll probably never know what Dad was thinking."

Frustration filled me, burning like acid in my stomach. No, we probably never would know the answer, because Fletcher was *dead*, tortured and murdered inside his own barbecue restaurant during one of my assassin jobs gone wrong. My mentor's death was arguably the greatest failure of my life, something that filled me with deep shame, unending guilt, and heartrending regret. Maybe if I hadn't been so sloppy back then, if I had seen the double cross coming, then I would have been able to save Fletcher, and he would have been here with Finn and me right now to explain things.

Instead, the old man had taken scores of secrets to his grave—secrets that kept coming back around to bite me on the ass—and I was starting to suspect that this latest discovery would be more of the same. More tiredness trickled through my body.

This didn't feel like a victory—more like another problem.

"Let's forget about the relatively paltry amount of cash and focus on what's really important right now," Finn said.

I sighed, knowing I was going to regret asking the question, but I voiced it anyway. "And what would that be?"

He grinned, grabbed my right hand, and slapped the hundred-dollar bill he'd pulled out of the plastic-wrapped brick into my palm. "How we're going to get all this loot out of here."

I curled my fingers around the bill, then glanced around. "I have no idea. It's not like we can just stuff the cash, coins, and jewelry into our pockets, take the elevator back upstairs, and stroll out the front door. And I seriously doubt that Drusilla and Charles Yang will let us bring wheelbarrows down here to haul it all away at once."

"Hey, you never know until you ask. There's a hardware store a few blocks over. I'm sure they have wheelbarrows." Finn's face lit up. "Or maybe even those little colored wagons that kids play with. Those would be fun. Then we could move the money out of here with *style*."

"How, exactly, does a kid's toy have style?"

Finn ignored my question and waved the brick of money at me again. "You're the one who was so eager to find Dad's loot. Don't blame me because it's not all ones and zeroes in an electronic account. Besides, we both know that more than one person saw you in the lobby. Sooner or later, word will get back to Mason that Gin Blanco was at the Bellum Bank, and he'll start wondering if his stolen money is here. So you can't just leave all this stuff behind. Not for long. We need to move the valuables out of this vault and get them somewhere safe as soon as possible."

The sly gleam in his eyes indicated that he already had a location in mind.

I huffed and crossed my arms over my chest. "Let me guess. You think *somewhere safe* is your own personal account at First Trust."

"Exactly!" Finn beamed at me. "After all, I *am* the investment banker in our circle of friends, so I'm the most logical choice to help you turn this loot into electronic currency. Why, I'll even give you the friends-and-family discount when it comes to my usual commission."

"Wow. Thanks, *Bro*," I said in a snide tone.

"Anytime, *Sis*."

Finn grinned at me again. Then he leaned down over the

table, grabbed the extra penny in the center of the spider rune that dotted the *i* in *Gin*, and flipped it over to me. I caught the coin and slid it into my pants pocket, along with the hundred-dollar bill he'd slapped into my hand.

My brother started wandering around the vault, whistling with happiness as he shoved bricks of cash into his jacket pockets, but I remained beside the table, staring out over the mounds of bills, bags of coins, and trays of jewelry.

Earlier, I had been worried that this was just another pit stop on the complicated road map Fletcher had left behind, but now that I was in the vault, it felt more like a final destination. This wasn't some safety-deposit box or ledger or other small clue that led to something bigger. This was the largest and most important clue of all. I didn't know what else the old man could have possibly left behind that could ever top this.

Despite my satisfaction at finding the money, I still felt like I was missing something, like there was one more puzzle in here that I needed to solve. Or maybe that was simply my own paranoia nagging at me, the way it always did.

My gaze darted back over to the fake *Reverie in Gray* painting, then dropped to the *Gin* coins laid out on the table. If Fletcher had left me a message, then he had been much more cryptic about it than usual. Whatever the old man was trying to tell me, I wasn't going to figure it out today.

But I had most definitely put myself in very real danger by coming here, and I could still hear that countdown clock steadily ticking away in my mind. Gossip traveled fast in the Ashland underworld, and it was only a matter of days, maybe even hours, before Mason heard that I had visited the bank. Finn was right. We needed to figure out how to move all this stuff out of here before my uncle came after it—or worse, came after my loved ones.

I might have finally found Fletcher's secret stash of Circle cash, might finally have some tenuous leverage over Mason, but I couldn't help but wonder how much more pain, heartache, and suffering the money would ultimately end up costing me.

Finn and I floated several ideas, but try as we might, we just couldn't come up with a safe, easy way to remove the valuables from the vault without attracting even more unwanted attention than we already had.

Drusilla Yang had said there were no cameras on the vault level, but they certainly covered the rest of the bank, including the lobby, which was also full of folks with cell-phone cameras. I didn't want a security guard, a bank teller, or an underworld minion to see me walking out the front door with bricks of cash stacked up in my arms and decide to text a photo to their friends.

Besides, even if Finn and I discreetly removed some rolls of cash by hiding them in our pockets, there were still hundreds more to go, not to mention the dozens and dozens of bags of coins, stacks of gold bars, and trays of jewelry. It would take hours, maybe days, to remove all the loot that way, and we simply didn't have that kind of time, not when Mason could strike out against us at any moment. And my murderous uncle wasn't the only danger. Some enterprising underworld boss might start wondering what I had stashed in the bank and try to rob me themselves, which would be yet another headache that I didn't need.

Since we couldn't figure out a way to safely remove the goods, I decided to just leave them in the vault. It was the only option we had right now.

I stepped back out into the hallway. Finn reluctantly

followed me, and together we closed the mirrored door. Several *clicks* sounded, indicating that the vault had locked, and the two of us faced our own reflections again.

Finn flattened his palm against the glass. "Soon," he whispered. "I'll be back for you soon, baby."

I rolled my eyes. "Come on, *baby*. We've already been down here too long. Owen and Silvio are probably worried sick by now."

We walked along the corridors, following the green arrows embedded in the floor back toward the freight elevator. Our shoes tapped against the stone, which started murmuring again, adding my worry and Finn's greed to the low, constant chorus of dread, fear, and paranoia that was already rippling through the marble. The sound made me wonder what other dark, dangerous secrets were housed behind all these smooth, shiny mirrored doors.

Finn pulled his phone out of his jacket pocket. "I know Drusilla said there's no service down here, but maybe I can get a signal once we reach the elevator."

"See if Silvio has spotted any sudden influx of underworld bosses or minions flooding the lobby or loitering around outside the bank. I'd like to get out of here without being waylaid."

Finn nodded and started fiddling with his phone, scrolling through screen after screen.

Ding.

In the distance, the elevator chimed out its arrival. The metal gate creaked back, and then a couple of voices sounded, along with footsteps. It seemed as though Drusilla was escorting someone else to their vault while Finn and I were still down here. So much for absolute privacy.

Either that, or she'd come back with more guards to try to kill us.

Neither option was ideal, but there was no place to hide, and as far as I could tell, the elevator was the only way out of this underground labyrinth. So Finn and I had no choice but to keep moving forward and step around the corner into the next hallway.

"As you can see, our security is quite comprehensive." Drusilla's voice floated over to me.

She strode into view at the opposite end of the hallway, along with the two guards who had been stationed by the elevator earlier. My gaze skipped past the guards and locked onto the person Drusilla was talking to—a seven-foot-tall giant with a sleek bob of blond hair, hazel eyes, and milky skin dotted with freckles.

The sight of the female giant stopped me dead in my tracks. This was no mere criminal, no uppity underworld boss. This was a much more dangerous brand of trouble.

Emery Slater, Mason's number one enforcer, who hated me with a burning passion and wanted to kill me more than anything else.

❋ 4 ❋

I froze. Out of all the people we could have run into, Emery Slater was just about the worst possible one.

And why was she here? Why *now*? Had Mason made some secret deal with the Yangs? Was Emery coming to kill Finn and me and loot Fletcher's vault? The questions crowded into my mind, with each possible answer more troubling— and deadly—than the last.

"Each vault is locked with a two-step verification process…" Drusilla explained, while she gestured at the mirrored vaults that lined the corridor.

She wasn't looking in this direction. Neither were her two guards, who were squarely focused on Emery.

The female giant stopped, turned, and gestured at someone behind her. My breath caught in my throat, and my heart sputtered to a stop.

Was *Mason* here too?

A male giant wearing a black suit shuffled into view. My breath spewed out of my lips, but my relief was short-lived.

This was bad—so very, very bad.

My brain finally kicked back into gear, and I grabbed

Finn's suit jacket. He was still focused on his phone, trying
to get a signal, and he hadn't looked up this whole time. Finn
let out a surprised, strangled sound, but I dragged him back
around the corner, out of sight of Emery Slater.

He stumbled away and opened his mouth, probably to
lecture me about wrinkling his jacket, but I put my index
finger against my lips, warning him to be quiet, then pointed
to a mirror mounted on the opposite side of the corridor I had
just pulled him out of. Thanks to its position and all the other
mirrors in the corridor, I could clearly see Emery coming
toward us, along with Drusilla and the other giants.

Finn's eyes widened, and he swallowed his protest and
flattened himself up against the wall beside me.

"What is Emery doing here?" he whispered. "Do you think
Mason knows we're inside the bank?"

"I have no idea," I whispered back. "Mason could have a
spy here. Maybe one of the tellers or guards spotted us and
texted him. Either way, we need to be ready in case Emery
sees us."

I palmed one of the silverstone knives tucked up my
sleeves, while Finn plucked his gun out of the holster nestled
in the small of his back. Together, we held our positions up
against the wall, stared into the mirrors, and watched Emery
Slater amble down the corridor.

The giant was wearing a dark blue pantsuit that outlined
her tall, strong body, along with blue ballet flats. She wasn't
carrying any weapons, but she didn't really need a gun or a
knife. Thanks to her giant strength, Emery could easily snap
someone's bones like twigs—before she beat them to death
with her fists.

"I should mention something important about the Bellum
Bank," Finn murmured. "Something I probably should have
told you before now."

"What?" I asked, never taking my gaze off Emery's reflection, which was slowly getting larger and closer, just like the giant herself was.

"No violence is permitted inside the bank," Finn replied. "No brawls, no fisticuffs, no physical assaults or threats of any kind. You can't give someone so much as a paper cut in the lobby. There are consequences for people who break the rules."

Once again, I knew I was going to regret it, but I asked the question anyway. "What kind of consequences?"

"Supposedly, Charles Yang likes to use his Fire magic to make examples out of people who break the bank's no-violence rules," Finn whispered. "At least, that was the story until a few years ago."

For the third time, I asked a question I knew I was going to regret getting answered. "And what's the story now?"

"That Drusilla has taken over that particular duty from her father."

"And?"

Finn sighed. "And that she makes even more...vivid and... permanent examples out of rule breakers than her father did."

I ground my teeth. Of course she did. Drusilla Yang was a much more powerful elemental than her father, so it only made sense that she would use her Fire magic to its fullest extent, especially to protect her family's bank and reputation. Combine Drusilla's power with Emery's hatred of me, and there was a very real chance Finn and I wouldn't get out of here alive.

"Back," I whispered. "Go back to Fletcher's vault. Now. As quickly and quietly as you can."

Finn scurried in that direction. I fell in step behind him, wincing at the steady taps of his wing tips against the floor, along with the soft, answering squeaks of my boots.

Behind us, more footsteps rang out, along with Drusilla's voice.

"We have a variety of vault sizes," she said. "Of course, the larger vaults do cost more. There are also additional costs if your contents need to be stored at a certain controlled temperature, like with fine wines..."

I frowned. Drusilla sounded like she was giving Emery a tour, instead of leading the giant straight to us. But why would Emery be interested in the vaults? Unless, of course, she was here at Mason's behest, looking for a safe place to stash something important that belonged to him. My steps slowed, and I tilted my head to the side, straining to hear their conversation.

Arrogance will get you, every single time, Fletcher's voice whispered in my mind.

The old man had said that more than once over the years, and he was just as right now as he had been all those times back then. Learning why Emery was here wasn't worth getting Finn and myself killed, so I picked up my pace, following my brother around the last corner and into the corridor that ended at Fletcher's vault.

Finn rushed over to the keypad and entered the *Pork Pit* code, but the three lights all flickered to red, and the keypad beeped in warning. "Why isn't it working?" he hissed.

"Drusilla has to use her skeleton key first, remember? The vault won't open otherwise."

Finn's jaw clenched, and he shot the keypad a disgusted glare.

"Is someone else down here?" This time, Emery spoke, her voice much louder and harsher than Drusilla's soft, dulcet tones. "I thought I heard footsteps. Like someone running away."

I snapped up my hand, telling Finn to keep quiet. He

nodded and hefted his gun a little higher. Then I tiptoed forward to the end of the corridor and plastered myself up against the wall so that I could peer into the mirrors again. Finn did the same thing, easing up beside me.

Emery Slater was standing in the middle of the next corridor, her hands planted on her hips, facing this direction. A suspicious scowl twisted her face.

I tightened my grip on my knife, making the spider rune stamped into the hilt press into the larger matching scar embedded in my palm. The sensation steadied me, the way it always did. No matter what happened, I was *not* letting Emery anywhere near Finn. If Drusilla roasted me with her Fire magic for violating the bank's no-violence rules, then so be it.

Drusilla stepped up beside Emery. Her guards started to follow, but she waved her hand, telling them to hang back. The two men obeyed her silent order and focused their attention on the giant Emery had brought along.

"People come and go as they wish," Drusilla said. "Someone is always at the bank, so the vaults can be accessed twenty-four hours a day. I thought your employer would appreciate that, since you said that he prefers to keep odd hours."

"Yes, he does." Emery kept staring in this direction. "And he values discretion above all else."

I held back a derisive snort. Mason valued power above all else—power that he could use to bribe, cajole, threaten, torture, or kill anyone who got in his way.

"Don't worry," Drusilla replied, her tone smooth and even. "There are no cameras down here, and we don't monitor our clients' comings and goings or what they store in their vaults. We take our clients' privacy very seriously."

Emery huffed. "You should, as much as you're charging for it."

Annoyance flickered across Drusilla's face. "The Bellum Bank *is* the best and most discreet in all of Ashland. Such service and security come at a premium price."

Emery huffed again, then took a few steps forward. "What's down that way?"

I shifted my stance, getting ready to strike should Emery decide to mosey around the corner and wander into this corridor. Maybe I could take the giant by surprise and kill her before she realized what was happening. After that, well, I didn't know what Emery's goon would do, or Drusilla and her two guards. Perhaps I could deal with them all in a less lethal manner. Drusilla hadn't wronged me—yet—and I didn't want to hurt her or her people unless it was absolutely necessary.

Emery kept creeping forward. Her eyes narrowed, and more suspicion filled her face. The giant seemed bound and determined to see every single inch of the vault level—

Drusilla stepped in front of Emery, stopping the other woman from going any farther down the corridor. "More vaults are down that way. Some of our smaller units. But given what you've told me, I think your boss would be happier in a different section. One with more spacious units. Now, if you'll follow me, I'll show you to that area."

Drusilla strode past the giant, heading to the opposite end of the corridor, but Emery kept staring in this direction, as if she could sense me lurking around the corner, just longing to kill her.

My fingers curled a little tighter around my knife. Part of me wanted to throw caution to the wind, charge forward, and bury my blade in her chest. Killing the giant would eliminate one of my most pressing, dangerous problems, as well as being a serious blow to Mason. But I was all too aware of Finn standing beside me, his gun in his hand, and the two bank guards, who had their hands on their own weapons and were watching Emery and her minion.

Any sort of confrontation would end badly—for everyone.

"Are you coming?" Drusilla called out.

Instead of answering, Emery shifted on her feet, as though she was going to ignore the other woman and head this way. I drew in a breath and got ready to move—

"Yeah, sure," Emery muttered. "Show me this big fancy vault."

She stared in this direction a second longer, then turned and headed to the opposite end of the corridor, where Drusilla was waiting. Emery's man followed her, as did the two bank guards. The five of them vanished around the far corner, and their voices and footsteps faded away.

Beside me, Finn blew out a long, tense breath, stepped away from the wall, and tucked his gun back into its holster. "That was close."

"Too close," I agreed.

"What do you think Emery is doing here?" he asked. "Is she really looking at vaults for Mason, like she claimed?"

I shook my head and slid my knife back up my sleeve. "I have no idea, but we need to get out of here before she comes back."

Keeping an eye out for Emery and the others, Finn and I followed the green arrows in the floor back to the elevator. The metal grate was standing wide open, but a new, third bank guard was stationed there now. The man watched us approach with a wary expression on his face and his hand on his gun. He seemed just as well trained as the two men guarding Drusilla.

"All done," I chirped, giving the giant a bright smile. "Ready to head back up to the land of the living."

The guard eyed us, still wary, but he gestured for us to get into the elevator, then reached inside and punched a button on the panel. The guard drew back, the grate rattled shut, and the elevator started to rise.

I half expected the car to screech to a halt, trapping us, but a few seconds later, the elevator floated to a stop, and the grate automatically rattled back. Finn and I both glanced out into the corridor beyond, but it was empty, so we moved forward.

Instead of arrows in the floor, green signs on the walls told us which way to go. We quickly scurried through the corridors, finally reaching yet another guard standing in front of a metal door. This giant also eyed us with suspicion, but he shoved the door open at our approach.

Finn and I stepped back out into the lobby. We both glanced around, but I didn't spot Mason or any black-suited giants among the crowd, so we hurried forward.

As we walked along, both of our phones started *chime-chime-chiming* with texts, drawing the attention of several folks waiting in the teller lines. I grimaced, berating myself for not setting my phone to silent earlier, but I kept moving at a steady pace, as though nothing was wrong and I didn't care that so many people were staring at me. Several long, interminable seconds later, Finn and I pushed through the glass doors and made it outside.

Once again, I glanced around, but I didn't see Mason or any other potential enemies trudging up the bank steps, loitering on the street corners, or sitting on benches in the grassy park in the center of the roundabout. I couldn't relax, though. Not until we were away from here.

Finn looked at his phone. "Eight—no, nine texts from

Silvio, each one increasing exponentially in numbers of exclamation points and degrees of panic, starting with wondering what's taking so long, then seeing Emery entering the bank, then wondering if we're still alive."

"Less talking, more walking," I muttered, still scanning the area for enemies.

I hurried down the steps, with Finn hot on my heels. A car zoomed up the street and pulled over to the curb right in front of us. I tensed and started to palm a knife, but then I spotted Owen behind the wheel.

"Get in!" he called out through the lowered passenger's-side window.

Finn opened the door and slid into the back, while I got into the front. The second I closed the door, Owen glanced in the rearview mirror, checking the traffic, then pulled away from the curb.

"I saw Emery go into the bank," Owen said. "Are you two okay?"

"We're fine," I replied. "It was a close call, but I don't think she spotted us. Otherwise, things would have ended much differently."

"Yep, with screams, gunfire, blood, and death," Finn chirped in a cheerful voice.

I glared at him over my shoulder, but he shrugged in return.

"Hey, don't blame me, because that's the Spider special. Why, you should put it on the menu at the Pork Pit." Finn snickered at his bad joke.

I rolled my eyes, but he was right. Like it or not, screams, gunfire, blood, and death *were* my specialties as the Spider.

Owen shot me a worried glance, so I reached over and squeezed his hand.

"We're fine," I repeated. "Truly. All that matters is that we got out of there alive."

He nodded, and some of the tension eased out of his shoulders. "I have to go back to the garage and pick up Silvio."

"Good. That will give us the perfect vantage point."

Owen frowned. "To do what?"

"Spy on Emery."

Owen drove the car back up to the third level of the garage and parked it in the same spot we'd started out from an hour ago. The three of us got out of the car and went over to the railing where Silvio was still stationed.

I glanced down at the area below. People scurrying along the sidewalks. Vehicles cruising along the streets and flowing through the roundabout. Vendors opening up food carts full of pretzels, hot dogs, and ice cream in the park. Everything looked the same as before, and I didn't see any telltale black SUVs idling at the curbs that would indicate that more Circle goons were in the area.

Some of the tight knots of worry in my chest loosened, and I turned to Silvio. "Any sign of Mason?"

My assistant swiped through a few screens on his tablet, then shook his head. "Nothing on the traffic cams. I was holding my position here when I spotted Emery going up the bank steps. I texted you and Finn that she was heading inside, but neither one of you responded."

"There's no cell service on the underground vault level. Believe me, the heads-up would have come in handy."

I told Owen and Silvio everything that had happened inside the bank, from Finn and me meeting Drusilla and Charles Yang, to finding Fletcher's vault full of valuables, to almost running into Emery Slater.

"You're lucky she didn't see you," Owen said.

"It was a close call," Finn agreed.

"Too close," I muttered.

"Why was Emery at the bank?" Silvio asked. "Do you think someone tipped her off that you two were inside? That she followed you down to the vaults to see what you were doing? To find out if Mason's missing money was there?"

"Or maybe she just wanted to kill Gin," Owen rumbled, a concerned look on his face. "We all know how much Emery hates you."

Hate was putting it mildly. Emery absolutely *despised* me for killing her beloved uncle, Elliot Slater, a vicious giant who used to work for Mab Monroe. What Emery didn't know was that I hadn't actually killed her uncle. That had been Roslyn Phillips, a vampire and friend of mine Elliot had been stalking and terrorizing. Still, I'd taken the blame for Elliot's death to protect Roslyn, and I was glad that I had. Otherwise, Emery would be targeting my friend instead of me.

I shook my head. "I don't think Emery was there to murder me. We had only been on the vault level for about thirty minutes when she showed up. The criminal gossip grapevine in Ashland might be fast, but it's not *that* fast. No, I think she came to the bank for some other reason."

In the distance, the bank's glass doors opened, and Emery strode outside, as if my invoking her name had magically summoned her, like conjuring an evil spirit. The black-suited male giant also stepped outside, as did Drusilla Yang.

The two women stopped and faced each other. Drusilla smiled and started talking, gesturing over at the bank, but Emery planted her hands on her hips and stared down her nose at the shorter woman. The giant was clearly not buying whatever the banker was selling.

After several more seconds of one-sided conversation, Drusilla stuck out her hand, which Emery gave a perfunctory shake before spinning around and trudging down the steps.

The male giant followed her, and the two of them walked down the block, rounded the corner, and disappeared from sight.

My gaze snapped back over to Drusilla. The second Emery vanished, the smile dropped from the Fire elemental's face, and she crossed her arms over her chest and started tapping her right foot in a quick, staccato rhythm. I couldn't tell if she was annoyed or worried or both. Either way, Drusilla didn't seem to be a fan of Emery Slater. Well, at least we had that in common.

Drusilla moved over to speak to the giant still guarding the entrance. The man straightened up, even more vigilant than before. Drusilla nodded, as if satisfied, then pushed through the glass doors and vanished back inside the bank.

"It doesn't seem like Emery got whatever she wanted from the Yangs," Owen said.

"No, it doesn't," I replied. "And why did Emery come here? Why today, of all days? If she had been following me, then I would at least know that she came here to kill me."

Silvio huffed. "Only you, Gin, would be satisfied knowing that someone was plotting to kill you."

I shrugged. "Knowing someone is gunning for me is always better than *not* knowing."

Silvio huffed again, but he couldn't disagree with my logic.

"Emery was talking to Drusilla about renting a vault for her boss," Finn chimed in. "Maybe Mason has something valuable he wants to store at the bank."

"Like what?" Owen asked. "What could Mason be so protective of or worried about that he would let someone else watch over it instead of Emery and his own men?"

None of us had an answer for that. Worry spiked through me, as sharp as nails being driven into my body. Ever since Mason had revealed himself, ruined Mosley and Mallory's wedding reception, and almost killed me, I had spent my days and nights fretting about what he might do next, how he might strike out at me, and especially when he might decide to murder everyone I cared about.

More than once, I'd woken up in a cold sweat, heart hammering and a scream stuck in my throat because I'd dreamed that Mason was torturing Owen, Finn, Silvio, or someone else I loved with his Stone magic. All that continued worry and all those vivid nightmares made my head pound with dread and my heart ache with bone-chilling fear, even now, in the daylight.

I couldn't stop the nightmares from hijacking my sleep, but worry was a useless emotion, just like tears were a waste of time, energy, and resources. Fletcher had told me both those things more than once, but somehow Mason had made me forget them, made me forget *myself*. For the past few weeks, I had been trapped and treading water in my own cold tank of worry, fear, and dread.

Well, no more. I was Gin Blanco. I was the Spider. Patience might be one of my virtues, but now it was time to *act*.

First up on the agenda: figuring out exactly what sort of scheme Mason had cooking with the Bellum Bank. Oh, I didn't know the answer any more than I had a few minutes ago, but I did have access to someone who might be able to shed some light on things.

"What do you want to do now, Gin?" Silvio asked. "Watch the bank and see if Emery comes back with Mason?"

I shook my head. "No. It could be hours, or even days, before that happens. Let's go. I have barbecue to cook."

❋ 5 ❋

We all piled back into Finn's car, and he drove us out of the garage. We'd come to the bank early, in hopes of blending into the morning rush, but now it was after ten, and everyone needed to get to work.

Finn dropped Owen off outside his office building before leaving Silvio and me at the Pork Pit, my barbecue restaurant. My brother waved good-bye, then pulled away from the curb to head over to First Trust bank, since he was running things while Stuart Mosley enjoyed his honeymoon.

I glanced up and down the street, but the foot and vehicle traffic was flowing normally, and no one looked like they wanted to lunge out of the crowd of people hurrying along the sidewalk and try to murder me. A refreshing change.

So I focused on the front door, examining it and the storefront windows for rune traps, bombs, and any other nasty surprises an underworld boss might have left for me overnight. But the restaurant was clean, so I unlocked the door and stepped inside. Silvio followed me.

The bell over the door jingled, announcing our arrival. Silvio stepped forward, moving past the blue and pink booths that lined the storefront windows, along with the tables and chairs in the middle of the restaurant. He followed the blue and pink pig tracks on the floor over to the long counter that ran along the back wall. Within seconds, Silvio had shrugged out of his long gray overcoat, had shed his gray plaid scarf, and was ensconced on his usual stool close to the old-fashioned cash register that perched at one end of the counter.

I stripped off my own fleece jacket and walked over to the counter, breathing in deeply and letting the spicy cumin scent of Fletcher's secret barbecue sauce fill my nose and sink deep down into my lungs.

Behind the counter, a woman watched a large vat of said barbecue sauce that was bubbling away on one of the stoves. She was a dwarf, a little more than five feet tall, with a thick, strong body, and the muscles in her arms bulged every time she stirred the sauce. Neon-blue streaks shimmered in her black hair, while matching glitter eye shadow and liner made her black eyes pop in her pale face. A blue crystal heart dangled from a black velvet ribbon that ringed her neck, and smaller matching hearts also covered her black apron, along with her short-sleeved black T-shirt. Black jeans and boots with neon-blue laces completed her cool Goth ensemble.

"How can I help?" I asked.

Sophia Deveraux, my head cook and the best body disposer in Ashland, pointed to the tomatoes, carrots, red onions, and cabbages piled on the counter. "Slice those up for sandwiches and coleslaw," she rasped in her eerie, broken voice.

I nodded, hung my jacket on a nearby coatrack, and tied a blue apron on over my clothes. Then I grabbed a knife, along with a cutting board, and started filleting the vegetables. Thick round slices for the juicy red tomatoes. Thin matchstick pieces for the sweet orange carrots. A neat tiny dice for the aromatic red onions. I even broke out a mandolin and scoured the green and purple cabbages against the sharp blade, reducing the leaves into long, thin, julienned strips.

While I chopped vegetables, the waitstaff trickled into the restaurant, and soon it was eleven o'clock and time to open. Given the early March chill, several people had a hankering for barbecue, and customers streamed inside the restaurant as soon as I unlocked the front door.

I spent the next few hours waiting on tables, helping Sophia plate up food, and cashing out customers. All the while, I kept an eye on the front door and the windows, wondering if Emery—or maybe even Mason himself— might appear, especially given my near miss with the giant at the bank earlier. But neither of them darkened my door, and the lunch rush zoomed by like normal.

Around two o'clock, the front door opened, making the bell chime, and a woman strolled into the restaurant. She was in her mid-twenties, about five years younger than me, and quite pretty, with short, shaggy blond hair, blue eyes, and rosy skin. She shrugged out of her navy peacoat, revealing a shiny gold badge and a gun holstered to her black leather belt. She was wearing a navy-blue turtleneck sweater, along with dark jeans and brown boots. A silverstone pendant shaped like a primrose, the symbol for beauty, dangled from the chain around her neck, while two rings gleamed on her left index finger—one band ringed with snowflakes and the other with ivy vines.

Detective Bria Coolidge, my baby sister, slid onto the stool beside Silvio, who gave her an absentminded nod. My assistant was absorbed in his tablet, looking at the traffic-camera footage and trying to track where Emery had gone after she'd left the bank. Still staring at the screen, Silvio nibbled on an oatmeal-raspberry cookie, then washed it down with a sip of the dark hot chocolate laced with raspberry syrup I'd made for him.

"What can I get you?" I asked my sister.

Bria ordered a platter with shredded barbecue chicken, baked beans, potato salad, and some of Sophia's delicious sourdough rolls. I fixed her food, then made myself and Sophia the same plate, since neither one of us had eaten lunch yet. I sat on my own stool behind the cash register and wolfed down my food, while Sophia leaned against the counter and did the same with hers.

Thanks to Fletcher's barbecue sauce, the chicken and the baked beans were both filled with layers of deep, intense flavor, while the potato salad was a cool, creamy contrast, with its celery crunch, refreshing notes of dill, and bright splash of lemon juice. Sophia's warm, soft, yummy rolls were the perfect way to sop up all the last bits of food and sauce on my plate, while the raspberry lemonade I'd made had just enough sugar and tang to cut through the rich, heavy meal.

I popped the last bite of roll into my mouth and sighed with happiness. I *never* got tired of barbecue. Meat, sauce, and smoke, with both sweet *and* spicy notes. Barbecue truly was the perfect food.

Bria also sighed with similar contentment, fullness, and happiness and pushed her own empty plate away. So did Sophia. Silvio had eschewed the chicken and other dishes in favor of nibbling on more cookies and slurping down a second mug of hot chocolate.

Bria planted her elbows on the counter. "How did things go at the bank?"

Food first, business later. My sister had her priorities exactly right.

"Good, bad, and ugly, like most things in my life," I drawled.

I filled Bria and Sophia in on everything that had happened at the Bellum Bank, while Silvio cued up the photos I'd taken of Fletcher's secret vault on his tablet. He showed the screen to Bria and Sophia, who both let out low whistles of appreciation.

"That's a lot of money," Bria replied.

"A whole lot of money," Sophia agreed.

"Finn estimates that the cash alone is worth about ten million dollars, but according to *my* calculations, it's worth more," Silvio replied, still staring at his tablet. "I'd say the grand total is closer to twelve or maybe even thirteen million, if you include the bags of coins."

Bria, Sophia, and I all grinned at one another. Just like Finn and Drusilla Yang, my brother and my assistant also had a relationship that bordered on *friendly rivals*. Due to their competitive natures and unending needs to be right, Finn and Silvio were constantly correcting and trying to one-up each other, although their relationship was far warmer than Finn's was with Drusilla Yang.

"Of course, I can't tell *exactly* how much money there is in coins, especially since it looks like Fletcher just shoved whatever loose change he had into some of those bags." Silvio shook his head. "Why would he even bother storing coins in the vault? They're so awkward and heavy to haul around, not to mention extremely tedious to count out. Sometimes I think your mentor was a very strange man, Gin."

"Heh. You're telling me. You're not the one Fletcher sent on this wild-goose-chase-slash-treasure-hunt in the first place."

Silvio nodded his agreement, still staring at the vault photos.

Bria looked at his screen for a few more seconds, then raised her gaze to mine. "Ten million dollars? That's all? The way Mason described it when he had Emery kidnap us, you would have thought Fletcher had stolen *tens* of millions of dollars from the Circle."

Her words echoed my own concerns. "I know. Even though we found the vault, and Finn and I didn't see any more clues or letters from Fletcher, I still feel like I'm missing something. That the old man left me one final message inside his vault, something only I would understand. But so far, I'm stumped about what it might be."

Frustration filled me, simmering in my veins just like Fletcher's barbecue sauce had bubbled away on the stove earlier. "But if I'm wrong, and there *aren't* any more clues from Fletcher…well, I don't know what to do with that vault full of loot. Ten million dollars probably isn't enough money to undercut whatever horrible thing Mason is plotting."

Sophia reached over and gently squeezed my arm, careful not to hurt me with her dwarven strength. "You'll figure it out."

"Absolutely," Bria agreed. "And look on the bright side. You found the vault, so you can access the money now."

Her cheerful tone and positive words didn't match her serious expression, so I arched an eyebrow at her. "And on the dark side?"

My sister grimaced. "Emery Slater was there."

"And we still have no idea why," Silvio chimed in.

Bria shot Silvio a sour look, but he shrugged in return. My assistant was never one to sugarcoat things.

"You're both right," I said. "We need to know why Emery was at the bank, and especially why Mason is suddenly so interested in doing business with the Yangs. And I have just the thing to help us figure it out."

I turned around, grabbed a large cardboard box off the back counter, and set it down in front of Bria and Silvio. Various containers filled the box, along with napkins, silverware, and more.

My sister frowned. "How is a box of barbecue going to help you get answers?"

"Don't you know? Barbecue makes *everything* better," I drawled. "Especially when it comes to getting answers out of recalcitrant people."

Understanding flashed in Bria's blue eyes. "You're going over *there*? To see *him*?"

I nodded. "Yep. I've been going around this time every day for the past few weeks. Want to tag along?"

Anger flickered across her face, making her eyes burn an even brighter blue. "Definitely. We still have unfinished business."

Silvio shook his head. "I never thought I would say this, but I almost feel sorry for that poor bastard right now."

"Beware of Greeks bearing gifts, and especially of Gin bearing barbecue," Sophia rasped, winking at me.

I grinned at my friends. "Absolutely."

Silvio opted to stay behind and keep studying the vault photos, so I left the Pork Pit in his and Sophia's capable hands, grabbed my box of barbecue and my fleece jacket, and skedaddled. We took Bria's car, and she circled through the downtown loop three times before I was satisfied that no one was following us.

"We're clear," I said.

Bria made the turn that would take us toward our ultimate destination. She stopped at a red light and eyed me. "So...do you want to tell me what's bothering you? Or am I going to have to pry it out of you like usual, oh recalcitrant one?"

"Hey, no fair using my own words against me. And I am *not* recalcitrant."

She snorted. "Oh, no, Gin. You would just rather have a root canal, walk barefoot across hot coals, *and* swim in a tank full of hungry sharks than talk about your feelings. That's not recalcitrant *at all*."

"You're wrong," I protested. "I'd swim in the shark tank first. That way, if the sharks did eat me, then I wouldn't have to worry about the root canal or the hot coals. Win-win for me *and* the sharks."

Bria kept staring at me, unimpressed with my warped logic. "Don't try to change the subject. Spill. Now."

My sister was as stubborn as I was recalcitrant, so I sighed, giving in to the inevitable. "Is it that obvious?"

"Only because you looked like someone was twisting one of your own knives into your side when Silvio was showing off the vault photos," Bria replied.

I sighed again. I thought I'd done a better job of hiding my disappointment and frustration, but apparently not. "It's the same thing you said earlier, and Finn and I talked about it at the bank too."

"What?"

"That the money in the vault just doesn't seem like… *enough*."

"Why? Because Mason made it sound like it was a lot more than ten million dollars when he held us hostage at the Mitchell mansion?" Bria shook her head, making her blond hair dance around her shoulders. "You can't trust a word he says. Maybe Mason was trying to make the missing money seem bigger and more important to motivate you into finding it. Maybe he was just being petty and screwing with you because Fletcher got the better of him all those years ago. We both know Mason is capable of that—and far, far worse."

Images of my father's body flickered through my mind. The black-and-blue bruises that had dotted Tristan's arms and legs like ornaments on the most macabre Christmas tree ever. His broken bones poking up at impossible angles, like arrows about to shoot out of his skin. His purple, swollen, dislocated fingers. How thoroughly *crushed* he had been from head to toe, with only his face left strangely, unnaturally intact. Mason fucking Mitchell had inflicted unspeakable pain on his own twin brother, and my uncle was more than capable of doing the same thing to me and everyone I loved.

My heart twisted, my chest tightened, and my stomach churned. I quickly rolled down the window, trying not to vomit. The cold March air slapped me in the face, easing some of my nausea, but it didn't wash away the awful images that were burned into my brain.

Nothing could ever do that.

"Besides," Bria continued. "Fletcher stole that money from Mason years ago. Maybe ten million dollars meant a lot more to the Circle back then. And if the cash has just been sitting in the vault, then it's not like it's been earning interest and increasing in value."

Her eyes were on the road, and she didn't seem to have noticed my mini-meltdown, so I rolled the window back up and forced myself to answer her in a light, playful voice.

"Now you sound like Finn," I teased.

A sly smile curved her lips. "Well, when you date an investment banker, you're bound to pick up a few things."

Finnegan Lane might be an incorrigible flirt, but Bria held his heart in the palm of her hand, and he gripped hers just as tightly in his. In many ways, they were complete opposites. Finn was greedy, charming, and whimsical, while Bria was righteous, serious, and determined. But somehow their differences made them complement each other perfectly.

I was so glad they had found each other, especially now, when my own future was so very uncertain. I still wasn't sure if I had the strength and smarts to kill Mason, and if I died trying, then at least Finn and Bria would have each other to lean on. Maybe the two of them could even help Owen deal with whatever bad thing that happened to me.

Yep, that was me, looking on the bright side, instead of dwelling on the very dark, very real possibility that Mason might end up murdering me the same way he had my father. More nausea roiled in my stomach, but I ignored it the best I could.

"Here we go," Bria murmured.

She slowed the car, and we both glanced around. We had left the gleaming skyscrapers and historic downtown buildings behind and were now firmly in Southtown, the part of Ashland that was home to gangs, drug dealers, and other violent, dangerous folks.

Including the people we had come to see.

I checked the passenger's-side mirror again, but no vehicles were creeping along behind us. "We're still clear."

Bria steered her sedan into a paved lot that fronted a small park and wooded area. Given the chilly, windy day, only a few die-hard fitness folks were walking, jogging, and biking through the area, but I still pulled a black toboggan out of the pocket of my gray fleece jacket and pulled it down over my head, hiding my dark brown ponytail from sight. Bria pulled a similar blue toboggan down over her own head. We both also wrapped scarves around our necks, obscuring the bottom halves of our faces, before getting out of the car.

Several guys in their late teens and early twenties were sitting on some blue fiberglass picnic tables at the park entrance. They were all wearing winter jackets, and they quickly stuffed their hands—and bags of drugs—into their pockets as we walked toward them.

Normally, the guys probably would have called out and tried to get us to buy some of their pill and powder merchandise, but Bria's navy sedan screamed *cop car*, so they kept quiet. In Ashland, many of the cops were even more dangerous and crooked than the city's criminals, and it was usually a good idea to steer clear of the po-po whenever possible. Bria was one of the few exceptions who were truly dedicated to protecting and serving, instead of lining their pockets with bribes, but these dealers didn't need to know that.

Bria stopped in front of the tables, jerked her navy peacoat up to reveal her gold badge and gun, and stabbed her blue-gloved finger at the dealers. "Little kids play in this park," she growled. "Don't be here when I come back."

Her low, angry voice had the guys scrambling off the tables and scurrying away. They quickly left the park, crossed the street, and vanished around the corner of the closest building.

"I thought we were going to keep a low profile," I said. "Not roust some low-level dealers and make ourselves memorable."

Bria kept glaring in the direction the dealers had gone, like she wanted to chase after and arrest the lot of them. "You know I can't just walk by guys like that and not say anything."

"And that's one of the reasons I love you." Even though she couldn't see it, I grinned beneath the scarf covering my chin. "Plus, it's always so much fun watching you be a hard-boiled badass."

"Hard-boiled? What am I, a freaking egg?" Bria scoffed, but I could hear the smile in her voice. "Come on. The coast is clear, so let's deliver your food before it goes completely cold."

We left the park behind, stepped onto a winding path, and headed into the nearby woods. No one was walking, jogging, or biking through this area, and the only sound was the soft scuffing of our footsteps, along with an occasional whistle of wind that made the tree branches moan and groan, like old folks crankily complaining about the weather.

We reached the end of the path, moved through another small, wooded park, and wound up at a ten-foot chain-link fence that cordoned off this area from the neighboring industrial zone. Bria pulled back a cut section in the fence, and we both slipped through to the other side.

And just like that, the landscape morphed from pleasant woods into a shipping yard crammed full of metal containers in various shades of rusty red, faded yellow, and burnt orange. It was after three o'clock now, and business was still going strong. Shouts filled the air, along with the loud answering rumbles and belching, acrid exhaust of heavy machinery.

Bria and I quickly moved from one row of containers to the next, but we didn't run into any workers. Finally, we reached a lone box sitting off by itself under a large maple. Unlike all the others, this container was dented in several places, as though it had been dropped on its side one too many times and was no longer usable, and its isolated location made it look like an oversize building block a child had tossed aside in a tantrum.

Bria stopped and pointed her finger at the container door, which was standing open. She shot me a worried look, then unbuttoned her coat and yanked her gun out of its holster. I shifted my cardboard box to the crook of my left elbow, then palmed the knife hidden up my right sleeve. Together, Bria and I crept over to the container.

The shipyard workers must have decided to take a break, because their shouts faded away, as did the rumble and belch of machinery. After all the noisy commotion, the sudden, abrupt silence seemed odd and sinister—

"Exactly how long do you plan on keeping me here?" a man's low, grumpy voice echoed from the open door.

"Oh, I don't know," a woman answered in a tart tone. "Probably until you stop being a jackass. So I suppose that means the tenth of never?"

Bria looked at me and rolled her eyes before holstering her gun. I tucked my knife back up my sleeve, knowing that the only danger here was acerbic insults. Then we both stepped forward so that we could peer inside.

Instead of being a barren shell, the shipping container boasted a surprising amount of furniture: a cot covered with cozy fleece blankets, a table with several chairs, a small TV, an even smaller radio, and a box full of books. Bare bulbs had been strung up overhead, and a couple of electric heaters were tucked into the back corners, blasting out some much-needed warmth.

A man was sitting on the cot, with his back against the metal wall. He was in his fifties, although he had one of those ageless faces that would make him appear handsome no matter how old he got. His black hair and goatee gleamed under the lights, and he was wearing a thick navy fisherman's sweater over a pair of light blue corduroy pants, which was most definitely dressing down from his usual slick, dark suits. His tan skin was still unnaturally pale, and he had the weak, sickly look of a man who'd recently been more dead than alive.

Hugh Tucker used to work for Mason as the Circle's number one enforcer, and the vampire had been my nemesis for all the months I'd been investigating the evil group.

Although I was starting to think he was someone else's problem now, especially given the hungry look in his black eyes as he stared at the woman sitting at the table, calmly typing away on a laptop.

The woman was my age, early thirties, and quite pretty, with blue eyes, pale skin, and black hair pulled back into a French braid. She was wearing a royal-blue turtleneck sweater, along with dark jeans and boots. A diamond rose-and-thorn ring glinted on her finger, a symbol of how dangerous beauty could be.

And attraction too, especially when it came to the two of them.

"A mere jackass? And here I thought I was the big bad, the ultimate evil, the stuff of your worst nightmares," Tucker drawled in a wry tone.

Lorelei Parker didn't even glance up from her screen. "Well, I suppose it's never fun to be downgraded, but when it comes to evil, you are barely a blip on my radar," she drawled right back at him. "Especially since you're still as weak as a puppy."

A low noise that sounded suspiciously like a frustrated growl erupted out of Tucker's throat. Silence. Then he spoke again. "I'll admit that I'm not at my best right now, but that will change soon. And then…"

His voice trailed off, although I couldn't tell if his words were a threat or a suggestion or both. More silence.

Lorelei's fingers stilled on the laptop keys, and she finally glanced up at him, her eyes narrowing. "And then *what?*"

"Why, you'll just have to wait and find out, Ms. Parker." Tucker's eyes glittered with heat.

An answering flush swept over Lorelei's cheeks, turning them a pretty pink, but she huffed, focused on her laptop, and started typing again. "Promises, promises," she mocked.

"Promises that I intend to keep, just as soon as I am able," he answered in a low, husky voice.

Lorelei's fingers stuttered to a stop, but she kept her gaze fixed on the screen. After a few long, tense, silent seconds, she started typing yet again, her fingers stabbing the keys a little quicker and more violently than before, as if she was trying to drown out...whatever Tucker had been talking about.

I loudly cleared my throat, knocked on the open door, and stepped inside the container. I pulled my scarf down so that Tucker and Lorelei could see my face, then yanked the toboggan off my head and stuffed it into my coat pocket. Bria followed me and also shed some of her winter gear.

"How is our patient?" I asked, pretending I hadn't heard the two of them sniping and flirting with each other.

"Getting better and mouthier every single day," Lorelei muttered.

"I was just asking Ms. Parker how much longer I have to enjoy her fine Southern hospitality," Tucker replied in his smooth, silky voice.

"Well, that depends entirely on you, Hugh, and what information you have for me."

He sighed. "Come to ask me more pointless questions about Mason and the Circle?"

"The questions wouldn't be so pointless if you would actually *answer* them," Bria snapped.

Tucker looked at her and winced a bit, the way he always did. With her blond hair and blue eyes, Bria was the spitting image of Eira Snow, our mother, whom Tucker had been in love with for years—until Mab Monroe had murdered her.

Sometimes I thought Tucker felt more guilt about that and was even more haunted by my mother's and Annabella's deaths than I was. Part of me hoped he *did* agonize about that fateful night, that he hurt and grieved just as badly and deeply as I still did. The other part of me just felt sorry for him, for all he had lost, suffered, and endured. Like it or not, Hugh Tucker was another one of Mason's many, many victims.

"As I've told you before, Bria, I am no longer in Mason's inner circle, so to speak, so any information I might provide has probably been rendered useless by this point—or might lead you and Gin into a trap." Tucker shook his head. "And none of us wants that."

Bria crossed her arms over her chest and glared at him. "I have absolutely no idea what you want."

For the briefest instant, Tucker's eyes flicked to Lorelei. No one seemed to notice the telltale motion but me, though.

"What I want is irrelevant," the vampire replied, his voice as smooth as ever. "I've made my bed, and now I have to lie in it. And I can tell you that it's quite uncomfortable."

We all knew he wasn't talking about the cot, which admittedly wasn't the softest one around, but rather about the choice he'd made in the Circle cemetery to finally rise up against Mason. Tucker had almost died shielding me from my uncle's Stone magic, and the vampire and his incredible speed were the only reasons I was still alive. Tucker had taken an alarming amount of Stone shrapnel in the back to protect me, and I wouldn't—*couldn't*—forget that selfless action, that willing sacrifice, no matter how many times he had tried to kill me in the past.

I set the cardboard box on the table. "Well, just because your bed is uncomfortable, that doesn't mean your belly can't be full."

Tucker eyed the box with suspicion. "I expected you to simply slit my throat, Gin. Not try to poison me."

"If I wanted you dead, then dead you would be." I stabbed my finger at him. "And don't you *dare* malign my barbecue.

People pay good money for my cooking. Now, sit down, and eat up."

Tucker gave me a sour look, but he hoisted himself up off the cot and slowly shuffled over to the table. It wasn't that far, no more than a few feet, but his legs wobbled, and his breath was puffing out of his mouth by the time he pulled out a chair and collapsed down into it.

Lorelei closed her laptop and scooted it off to the side so that I could lay out the food: shredded barbecue chicken, along with baked beans, mac and cheese, potato salad, coleslaw, and plenty of Sophia's sourdough rolls. I'd even brought along a gallon of raspberry lemonade and a dozen oatmeal-raspberry cookies.

I handed paper plates, silverware, and napkins to both Tucker and Lorelei and snitched some cookies for Bria and myself. Lorelei quickly cleaned her plate, while Tucker downed three big helpings of everything. When he had finished eating, I reached into the box and pulled out one final item: a bag of blood.

I slid it over to the vampire. "Here. A gift from Silvio. To help build up your strength."

Tucker shuddered. "Did you know that Mr. Sanchez puts sugar in his blood? It's *disgusting*, like drinking sweet, luke-warm, liquid copper."

"And how *do* you like your blood, Mr. Tucker?" Lorelei sniped. "Ice-cold and served in a crystal flute?"

"Oh, no, Ms. Parker," he purred, his gaze dropping to her neck. "I like my blood straight from the source. It can be *quite* a heady experience, when both parties are willing."

Once again, a pink flush swept over Lorelei's cheeks, while answering heat sparked in Tucker's eyes.

Bria crinkled her nose, apparently missing the subtext between the two of them. "Ewww. I don't know which would be worse, drinking cold sugared blood or warm fresh blood. Blech."

Lorelei and Tucker ignored my sister's disgust and kept eyeing each other, tension crackling in the air between them. As amusing as it was to watch them bicker, or whatever they were truly doing, I needed answers, so I leaned forward, breaking up their silent staring contest.

"So, Hugh. What can you tell me about the Bellum Bank?"

Tucker's gaze swung around to me, and genuine surprise filled his face. "Why are you asking about that?"

"Because I spotted Emery Slater there earlier today. She seemed quite interested in the bank's services."

Tucker's eyes narrowed. "And what were *you* doing there, Gin? Because you are most definitely not one of the Yangs' usual clients."

I kept my face blank, but Tucker was smart, and I couldn't stop the wheels from turning in his mind. Understanding flickered across his face.

"Ah, I see. You finally found Mason's money. Fletcher hid it at the Bellum Bank, didn't he? Clever, clever. The Yangs are among the few elemental families in Ashland who wouldn't be afraid of the Circle, if they knew it existed. Plus, they have a code. Once Fletcher brought the money to the Yangs, then they would have been honor-bound to keep it safe, no matter how badly Mason threatened them."

I resisted the urge to grind my teeth. Every time I tried to question Tucker about Mason and the Circle, the vampire twisted things around to his own advantage, squeezing far more information out of me than I did out of him. So far, my current interrogation—or lack thereof—was following a similar, disappointing pattern.

"If Fletcher hiding the money at the Bellum Bank was so

clever, then why didn't *you* think to search there for it?" Bria asked.

Tucker looked at her, but his gaze quickly skittered away from her face, the way it always did. "Of course, I thought the money might be hidden there, but the Yangs are powerful Fire elementals, especially Charles and Drusilla. Trying to break into their bank to search for the money would have been a suicide mission, and harming either one of them would have started a war with the rest of the Yang family— one that Mason might not have been able to win."

Well, it was good to know that Mason was wary of the Yangs, although Tucker's info made me even more curious about why my uncle would want to store something at their bank.

Tucker's eyes narrowed in thought again. "But you didn't find *all* of Mason's money, did you? Otherwise, you would be crowing about it right now. Rubbing my face in the fact that you found the money in a few weeks when I had spent years searching for it."

"Well, I suppose I *am* just a tiny bit smarter than you are, Tuck," I drawled, trying not to let him get under my skin again. "Yes, I found the missing money, and I did it without breaking into the bank or kidnapping and torturing someone to death."

He harrumphed. "And so the crowing begins."

I ignored his insult. "Forget about the money. It's not going anywhere. My main concern right now is what Emery was doing at the bank."

Tucker's lips puckered as though he'd bitten into something sour. No love was lost between the vampire and the giant, especially since Emery had taken Tucker's place as the Circle's number one enforcer. "I can only speculate about Emery's presence at the bank. Mason always keeps his most sensitive schemes to himself, right up to the very last minute. He never reveals anything he doesn't have to, not even to me, and I know him better than anyone."

"But you know *something*," Bria snapped. "You always do."

"Surely, after all these years, you have some inkling of what Mason's endgame is," Lorelei chimed in. "Otherwise, what was the point of working for him?"

Tucker's lips puckered again. "My reasons for working for Mason are my own."

Those reasons had a lot to do with Tucker's father gambling away their family fortune and becoming indebted to Mason and the other Circle members, but I kept quiet. That pain was the vampire's to bear, and the decision about whether to share the information was his, not mine.

Still, I was fed up with Tucker's word games, so I decided to remind him of some pertinent facts. "You might have saved me from Mason's Stone magic in the Circle cemetery, but I saved you too. You would be dead right now if I hadn't used my Ice magic to freeze your wounds until Jo-Jo Deveraux could heal you."

A muscle ticked in his jaw. "And I have thanked you multiple times for that benevolence, even though I've spent the past few weeks staring at the inside of this damn box."

"I don't want your thanks," I snapped. "I want some *answers*. So far, I've let you eat my barbecue and dance around the truth while you slowly recovered, but playtime is over. If you know something about what Mason is plotting, then you need to tell me. Right now."

The vampire leaned back in his chair and crossed his arms over his chest. He looked at me, and I stared right back at him. Tucker might be a recalcitrant bastard, but I excelled at being patient, at watching and waiting until the right moment presented itself for the Spider to eliminate a target. Now that I'd found Fletcher's vault, the moment to strike out at Mason was tantalizingly close, but I wasn't going to blow it by rushing headlong into a situation I didn't fully understand.

"I can sit in this chair all afternoon, Hugh," I drawled. "But I doubt that you can do the same. Why, you look like you're about three seconds away from keeling over onto the floor."

I wasn't exaggerating. Tucker's body was trembling, just the tiniest bit, and a fine sheen of sweat had formed on his forehead.

Still, he was stubborn to the end, and several more seconds ticked by in silence before his shoulders finally slumped, betraying his exhaustion.

"Fine," he muttered. "But my telling you what Mason is planning won't do it justice. It's better if you see it for yourself. Give me a pen and a piece of paper."

Bria reached into her coat pocket and drew out the pen and small pad she always carried to jot down notes at crime scenes. She slid them across the table to Tucker, who scribbled something, then tore the top sheet off the pad and handed it to me.

I glanced down at the paper. *Nineteen Bluff Street, tenth floor.* I recognized the address as belonging to one of the downtown office buildings. "What's there?"

A cold, thin smile creased Tucker's face. "Ambitions."

The cryptic answer puzzled me, but I held my tongue, not wanting to give him the satisfaction of asking any more questions. He probably wouldn't answer them anyway, given how little he had revealed so far.

"This had better not be some snipe hunt, some wild-goose chase," Bria warned.

Tucker arched an eyebrow at her. "Or what? Gin will come back and slice me to ribbons with her knives? Fine by me. A good spot of torture would be a welcome change from the monotony of being cooped up in here."

Bria opened her mouth to snap at him again, but I held up my hand. Tucker was right. I could whip out my knives and threaten to torture him unless he coughed up some answers, and I could actually go through with it and start carving him up like a Christmas ham. Oh, yes. I could torture Hugh Tucker until his blood dripped off the walls and he didn't have breath left to scream, but it wouldn't do any good.

Tucker had survived years of emotional abuse from Mason, not to mention all the dark deeds he'd done on my uncle's behalf. No torture I could inflict on the vampire would ever be worse than all of that—or the guilt and grief he still felt over my mother's murder.

So I slid the paper into my coat pocket and got to my feet. "Thank you."

Tucker's smile vanished, and his entire body sagged, making him look even more wobbly and exhausted than before. In that moment, he almost seemed…fragile. "*Never* thank me," he growled. "I don't deserve it."

Maybe he didn't, but I'd said the words, and I wasn't going to take them back. Besides, I thought that deep, deep, *deep* down, Hugh Tucker was more like me than he wanted to admit—someone who walked in the shadows but was still capable of goodness, on occasion.

I glanced over at Lorelei. "I'll check in with you later. Okay?"

My friend nodded, cracked her laptop open again, and returned to her typing. Tucker also remained at the table, eyeing the bag of sugared blood with a wary expression, his lips curling like he was trying to talk himself into drinking it, no matter how disgusting it might be.

Bria dumped the dirty plates into a trash can, while I

gathered up the food containers, packed them back into my cardboard box, and hoisted the whole thing up into my arms.

Bria headed for the door, and I followed her. I had just reached the opening when Tucker called out to me.

"Gin?"

I glanced over my shoulder at him. "What?"

"Be careful, and take some backup with you," he replied in a serious voice. "You'll probably need it."

Tucker gave me another thin smile, but this one seemed more pitying than mocking, and sympathy softened his eyes, almost as if he knew that he was leading me straight into a trap—one that would screw me over and shred my heart yet again.

✵ 6 ✵

ria and I left Tucker and Lorelei behind in the container, slipped out of the shipping yard, and went back to her car. The guys who'd been dealing drugs earlier were nowhere in sight, although they would probably resume their perches and trade on the picnic tables the second we left. Still, at least Bria had tried to make the park a little safer.

We slid into Bria's car, and she cranked the engine. "Now what?" she asked.

"Now we see if Tucker's information is any good."

I stared at the address the vampire had written down: *Nineteen Bluff Street, tenth floor.* Then I pulled out my phone and looked it up online.

Yep, it was one of the downtown office buildings, just like I'd thought, although my quick search didn't reveal what businesses—or "ambitions," as Tucker had so mysteriously called them—might be on that particular floor.

"Please tell me you're not actually thinking about going to that address," Bria said. "We both know you can't trust a word Tucker says. He might not be working for Mason anymore, but Tucker always has his own agenda."

"True," I replied. "But the best thing that could happen to Tucker would be for me to kill Mason as soon as possible. Our dear uncle will send Emery to murder Tucker the second he realizes that the vampire is still alive. So we can safely assume that Tucker's interests are aligned with ours—for now."

Maybe even for longer than that, given the way he was looking at Lorelei earlier, but that wasn't for me to decide. The vampire and my friend would have to work out their obvious attraction between themselves. But if Tucker hurt Lorelei, then I would gut him with my knives and watch him bleed out all over my shipping container, no matter how much information he might have on Mason.

But for right now, Tucker had given me a lead, and I needed to follow it.

I looked at Bria. "I can't sit around waiting for Mason to show his smug face. We need to go on the offensive and undercut him before he tries to kidnap one of us again—or worse."

She shook her head. "I still don't like it."

"I don't like it either, but it's the only move we have. Finn and Silvio haven't been able to find the smallest trace of Mason anywhere in Ashland, and our man inside the Circle hasn't been able to find out much either. Certainly not enough info for me to make a solid plan to assassinate Mason."

"All right, then. Where to?" Bria stabbed her finger at me. "And don't even *think* about arguing that it's too dangerous for me to come along. You heard what Tucker said about needing backup."

Love and gratitude warmed my heart, and I grinned at her. "Why, I couldn't think of better backup than a badass, hard-boiled detective."

Bria groaned. "I'm still not an egg."

My sister shot me a sour look, but her lips twitched upward into a smile as she threw the car into gear and steered out of the parking lot.

While Bria drove, I texted Owen and Finn, telling them what Tucker had said and the building we were going to investigate, but neither one of them responded. They were both probably busy with work. I also texted Silvio, who immediately messaged me back.

Want me to meet you there?

I quickly replied. *Nope. Stay put, and keep an eye on the Pork Pit in case Emery or Mason shows up.*

Okay. But text me the second (!) you two are out of the building.

I rolled my eyes. Even though it was only a message, I could still hear his chiding tone loud and clear. *Sure thing, Mom.* ☺

Silvio replied with a red glaring face emoji, as though he really were a mom giving me a stern, disapproving look.

By the time I slid my phone into my jacket pocket, Bria was steering the car into a parking garage—the same one Finn had parked in when we'd gone to the Bellum Bank this morning.

Unease churned in my stomach. The address Tucker had given me was only a couple of blocks from the bank. I didn't believe in coincidences, and I couldn't help but wonder how whatever was in that building tied in with both Mason and the Yangs.

Time to find out.

Bria and I got out of the car, left the garage, and walked over to Nineteen Bluff Street. Unlike most of the surrounding structures, which dated back more than a hundred years, this building was all sleek, modern chrome, along with gleaming glass windows. It even boasted a tall metal spike with a bright blue light burning at the very tip-top, as though it were a real skyscraper, instead of just a fifteen-story pretender.

Most buildings, especially the ones made largely of stone, hummed with emotional vibrations. Sure, those vibrations weren't always pleasant, like the greed, malice, and tension that rippled through the Bellum Bank, but at least those buildings had *personality*. All this chrome and glass was eerily quiet. Soulless, just like Mason.

"You sure you want to do this?" Bria asked.

We were loitering near a coffee cart on the street corner, as though we were waiting in line to get an overpriced drink and a stale bagel. My gaze flicked over the people hurrying along the sidewalks, but their heads were down and their eyes were on their phones. Next, I glanced out over the street, but cars cruised by at a normal rate of speed, following the traffic patterns. Finally, I looked at the building entrance, but folks pushed through and exited the revolving doors at a steady clip, and no one seemed particularly worried or nervous—or on the lookout for trespassers.

"It's creeping up on five o'clock," I said. "People will be focused on wrapping up their work for the day, so they shouldn't pay too much attention to us. Besides, we'll have an easier time getting into the building now, rather than after office hours. Let's do this."

Bria nodded and fell in step beside me. Together, we strolled along the sidewalk, pushed through one of the doors, and stepped into the lobby.

The inside of the building matched the outside—all chrome walls and glass windows, although the floor was a nice pale blue granite. I reached out with my magic, but I barely heard a whisper of sound from the stone. No wonder, since it was buried in the midst of all these modern trappings like a granite needle in a metal haystack. This building was most definitely soulless, just as I'd thought. Shame.

Several businesses were located in the lobby, including a sandwich shop, a more upscale dine-in steakhouse, and a jewelry store selling overpriced trinkets. People flowed in and out of the businesses, but my gaze zoomed over to the right side of the lobby, where there was a long counter with three giant security guards stationed behind it. Two of the men were leaning back in their chairs, slurping down sodas, and thumbing through magazines, but the third man was standing straight and tall, his hands resting on his gun belt, his eyes flicking back and forth as he studied everyone who walked by him.

"Guards at your three o'clock," Bria murmured.

"I see them. Follow me."

In a situation like this, confidence was everything, so I marched right by the guards' desk as though I had every right to be here. I even smiled and nodded at the giant keeping watch. He nodded back to me, then scanned the rest of the lobby.

I stopped in front of a directory mounted on the wall beside a bank of elevators. Doctors, lawyers, a few accountants... All the business names seemed perfectly ordinary and exceptionally boring. Plus, I just didn't see how *Fred's Fine Feet Podiatry* could help Mason enact his evil master plan, whatever it was. So instead of names, I started looking at the floor numbers listed on the board—*1, 13, 7, 5, 9... 10.*

I glanced over at the corresponding name—Carpenter Consulting. Well, that was pretty vague. What kind of firm was it? And what did the employees consult on?

I scanned the rest of the directory, but Carpenter Consulting was the only business listed on the tenth floor, so I jerked my head at Bria. "Come on. Let's see if Tucker's lead is legit."

We stepped into a waiting elevator, and I punched the button for the appropriate floor.

"What are you going to do?" Bria asked. "Just waltz into Carpenter Consulting like you cruised through the lobby?"

I grinned. "Hey, if it ain't broke…"

She snorted.

"Oh ye of little faith," I chided her. "I do have slightly more of a plan than that."

Bria arched an eyebrow. "Which would be?"

"We'll scope out the place, and if someone asks what we're doing, then we'll play dumb and say we got off on the wrong floor and are looking for Fred's Fine Feet. It probably happens all the time in a building with this many offices."

Bria's eyebrow arched a little higher. "And if that doesn't work and people start asking us more pointed questions?"

"Then it's a good thing you've got a badge and a gun, Detective."

"So that's why you let me come along—so you can use my credentials to get out of a sticky situation, if need be."

I slung my arm around her shoulder. "What are sisters for?"

She snorted again. "Now you sound like Finn."

The elevator floated to a stop. I dropped my arm from Bria's shoulder and stepped in front of her, putting myself between my sister and whatever might be waiting on the other side of the door. Just because we were in an office building, that didn't mean there were no dangerous people around—far from it.

The elevator cheerfully *dinged*, and the door slowly slid back to reveal…

Another lobby.

Well, it wasn't a lobby so much as it was a waiting area. Several gray leather couches and chairs were arranged around low frosted-glass tables covered with neat stacks of colorful magazines. A higher, larger glass table boasting a coffeepot, blue ceramic mugs, and bottles of water stood against the right wall, while a couple of spindly-looking palm trees lined the left wall. A secretary's desk squatted in the center of the open space, standing guard in front of chest-high gray cubicle walls that cordoned off the work spaces beyond. Gray carpet covered the floor, giving the entire level a dull, washed-out look.

The waiting area was deserted, so Bria and I moved forward, stopping in front of the secretary's desk. I didn't see anyone typing on a laptop or murmuring into a phone in one of the cubicles, and the lights in the glass-fronted offices embedded in the walls were turned off, casting much of the area in shadows. The whole floor had an empty, deserted feel, as though all the worker bees had already gone home. Odd. It wasn't five o'clock yet, so a few folks should still be here, burning the daylight oil—

"Can I help you?"

Bria and I both whirled around, startled by the high, reedy feminine voice.

A woman was standing in front of us, having stepped out of an open door I hadn't noticed beside the palm trees. The woman looked to be in her sixties and gave off the no-nonsense vibe of a professional assistant. Her silver hair was pulled back into a sleek bun, and silver glasses perched on her nose, making her blue eyes look as big as quarters. She was wearing a cream-colored pantsuit and black kitten heels, and several manila folders were nestled in the crook of her left elbow.

"Can I help you?" the woman repeated, an irritated look on her pale face, as though she had better things to do than deal with the likes of us.

Sometimes I thought *Can I help you?* was really just polite Southern code for *What the fuck are you doing?* Especially since the woman was eyeing us with obvious suspicion.

Bria glanced at me, and I sucked in a breath to launch into my story about looking for Fred's Fine Feet—

"Are you here for the meeting?" the woman asked, her voice a tiny bit less hostile than before, as though it had just occurred to her that we might actually be here on legitimate business.

"Yes! The meeting!" I seized on her words. "We're here for the meeting."

Bria's eyebrows shot up in surprise, but I smiled at the woman as though nothing was wrong.

"We *are* expected," I continued in a cool tone, as though I were used to people obeying me with no questions asked.

The woman gave me a brisk nod. "Of course. You're about thirty minutes early, but I can go ahead and put you in the conference room. You can wait there for the others to arrive."

She moved past us and stepped behind the desk. The woman, Mildred, according to a gleaming brass nameplate, set her folders down, arranging them in a neat, precise pile. While she was distracted, Bria shot me an incredulous look, but I shrugged back. We still had no idea what Carpenter Consulting did, and pretending we were here for some meeting might be our only chance to find out.

Mildred finished organizing the folders and gestured with her hand. "This way."

She strode into the maze of cubicles, and Bria and I followed her. As we walked along, I glanced at the various desks, many of which were covered with large sheets of paper filled with all sorts of lines and squiggles. Those looked like...blueprints.

I frowned. What was this place?

Mildred ushered us into a large conference room in the back of the office. More than a dozen chairs were arranged around a long, rectangular table, with a manila folder, a pen, and a notepad lined up at each seat. Several smaller tables were along the walls, filled with everything from reams of paper to boxes bristling with pens to cases of bottled water, while a couple of tall, wide filing cabinets clustered together in the back corner.

Mildred gestured at the main table. "Please make yourselves comfortable. The others should be here shortly. In the meantime, I need to talk to the caterers and make sure the champagne and other refreshments will be served as scheduled."

A smile split her face, making her look much happier and ten years younger. "After all, it's not every day our firm closes a deal that's going to change the landscape of downtown Ashland forever."

Even though I had no clue what she was talking about, I smiled back at her. "You're absolutely right."

Mildred smiled at me again, then left the conference room and pulled the frosted-glass door shut behind her, leaving Bria and me alone.

"What *is* this place?" Bria whispered, echoing my earlier thought.

"I have no idea, but we need to find out—fast. Whoever Mildred is expecting will be here soon."

Bria hurried over to the conference table, opened one of the folders, and started scanning through the papers inside. I prowled around the room, eyeing the smaller side tables and looking for a brochure or some other document that would tell me what Carpenter Consulting actually *did*.

I didn't find anything like that, but a large white sheet was draped over one of the tables along the wall. Strangely enough, the sheet wasn't flat, like a tablecloth, but rather filled with peaks and valleys, as though it had been draped over something to hide it from sight. Curious, I headed over there.

Up close, the sheet boasted two big, blue *C*s inside a blue box, which I assumed was the logo for Carpenter Consulting. Written in blue beneath the logo was a corporate slogan: *Building your dreams from the ground up.*

Cubicles full of blueprints, and now this talk of building dreams. Unless I was mistaken, Carpenter Consulting was some sort of architectural or construction firm. Was Mason hiring them to rebuild the Circle cemetery? Or the pavilion that contained my father's tomb?

Mason had used his magic to shatter many of the cemetery's tombstones so he could pummel me with the shrapnel, and he'd blasted the pavilion roof to pieces in hopes of using the resulting rubble to crush me to death. But if Mason wanted those things repaired, then why not hire a firm that specialized in graveyard restorations?

Nothing about this made any sense, but the peaks and valleys in the white sheet increased my curiosity, so I reached out, took hold of the fabric, and yanked it down, revealing...

A diorama—the largest diorama I had ever seen.

The diorama took up the entire table, stretching out more than nine feet long and three feet wide. It was *enormous*, and I was willing to bet that it had been pushed up against the wall to keep it out of the way until the big unveiling, which was probably going to happen during this upcoming mystery meeting.

"Bria," I said. "Come take a look at this."

She walked over to stand beside me, and then we both crouched down and studied the miniature landscape.

Tiny cars and trucks parked on gray streets. Prickly green pine trees clustered together in grassy parks. Old stone buildings sitting next to shimmering silver skyscrapers. The diorama was a perfect replica of downtown Ashland, right down to the ribbon of blue water that curled through the landscape as the Aneirin River. There was even a tiny white boat on the blue strip of water, representing the *Delta Queen* riverboat casino, which was owned by my friend Phillip Kincaid. The detail was truly stunning, like I was seeing a bird's-eye view of the city I loved and had lived in my entire life.

"Why would Mason have a diorama?" Bria asked. "He doesn't strike me as the type to be into role-playing fantasy games, not like those people at the renaissance faire were."

I shuddered. "Don't remind me."

A couple of months ago, Darrell Kline, an accountant who worked for Owen, had lured my significant other to the Winter's Web Renaissance Faire as part of a plot to kidnap Owen, drain his bank accounts, and then murder him. Of course, I'd come to Owen's rescue, and he to mine, and we'd managed to turn the tables on Darrell and his costumed friends.

But Bria was right. Darrell and his crew had had a diorama much like this one in their secret lair, although theirs had been of a fantasy kingdom, not streets and buildings I walked and drove by every day.

What did this diorama have to do with Mason and the Circle? What was my uncle plotting?

Bria straightened up, went back over to the table, and started reading through the documents in the folder she'd opened. "According to these memos, Carpenter Consulting is about to break ground on some big development project in downtown Ashland. I haven't heard anything about new construction downtown. Have you?"

"Not a word."

I turned my attention back to the diorama. Maybe it was strange, but I found the familiar locations disconcerting and a bit creepy. I could easily imagine Mason looking down on the landscape, as though he were some old mythological god deciding which people he was going to favor—and which he was going to utterly destroy.

My gaze locked onto the *Delta Queen* riverboat, and I followed the curve of the blue water down to Underwood's restaurant and then over a few blocks to the Pork Pit—

It wasn't there.

I blinked and reared back, wondering if I was looking at the wrong part of the diorama. But no, if the riverboat and Underwood's were over *there*, then the Pork Pit should be right *here*.

But it wasn't.

Instead of a street lined with brick storefronts and other old, historic structures, a chrome-and-glass building dominated the landscape, one that looked eerily similar to the building Bria and I were currently in, right down to the metal spike and the tiny blue light winking on the very tip-top.

Smaller but similar chrome-and-glass buildings spiraled out from that main one, all of them connected by glassed-in pedestrian walkways that stretched over the streets below. Still more walkways on the ground level led to grassy parks featuring everything from tiny swing sets to splash pads and carousels. I even spotted a Ferris wheel next to a roller coaster.

The new building seemed to be the centerpiece not just of the diorama but of the entire downtown area, and it squatted on the table like a silver spider in the middle of a glittering glass web.

Over at the conference table, Bria sucked in an audible breath. "According to this memo…" Her voice trailed off as she read a few more lines. "You're not going to believe this, but it looks like…"

"Mason is behind Carpenter Consulting's new construction project," I finished for her. My heart dropped, and a sick, sick feeling flooded my stomach. "This is *his* meeting. To talk about *his* plans for downtown Ashland."

Bria nodded, a worried look on her face. "He's mapped out some huge development. Shops, restaurants, parks with rides, games, and more."

My gaze zoomed from one side of the diorama to the other and back again. Everything she was talking about was laid out before me in tiny, precise, nauseatingly perfect detail.

"There's something else," Bria continued. "Mason's name is all over these memos, and the project has been dubbed the Mitchell Mile. He's not hiding in the shadows anymore. Mason is putting his name and face on the entire development."

"This is it," I whispered, a hard knot of certainty lodging in my throat. "*This* is Mason's grand plan. This is the thing he's been working toward all these years. He's going to rebuild downtown Ashland to his own liking—and wipe the Pork Pit off the map."

✵ 7 ✵

I kept staring down at the diorama, at the space where the Pork Pit, *my* restaurant, should be. But it was gone, swallowed up by this sprawling, gleaming monstrosity, buried in a sea of soulless chrome and glass and crass commercialism.

A while back, Madeline Monroe, Mab's daughter, had burned the Pork Pit down to the bare brick walls in an effort to kill me, but this was *worse*.

It was like the restaurant had never existed—like *Fletcher* had never existed.

And suddenly, I knew that was one of the driving reasons behind Mason's pet project. Oh, I was sure my uncle would greatly enjoy the fame and fortune this development would bring him, especially since the Circle's coffers had been so severely depleted in recent months. But it would also give him a way to eliminate every last remaining trace of Fletcher from downtown Ashland, from the city they had both called home.

Mason hadn't been able to beat Fletcher in life, so he was going to destroy the Pork Pit, now that the old man was dead and couldn't defend his beloved restaurant. My uncle was such a small, petty bastard.

Bria came over and put a comforting hand on my shoulder. "Oh, Gin. I'm so sorry. The thought of losing the Pork Pit must break your heart."

Break my heart? More like completely, utterly, irrevocably *shatter* it.

The restaurant was one of the few tangible things of Fletcher's that I had left, and I never felt closer to the old man than when I was making his barbecue sauce or sitting behind the cash register and reading a book, the way he so often had. Even more important, Fletcher had given me the Pork Pit because he'd known that I would carry on his recipes, his traditions, his *legacies*, both as the purveyor of the finest barbecue in Ashland and as the Tin Man, the mysterious assassin with a heart of gold who helped people who couldn't help themselves.

Now both those legacies were hanging by a thread.

Before I'd gone into the Bellum Bank this morning, I'd told Owen that I wanted to know that everything I'd been through, everything I'd suffered, had been worth it. That all the pain, torture, and heartbreak I'd endured at the hands of all the bad, bad people I'd faced down over the past few years had mattered. That I had made a difference and changed Ashland for the better in some small way.

Losing my life battling Mason had always been a possibility. One that I'd accepted and even made peace with. I just never thought I could lose such a big piece of *myself* before the end.

The Pork Pit was just as much a part of me as an arm, a leg, or an eye. It was where I had first met Fletcher, where he had taken me in, where he had died, and where I had almost died too. The restaurant was my heart, my rock, my *foundation*.

And now Mason wanted to destroy it just as he had destroyed my parents, my family, all those years ago. And if he succeeded…well, I didn't know how I would ever recover from it.

Hot tears stung my eyes, but I blinked them back and straightened up. "How can Mason do this? You'd have to level several city blocks before you could even break ground on this project. What about zoning permits and things like that?"

Another thought occurred to me. "And bribes. He'd have to bribe a whole lot of people to make something like this happen. Everyone who's anyone in Ashland would want a piece of this pie."

Bria gestured over at the open folder on the conference table. "I don't understand it all, but the project sounds like it's a done deal. Mason must have already gotten whatever zoning permits and everything else he needs. According to the memos, today's meeting is just a formality to dot a few final i's and cross some t's."

She gestured over at the table again. "As for bribes, there are names on the folders. The mayor, the city planner, even the police chief. They're all coming to this meeting, so they all know about the project."

I could hear what she wasn't saying. "Which means that Mason has already paid them off, either with cash now or kickbacks from the construction contracts or promises of future profits once the development is open and business is booming. Maybe even all three." I frowned. "But where is he even getting the money for the bribes? Or to start the project?"

"Mason took out a massive loan from the Bellum Bank," Bria replied. "We're talking tens of millions of dollars. Charles and Drusilla Yang's names are on several of the memos."

"So Mason has already made a deal with the Yangs too," I muttered. "Terrific. Just terrific. Although I suppose that explains what Emery was doing at the bank this morning."

"What do you mean?" Bria asked.

I stabbed my finger at the diorama. "Emery was probably looking at vaults to store this monstrosity, along with all the files related to this so-called Mitchell Mile. Mason would want to keep the project under wraps for as long as possible, and storing the info at the Bellum Bank would be one way to do that. Besides, if he started using the bank for more than just a hefty loan, then he could further ingratiate himself with Charles and Drusilla."

Bria nodded. "Well, he's not planning to keep it under wraps for much longer. I spotted an invitation in the folder. The project is being publicly announced and celebrated at a gala in a few days' time." She hesitated. "The party is taking place at the Mitchell family mansion."

I bit back the vicious curse dangling on the tip of my tongue. A few weeks ago, Emery Slater had kidnapped me, Bria, and Lorelei and taken us to the mansion. That was where I'd first met Mason face-to-face and where he had revealed all the ugly secrets about how the Mitchell family was one of the founding forces behind the Circle, along with other old, prominent, powerful Ashland families like the Snows, Monroes, Shaws, and Riveras.

Mason had also calmly detailed how he had used his Stone magic to kill Tristan because my father had dared to question Mason's leadership and because Tristan and my mother, Eira, had wanted to use the Circle's resources for good rather than evil. And for the final, cruel kicker, Mason had shown us the sick shrine he'd built to showcase Tristan's tomb in the middle of the Circle cemetery in the woods behind the mansion.

If there was any place in Ashland that should be utterly destroyed, then it was the Mitchell family mansion.

Bria rubbed her hand across my back, still trying to comfort me. "I'm sorry, Gin. So sorry. I didn't know what I was expecting to find here, but it wasn't *this*."

"Me neither," I whispered back. "Me neither."

Bria kept rubbing my back. I stared down at the diorama again, my gaze focusing on the spot where the Pork Pit should be. More tears stung my eyes, but I ruthlessly blinked them back. I didn't have time for tears or heartache or anything else that didn't help me figure out how to stop this project.

Another thought occurred to me, and a bitter laugh spewed out of my lips. "Tucker was right, though. I wouldn't have believed this if I hadn't seen it for myself."

"What do you want to do now?" Bria asked.

I blinked back a few final tears, then glanced at the clock on the wall. We'd already been in the conference room for more than ten minutes. Once again, the steady *tick-tick-tick* of that countdown clock filled my mind, louder and faster than ever before.

"Gin?" Bria asked again.

I looked at my sister. "We need to find out as much about the project and the people involved as possible, then get out of here before Mason or anyone else shows up."

Bria returned to the conference table, using her phone to snap photos of the documents inside the open folder. I pulled out my own phone and took shot after shot of the diorama, trying to capture the scope of the Mitchell Mile. Ugh. What a horrible, cliché name. Not only was Mason small and petty, but he was an egotistical narcissist too.

Once I was done with the diorama, I hurried over to the filing cabinets in the back corner. I wrenched open first one drawer, then another. Surprise, surprise, they were all filled with manila folders stuffed with papers. I riffled through some of the folders, but I didn't see Mason's name on any of them. I didn't have time to pull out the folders, look through the documents inside, and do a more thorough search, so I snapped some photos of the names on the tabs, hoping there might be a clue in them.

When I finished, I closed the drawers and turned around, staring out over the conference room again and wondering where else I could look for information. Maybe there was something on the diorama that I'd missed.

I started to head in that direction, but I wasn't watching where I was going, and my boot clipped the edge of one of the filing cabinets. Pain exploded in my toes and rippled up into my ankle, making me hiss. My clumsiness also jostled a couple of folders on top of the cabinet, sending pieces of paper flying through the air like feathers out of a fat pillow.

"You okay?" Bria asked.

My sister had finished with the documents and closed the folder. Now she was moving around the conference table, snapping photos of the names on the other folders.

"Fine," I muttered. "Just bruised my pride."

She nodded and kept working.

I hobbled forward, snatched the loose pieces of paper up off the floor, and turned back to the filing cabinet. I started to stuff the papers back into the topmost folder, but some bright blue words on one of the sheets caught my eye.

MM—Phase 2.

Was that part of Mason's project? Or some other deal that Carpenter Consulting was involved in? I didn't have time to look right now, so I crammed the papers into my jacket pocket. Then I stuffed the remaining wad of papers into a folder and shoved it farther back on top of the filing cabinet.

Once that was done, I surveyed the conference room again, and the gleaming buildings on the diorama caught my eye. This time, instead of shock and heartache, anger and revulsion coursed through me. Even though I wanted nothing more than to tear the miniature buildings off the table and grind them to pieces under my boots, there was no time for such pettiness, so I hurried over, grabbed the white sheet from the floor, and draped it back over the display. It wasn't the best or neatest job, but maybe no one would wonder why the fabric wasn't evenly spread out over the atrocious landscape.

I didn't see anything else to do or investigate, so I eyed the clock on the wall—five minutes until five. "We need to leave. Now."

Bria snapped a final photo. "I'm done. Let's go."

I cracked open the door, staring out over the cubicles, but I didn't see Mildred or anyone else. "We're clear."

Bria and I slipped out of the conference room and hurried past the cubicles. I glanced left and right, looking for another exit so we wouldn't have to walk by Mildred's desk, but there was only one way in and out of the office. Maybe the assistant would still be off talking to the caterers, and we could slip out of here unseen...

No such luck. I rounded the corner to find Mildred sitting at her desk, sorting through a stack of folders.

"Gin?" Bria whispered.

"Just keep going."

Mildred looked up at the soft scuffing of our footsteps on the carpet, and her eyebrows drew together in confusion. "Where are you going? The meeting is about to start, and the other guests should be here any minute."

I gave her an airy wave. "Oh, I left my phone in the car. Can't live without that. Don't worry. I'm just going to pop downstairs and get it. We'll be back in a jiffy."

Perhaps it was my jaunty wave, too-bright smile, or ill-advised use of the word *jiffy*—or all of the above—but Mildred's blue eyes narrowed behind her glasses, and I could almost see the proverbial cartoon light bulb click on over her head as she realized that we hadn't been invited here.

She shoved her chair back from her desk and shot to her feet. "Security! Security!"

In the distance, at the end of a long hallway, a couple of giant guards ambled out of a break room, judging from the mugs and magazines they were both clutching. The two men seemed genuinely confused by Mildred's bellows, but I knew they would catch on quick.

"Go!" I hissed at my sister. "Now!"

Bria abandoned all pretense of stealth, zoomed past Mildred's desk, and sprinted right on past the elevators. For a second, I wondered where she was going, but then I spotted a red *Exit* sign burning over a door at the far end of the lobby. Bria shoved open the door, then stopped, waiting for me.

"Hey! You there!" a male voice yelled.

I glanced to my right. The two giants had set their mugs and magazines down on a table and were quickly striding toward me, with their hands on their belts. I couldn't tell if they had real guns or merely stun guns, but I wasn't going to stick around to find out.

"Gotta jet, Millie!" I called out to the assistant. "Catch you later!"

She glowered at me and reached for the landline phone on her desk, probably to call for reinforcements. I didn't have time to slap the phone out of her hands, so I ran through the waiting area and over to the emergency stairs where Bria was standing.

My sister slipped into the stairwell. I followed her and slammed the door shut behind me. The second it was closed, I wrapped my hand around the knob and sent out a blast of Ice magic. Cold crystals shot out of my palm and zoomed into the lock, freezing it in place. I sent out another blast of magic, and the rest of the door Iced over, including the frame and part of the wall. That should be enough to keep the giants from chasing us—

Bang!

The door shuddered, and bits of Ice cracked off the frame and zipped through the air, including one that stung my cheek like a cold bee. One of the giants must have shoved his shoulder into the door, trying to force it open.

Bang! Bang!

The door shuddered again, then again, but my Ice held it in place—for now. It was only a matter of time before the giant's strength cracked away the cold crystals.

I whirled around. "Go! Now!"

Bria started pounding down the steps. The sharp, jerky motions made her shaggy blond hair swing wildly from side to side, as well as slap against first one shoulder, then the other. I was right on her heels, listening to the continued bangs behind us.

Bria and I raced down one flight of stairs. Then another, then another...

Even though it seemed like forever, we reached the bottom of the stairs less than two minutes later. Bria stopped, her cheeks pink, breathing hard. She started to wrench open the ground-level door, but I held up my hand, stopping her.

"Walk through...the lobby...like everything...is normal," I replied, huffing and puffing for air just like she was. "Mildred might have already...alerted the guards down here.

Don't give them any reason...to be suspicious. Our best chance to escape...is to blend in with everyone else."

Bria nodded and sucked down a couple more breaths. Then she straightened her shoulders, opened the door, and stepped out into the lobby. I sucked in some more air too, then followed her.

It was right at five o'clock now and officially quitting time for most folks. The elevators *ding-ding-dinged* one after another, depositing dozens of people in the lobby. Some folks drifted off toward the sandwich shop and the steakhouse to grab a bite to eat, but most headed straight for the exits, ready to go home.

Bria and I fell in with the flow of people streaming toward the exits. Our route took us right by the three giant security guards stationed behind the counter. One of them was clutching a phone to his ear. The giant's mouth flattened out into a thin line, and his dark eyes started flicking left and right. Unless I missed my guess, Mildred was telling the guard to detain us.

"Gin," Bria said in a warning voice. She had also spotted the guard.

"Just keep walking. There are too many people in the lobby for us to take on those giants or for them to do the same thing to us."

Bria and I strode past the security counter, still in the middle of a pack of people. By this point, the first guard had put the phone down and was talking to the other two giants, who climbed to their feet and dropped their hands to the weapons on their belts. Unlike the guards in the Carpenter Consulting office, I could clearly see that these three men were carrying very real guns that were no doubt loaded with very real bullets.

Bria and I kept going, walking, walking, walking...

The three guards stepped around the counter. I held my breath, wondering if they might stride forward, raise their hands, and order everyone to stop. But there were simply too many people, and the giants were forced to hold their positions, although they kept their hands on their guns and started scanning the crowd. Bria and I swept right on by them and kept going, still heading toward the doors.

I turned my head, tracking the giants out of the corner of my eye. They finally waded into the crowd, pushing past the flow of people and heading toward the stairwell that Bria and I had exited. Mildred must have told them that we were coming down the emergency stairs, but it didn't seem like the giants had seen us enter the lobby. I let out a quiet sigh of relief and moved on.

My sister and I made it to the doors and streamed outside along with everyone else. The sidewalk and the street beyond were busy too, with most folks walking to their next destinations, while others hailed cabs or got into waiting town cars.

"This way," I said, moving in front of Bria. "We need to get off the main street as fast as possible—"

I was looking at my sister instead of watching where I was going, and I rammed straight into a man heading in the opposite direction toward the building. I bounced off him and stumbled back, stepping on Bria's foot. She yelped and staggered to the side.

"Oh, excuse me. I'm…so…sorry…" I looked at the man I'd run into, my voice trailing off and my apology dying a slow, painful death on my lips.

The man was in his mid-fifties, the same age my father would have been if he hadn't been killed by his own twin brother. This man was quite handsome, with dark brown hair, tan skin, and the same gray eyes my father had had—and that

I had too. His long navy overcoat was tailored to his tall, muscled figure, as was his matching navy suit underneath, and his black wing tips were as glossy as wet ink.

The only thing worse than this man's uncanny resemblance to my father was his Stone magic. Even now, when he was simply standing on the sidewalk, raw power still surged off him and crashed into me, like rock-hard fists pummeling my body with every breath we both took.

The cold, hard force of his magic was eerily similar to my own Stone power, although this man was far, far stronger in his magic than I was in mine. With just a wave of his hand and a few blasts of his power, this man could do whatever he wanted to any stone in the vicinity, from making bricks fly out of a nearby storefront wall, to splintering the sidewalks under our feet, to reducing the surrounding buildings to rubble.

"Watch where you're going..." the man snapped, clearly annoyed that I had plowed into him, although his words also stuttered to a stop on his lips, just as mine had. His eyes widened in surprise, then quickly narrowed.

For the second time today, I had run straight into an enemy.

Mason fucking Mitchell.

8

For a heartbeat, Mason and I stood there on the sidewalk, staring at each other. Then the image of that diorama flashed through my mind. Rage boiled up like venom in my veins, scorching through the last of my shock, and a low, angry growl erupted from my throat.

I palmed a knife, raised it high, and sprang forward, bringing the weapon down in a vicious arc, determined to ram it straight into Mason's cold, black heart—

Tink.

My silverstone knife cut right through my uncle's coat, jacket, and shirt, but instead of plunging deep into his chest, the blade skittered off his skin, as though I were trying to stab a toothpick into a cement block.

Magic burned in Mason's eyes, making them gleam like liquid silver, and power surged off him—more power than I had ever felt from any other elemental, even Mab Monroe. My uncle had used his Stone magic to transform his skin, his body, into a hard, impenetrable shell, something I had done countless times with my own Stone magic. Another growl spewed out of my throat. I hated the irony.

"Oh, Gin," Mason purred, his smooth, silky voice completely calm, despite the fact that I'd just tried to kill him. "You should know by now that you can't hurt me with those pitiful little blades."

I yanked my knife back, but before I could snarl out a response, another voice cut me off.

"What's going on?"

My gaze darted to the left. Charles Yang was also standing on the sidewalk, along with Drusilla.

Charles frowned at me, but Drusilla immediately stepped in front of her father. Magic flared in her eyes, making them glitter like dark topazes, and the hot, scorching, invisible waves of her Fire magic blasted over me. Drusilla was ready to fry me with her power if I made any sort of threatening move toward her or her father.

I silently cursed my exponentially increasing bad luck. Of course the Yangs would come to the meeting. No doubt Charles and Drusilla wanted to see the diorama and exactly what my uncle was planning to do with all the money they were loaning him. And of course I would run into both them *and* Mason when Bria and I had been seconds away from escaping. Lady Luck was really screwing me over today.

Bria had finally regained her balance, and she eased up beside me. Ice magic rippled off my sister, and she glared at Mason, ready to unleash her power, even though it wouldn't penetrate his Stone-hardened skin any more than my knife had.

"Sir!" another voice sounded. "I asked you to wait by the car while I scouted the area."

A man hurried up and stopped beside Mason. He was in his forties, with blue eyes, tan skin, and dark brown hair shot through with a few silver threads. He too was tall and muscled and was wearing a gray overcoat over a matching suit. He looked every inch the professional businessman, just like my uncle did, but tension charged the air around this man, a watchfulness that whispered that he was constantly studying everyone and everything around him and assessing whether they were potential threats. Then again, that was his job as Mason's new security consultant.

Liam Carter froze, his eyes going wide at the sight of me. A second ticked by. Then another one. Then a third. Liam's gaze flicked to the knife in my hand. His brain must have finally kicked into gear, because he cursed and reached for the gun holstered on his belt.

I couldn't kill Mason with my knife, but I could definitely hurt Liam with it, so I lashed out with the blade, aiming for his gun hand. Liam cursed again and lurched to the side, his long gray overcoat flapping around his legs.

"Guards!" Liam screamed. "Guards!"

Farther down the sidewalk, several black-suited giants were loitering beside a couple of SUVs, but Liam's yells made them snap to attention and charge in this direction. Between the incoming giants, Liam, Mason, Charles, and Drusilla, this was a fight that Bria and I didn't have a chance of winning. As much as it pained me, we had to retreat, to run away and hope to kill another day.

I might not be able to break through Mason's Stone-hardened skin, but I could still knock him down, so I lowered my shoulder, surged forward, and rammed straight into the bastard with all the determination of a football linebacker making a game-winning tackle. The move took my uncle by surprise, his feet flew out from under him, and his ass hit the sidewalk.

By this point, Liam had finally pulled out his gun, and he stepped forward, aiming it at my chest. He winced a bit, as though he didn't like what he was about to do, but his finger curled around the trigger—

"Gun!" someone screamed. "That man has a gun!"

Their words blasted through the air like a foghorn. For a split second, all noise and conversation ceased, and everyone moving along the sidewalk froze, as though they were all part of a movie that had been abruptly paused. Then everyone panicked at once.

"Gun! Gun!" People yelled and screamed as they stampeded away.

Most folks bolted in the opposite direction, while some scurried back into the office buildings they'd just exited or ducked behind the food carts spaced along the sidewalk. A few people even hurried out into the street, making the cars going by screech to sudden stops to avoid hitting them.

Guilt punched me in the stomach, hitting me even harder than Mason's magic had. The last thing I *ever* wanted to do was put innocent people in danger. That went against everything Fletcher had ever taught me about being an assassin—and a decent person too.

But there were too many people running in too many different directions, and I couldn't shepherd any of them to safety. No, the best thing I could do for all the innocent bystanders was to get out of here as fast as possible. I might avoid collateral damage at all costs, but Mason had no such qualms, and he would order his giants to kill whoever got in the way of them killing me.

"Gin! Gin!" Bria's voice rang out above the yells and screams.

The crowd pushed my sister back, sweeping her away from me, but I didn't mind, because that got her farther away from Mason as well.

Heat pulsed through the air, and I spotted a flash of elemental Fire out of the corner of my eye. My head snapped in that direction. Drusilla was still standing in front of her father, with red-hot flames now flickering on her fingertips. Her eyes narrowed, and she lifted her hand to hurl her magic at me.

I could have thrown my knife at her or blasted her with jagged Ice needles or hurt her half a dozen other ways. But Drusilla wasn't the villain here, and she didn't deserve to die for mistakenly picking the wrong side. So I simply shook my head, silently asking her to reconsider.

Oh, I wasn't afraid of Drusilla or her power. I could always use my Stone magic to harden my skin to protect myself from her elemental Fire, but the flames would probably shoot off my body, and I didn't want anyone else to get scorched by her power.

Drusilla hesitated, and confusion flickered across her face, much the same way the flames were still dancing along her fingertips.

But Mason did not hesitate.

My uncle was still sprawled across the sidewalk, and he slapped his hand down onto the stone. A wave of magic surged off him and raced toward me, and the sidewalk rippled ominously under my feet, as though it were suddenly made of water, instead of thick, solid concrete. My boots skidded on the undulating surface, and I had to windmill my arms to keep my balance.

More magic surged off Mason, and a chunk of the sidewalk flew up through the air and slammed into my left shoulder. The hard, brutal impact hurt plenty all by itself, but he sent out a third blast of power, shattering the stone. Razor-sharp bits of shrapnel battered my entire left side, slicing through my clothes and stinging my skin like dozens of tiny daggers.

I hissed with pain and staggered back. Memories flooded my mind, even sharper, harsher, and more painful than my current injuries. A few weeks ago in the Circle cemetery, Mason had shattered several tombstones and then pelted me with the resulting debris, cruelly battering and cutting me to shreds. He'd almost killed me back then, and he seemed determined to finish the job now.

"Secure the principal!" Liam yelled. "Get him out of here!"

Two black-suited giants hurried forward, grabbed Mason's arms, and hauled him upright. The motion must have surprised my uncle, because he lost his grip on his magic, the sidewalk solidified, and no more chunks of stone flew up at me. Mason growled and tried to shake off the two men, but the giants were much stronger than he was, and they easily dragged him backward.

I snarled, lifted my knife high, and charged forward, as though I were trying to kill Mason again. That would have been nice, but my knife was absolutely useless against his Stone magic, as he'd so smugly pointed out. No, this attack was about saving face—and helping my inside man maintain his cover.

Just as I'd expected, Liam Carter stepped in front of me, blocking my path. Liam lifted his gun to shoot me, so I adjusted my aim, plunging my knife deep into his right arm. Liam grunted with pain, and his gun slipped from his fingers and clattered to the sidewalk. More guilt filled me, but I pushed it away and focused on playing my part to the hilt, so to speak.

"Die, you traitor!" I screamed at the top of my lungs.

I yanked my knife out of his arm and raised it for another strike, but Liam growled, drew his left fist back, and surged forward. He wasn't pulling his punch, so I reached for my own Stone magic, using it to harden my skin.

Liam's fist plowed straight into my face. Thanks to his mix of giant and dwarven blood, he was exceptionally strong, and the blow would have shattered my jaw if not for the protective shell of my magic. Even then, it still felt like someone had driven a sledgehammer into my chin. White stars erupted in my eyes, and I drunkenly stumbled around, trying to regain my balance.

By this point, the giants had dragged Mason over to the SUVs farther down the street, although he was still yelling at them to release him. I blinked away the last of the stars, shook off my daze, and started forward, but Liam blocked my path again.

"Give it up, Blanco!" Liam yelled.

I snarled and lashed out with my knife. This time, Liam stepped up to meet me, catching my wrist in his left hand and stopping me from plunging my blade into his chest. We seesawed back and forth on the sidewalk, with me trying to shove my knife into his heart and him trying to break my wrist.

"Sorry about the arm," I whispered.

Liam winked at me, then grimaced. "Just make it look good."

"You got it."

I snapped up my left hand and slammed my Stone-hardened fist into Liam's stomach, making him grunt and gasp for breath. His grip loosened, so I yanked my wrist free, then kicked out, driving my boot into the side of his knee and sending him tumbling down to the sidewalk.

I stepped over Liam, my murderous gaze swinging back to Mason, who was glaring right back at me. More of that venomous rage boiled up in my veins, and my hand tightened around my knife. Maybe I could kill him after all. I certainly wanted to try—

A hand latched onto my shoulder. "The cops are on their way!" Bria yelled. "We have to get out of here!"

I knew she was right. The cops in Ashland were notoriously crooked, and there was no telling how many of them were on Mason's payroll. Getting caught and arrested was a surefire way to end up in a holding cell—one that I would probably never leave alive.

But that knowledge didn't stop frustration from zipping through me, and the bitter taste of defeat burned like acid in my mouth. Mason was right *here*, within my grasp. All I had to do was figure out some way to kill him, and the threat against me, my loved ones, and the Pork Pit would end.

My gaze locked with Mason's rage-filled one again, but the giants finally shoved him into the back of one of the SUVs. Charles and Drusilla Yang had also vanished, probably into another SUV. At the end of the block, a police car screeched to a halt, its blue and white lights flashing. A couple of uniformed cops jumped out of the car.

"Gin!" Bria yelled, yanking on my shoulder. "We have to leave! Now!"

Cursing, I tucked my knife back up my sleeve, then whirled around and followed her, sprinting in the opposite direction and running away from my enemies.

✧ 9 ✧

Bria and I raced down to the end of the block.

"Left!" I yelled. "Go left!"

Bria veered in that direction. We sprinted about halfway down that block, and then I pointed to an alley across the street. Bria slowed down long enough to make sure no traffic was coming, then hurried in that direction. I followed her.

We ran through that alley, then another one, then another one. Eventually, we made our way back to the parking garage. Bria and I looked around, both of us huffing and puffing for air, but the garage seemed to be empty, so we kept moving. We trudged up the stairs to the third level, then rounded the corner to head back to my sister's sedan—

A man was waiting for us.

A giant, roughly seven feet tall, with a strong, muscled body, was checking his phone and leaning against the hood of the car that was parked next to Bria's sedan. His shaved head, ebony skin, and dark eyes gleamed under the garage's dim lights, as did the gold badge clipped to his belt. A black leather jacket stretched across his broad shoulders, and a pair of aviator sunglasses was hooked into the top of his dark green sweater. Black jeans and boots completed his casual but cool ensemble.

Xavier, Bria's partner on the force, glanced up from his phone and waved us over.

The giant eyed Bria and then me. His gaze focused on my face, before dropping to my left arm. I looked down. My fleece jacket was torn and ripped, as was my suit jacket underneath, and angry red cuts and scrapes crisscrossed my skin from my shoulder down to my elbow, like I'd been dragged across a bed of broken glass.

"You okay, Gin?" Xavier asked in his deep, rumbling voice.

I moved my arm, then wiggled my jaw. More pain bloomed in the cuts and scrapes caused by Mason's shrapnel, and a dull ache pounded through my face from where Liam had punched me, but nothing seemed to be broken, and none of my teeth were loose. Small favors, but I'd take what I could get after that disastrous encounter.

"Never better," I chirped.

Bria shot me a concerned look, but I shrugged back. All things considered, I'd gotten off pretty easy.

She turned back to the giant. "What are you doing here?"

Xavier waggled his phone at us. "Silvio texted me that the two of you might need some backup, so I tracked Bria's car here."

I glanced over at my sister. "Silvio put a tracker on your car too?"

My assistant had apps on his devices that let him monitor my car and phone, but I didn't realize that he was keeping tabs on my sister too. Sometimes I thought Silvio was even more paranoid than I was.

Bria shrugged. "Mine and Xavier's cars. We also let him

access our phones. Given everything that's been going on with Mason, it seemed like a wise precaution."

Xavier waggled his phone again. "From the texts I've been getting from the police department, the two of you caused quite a ruckus over on Bluff Street."

Bria grimaced. "You could say that."

She quickly filled him in on everything that had happened.

When she finished, Xavier let out a low whistle. "Mason showed up and attacked you all in broad daylight? I thought he was more of a creep-around-in-the-shadows type of bad guy."

"To be fair, I did attack him first," I said.

"Let me guess. You tried to shove one of your knives into his chest?" Amusement filled the giant's face.

"Yeah. Too bad it didn't stick," I drawled.

Bria rolled her eyes at my bad joke, but Xavier laughed, the loud, hearty sound booming through the garage. I grinned back at him. At least someone appreciated my twisted sense of black humor.

Bria looked at her partner again. "I need you to do me a favor."

"Let me guess," Xavier repeated. "You want me to get the security footage from the buildings and traffic cameras on that block. Anything that could be used to identify you and Gin."

"Yeah," she replied. "I want all the footage from before, during, and after the fight. Maybe we'll get lucky, and we can use it to somehow track Mason. See where he was coming from or where he went."

"On it," Xavier replied. "I'll text you when it's done."

I reached out and touched his shoulder. "Thank you, Xavier. You're a good friend."

He winked at me. "Good friends take care of each other."

The giant got into his car and left the garage.

I looked at Bria. "You should go with Xavier to watch his back and help him get the footage. I can call Silvio to come pick me up."

She shook her head. "Nope. I'm not leaving you, especially not when your arm looks like ground sausage. We're going straight to the salon to get you healed."

I glanced down at the cuts and scrapes, many of which were oozing blood. Yeah, *ground sausage* was an appropriate description. Maybe a trip to the salon wasn't such a bad idea, although I hated to interrupt Jo-Jo's day when I was still mostly in one piece.

Bria marched over to her sedan and opened the passenger's-side door. "Good sisters take care of each other too. So get in."

Despite my protests that I was only mildly injured, my sister wouldn't take no for an answer, and she herded me into her sedan. Then she slid into the driver's seat, pulled out her phone, and started texting.

"I'm telling Silvio what happened," Bria explained. "He can get in touch with Finn and Owen and have them meet us."

I sighed, knowing that I couldn't stop my friends from descending on the salon en masse. Since the party was already getting started, I might as well invite the rest of the gang, so I pulled out my own phone.

"Who are you texting?" Bria asked.

"Lorelei."

My sister frowned. "Why? We just saw her a couple of hours ago."

Anger flooded my body, drowning out the pain of my injuries. "Because I want to have another word with Hugh Tucker."

Bria and I both put our phones away, then she cranked the engine, steered out of the garage, and headed for the more genteel confines of Northtown.

Twenty minutes later, she coasted through a subdivision, steered her sedan up a hill, and parked in front of a sprawling white house. A van was already sitting in the driveway, and Silvio was waiting for us on the front porch. My assistant rushed over to open my door. He even tried to help me out of the car, although I waved him off.

"I'm fine. More or less."

Silvio arched an eyebrow. "It definitely looks like *less* to me. What happened?"

"We were about to get away scot-free when I ran smack-dab into Mason. Naturally, there was an incident."

"*Incident?*" he asked. "It looks like someone took a cheese grater to your arm and then slammed a brick into your face for good measure."

"Mason exploded part of the sidewalk and pelted me with the shrapnel, hence my arm."

Silvio's eyebrow rose a little higher. "And your face?"

I gingerly touched my jaw, which now featured a throbbing goose egg. Once again, a dull ache rippled through my skull, making me wince. "That was Liam, playing the part of the loyal bodyguard. He clocked me pretty good."

Silvio's gray eyes widened. "Liam was *there*? With Mason?" He hesitated. "Is Liam...okay?"

The concern in his voice made my heart squeeze tight and my stomach churn with guilt. I wasn't the only one with something to lose in this dangerous game I was playing with Mason. Silvio and Liam were...well, I wasn't quite sure what they were. Definitely interested in each other. They might even have been something more by now, if Liam hadn't agreed to work for Mason and spy on my uncle for me.

"Liam's fine," I replied, trying to reassure my friend. "He got off with some bruises and a stab wound."

Silvio's eyes widened even more. "You *stabbed* Liam?" he asked in an incredulous voice.

I grimaced. *Way to say the wrong thing, Gin.* Still, I kept talking, trying to explain. "Well...yeah. I had to keep up appearances. I couldn't just ask Liam nicely to step out of my way. Mason would have been suspicious of that."

"She only stabbed him in the arm," Bria piped up, trying to be helpful. "And just the one time, right, Gin?"

"Right," I replied, grasping onto the lifeline she was throwing me. "Plus, Liam shot me at Mallory and Mosley's wedding reception to prove his loyalty to Mason. So you could say we're even now."

Silvio threw up his hands in frustration, then started pacing back and forth and muttering to himself. I didn't catch everything he said, although I definitely heard "I'm surrounded by crazy people" at some point in his tirade. After several seconds, he stopped pacing, yanked his phone out of his pocket, and sent a text. I didn't ask who he was contacting—it was obviously Liam.

My assistant stared down at the phone, worry pinching his face. The more seconds that ticked by, the tighter his features became, as if he was steeling himself to receive the worst possible news. My heart squeezed again, and more guilt churned in my stomach. If Mason hadn't bought our act, then Liam could be in serious trouble—

Silvio's phone beeped. He flinched, then slowly raised the device, his gaze locked on the screen. "Liam is okay. He's helping Emery and her giants move Mason to a secure location."

Silvio blew out a breath, and some of the tension leaked out of his body. He sent another text to Liam. I didn't ask what he'd said. It wasn't any of my business, but his phone beeped again a few seconds later, and the barest hint of a smile curved his lips. The vampire realized that Bria and I were watching him, and he cleared his throat and slid his phone back into his pocket.

"We should get Gin inside," Silvio said, changing the subject.

He once again offered to help me, as did Bria, but I waved them both off and climbed up the porch steps, with the two of them following along behind me. Silvio knocked politely on the front door, then turned the knob. It was open, so he, Bria, and I went inside, walked down a long hallway, and stepped into a large room.

An old-fashioned beauty salon took up the back half of the house. Cherry-red chairs lined most of the far wall, surrounded by low tables boasting stacks of colorful magazines. Still more magazines covered the tables next to the love seats and other chairs.

Combs, scissors, curling irons, flat irons, brushes, and other beauty tools were scattered across the long counter that ran down another wall, along with pink plastic tubs filled with bottles of nail polish, tubes of lipstick, and other makeup. The air smelled like soft vanilla mixed with harsh chemicals, but the strange combination of soft and stringent aromas always soothed me and let me know that I was safe.

At the sight of me, Silvio, and Bria, a black-and-brown basset hound lifted his head from where he was curled up in a white wicker basket in the corner. He wagged his tail and let out a loud, welcoming, hopeful *woof!* Rosco waited a few seconds, but when it became obvious that none of us had a treat, he snuffled out his displeasure, laid his head back down, and returned to his nap.

A woman was sweeping the salon floor. She was a dwarf, a little more than five feet tall, with a thick, strong body. Even though it was creeping up on six o'clock, her white-blond curls were still exceptionally springy and perfectly in place, and her makeup looked as fresh and dewy as if she'd just applied it. A string of gleaming white pearls hung around her neck, and a pale pink dress patterned with small yellow sunflowers covered her body. Despite the March chill outside, her feet were bare, and her toenails gleamed a bright neon pink.

Jolene "Jo-Jo" Deveraux looked up and her pale, middle-aged face creased into a smile. "Hey! What are y'all doing here?"

Bria gestured at me. "Getting Humpty Dumpty put back together yet again."

"I am *not* a nursery-rhyme character."

She grinned. "Oh, consider the nickname as payback from this 'hard-boiled badass.' You know, from one bad egg to another."

I huffed at her teasing, then shuffled forward.

Jo-Jo's clear, almost colorless eyes widened as she got a better look at my bruised face, along with my shredded arm. "Darling! Come sit down before you fall down," she said, ushering me over to one of the salon chairs.

"It's not *that* bad," I protested.

Jo-Jo exchanged a quick look with Bria and Silvio. Apparently, they all disagreed with my injury assessment.

"Well, no matter how bad it is, I'll fix you right up," Jo-Jo replied.

I lay back in the salon chair while the dwarf washed and dried her hands. She pulled over a stool and sat down next to me. She also clicked on a freestanding light and angled it so that the glow fell on my face. I grimaced at the sudden brightness, which tweaked the goose egg on my jaw and added to the throbbing ache in my head.

"Who did this to you?" Jo-Jo asked.

"The one-two combo of Mason Mitchell and Liam Carter. But don't worry. It looks worse than it is."

Jo-Jo shook her head, still not agreeing with my assessment. She lifted her hand. "Just try to relax, darling. I'll make this as quick and painless as possible."

A milky-white glow sparked to life on her palm, and the same power flared in her eyes, as though wispy clouds were floating through her field of vision. Jo-Jo was an Air elemental, which meant that she could grab hold of oxygen and all the other natural gases in the air and use them to fade out bruises, heal cuts, straighten broken bones, and generally put Humpty Dumpty Gin back together again, just like Bria had said.

Jo-Jo leaned forward, and her magic washed over me. Unlike Mason's power, which was almost exactly the same as my own cold, hard Stone magic, Jo-Jo's Air power felt like dozens of red-hot needles stabbing deeper and deeper into my body and pulling, yanking, and stitching my shredded skin back the way it should be. Despite the intensely uncomfortable sensation, I gritted my teeth and held still while the dwarf fixed all the damage that Mason had gleefully and Liam had reluctantly done to me.

A few minutes later, Jo-Jo leaned back. The milky-white magic faded from her palm, the matching glow leaked out of her eyes, and those red-hot needles finally stopped stabbing into my body. I let out a quiet sigh of relief.

"There you go, darling," she said. "Good as new."

I nodded, sat up, and swung my legs over the side of the chair. "Thank you, Jo-Jo."

She gave me a bright smile, then went over to the sink to wash her hands again.

From the front of the house, a sharp knock sounded, along with the faint creak of the door opening and the scuff of footsteps.

"Gin?" Owen called out.

"In the salon!"

More footsteps sounded, picking up speed. A few seconds later, Owen burst into the salon, with Finn hot on his heels. My significant other rushed over to me, and I got to my feet and hugged him tight, drinking in the strong, comforting warmth of his body pressed up against mine.

Owen drew back, his hands curling around my waist. His violet gaze scanned my face, along with the rest of me. "Are you okay? What happened?"

I made everyone sit down, and I told Owen, Finn, Silvio, and Jo-Jo about the fight with Mason, as well as what we'd found in the Carpenter Consulting office. Bria and I handed our phones over to Silvio, who transferred the photos we'd taken onto his tablet, connected his device to Jo-Jo's printer, and made color copies for everyone.

Finn stared at one of the diorama photos. "This is bad, Gin," he said in a low, strained voice. "Really, really *bad*."

His face twisted, as though he was about to be sick. Fletcher might have left me the Pork Pit to run, but Finn had grown up inside the restaurant just like I had, and it meant just as much to my brother as it did to me. Maybe even more, in some ways, since it was the place where Finn had spent so much time with his dad, the only parent he'd ever really had.

If the Pork Pit was my foundation, then it was my brother's security blanket. A place where he was always welcome, safe, loved, and protected.

"I know *exactly* how bad this is," I replied. "But the deal hasn't gone through yet, which means we still have a chance to stop it, right?"

Finn tried to smile, but his face twisted into another sick grimace, and doubt filled his eyes—the same doubt that was relentlessly beating in my own heart.

Another knock sounded on the front door, which creaked open again, and more footsteps headed in this direction, followed by a series of slow, steady *tap-tap-tap-taps*.

"Who is that?" Owen asked.

"Jo-Jo's other patient," I replied in a snide voice.

Several seconds later, Hugh Tucker appeared in the salon doorway. He was dressed in the same fisherman's sweater, corduroy pants, and boots as when Bria and I had seen him in the shipping container earlier, although he had a new accessory: a wooden cane he was leaning heavily on.

It wasn't all that far from the driveway to the salon, but sweat covered Tucker's forehead, he swayed from side to side, and his breath puffed out in thin, ragged gasps.

Lorelei was standing beside him. She reached out, as though to steady him, but Tucker jerked away. Annoyance flickered across Lorelei's face, along with the faintest flash of hurt, but she shrugged and moved forward, as if she didn't care whether he fell flat on his face.

The vampire grimaced, a muscle ticked in his jaw, and his hand curled a little tighter around the top of the cane. As much as I hated to admit it, Hugh Tucker and I were alike in a lot of ways, and few things would have made me more angry, frustrated, and embarrassed than to be so unsteady and helpless, especially around someone I was so strangely, strongly, reluctantly attracted to.

"A field trip," Tucker drawled, staring out over everyone gathered in the salon. "How exciting."

"Oh, shut up, and sit your ass down," Finn snapped.

Tucker arched a black eyebrow at him. "Temper, temper, Finnegan."

My brother surged to his feet and took a menacing step toward Tucker, but the vampire didn't so much as blink, despite his weakened state. After surviving the horror show that was Mason Mitchell, nothing that Finn or any of my friends could do, say, or threaten would so much as scratch Tucker's sardonic armor.

Still, he must have realized that we were in no mood to be mocked, because he slowly shuffled over and sank down onto the closest salon chair. He gasped for breath again, although his color was better, and he seemed quite a bit stronger than when I'd seen him earlier. Tucker must have given in and drunk the sugared blood Silvio had acquired for him, no matter how disgusting he claimed it was.

The vampire relaxed back in the chair as though he didn't have a care in the world, although he held on to his cane, laying it across his lap so he could use it as a weapon if need be. Smart. Given my current disposition, I felt more like stabbing him than questioning him.

"So," Tucker drawled again. "I take it things didn't go well at Carpenter Consulting?"

Bria glared at him. "No, they did not. Did you know Mason was going to be there? With his new best friends Charles and Drusilla Yang?"

His eyes narrowed in thought. "The Yangs were there? Curious. But no, I did not set you up, sweet Bria. I had no idea Mason would be there."

Bria kept glaring at him, her fingers twitching as though she wanted to blast him with her Ice magic. Tucker looked right back at her, still not concerned about when, if, or how any of us might try to hurt and kill him.

Silvio cleared his throat and held out the color copies he'd made. I grabbed them, then stalked over and dumped the stack of papers onto Tucker's lap.

"Tell me everything you know about the Mitchell Mile."

Tucker arched an eyebrow at me the same way he had at Finn, but he flipped through the papers, stopping on one of the diorama photos. "Well, this all looks more or less the same as the last time I saw it a few weeks ago."

Anger roared through me, but I forced myself to shove it down, down, down. Snapping at Tucker would only make him more hostile. "How long has Mason been plotting this?"

"You mean planning to raze the Pork Pit to the ground, along with most of downtown Ashland, and then rebuild it all to his liking?" Tucker shrugged. "As long as I've known him."

His answer surprised me. I'd thought this was Mason's way of taking a final bit of revenge on Fletcher, but if what Tucker was saying was true, then Mason had been planning this for years, and it was about much more than some petty retribution.

Owen frowned. "But I thought that the members of the Circle valued their anonymity above all else. That staying hidden in the shadows helped them accumulate even more money and power." He held up his own stack of papers. "Mason's name is all over these memos. Once this development deal is announced, he will never be anonymous again. Everyone in Ashland, underworld and otherwise, will know exactly who he is."

Tucker shrugged again. "Staying hidden in the shadows and pulling people's strings from afar was the Circle's preferred path and standard modus operandi for quite some time. But that hasn't worked so well ever since Genevieve killed Mab and refused to become the group's new figurehead."

I snorted. "I think you mean *puppet*."

He waved away my words. "You did far more damage to

the Circle by refusing to play Mason's game than you realize. Combine your obstinacy with the group's monetary troubles, and Mason is slowly losing his grip on the remaining members. He had to do something to reassert himself, to prove he is still in charge, and he saw the Mitchell Mile as the perfect way to do all of that and more."

"So I undermined his influence without even realizing it?" I drawled. "Why, I'd say that's a win for all of Ashland, especially everyone in the underworld."

Tucker shook his head. "Mason doesn't see it that way. He despises anyone who infringes on or undermines his power, even by accident, and he absolutely abhors anyone he can't control. In a nutshell, you, dear Genevieve, are everything Mason hates. Combine that with the fact that you are the daughter of Tristan and Eira, the two people who almost succeeded in wresting the Circle away from him..." The vampire's voice trailed off. "Well, I don't think there is a word strong enough to adequately convey the depths of Mason's loathing of you."

A shiver skittered down my spine at his eerily calm voice and matter-of-fact tone. All this time, I'd thought that Mason simply wanted to kill me the same way I wanted to kill him, but I was wrong. My uncle wanted to utterly *destroy* me and everything I represented, everything I loved, starting with the Pork Pit.

And he was well on his way to succeeding.

Another shiver swept through me, but I ignored it and gestured at the papers on Tucker's lap. "Mason hating me doesn't explain this project. Deals like this take years to set up. Mason didn't just dream up this development after he failed to kill me in the Circle cemetery a few weeks ago."

Tucker's nostrils flared, as though he'd just smelled something rotten. "Over the past few years, Mason has gotten...

restless. The other members of the Circle might be content to hide in the shadows and count their money, but he is not— not anymore. After all, if people don't know that you exist, then they don't know enough to fear you."

Understanding filled me. Not only was my uncle a sadistic control freak, but he also loved to remind people how powerful he was and how he could crush them with a mere wave of his hand.

"Not enough people are afraid of Mason, so he's going to build a monument to his own ego in downtown Ashland?" Bria shook her head. "That doesn't make sense to me."

Tucker shrugged for a third time. "It's not just about building a shrine to his own ego. Read the projections. The Mitchell Mile and all the new construction, development, and businesses it will create are worth tens of millions of dollars a year, if not more. Mason can use that money to replenish the Circle's coffers, get the other members back in line, *and* expand his influence. He doesn't just want to control Ashland—he wants to spread out as far and wide as possible."

"And the Pork Pit is ground zero for all his ambitions," Finn muttered, echoing Tucker's earlier words to me.

The vampire nodded.

Equal parts dread and frustration surged through me, and I yanked on the end of my ponytail, trying to release some of my pent-up emotions. "So how do we stop it? There *has* to be a way to stop it."

Pity filled Tucker's eyes, softening his cold black gaze. "While I was still in Mason's employ, most of the contracts had already been signed. I'm sure he's even farther along with the remaining contracts by now. Although..." His voice trailed off again.

"What?" I demanded, ready to catch whatever meager crumb of hope he threw me.

"I am surprised to hear that Mason was meeting with the Yangs."

Silvio held up a piece of paper. "According to this memo, the Yangs are loaning Mason the money for his development project. Why wouldn't they be there?"

"The Yangs were a last resort," Tucker replied. "Mason didn't want to borrow money from them unless he absolutely had to. He wanted the whole project to be legitimate from start to finish, and everyone in Ashland knows that the Yangs deal with criminals. He didn't want their reputation staining his own supposedly sterling one. Still, I suppose Mason had to take the Yangs' money since he didn't get his hands on the funds Fletcher stole from him."

He vampire paused, and a rare smile tugged up his lips. "Although I do find it deliciously ironic that Fletcher hid Mason's money in the Bellum Bank. That's where the funds are, right, Gin?"

His probing question reminded me of one of my own. "How much money *did* Fletcher steal from Mason?"

Tucker shifted in his chair, as though he was suddenly uncomfortable. "I don't know the exact amount."

"Bullshit," I accused. "You were in cahoots with Fletcher, and the two of you were trying to take Mason down together. Plus, Mason would have been screaming up one side and down the other about his missing money, especially to you, his right-hand man. So how much was it?"

Tucker shifted in his chair again. "Mason managed to keep the theft very, very quiet. None of the other Circle members ever realized it had happened, and he and Fletcher were the only ones who ever knew the exact amount."

"But?" Jo-Jo asked.

She crossed her arms over her chest and glared at him, while Rosco lifted his head and let out a low growl, as if warning Tucker to answer his mistress's question—or else.

Tucker eyed the basset hound with far more concern and wariness than he had shown me and my friends. "But from the things Mason let slip, I would estimate that Fletcher stole at least fifty million dollars, maybe more."

A stunned silence dropped over the salon. The amount even rendered Finn speechless, something that was extremely hard to do. But my brother recovered his voice first, the way he always did.

"Dad stole fifty million dollars?" Finn's voice screeched a little higher and louder with every word. "*Fifty million dollars?*"

Tucker winced, as though my brother's shrill tone was hurting his sensitive vampire ears. "Yes, fifty million dollars."

Finn blinked, and a soft, dreamy look filled his eyes. "Fifty million dollars back then was an *obscene* amount of money, but with interest, today it would be worth so much *more*. Even if you deducted whatever amount Dad was paying back to Mason every month."

"I believe the monthly repayment was about eighty-three thousand dollars, give or take," Tucker replied. "It was supposed to add up to one million dollars a year."

Finn threw back his head and laughed. "Oh, Dad. You sly, sly dog."

He laughed again, and then again, and again, until loud, merry chuckles were spewing out of his lips in a continuous stream. Tears leaked out of the corners of his eyes, and he clutched his stomach and doubled over.

Bria shot me a worried look. I shrugged in return. Finn was usually cheerful, but I'd rarely seen this level of hysterical mirth from him before.

"What's so funny?" Lorelei asked, eyeing my brother like he'd lost his mind.

Finn slowly quit laughing, then sat up and wiped away his tears, although a wide grin stretched across his face. "Let's be ultra-, ultra-conservative and say that Dad was getting two percent interest on that fifty million dollars. That's one million dollars every single year."

"So?" Lorelei asked.

"So Dad wasn't touching any of the principal. He wasn't actually giving Mason *any* of his money back. Not really. Not one lousy *cent* of it. He was just stringing Mason along and sending him the interest every single month. And probably not even all the interest he was earning, to add insult to injury. Dad always claimed that *I* was a greedy scoundrel. Please. *He* was conducting a master class in money management right under my nose, and I never even noticed." More tears gleamed in Finn's eyes. "Oh, how I miss him right now."

Bria reached out and squeezed Finn's arm. He caught her hand in his, then pressed a kiss to her knuckles.

"But the money wasn't in an account," Owen said. "It was just sitting in that vault, so how could it have been earning interest?"

Finn shrugged. "It wasn't in an account that we know of. Maybe Dad got spooked for some reason, turned all the money into cash and jewelry, and stuffed it into the vault. He could have done that at any time after he stole it from Mason. There's no telling when Dad got that vault."

"I hate to point out the obvious, but Fletcher has been dead for more than a year," Silvio said. "Which means his payments to Mason stopped, right?"

Tucker nodded, confirming the theory.

"So what?" Owen asked.

"So how did Mason secure such a big loan from the Yangs?" Silvio asked. "Charles and Drusilla Yang are smart businesspeople. They don't just hand out money to anyone, especially not the staggering amounts mentioned in these memos."

Finn shrugged again. "Mason probably had to put something up as collateral in case his project goes belly-up."

"Like the Mitchell family mansion?" Jo-Jo suggested. "That fancy house, the surrounding land, and all those old artifacts have to be worth several million dollars."

Finn nodded. "Mason could have put the mansion and its contents up as collateral. Or maybe he cut the Yangs in on future profits from the development deal." He looked at me. "Or maybe he's planning to pay them back with the money Dad stole from him."

I snorted. "Well, if Mason is counting on Fletcher's money to bail him out, then he is going to be sorely disappointed. There's not nearly enough cash in Fletcher's vault for Mason to pay back what he's borrowed from the Yangs—or to save him from the Fire elementals' wrath if his project does go sideways and they end up losing their investment."

Tucker's eyes narrowed. "How much money *is* in the vault?"

"None of your business," I growled.

"Oh, I think it is very *much* my business, Gin," Tucker growled right back at me. "If you believe nothing else I've said, then believe this: if Mason even *suspects* that you know where the money is, he will do whatever it takes to get his hands on it."

He leaned forward, spearing me with a hard look. "And it's not just the actual dollars he wants. Mason would love nothing more than to finally find that money, to finally take back what Fletcher stole from him, to finally fucking *win*."

Once again, the vampire's voice was eerily calm, and his matter-of-fact tone sent a new wave of chills sliding down my spine. I couldn't stop his words from ringing in my ears—or the truth of them from beating in my heart.

Tucker was right. To Mason, recovering his stolen money was a bonus at this point, and my uncle wouldn't let anything stand in the way of his new endeavor. Even worse, now that Mason knew that I knew about his project, it was only a matter of time before he tried to eliminate me.

No more half measures, no more near misses, no more escapes.

Mason would be playing for keeps now, planning, plotting, and scheming until I was dead.

❋ 10 ❋

We tossed out some more theories about what Mason might have promised the Yangs in order to get such a huge loan, but that's all they were—theories. And in the end, our theories didn't matter, since Mason had already secured the money. My friends and I also discussed how we might stop my uncle, but no one had any bright ideas about how to derail the Mitchell Mile.

It had been a long, long day, and rather than keep spinning our wheels at the salon, we split up for the night, still using the buddy system we'd been sticking to for the past few weeks, ever since Emery Slater had kidnapped Bria, Lorelei, and me from the Posh boutique parking lot.

Finn and Bria left to go to his apartment in the city, while Silvio agreed to come to Fletcher's house with Owen and me. I texted Sophia, making sure that she was on her way to Jo-Jo's house, then messaged several of our other friends, including Xavier, Roslyn Phillips, and Phillip Kincaid, reminding everyone to be careful.

Lorelei strode over to Tucker, crossed her arms over her

chest, and stared down at him. "Would you like some help?" she asked in a cool voice.

"No," Tucker replied, his voice as cool as hers. "I can manage on my own. Thank you."

He stabbed his cane against the floor and slowly hoisted himself to his feet. By the time he finished, he was sweating and wobbling again, and his knuckles were white around the top of the cane, as if it was the only thing holding him upright.

Lorelei let out an exasperated huff and strode down the hallway. Everyone else had already gone outside, which left Tucker and me alone in the salon, except for Rosco, who was once again snoozing in his basket.

"Stop it," I snapped.

"Stop what?"

"Being a jackass. Lorelei is just trying to help you, and you being insufferably rude won't get you what you want."

"And what do I want?" he muttered, staring down the hallway.

"Her."

Tucker jerked back as though I had slapped him, although he quickly schooled his face into its usual blank, remote mask. "I don't know what you're talking about."

I rolled my eyes. "I swear, sometimes I feel like I'm the only adult around here. It's so freaking *obvious* the two of you are attracted to each other. I can see why you like Lorelei. She's smart, tough, and strong. As for what she sees in you...well, I honestly have no idea. Perhaps she finds goatees attractive."

Tucker reached up and stroked his black goatee. I smirked at him. The vampire realized what he was doing, dropped his hand, and scowled at me.

"Either way, what goes on between you and Lorelei is your business. I won't get in the way, and I won't interfere. Why, I won't even bad-mouth you to her." I paused. "Much."

Tucker gave me a wary look. "But?"

I stepped closer to my former nemesis, letting him see exactly how cold my gray eyes were. "But...if you hurt or betray Lorelei in any way, shape, or form, then I *will* kill you. I might not be able to make it nearly as painful as Mason would, but your nine lives will officially run out, and you'll still be dead. Are we clear?"

Tucker tipped his head to me, a faint, mocking smile curving his lips. "Crystal."

"Excellent." I drew back. "You should head on outside, Tuck. I wouldn't want you to wear yourself out standing here trading insults and threats with little ole me, especially when you can't back them up."

Anger flared in his eyes, but for once he took my advice. He drew himself up to his full height and slowly limped out of the salon.

I made sure that Tucker got into Lorelei's car without collapsing, then said my good-byes to Jo-Jo. Owen drove me home, with Silvio following us in his van.

My assistant had been splitting time between his house and mine, as well as meeting with Liam Carter some nights, but given this afternoon's disastrous confrontation with Mason, I wanted Silvio under my roof, where I could protect him in case Emery Slater and her giants did attack.

Eva Grayson, Owen's younger sister, and several of her friends—including Violet Fox, Elissa Daniels, and Silvio's niece Catalina Vasquez—were currently on a spring-break trip in Cloudburst Falls, far away, where Mason couldn't hurt them. I was extremely glad that Eva and her friends were out of town. The fewer people I had to worry about, the better.

Owen turned off the curvy mountain road, steered his car up a bumpy gravel driveway, and parked in front of a house made of white clapboard, red brick, and dull, gray, weathered tin. The structure looked like something a child had shoved together from disparate building blocks, but I liked the odd mishmash of materials. The clapboard, brick, and tin were nothing fancy, but they had stood the test of time, and I felt safer at Fletcher's house, my house now, than I did just about anywhere else.

Owen killed the engine, and I stared through the windshield, reaching out with my Stone magic and scanning the dark landscape. But the rocks buried in the leaves in the woods only murmured about the scurrying of animals and the growing cold, as did the loose gravel in the driveway and the larger boulders that formed the steep ridge on the other side of the house. No one had been here since Finn had picked me up this morning.

"We're clear," I said.

Owen and I got out of his car, while Silvio climbed out of his van. I unlocked the front door, and we all trooped into the den.

Silvio immediately unpacked his briefcase, pulling out all the documents and photos he'd printed out at Jo-Jo's house. In less than a minute, several large stacks of papers covered most of the coffee table in the center of the den.

My assistant stepped back, planted his hands on his hips, and studied the den with a critical eye. "We need a whiteboard to properly display all this material. I'll grab the one I have stashed in my van and set it up in here."

Owen and I exchanged a look.

"You have a whiteboard in your van?" Owen asked the obvious question.

"Of course," Silvio replied in a no-nonsense tone. "A good assistant is always prepared for anything."

He ignored Owen's incredulous look, grabbed his tablet, and started tapping away on it.

I knew better than to argue with Silvio when he was in good-assistant mode, so I put my phone in its usual spot on the table to charge, then emptied my pockets. The first thing I pulled out was the papers I'd swiped from Carpenter Consulting. Next came the hundred-dollar bill Finn had given me from one of the bricks of cash in Fletcher's vault. And finally, there was the penny that had been part of my spider rune on the table in the vault.

Disgust rolled through me. I might have found Fletcher's secret treasure trove, but really, all I'd done today was make things worse. I dropped the papers, the bill, and the penny onto the table next to my phone, not particularly caring where they landed.

Silvio shot me a sharp, chiding look, as though I was imposing on his system, so I sighed and scooted the items off to the side of the table, out of his way.

"What are those?" Owen asked, also plugging his phone in to charge.

"Some money from Fletcher's vault, along with the rest of the detritus of the day. Nothing important." I glanced over at Silvio. "Do me a favor. Please don't stay up all night sorting through this stuff."

He gave me a distracted wave. "I won't stay up too late. I just want to get everything organized."

Of course he did. Silvio worked far too hard for his own good, but trying to reason with him was a lost cause, so I wished him good night and left the den.

Owen came with me, and we headed upstairs. I took a long, hot shower and put on my pajamas. So did Owen, and then the two of us crawled into bed.

He drew me into his warm, strong arms and smoothed my damp hair back from my face. "You're worried." He paused. "At least, more so than usual. Want to talk about it?"

I thought I'd done a better job hiding my concern, but Owen knew me far too well to be fooled by any happy, benign face I might put on. And no, I didn't want to talk about it—I *never* wanted to talk about my feelings. But I also knew that I *should*, and it warmed my heart that he had asked, rather than trying to pry the answers out of me.

I sighed, relaxing into his embrace. "Yes, I'm worried."

"About Mason's project?"

"His project, him working with the Yangs, Liam Carter still being undercover in the Circle. At this point, I don't know what I'm *not* worried about." I sighed again. "After all these months of investigating the Circle, we're down to the last round of the game between Mason and me. All the cards are finally laid out on the table for me to see, and right now, I have a losing hand."

Owen kept sliding his hand through my hair. "Look on the bright side. At least you found Fletcher's money. Maybe you can use it to stop Mason's project and save the Pork Pit."

"Maybe."

"But?" he asked, hearing the doubt in my voice.

"But I'm starting to wonder if my finding Fletcher's money is just going to lead to more problems."

"How so?"

"Tucker is right. Sooner or later, Mason is going to realize that I found the money, and once that happens, he'll stop at nothing to get it." A third sigh escaped my lips. "And that's not even what worries me the most."

Owen frowned. "What would that be?"

"How Mason is going to react when he realizes there's not enough money to cover what Fletcher stole from him all those years ago or to pay back the loan he took out from the Yangs."

"Maybe Finn got his math wrong," Owen suggested. "Maybe there's more cash in the vault than what he estimated."

"Finnegan Lane get his math wrong about a vault full of money?" I snorted. "*Never*. Oh, Finn might be off by a million or two, like Silvio said, but that's not enough to make a difference to Mason. Not when Fletcher stole *fifty million dollars*."

Owen's black eyebrows creased together in thought. "Well, we both know how much Fletcher loved puzzles and surprises. Maybe the rest of the money *is* in the vault. You said that you and Finn just glanced at the shelves. Maybe the gold bars are worth more than the cash. Or maybe Fletcher hid something in one of the bags of coins. Or maybe there's a secret compartment filled with diamonds in one of the walls."

"Maybe," I replied. "But if Fletcher *didn't* hide something in the vault or he *didn't* leave me another message, then I don't know where else to look for the rest of the money. This is the end of the rainbow, only there's no pot of gold, just a lot of loose change."

Owen slid his hand through my hair again. "You'll figure it out, Gin. You always do."

I forced myself to smile at him, even as my stomach churned with worry. "Well, I need to figure it out fast. Because once Mason realizes that the majority of his cash is most likely gone forever, he'll cut his losses. He might not be able to recover his money, but he can still extract more than a pound of flesh from us. You, me, Finn, Bria, Silvio,

Sophia, Jo-Jo, Lorelei, even Tucker. Everyone who's been helping us. Everyone we care about."

"Let the bastard come," Owen growled, a fierce light flaring in his violet eyes. "You killed Mab Monroe. And Madeline Monroe. And everyone else who's threatened us. You'll figure out a way to kill Mason too. I know you will, Gin."

Hot tears stung my eyes, and my throat closed up with emotion. Owen's unwavering, unshakable faith meant more to me than he would ever know, more than I could ever properly put into words. So I decided not to bother with words at all. Not tonight. Not when I could still hear that clock relentlessly ticking away in my mind, counting down the seconds until Mason lashed out at me again and finally put me in the ground for good.

So I scooted forward, staring into Owen's eyes. I cupped his cheek in my hand, then trailed my fingers down his neck, enjoying the faint prickle of his dark stubble against my palm. A low rumble of pleasure sounded deep in Owen's chest, and he leaned into my touch. I leaned in as well and pressed my lips to his.

My kiss was soft, gentle, sweet even, just a brush of my lips against his, but it was packed with pure, raw emotion. I kept kissing Owen, trying to show how much I cared for him, how much I felt for him. With every press of my lips against his, I poured out a little more of my heart, along with all those pesky feelings that I had such a hard time sharing, such a hard time putting into words. Care, concern, respect, appreciation, admiration, and, most of all, love.

So much love.

Owen let out another low rumble of pleasure, one that vibrated out of his body and into mine, as though we were tuning forks resonating at the same frequency. Then he wound his hand into my still-damp hair and drew me down on top of him.

We lay like that for a long time, just exchanging those slow, sweet, powerful kisses, each of us showing the other the true depths of our feelings. Maybe it was the third kiss, or the thirteenth, or the thirtieth, but the sweetness faded, burned away by a bright flare of passion.

I nibbled on Owen's lower lip, and his tongue darted out to meet mine. Our kisses grew deeper, longer, harder, even as our hands starting moving over each other's body. Even though we had been together countless times, I always found something new to admire, appreciate, adore about Owen, whether it was the hot stroke of his tongue teasing mine, or the firm press of his muscles against my own, or the way his fingers so carefully, thoughtfully glided over my skin, as though I were the finest, most delicate treasure he had ever touched.

"You're wearing too many clothes," Owen murmured against my mouth, reaching for the bottom of my shirt.

I was already wrestling with his. "I was just going to say the same thing about you."

We both laughed and quickly shed our pajamas, then Owen grabbed a condom from the nightstand drawer. I took my little white pills, but we always used extra protection. Then, when we were both ready, we came together again.

Owen kissed his way down my neck, then cupped my breasts in his hands. He caught one of my nipples between his teeth, sucking hard. Pleasure spiked through me, and heat pooled between my thighs. I dug my fingers into his hair and arched back to give him better access. While he kept lavishing attention on my breasts, I slipped one hand between us and grabbed his thick, hard length.

Owen's breath hitched in his throat, and he raised his head

and stared at me, desire making his eyes blaze like violet suns. I kept stroking him, feeling every twitch and flex of his muscles from top to bottom as he lay against me.

"I love it when you touch me like that," he rasped.

"I love it too," I replied in a husky voice, still stroking him. "But not nearly as much as I love you."

"Well, that feeling is definitely mutual." A wicked grin curved his lips. "Now, let's see what else I can do about giving you some other mutual feelings."

This time, his hand was the one that slid lower...and lower...and lower. Owen carefully eased my thighs apart and started caressing that most intimate part of me.

Waves of pleasure zipped through me, and my breath hitched in my throat, much like his had. I grasped his back, digging my fingers into his skin and pulling him closer.

"That's...not fair," I rasped. "Using...my own moves... against me."

Owen gave me another wicked grin. "Oh, it might not be fair, but it sure is fun."

He leaned down and put his mouth where his hand had been. The first long, slow lick of his tongue sent a hot electric shock through me. I cried out and arched back, but Owen kept going, teasing me with his fingers and tongue. Each new touch, lick, and caress sent more pleasure spiking through me—pleasure that quickly coalesced into sharp, throbbing, aching need.

Finally, when it was too much, I dug my hands into his hair and lifted his head. "I want you inside me. Now."

Owen nodded and covered himself with the condom. He reached for me again, but I pushed him over onto his back and straddled him. We kissed again, slow and sweet, and I slid forward, taking him inside me. This time, Owen was the one who arched back.

"More, Gin," he rasped. "More."

So I gave him more, rocking my hips back and forth until we both fell into that quick, hard rhythm we knew so well. I cried out first, finding my release. Owen joined me a moment later, and in an instant, we were both lost in our explosions of mutual feelings.

✿ 11 ✿

*A*fterward, we snuggled in bed, with Owen lying on his back and my head resting on his chest. The strong, steady thump of his heart reassured me. Owen was still here, still alive, and so was I.

Despite my disastrous run-in with Mason earlier, my uncle hadn't gotten the best of me—yet. As long as I was still breathing, then I still had a chance to fix things, to kill Mason and end his reign of terror. Maybe Fletcher's money would help with that. Maybe not, but at least it gave me some options, providing I could figure out how to get the cash, coins, and valuables out of the Bellum Bank undetected.

But that was a problem for later. Right now, I was warm and comfortable, and my eyes fluttered shut. I quickly drifted off to sleep, and sometime later, I started to dream, to remember...

"Well, that was easy."

I waved my bloody knife at Fletcher. "You think this was easy? Are you kidding me?"

The old man grinned, his green eyes glimmering in his tan, wrinkled face. "Well, easy is a relative term."

I snorted and stared out over the dead bodies littering the library.

Half an hour ago, Fletcher and I had snuck into the mansion of Ivan Gere, a dwarf who was one of Ashland's most ruthless and notorious loan sharks. Ivan was sprawled across his desk, his blood oozing over the wood from where I had snuck up behind him and cut his throat. The three dwarves who had served as Ivan's bodyguards were slumped on couches around the library, dead from the bullets Fletcher had pumped into their chests.

"C'mon, Gin," he said in a wheedling tone. "Admit it. This was one of the easiest jobs we've done in a long time. Nobody laid a finger on either one of us."

Well, okay, maybe this job had been easier *than usual, since neither Fletcher nor I was bruised, battered, and bleeding, but we'd still spent days planning, researching, and learning everything we could about Ivan and his operation.*

And we'd still come up one body short.

"What about Ethan?" I asked. "The plan was to take them all out at once."

Ethan, Ivan's brother, was supposed to have been here too, but he must have gone out to party the night away at Northern Aggression. Ethan had a not-so-small and not-at-all-secret drug habit.

Fletcher shrugged. "Ivan was the brains of the operation. Ethan is just the muscle. Besides, Ethan is too interested in putting his money up his nose to cause any real trouble."

I frowned. That hadn't been my assessment of the brothers Gere. If anything, I thought that Ethan was the far more dangerous dwarf. Ivan had been a greedy loan shark who cared about profits more than anything else, and he knew that you couldn't squeeze money out of dead people. But I hadn't gotten that same vibe from Ethan. No, I thought Ethan Gere liked hurting people far too much to listen to any kind of common sense.

Still, I pushed my unease aside. This was Fletcher's mission, not mine, and I shouldn't question his judgment, especially since he'd been right about everything so far, from when we should break into the mansion, to the kind of alarm system Ivan had, to what room he and his bodyguards would be in.

Fletcher reached out and started sliding stacks of money around, making sure to keep the bills out of the growing pool of blood on the desk. He finished, then swept his hand out over the desk. "Voilà!"

I frowned at the odd pattern he'd created. "What is that?"

The grin faded from his face. "It's your spider rune. Can't you see it?"

I tilted my head to the side, looking at his odd, impromptu creation from a different angle. Fletcher had arranged several stacks of cash in a rough circle and surrounded them with eight more stacks of cash shooting out in various directions. If you squinted at it real hard, you might think it was my spider rune...or you might think Ivan had a really weird way of counting his money.

"Oh, yeah," I replied, not wanting to hurt the old man's feelings or artistic pride. "I see it now. Of course it's my spider rune."

Fletcher beamed at me, then walked over to the fireplace. "And now, to get what we came here for."

The old man lifted a small silver-framed painting off the mantel above the fireplace. He turned around and showed it off to me. "Ain't she a beauty?"

The she *in question was a woman in a light gray dress who was clutching a bright blood-red book in her lap. The* woman was perched on a gray rock and surrounded by a field of grayish wildflowers, with a gray castle and mountains lurking in the background.

The painting was called A Lady's Reverie in Gray and was a portrait of the artist's daughter. I'd never been much for art, but even I liked this work, probably because I lived so much of my life in the gray, in the shadows, just like the woman in the painting seemed to.

Fletcher had told me about the painting's history and artistic significance, although I'd largely tuned out that information. Other than its stunning beauty, the only thing truly important about the Reverie in Gray painting was that it dated back to the 1800s and was worth more than three million dollars.

But the piece's value paled in comparison to its sentimental worth. The painting had been gifted from mother to daughter through several generations of the artist's family, including its current owner, Blanche Langley, a seventy-something retiree who enjoyed traveling, taking photos, attending kickboxing classes, and spending time with her friends and family.

At least, until the Gere brothers had come along.

Benji, Blanche's twenty-something grandson, had gone to an underground casino run by the Geres—the kind of place where the drinks were spiked and the games were rigged. The next morning, Benji had woken up and found himself more than fifty thousand dollars in debt. Instead of coming clean to his grandmother, Benji had decided to avoid the Geres, who were known for getting either money or blood from their victims, whichever was easier to obtain.

The Geres had quickly caught up with Benji, who had started blubbering about his grandmother's valuable painting. When Blanche had refused to give Ivan her family *heirloom, Ethan had beaten her to a bloody pulp, along with Benji, and had taken the painting.*

Ivan had warned Blanche not to go to the cops, but she'd heard stories about the Tin Man, the assassin who could help people when the legal system couldn't. Blanche wanted her painting back, and she wanted the Geres to pay for what they'd done to her and her grandson. Eventually, Blanche's story had found its way to Fletcher's inquisitive ears, and here we were tonight, retrieving the painting and eliminating the Geres for conning and terrorizing an innocent family, along with all their other victims.

"If we hurry, we can drop this off at Blanche's house and then head over to the salon for movie night," Fletcher said. "I think Jo-Jo and Sophia were going to watch The Sting *or some other heist movie."*

I gestured at Ivan's body. "But what about Ethan? What if he comes home and decides to look for the people who killed his brother? Plus, he's sure to notice the painting is gone. He might go after Blanche as payback."

Fletcher shook his head. "Nah. Ethan is probably paying his dealer for something new and exciting to snort up his nose. He shouldn't come home for hours. Besides, we'll stick to our plan and make it look like a robbery. Blanche will be in the clear. Trust me."

I did trust the old man, more than anyone else, but he had also taught me to trust in one very basic principle: bad guys didn't change their bloody stripes. Fletcher even had a saying about it. Always expect the bad guys to do the worst, most inconvenient thing possible. *Something he seemed to be forgetting right now.*

Fletcher leaned the painting up against the fireplace, then strode back over to Ivan's desk. He admired the spider rune he'd made from money, then picked up the bricks of cash and stuffed them into the pockets of his blue coveralls. "This should take care of Blanche's and Benji's medical bills. Let's see what else is worth stealing. I feel like making some donations."

He winked, coaxing a laugh out of me. We might be assassins, but we weren't greedy. Whenever we made a hit look like a robbery gone wrong, Fletcher always donated whatever we stole to one charity or another. Everything from soup kitchens to animal shelters to literacy programs had benefited from his largesse.

Fletcher shoved Ivan off to the side, then started rifling through the desk drawers. More bricks of cash, several gold watches, a couple of diamond necklaces in velvet boxes, even some plastic sleeves filled with rare stamps. Ivan's desk was a veritable treasure trove. I wondered if any of the watches, necklaces, and stamps had saved their previous owners from Ethan's wrath. Probably not.

"Hey, Gin. Come put some of this stuff in your bag," Fletcher said. "I'm not going to be able to carry it all."

I had crammed a canvas bag into my jacket pocket for this very purpose, so I pulled it out, snapped it open, and started sliding the valuables off the desk and down into the bag.

Fletcher moved over to a freestanding safe tucked in the back corner. The safe was standing wide open, and he started pulling out more bricks of cash and tossing them over to me.

The larger the bag of loot grew, the more worried I became. Fletcher had been right earlier. This had been easy—way too easy—and I found myself waiting for the proverbial other shoe to drop and for trouble to come crashing down on us like it always did...

My eyes slowly fluttered open. For once, my dream, my memory, had ended on a quiet, nonviolent note, although the worry I'd felt all those years ago matched what was currently churning in my stomach. My sleep might have been peaceful, but it hadn't been restful.

I glanced to my right. Owen was lying on his back, eyes closed, with little puffs of air escaping out of his open mouth. I exhaled, relieved that I hadn't yelled, screamed, thrashed around, and woken him up the way I so often did whenever my brain dredged up some long-ago battle.

Of course, it was painfully obvious why this particular fight had popped into my mind. I had remembered it as soon as I'd seen the replica of *A Lady's Reverie in Gray* in Fletcher's vault.

Once again, I wondered why the old man had left the fake painting in the vault. Had he been planning to pass it off to someone as the real deal? Maybe even give it to Mason as part of his monthly repayment of the Circle's money? Or was the painting one final message to me? If so, what was the message? And how could it help me stop Mason's plans for the Pork Pit?

I stared at the ceiling, more and more questions crowding into my mind and more and more worry flooding my body. Just like the woman in the painting, I was drowning in a sea of gray, with no bright, hopeful colors in sight.

I couldn't go back to sleep, so I slipped out of bed, threw on my pajamas and a fleece robe, and headed downstairs. I moved from room to room, peering out the windows, but no one was lurking in the woods, and the midnight landscape was cold and quiet. Mason wasn't going to attack us tonight.

So I padded into the den, grabbed my phone, and sat down on the couch. Other than a couple of texts from Bria, saying that she and Finn were back at his apartment, none of my other friends had reached out. Everyone seemed to be safe—for tonight. As for tomorrow, well, that would bring more chances of death and danger for all of us.

It always did.

I set my phone back down on the table, and something bright and shiny caught my eye: the penny Finn had tossed at me earlier, the centerpiece of my spider rune that Fletcher had arranged on the vault table.

The sight of the shiny coin made me sigh with frustration. Once—just once—I would have liked to have seen one of Fletcher's little puzzles and immediately known what it meant. But here I was, yet again, sitting up late and wondering what he was trying to tell me with a fake painting, a table covered with coins, and shelves filled with money and assorted trinkets.

Or maybe Fletcher wasn't trying to tell me anything. Maybe the vault had just been a repository for the loot he'd stolen as the Tin Man, all the things he hadn't had the time or inclination to fence for cash before his death.

Cold sorrow washed over me. As frustrated as I had been by Fletcher's byzantine codes that only seemed to lead to more byzantine codes and his painstaking approach to only revealing a few pieces of the Circle puzzle at a time, part of me had absolutely *loved* chasing down his clues and trying to figure out what his cryptic messages meant.

Over the past few months, I'd dug up graves, opened safety-deposit boxes, and found ledgers in unexpected places. The long, winding treasure hunt had almost made it seem like Fletcher was still alive, instead of dead and buried in Blue Ridge Cemetery.

But I supposed that all good things had to end, even Fletcher's trail of clues, and I was going to miss them far more than I'd ever thought possible.

More cold sorrow flooded my heart, but moping about Fletcher wasn't going to solve my myriad problems, so I focused on the other two things I'd picked up during the day's adventures: the hundred-dollar bill Finn had slapped into my hand in the vault and the memo I'd swiped from Carpenter Consulting.

The bill was exactly what it appeared to be—one hundred dollars—with no notes or messages scribbled on it, so I set it next to the penny. Then I picked up the papers, unfolded them, and scanned the contents.

MM—Phase 2... NOT for public distribution...will require independent monetary assets...

The papers included a memo, along with some artist renderings, about the cursed Mitchell Mile, and the corporate double-speak made it sound as though my uncle was already planning to expand his evil empire. I snorted and tossed the papers back down onto the table. Of course he was. Hugh Tucker was right. Mason wouldn't be happy until he had all of Ashland under his thumb.

Since I'd struck out with my clues, such as they were, I got up off the couch and walked over to the fireplace. Silvio had indeed brought a freestanding whiteboard into the den, and he'd already covered it from top to bottom with copies of the photos I'd taken of Fletcher's vault, as well as the pictures I'd snapped of Mason's diorama and the ones Bria had taken of the documents in the Carpenter Consulting conference room.

I focused on the vault photos. The shrink-wrapped bricks of cash sitting on the shelves. The rings, necklaces, and bracelets glinting on their white velvet trays. The fake *Reverie in Gray* painting propped up on the table. The shiny coins that spelled out *Gin*, along with my spider rune.

The photos and items looked exactly the same as before,

and I didn't see anything new or different in the images.

I kept staring at the pictures, prioritizing my various problems in my mind. If Silvio had still been awake, I might even have asked him to make me a troubleshooting list, something that probably would have made my assistant extremely happy—and something that he would never let me live down.

Right now, I didn't know what, if anything, was special about or hidden in Fletcher's vault, I didn't know how to stop Mason's scheme to destroy the Pork Pit, and I still hadn't figured out a way to kill my uncle.

Those three items on my mental list all had big red question marks beside them, so I moved on to my most pressing immediate concern and the one thing I might actually be able to accomplish: keeping the vault valuables away from Mason. Even if the dollar amount wasn't nearly as much as it should be, my uncle could still do a lot of damage with the money, and I couldn't afford to let him get his hands on it.

The only problem was that I didn't see a way that *I* could get my hands on it either.

Oh, sure, Finn had smuggled a couple of bricks of cash out of the vault earlier, but it would take hours, maybe even days, for the two of us to remove all the money on the sly, not to mention the trays of jewelry, the heavy bags of coins, and the fake painting. Even if I enlisted Owen, Silvio, and Bria and we all used duffel bags, we'd still have to make several trips in and out of the bank, and that was if the Yangs would even let us back into their building now, after the battle on the sidewalk.

Finn had said that the Yangs had a code, just like we did, but given Charles and Drusilla's affiliation with Mason, they might have decided to break their own rules and sell me out.

They might have already told Mason about Fletcher's vault. They might have already opened it up for him.

Arrows of worry shot through my heart, but I forced myself to shove aside my concern. Drusilla had claimed that she couldn't access the vault without Fletcher's password. At least, not without having it drilled open. So I was going to assume that the détente was holding and the money was still safe in there—for now.

Besides, my uncle was a devious bastard who liked to prove how much smarter he was than everyone else. If I were Mason, I would let me and my friends open the vault, bring the money out of the bank, and *then* take it away from us.

"Why did you do it, Fletcher?" I muttered. "Why did you make the money so hard to access? Why didn't you just put it in an account like a regular person?"

My harsh words quickly faded away, but saying them made me look at the vault photos in a new light, just like I'd finally seen the spider rune Fletcher had arranged on Ivan Gere's desk so long ago. Maybe this being so difficult *was* the answer—or at least *part* of the answer.

I didn't know how my friends and I were going to remove the cash, coins, and other items from the vault without getting caught, robbed, and potentially killed, either by Mason, the Yangs, or some greedy underworld boss. But if we couldn't get the money out of the bank, then Mason would have a hard time getting his hands on it too.

Maybe that was why Fletcher had stuffed that vault full of cash, coins, and jewelry. Not to hamper me when I found the money but to keep Mason from immediately stealing it away. After all, a regular bank account was simply ones and zeros, just like Finn had said. All you needed was a willing banker, some account and routing numbers, and a few passwords, and you could transfer—*steal*—millions of dollars in a minute, two tops. And once that money was out of an account, it was *gone*, and there was no putting it back. The whole process was clean, simple, easy.

But there was nothing clean, simple, or easy about physically moving a vault full of loot. Not even for someone as powerful as Mason.

The more I thought about it, the more sense it made. Fletcher must have realized that either Mason or I would find the valuables sooner or later, and he'd wanted to protect them as much as possible. Part of me admired the old man's cleverness in stockpiling the cash and goods, even if his brilliance was thwarting me now.

Frustrated, I stalked past the whiteboard and went over to several framed rune drawings sitting on the mantel. One of them was of a pig holding a platter of food, the sign that hung above the front door of the Pork Pit—my symbol for Fletcher and everything he had meant to me, everything he had given to me, everything Mason was threatening to take away.

My gaze zipped over to a more recent addition to the mantel: a letter Fletcher had written to me that had been in the black ledger he'd hidden under the porch steps at Jo-Jo's house. I'd framed it as yet another reminder and memento of the old man, and my gaze scanned the familiar lines.

We might not always be richer or stronger than our enemies, but we can always fight smarter.

Fletcher had urged me to be smarter than Mason, to outthink my uncle, but so far, my brain cells were firing on empty, and I just couldn't see a way to do it. At least, not when it came to the vault valuables. Then again, I was more of a doer—a killer—than a thinker.

Roxy Wyatt, Brody Dalton, Bruce Porter, Alanna Eaton. I'd used a combination of my Ice and Stone magic, assassin skills, sheer determination, and a little bit of luck to best the other Circle baddies, but none of my previous tricks would work on Mason. I couldn't—wouldn't—risk my life or especially my friends' lives on the thread-thin hope that I could find some way to kill him before he crushed me. No, I needed a plan before I faced my uncle again. If only Fletcher had stored one of those in his vault along with the rest of the valuables.

I sighed and moved past the letter, as well as a drawing that featured Bria's primrose, and focused on two other drawings: a snowflake, the symbol for icy calm, which represented my mother, Eira, and an ivy vine, the symbol for elegance, for my older sister, Annabella.

Two matching silverstone rune pendants—a snowflake and an ivy vine—were draped over their respective drawings. I plucked the pendants off their perches. Each one pulsed with Ice magic—my Ice magic.

Despite Mason almost killing me in the Circle family cemetery a few weeks ago, I had learned something important from his attack: I couldn't beat him with my Stone magic. He was simply too strong and had too much raw power to battle that way. But Mason had to be able to sense the stones to use them against me, something my Ice magic had prevented him from doing.

So ever since that night, I had been adding more and more of my Ice magic to my spider-rune pendant and ring, as well as to my mother's snowflake and Annabella's ivy vine. I wasn't quite sure how, or even if, I would weaponize the jewelry, but building up the Ice reserves made me feel like I was at least doing something useful, instead of just waiting for Mason to attack again.

So I clutched the snowflake pendant in one hand and the ivy vine in the other. Then I reached for my Ice magic, letting it flow out of my palms and coat each rune with a thick layer of cold crystals. The crystals sank into the silverstone, so I coated them with another layer of Ice magic, and then another one, and then another one, until I had almost exhausted the natural power in my own body.

The pendants glowed a bright silver, although they quickly faded back to their duller, dimmer color. Once I was sure they had absorbed my magic, I hung them back on their drawings.

A sapphire paperweight was also on the mantel, and it too pulsed with magic—Mason's magic. Just staring at the paperweight made me shudder, and the cold, hard feel of his power continuously rippling off the jewel made me flash back to how brutally he'd battered me with his magic.

More than once, I'd thought about going outside, rearing my arm back, and chucking the paperweight off the side of the ridge. That would have been one way to get rid of it, if not the memories that came along with it. Still, I couldn't quite bring myself to do that. The sapphire might stir up bad feelings, but it was also chock-full of magic and thus too valuable to throw away.

I reached out with my own magic and focused on the paperweight, hoping it might give me some idea for how I could use its magic against Mason, but the sapphire only smugly whispered about its own deep blue beauty, as well as all the power it contained. The gleaming facets and sly murmurs didn't offer me any answers.

Nothing in here had given me any answers.

Disgusted, I whirled away from the mantel, slapped off the lights, and stormed out of the den, all the while knowing that my worries and problems were going to follow me back to bed—and beyond.

✤ 12 ✤

I didn't think I would get much sleep, but the fight with Mason and Liam must have taken more out of me than I'd realized, because I crawled back into bed next to Owen and drifted off almost immediately. Even better, no more memories interrupted my deep, soothing sleep.

When I rolled over the next morning, Owen was gone, and the clock on the nightstand said that it was creeping up on nine o'clock. I sighed, wishing I could stay in bed for the rest of the day, week, month, year, but I had a restaurant to run, a vault full of money to steal, and a sadistic uncle to kill, so I threw back the blankets, took a hot shower, and donned my usual long-sleeved blue T-shirt, dark jeans, and boots.

The whole time I was getting ready, I could hear Owen and Silvio talking and moving around downstairs. They were probably waiting on me, so we could all leave to go to work, so I rushed through everything, then went downstairs.

"Guys?" I called out.

"In the den!" Owen answered.

I walked down the hall and stopped at the den doorway.

Owen and Silvio both turned toward me, grinned, and swept their hands out to their sides.

"Ta-da!" they exclaimed in unison.

My gaze fell to the coffee table between them. Last night, the table had been empty, except for my phone and Owen's, along with the penny, the hundred-dollar bill, and the papers I'd picked up during yesterday's misadventures. But all those items had been removed, and the table was now covered with food—waffles with fresh strawberries, bagel sandwiches, smoked sausages, cherry Danishes, mini cinnamon rolls, chocolate croissants. There was even a pitcher of orange juice and a thermos of hot chocolate. It was like someone couldn't decide whether they wanted breakfast or dessert and had opted for both.

Owen offered me his arm, which I took, and escorted me over to the couch. He gestured for me to sit down, then slid the coffee table in front of me. "This is for you, Gin. You always do so much for everyone else, especially when it comes to cooking, so Silvio and I thought we'd treat you to breakfast."

I eyed the food. "You two cooked all of this?"

"Well..." Silvio's voice trailed off. "If by *cooking* you mean that Owen and I went to the Cake Walk and picked up everything, then yes, we *cooked* it all."

The Cake Walk was another downtown Ashland restaurant that served food that was almost—*almost*—as good as what I dished up at the Pork Pit. Then again, I was more than a little biased when it came to my own cooking. Still, anything from the Cake Walk was a treat, especially the mini cinnamon rolls, which were among my favorites.

My mouth watered, and my stomach rumbled in anticipation, but the longer I looked at the food, the more my hunger waned. The Cake Walk was another business that would be wiped off the map if I didn't stop Mason's development project.

"Gin?" Owen asked. "Is something wrong?"

I pushed away my worry and smiled at him and Silvio. "What could possibly be wrong when I have waffles *and* sausages *and* cinnamon rolls?"

The guys pulled some chairs up to the low table, and we all filled our plates high.

The food was even better than it looked. The waffles were light and fluffy, while the bagels were soft and chewy and stuffed with scrambled eggs, crispy bacon, and melted cheddar cheese. For dessert, if you could even call it that this early in the morning, I had not one, not two, not three, but five mini cinnamon rolls, each of which was topped with a small, perfect dollop of gooey cream-cheese icing. Mmm-mmm-mmm. There was nothing better on a cold morning than soft bread, warm cinnamon, and sweet icing all rolled into one.

Thirty minutes later, I popped the last bite of cinnamon roll into my mouth, then washed it down with a final sip of orange juice and sighed with happiness. "Thank you, guys. This really hit the spot."

Owen grinned. "Everyone needs a break, Gin, even you."

I grinned back at him. Once again, he was right. I was pleasantly full, and everything seemed a little brighter and more hopeful now. Or maybe that was just the cinnamon rolls talking. Either way, I was ready to face another day of trouble, danger, and deceit.

Owen and Silvio took the leftover food into the kitchen, while I grabbed my phone, which Silvio had relocated to the mantel, along with the penny, the hundred-dollar bill, and the papers. I didn't see anything new in the items, so I left them on the mantel and went to help the guys finish cleaning up.

Silvio and I dropped Owen off outside his office building, then headed over to the Pork Pit. I did my usual checks for rune traps and bombs, but the storefront was clean, so we stepped inside.

Sophia was already there, cooking a large vat of baked beans in Fletcher's barbecue sauce. I pulled a blue apron on over my clothes, while Silvio settled himself on his usual stool, pulled out his tablet, and updated me on the underworld bosses and their various shenanigans. We might currently be battling Mason, Emery, and their goons, but there were still plenty of other criminals in Ashland to worry about.

Once Silvio had finished with his updates, I opened the restaurant and started cooking, cleaning, and cashing out customers. But my brief bout of happiness and my cinnamon-roll sugar rush from breakfast quickly wore off, and my mind started churning as I tried to figure out how I could get Fletcher's money out of the Yangs' bank and keep it away from Mason afterward.

Given the bitter cold, howling wind, and bits of snow swirling through the air outside, the lunch crowd died down around one o'clock, which was earlier than usual, so I sent the waitstaff into the back to take a break.

I wasn't particularly hungry, but I'd brought some of the cherry Danishes from breakfast to the restaurant, so I plated up one each for me, Sophia, and Silvio. The dwarf merely nibbled on her pastry, but the vampire dove right into his, polishing off the whole thing before I'd even taken one bite of my own Danish.

Silvio dabbed at his mouth with a napkin, then carefully set it aside. "I love your cooking, Gin, but that Danish was exceptional."

"You're just saying that because you're addicted to sugar," I teased. "We all know you put it in the blood you drink.

Something Hugh Tucker does *not* approve of."

Silvio huffed. "Hugh Tucker can go jump in the Aneirin River for all I care." Then his face turned serious, and his gray eyes narrowed in thought. "What *are* you going to do about Tucker? He's getting better every day. It won't be long before he's back to full strength. You can't keep him in that shipping container forever."

I sighed. "I know."

Tucker was yet another item on my ever-growing list of problems. Silvio was right. I couldn't keep the vampire in that shipping container forever, but I had no idea what he would do if I let him go. Tucker certainly couldn't return to Mason and the Circle, but I didn't want him working for one of the other underworld bosses either.

I took another bite of my Danish, hoping the flaky, buttery pastry, with its rich vanilla-bean cream filling and tart cherry topping, would travel through my taste buds and inspire my brain cells to conjure up a solution. Alas, it didn't work, but I took another bite, trying yet again—

The bell over the front door chimed out the arrival of a new customer. I glanced up and immediately froze, the bite of Danish wobbling precariously on my fork.

Mason fucking Mitchell was standing in the doorway of the Pork Pit.

My fork slipped out of my fingers and clattered onto the countertop, along with that final bite of Danish.

Even though I had been expecting Mason to show his face, his appearance this early in the day surprised me, especially since Silvio hadn't gotten a text from Liam Carter warning us that my uncle was coming here.

I dropped my hand down below the counter and palmed a knife, not that the blade would do me any good against Mason's Stone magic, as yesterday's fight had so painfully proven.

Mason calmly stripped off his navy overcoat and hung it on the rack by the front door, as though he were just another customer. He didn't so much as glance at me as he sat down in one of the booths next to the storefront windows. Arrogant bastard.

I held my position, my eyes locked on the front door, expecting Emery Slater and a couple of giants to stroll inside to join my uncle. But she didn't appear, and neither did any Circle goons. A finger of cold unease tickled my spine.

Something was wrong. At least, more wrong than my murderous uncle waltzing into my gin joint yet again like he owned the place.

Silvio glanced over his shoulder. He too froze, although his hands curled around his tablet, and his entire body tensed, as though he were ready to leap up, put himself between Mason and me, and defend me to his dying breath.

Behind the counter, a few feet away from me, Sophia was still nibbling on her own cherry Danish. She studied Mason a moment, then popped the rest of the pastry into her mouth and chased it down with a swig of lemonade, as though my uncle's appearance was no more important than the snow still swirling around outside.

Sophia drained her drink, although her fingers tightened around the glass, ready to use it as a weapon, just like Silvio with his tablet. The dwarf's black gaze locked with my gray one, and she gave me an almost imperceptible nod, telling me that she had my back no matter what.

Love for both of my friends flooded my heart, but it didn't banish my unease—or my worry that I was about to get the two of them killed.

"What do I have to do to get some service?" Mason's voice boomed like thunder through the restaurant.

A few folks were still eating their barbecue chicken sandwiches, sweet-potato fries, and onion rings, and they all glanced over at him, not realizing the danger they were in. I ground my teeth but tucked my knife back up my sleeve. Once again, all I could do was play along and pretend Mason was an ordinary customer and not a dangerous enemy.

So I grabbed a menu and headed over to his booth. I started to slap the menu down in front of him, but Mason airily waved his hand, as though he were a king ordering a servant to remove an unwanted dish from his dining table.

"I don't have time to eat, Gin," he purred. "I have several meetings to attend regarding my new development project."

My fingers strangled the paper menu. Too bad the edges weren't razor-sharp. Otherwise, in that mad, mad moment, I would have happily lunged forward and tried to paper-cut him to death, even though I knew how foolish and useless that would be. Mason might look unconcerned, but magic gleamed in his gray eyes. He was expecting me to attack, and he was ready to use his Stone power to protect himself.

Mason flapped his hand in another one of those airy, irritating gestures. "Sit down. Let's chat. We have so much to catch up on."

I ground my teeth again, but I tossed the crumpled menu down onto the table and slid into the opposite side of the booth. I glanced out the storefront windows, but I still didn't see Emery or any other giants lurking outside.

"Where's your entourage?" I asked in a snide voice.

"Oh, Emery and my men will be along soon enough," Mason replied. "They had to stop and deal with a small problem first."

His words were just cryptic enough to be highly worrisome,

although I couldn't imagine what Emery could be taking care of that was more important—or entertaining—than watching Mason threaten me yet again.

"I have to admit that I was quite surprised when we ran into each other yesterday," Mason said. "But I'm so glad we did. After our little run-in, I had a chance to sit down with Charles Yang, who told me about your visit to his bank."

My heart sank, and I had to swallow a long string of curses. This had already gone from bad to worse.

"I thought Finnegan Lane and Stuart Mosley handled all of your financial needs at First Trust. I wasn't aware you were also a customer of the Bellum Bank."

"What can I say? I'm looking to diversify my portfolio."

An amused chuckle spewed out of Mason's lips. "Oh, please. We both know you were at the bank because that's where Fletcher hid the money he stole from me."

I didn't respond. No lie I could spout would convince him otherwise. Not when he was right and the truth was so glaringly, painfully obvious.

"Clever of Fletcher to hide my money there," Mason continued. "The Bellum Bank is one of the very few places in Ashland where even my influence is limited. I always wondered if he might have stored the money there, but I could never confirm it one way or the other, and Charles and I weren't as good friends back then as we are now."

He shrugged, as though his lack of spies and tentacles inside the bank was of little consequence, but my brain started churning. Mason kept talking about Charles Yang, but he hadn't said one word about Drusilla so far. According to Finn, Drusilla was the one who ran things at the bank, not her father. Maybe Mason wasn't as good friends with Drusilla as he was with Charles. Either way, I found the oversight highly interesting.

Mason shrugged again. "But it doesn't matter now, since you're going to hand over the money, Gin."

"Why not get your new best friend, Charles Yang, to retrieve it for you?" I asked, my voice even more snide than before.

Annoyance flickered across his face. "Apparently, the Yangs have strict rules about that sort of thing, rules Drusilla doesn't want to break. Of course, I tried to convince Charles otherwise, but he sided with his daughter." Mason shook his head. "He really should put that girl in her place."

I'd never thought I would be grateful to Drusilla Yang for anything, but right now, I would have gladly sent her every last morsel of barbecue in the restaurant for sticking to her family's code—and keeping Fletcher's money out of Mason's hands for just a little while longer.

My uncle kept staring at me. "According to Drusilla, there is also the not-so-small matter of neither her nor Charles having the password to Fletcher's vault, although I feel confident that you *do* have it, Gin."

"And what are you going to do if I don't tell you the password? Kill me?" A bitter laugh spewed out of my lips. "You already tried that in the Circle cemetery, remember?"

More annoyance flickered across his face, and his lips pinched into a deep frown. "Yes, that whole evening was extremely disappointing, especially since so many of the original gravestones were destroyed, along with Tristan's pavilion. I blamed the destruction on random vandals, but the historical association is still nattering at me about fixing the damage."

Down under the tabletop, out of his line of sight, my hands curled into tight fists, my nails digging into the spider-rune scars branded into my palms. The thought of my father's tomb, of Mason's sick display of the brother he had tortured to death, made red-hot rage bubble in my veins, just like the baked beans had simmered away on the stovetop earlier.

Mason's gaze sharpened. "Speaking of the cemetery fight, how is Hugh? I've been wondering about him."

I opened my mouth, but he waggled his finger at me.

"And before you insult my intelligence by claiming that Hugh is dead, Emery did a thorough sweep of the cemetery, and she didn't find his body among the rubble." He waggled his finger again. "I know you, sweet little Genevieve, and especially your kind heart. The one you like to pretend is as hard as a stone but is really as soft as a marshmallow. You took pity on Hugh because he foolishly sacrificed himself to save you, so you saved him in return. Let me guess. Jolene Deveraux used her Air magic to heal him."

He was exactly right, but I didn't respond. No matter if they were lies or truth, my words didn't matter to my uncle, just as my father, his brother, his own flesh and blood, hadn't mattered to him. No, the only thing Mason cared about was power and the fear it inspired in others.

My uncle clucked his tongue in mock sympathy. "Oh, Gin. That marshmallow heart is going to be the death of you someday."

"Better a marshmallow heart than the empty black chasm in your chest," I snapped back at him. "Enough chitchat. What do you want?"

Mason steepled his hands on the tabletop. "I want what I've always wanted: my money. Back with me, where it belongs."

"So you can use it to help fund your development project? To destroy the Pork Pit? To evict innocent people from their homes and businesses?" I shook my head. "Nope. Not going to happen. My marshmallow heart would *never* allow such a thing."

"Oh, I know. Just like I know it would be a waste of time trying to torture the vault password out of you. So that leaves me with only one option."

Even though I knew that I really, really wouldn't like the answer, I couldn't help but ask the inevitable question. "And what would that be?"

A razor-thin smile creased his face. "Squeezing your marshmallow heart until it pops wide open."

Mason reached into his jacket pocket. I tensed, even though I knew he probably wasn't carrying a weapon. He didn't need one. He could always make a brick fly out of the wall and use it to bash in my skull. Why, Mason probably considered using a gun or a knife or some other ordinary weapon beneath him.

He pulled out his phone and texted someone. Then he returned the device to his jacket pocket, leaned back in his side of the booth, and smiled at me again. "Don't worry, Gin. Emery will be here any second, along with my special guest."

Special guest? I had a bad, bad feeling I knew exactly who he was talking about.

Mason glanced out the windows and waved his hand. "Why, here they are."

Emery Slater strode into view on the sidewalk outside. Blond hair, hazel eyes, milky skin dotted with freckles, tall, thick, strong body, blue pantsuit and matching ballet flats. The giant looked the same as she had at the bank yesterday.

Emery stopped and sneered at me, then stepped to the side and gestured with her hand. A couple of male giants strode into view, pulling a third man along with them, and the group stopped right outside the window, so that I had a crystal-clear view of them.

I didn't recognize the two giants, but I definitely knew the man standing between them, even though his head was bowed, as though he were staring down at something on the sidewalk.

Liam Carter.

✤ 13 ✤

I kept staring and staring at Liam, hoping against hope that my eyes were playing tricks on me. That I was dreaming. Hallucinating. Seeing anything but this.

My friend slowly lifted his head, and my marshmallow heart squeezed tight and then popped wide open, oozing soft, fluffy emotion everywhere, just like Mason had wanted it to.

Liam was a *mess*.

He had two black eyes, one of which was completely swollen shut. Purple bruises streaked across his skin like haphazardly applied makeup, and his nose had been broken so badly that it looked like puffy red putty clinging to the rest of his face. Both of his lips were split open, and blood had dribbled down and dried on his chin.

Liam's suit jacket and tie were missing, and his shirt and pants were both dirty, rumpled, and spattered with blood. Part of his broken left collarbone stuck out at an awkward angle, jutting up against his shirt, and his left arm dangled uselessly by his side. His right arm was curled around his chest, and he grimaced with every breath he took, as though his ribs were as battered and broken as the rest of his body.

All put together, Liam looked like a zombie who had come back to life.

Beside him, Emery flashed me a grin and slowly, deliberately cracked her knuckles, which were a bright, vivid red against the rest of her skin. She had obviously beaten Liam, and the bitch looked like she had enjoyed every second of the torture she had ruthlessly inflicted on him.

Cold, cold rage exploded in my chest, icing over the ruined remains of my charred marshmallow heart. My nails dug even deeper into the spider-rune scars branded into my palms, and I had to force myself to sit quiet and still in the booth, instead of palming a knife, storming outside, and burying the blade in Emery's rotten heart.

Liam blinked his one good eye and focused on me. He tried to smile, but his expression eased back down into the resigned, rueful look of a man who knew that he'd been found out.

This was all my fault.

I was the one who'd asked Liam to be my inside man in Mason's organization, which meant that *I* was the reason he'd been beaten to a bloody pulp. My rage vanished, buried beneath the hard, heavy bricks of guilt that were quickly piling up inside my chest. My stomach gurgled, and I had to swallow the hot, sour bile rising in my throat.

"As you can see, I discovered your little ruse with Mr. Carter," Mason said, his voice as smooth and calm as ever, as though he was discussing a football game instead of the brutal beating of another human being.

Instead of responding to his taunt, I looked over at Silvio, who was now standing beside the dining counter, still clutching his tablet.

Silvio's face was pale, and he kept blinking and blinking, as though he too were hoping that Liam's battered features were just an illusion. But with every second that passed, Silvio's shock dissipated, replaced by clear, undeniable anguish. More hard, heavy bricks of guilt piled up in my chest and crept up into my throat, choking me from the inside out.

"Of course, I had my suspicions about Mr. Carter from the very beginning, but the two of you played your parts extremely well," Mason continued. "Liam shooting you at the wedding reception was a nice touch, if a bit cliché. And he truly has done an excellent job with my security over the past few weeks."

I waited until I was sure my voice wouldn't shake with rage before I spoke. "So you had Emery beat Liam to a pulp because he's good at his job?" I asked, playing dumb in a desperate, last-ditch effort to help my friend. "That doesn't seem like a nice way to treat your employees."

Mason shrugged. "My employees know the risks in working for me, and they are handsomely rewarded for taking those risks. The one thing I demand is absolute loyalty, and it became very apparent yesterday that Mr. Carter was loyal to *you* rather than to *me*, despite the generous payments I had given him."

He paused, as if waiting for me to give in and confirm that Liam was in fact working for me, maybe even to beg for my friend's life, but I kept my mouth shut. Plausible deniability wasn't much in this situation, but it was all Liam had, and it was the only thing keeping him alive.

For now.

When it became apparent that I wasn't going to start blubbering, Mason crossed his arms over his chest and gave me a cool look. "As I said before, Mr. Carter had been doing an excellent job with my security, far better than even Emery, until that little incident on the sidewalk yesterday."

"What about it?" I asked, wondering where he was going with this.

"Liam Carter knows exactly how dangerous you are, Gin, and especially how much you want to kill me."

"So what? That's hardly news."

"So when he saw you yesterday, Mr. Carter hesitated. Not for long. Only for a few seconds. But Liam is a consummate professional, and he would *never* hesitate, not for one instant, not if his client's life was truly on the line."

"So maybe he had an off day," I replied. "Or maybe he didn't want to get a knife in the chest protecting you. Can't blame him for that."

Mason ignored my sarcasm. "Mr. Carter hesitated because he didn't care if I died. That's when I knew that he was really working for you and not me."

I bit back the multitude of curses dangling on the end of my tongue. Liam's hesitation had been a brief hiccup, the smallest mistake, the tiniest crack in his cover, but it had been more than enough to expose him to Mason. Now my friend was hanging on to his life by a thin, tenuous thread, one that could be cut at any moment, unless I found some way to appease my evil uncle.

"What do you want?" I asked again through gritted teeth.

"My money," Mason snapped. "You are going to go to the Bellum Bank right now, access Fletcher's account, and transfer the funds to my account. If you do that, then I might—*might*—let Mr. Carter live."

He didn't say what he would do if I refused. He didn't have to. We both knew that Mason would order Emery to kill Liam right here and now, and then the rest of my friends one by one, until I gave in and gave my uncle everything he wanted.

More bricks of guilt piled up inside me, but I forced myself to shove them aside and latch onto the icy calm that was the bedrock of my being, the very core of the Spider. Guilt, grief, and other raw, painful emotions wouldn't do me any good right now. No, the only way I was going to save Liam—or at least buy him a little more time—was to be cold and logical.

"I'm afraid I can't do that."

Mason's eyes narrowed. "Do *not* fuck with me, Gin. I will gladly do the same thing to Liam that I did to your father."

He casually flicked his fingers, and a wave of Stone magic surged off him and rippled through the storefront, making the walls vibrate ever so slightly. None of the customers seemed to notice the bricks shifting back and forth like an accordion, but Sophia stepped to the end of the counter, her hands curling into fists and her black gaze fixed on Mason. She was an Air elemental, so she'd sensed his magic, and it had probably felt as wrong to her as Jo-Jo's power always felt to me.

I shook my head, telling Sophia to stand down, then looked at Mason again. "I don't know what Charles Yang told you, but Fletcher's money isn't in a traditional account. I can't just go to the bank and wire it to you."

Mason's eyes narrowed a little more. "Okay, I'll play along. If the money isn't in an account, then where is it?"

"Let me show you."

I glanced over at Silvio, who was still staring at Liam. All sorts of emotions flickered across the vampire's face—despair, longing, heartache, rage. Liam stared back at him, peering at Silvio as best he could through his one not-quite-swollen-shut eye. More heavy bricks of guilt crushed my heart, but I forced myself to ignore the obvious feelings between the two of them.

"Silvio," I called out. "Can you come over here, please?"

The vampire flinched at the sound of his name, as though

my voice had snapped him out of a deep trance. He stared at Liam for a few more heartbreaking seconds, then straightened his shoulders and stiffly stalked over to the booth where Mason and I were sitting. Silvio's nostrils flared with anger, and his fingers curled around his tablet, as though he wanted to bash my uncle over the head with the device.

"Mason wants to see what Fletcher did with the money," I said. "Can you please pull up the pictures I took in the vault?"

Silvio gave me a sharp, single nod and silently swiped through a few screens on his tablet. Then he held the device out to Mason, who grabbed it and set it down on the tabletop.

"What the fuck is this?" my uncle muttered, scrolling through the photos.

"Fletcher took your money and turned it into cold, hard cash—literally. I found the black ledger that Fletcher stole from you, and a number inside led me to this vault at the Bellum Bank. As you can see, it's full of money, along with other valuables."

"You've got to be kidding me," Mason muttered, still scrolling through photos. "Why would Fletcher transfer the funds into cash and the rest of this junk? Why not just leave the money in a single account?"

"I don't know."

Mason glared at me. "If you're lying, if this is some trick—"

"It's *not* a trick," I snapped. "Believe me, I was just as pissed as you are to discover that Fletcher left me a vault full of cash—cash that I have no way of removing from the bank without you or someone else stealing it from me."

He kept glaring at me, and I stared right back at him, letting him see my own anger at Fletcher. For once, I was telling Mason the absolute truth, and Liam's life depended on my uncle believing me.

Mason started drumming his fingers on the table, and each soft, little tap made my heart wrench with worry. All he had to do was flick his fingers again, and he could easily send a brick flying out of the storefront wall and straight into Liam's skull.

Tap-tap-tap-tap...

Tap-tap-tap-tap...

Tap-tap-tap-tap...

Mason's fingers stilled. I tensed and reached for my Ice magic. If he lifted his hand, then I was going to blast him with every bit of cold power I had. Oh, I knew it wouldn't do any good and he would just harden his skin into an impenetrable shell, but maybe I could distract him long enough for Silvio to rush outside and try to save Liam.

"Fletcher always was clever," Mason grumbled. "I often wondered where he got all the tens and fives and ones he had delivered for my monthly repayment. Those small bills were always such a bitch to count and then transfer back into my own account. Well, at least now I know where all that small change came from. Petty bastard."

He glanced down at the tablet again, his lips puckering in thought. "Very well. Since Fletcher left you the money as cash, then I'll take it that way."

I frowned. "What do you mean?"

"You might not be able to get all the cash out of the bank without someone stealing it from you, but I certainly can." Mason leaned forward and stabbed his finger at me. "You will meet Emery in front of the Bellum Bank tomorrow at noon. You will go inside, open the vault, and let Emery and her men take every single dollar, watch, and necklace."

"And what about Liam?"

Mason shrugged and leaned back. "You do that, and I'll consider letting Mr. Carter go."

"*No*," I snarled. "Liam goes free, *right now*. Take me instead."

Over at the counter, Sophia sucked in a breath. So did Silvio, who was still standing beside the booth. Equal parts hope and guilt flickered across my assistant's face, although he quickly schooled his features into a more neutral expression.

"And risk you killing my men *and* potentially escaping *and* potentially finding some way to liberate Fletcher's money for yourself?" A merry laugh tumbled out of Mason's lips. "Oh, no, Gin. I'm not going to give you a chance to pull any of your Spider tricks on me. Besides, we all know you would much rather put yourself in danger than your precious friends, and I wouldn't want Mr. Sanchez and the rest of your motley crew to do something foolish like try to rescue you in the meantime. No, I'm going to hang on to Mr. Carter as collateral."

Frustration pounded through me like a red-hot sledge-hammer. I'd been hoping to do all of the above. Kill Mason's men. Escape his clutches. Figure out some way to get to the money before he did.

"You will come alone. No friends, no knives, no tricks. And if you do anything—and I do mean *any damn thing*—to stop me from getting my money, then one of my men will put a bullet in Mr. Carter's brain. And then I will have Emery do the same thing to you. Are we clear, Genevieve?"

Mason delivered his threats in a calm, conversational tone, which made them all the more chilling, and his gray eyes were as cold and hard as the pellets of snow still gusting around outside. More frustration pounded through me, but he had me cornered, and we both knew it.

"Clear as glass," I drawled, trying not to let him see how worried I was.

Another razor-thin smile curved his face. He didn't believe my bravado for one second. Yeah, me neither.

Mason slid out of his side of the booth and got to his feet. I stood up as well.

"Oh, I almost forgot something." My uncle reached into his suit jacket, making me tense again, but he only came up with a small, square piece of paper covered with fancy calligraphy done in bold black ink. He tossed the paper down onto the tabletop. "An invitation to my party in a few days formally announcing the Mitchell Mile. I'd *love* for you to come, Gin, along with all your friends."

Mason smirked at Silvio. "The ones who are still alive, anyway."

Silvio stepped forward so that he was standing inches away from my uncle, and his lips drew back in a silent snarl, revealing his sharp white fangs. Silvio didn't often flash his fangs at people, which told me exactly how enraged he was.

Mason looked down his nose at my assistant, completely unconcerned by the obvious threat. If he hurt—killed—Silvio because of my mistake with Liam...well, I didn't know how I would bear it.

"Silvio," I said in a low, warning voice.

The vampire's gaze dropped to Mason's neck, and his lips drew back a little more, as though he was thinking about lunging forward and trying to tear Mason's throat open with his fangs.

"*Please*," I said, my voice softer than before.

I didn't know if my plea penetrated his rage or if he simply realized that he couldn't murder Mason any more than I could, but Silvio blinked, and some of the anger dimmed in his eyes. He drew in a deep breath, as though steadying himself, then reluctantly eased away from my uncle.

Mason deliberately turned his back to Silvio, then buttoned

his suit jacket and gave me another smug look. "Tomorrow. Noon. Bellum Bank. Or Mr. Carter dies. Along with everyone else you care about, Gin."

He brushed past me, grabbed his coat from the rack, and opened the front door of the Pork Pit. The silver bell chimed out his exit, punctuating his many threats, all of which kept ringing in my ears and filling my heart with cold, cold dread.

Mason stepped out onto the sidewalk, shrugged into his coat, and strode away from the restaurant without a backward glance. Emery sneered at me through the windows again, then hurried after Mason. The two giants clutching Liam followed her, half dragging, half carrying my beaten friend out of sight.

Silvio's face pinched tight with anger, and he headed for the front door.

I lunged forward and grabbed his arm. "No. You can't go charging after them, no matter how much you might want to. Emery will kill Liam just for spite then."

"I can't just stand here and *do nothing*," Silvio growled, his voice cracking on the last few words. "Not when Liam is hurt. Not when Mason could decide to kill him anyway. Just to teach you a lesson."

Every word he said pierced my heart like an arrow, but I ignored the hard, stinging jolts, along with my own burning shame.

"Mason won't kill Liam. Not until he gets what he wants. As long as the money is in the Bellum Bank, we still have a chance to save Liam."

"So he dies tomorrow instead of today. Either way, Liam still *dies*." Silvio's voice cracked again, and the sheen of tears filled his eyes.

More arrows pierced my heart, but I reached up and put my hands on Silvio's shoulders. "I promise you that I am going to do everything—*every last thing*—in my power to save Liam. We might not have known him very long, but he's one of us now, and I will fight for him to my dying breath, the same way I would fight for you or Sophia or Owen or any of the rest of us who were taken. You have my word on that."

"Right now, I don't care about your word, Gin," he growled.

I had to grind my teeth to keep from flinching at his harsh tone. Still more arrows slammed into my heart, but I forced myself to keep talking. "Well, for right now, I need you to set your feelings aside and help me figure out a way to save Liam and stop Mason from getting his hands on the money. Can you do that for me? For Liam? Please?"

More anger pinched Silvio's face, and a muscle ticked in his jaw. He shifted on his feet, as though he were going to storm out the door anyway. I slowly dropped my hands from his shoulders and eased to the side.

I knew how much he cared about Liam, and I wouldn't stand in his way, not even if he would most likely get himself and Liam killed. If we were going to pull this off, if we had any hope of thwarting Mason, then Silvio had to choose to follow me, to believe in me, to trust in *us* and especially in our friendship.

Sophia stared intently at Silvio and me, but the customers kept eating their barbecue sandwiches, slurping down their iced teas, chatting with their companions, and checking their phones. None of them noticed the vampire and me staring at each other or picked up on the hostile tension and ugly emotions simmering in the air between us.

Silvio exhaled, and some of the anger leaked out of his face. "Fine," he growled. "We'll do it your way. But if we don't get Liam back…"

His voice trailed off, and he couldn't finish his thought. Yeah, me neither.

"I *will* find a way to fix this. I promise."

Silvio smiled, but it was a grim, humorless expression. "I know that you'll try."

His quiet, resigned tone cut me deeper than one of my silverstone knives ever could. I sucked in a breath to try to reassure him yet again, but Silvio turned away and picked up his tablet from where Mason had left it on the tabletop. He didn't look at me as he returned to the dining counter and slid back onto his usual stool. My assistant bent his head and focused on his tablet again, but his shoulders sagged, and he was leaning heavily against the counter, as if he needed its support.

Sharp daggers of regret stabbed into my heart, landing right next to those arrows of burning shame, as though I had an oversize pincushion of unwanted, prickly emotions lodged in my chest. Silvio was such a good, loyal friend, and he was hurting because of me. And Liam, well, Liam might *die* because of me.

But perhaps the worst part was that I didn't know how to fix any of this. I didn't know how to save Liam, or get Fletcher's money out of the vault, or stop Mason from razing the Pork Pit to the ground.

And if I didn't come up with solutions to all those problems in the next few hours, then Mason was going to end up with everything he had ever wanted and leave the rest of us with broken hearts—or dead.

❈ 14 ❈

By this point, it was after two o'clock, and for once, I didn't feel like slinging barbecue for the rest of the day. Not when Mason was holding Liam hostage and I had less than twenty-four hours to figure out a way to save my friend. So I asked Sophia to cover the restaurant. I also texted Owen, Bria, and Finn, and we all agreed to meet at Fletcher's house to decide our next move.

Thirty minutes later, Silvio steered his van off the road and into the gravel driveway. He hadn't said a single word during the ride, and I hadn't tried to coax him to talk. Nothing I could say would make this situation any better or his hurt, worry, and heartache any easier to bear. Just like nothing could lessen my own regret, shame, and guilt.

The van crested the ridge, and Fletcher's house popped into view. Silvio blinked in surprise, as did I. Cars filled the driveway, and people were milling around on the front porch—several more people than I had expected.

"What's going on?" Silvio finally spoke. "Did you ask them all to come?"

I shook my head. "No. I only texted Owen, Bria, and Finn."

Silvio squeezed his van into an empty spot in the driveway, and the two of us got out and walked over to the porch.

Owen, Bria, and Finn were here, just as I had expected, and Jo-Jo had also shown up, along with Xavier. But there were two new additions to the crowd: a tall man with blue eyes, tan skin, and blond hair slicked back into a low ponytail and a curvy woman with toffee eyes and skin and short black hair.

Phillip Kincaid was Owen's best friend and the owner of the *Delta Queen* riverboat casino, while Roslyn Phillips was Xavier's significant other and the owner of the Northern Aggression nightclub.

Owen, Bria, and Finn must have contacted our other friends, and they'd all dropped everything to come help us. My heart swelled with love and gratitude, and a little spark of hope ignited inside me. For the first time since I'd seen Liam's battered face, I felt like we might actually have a chance to save him.

"Phillip, Roslyn." I nodded at them.

"We're here for you, Gin," Phillip said.

Roslyn looked at me, then Silvio. "And you too, Silvio. Whatever you need."

I glanced over at the vampire. Tears glimmered in his eyes, although he quickly cleared his throat and blinked them away.

"Thank you," he replied in a strained voice.

Silvio gave everyone a tight smile, then opened the front door and headed inside the house, leaving the rest of us on the porch.

"He's taking this really hard," Bria said, sympathy rippling through her voice.

I sighed. "I know, and it's all my fault. I should have pulled Liam out of Mason's orbit the second we found the money."

"You didn't know you were going to run into Mason and that he was going to figure out that Liam was really working for you," Owen said, putting his arm around my shoulder. "No one could have predicted that, not even you, Gin."

He was right, but his words didn't ease my guilt or stop Liam's battered face from flashing through my mind. Still, I let myself lean on Owen, soaking up his warm reassurance and unwavering support. He wrapped his arms around me, and I breathed in, drawing his rich, metallic scent deep into my lungs.

I could have stayed in his comforting embrace forever, but Silvio and Liam were counting on me, so I pressed a kiss to Owen's cheek. He looked down at me, understanding flaring in his eyes. He brushed his own kiss against my lips, then released me.

I jerked my head at the others. "Let's get to work."

We all trooped into the house. I started to head into the den with everyone else, but Finn flapped his hands at me.

"How about you go make us some snacks, Sis?" he suggested.

I slapped my hands on my hips. "I might own a restaurant, but I am not your personal chef, *Bro*. Besides, we have far more important things to worry about right now than snacks."

Finn sucked in a breath and dramatically clutched his hand to his heart, as though my words had gravely wounded him. "*Nothing* is more important than snacks. No one ever figured anything out on an empty stomach, and we will all think much better with full tummies. Besides, you're the one who always claims that cooking relaxes you. So go, cook, relax. And then we'll get busy scheming."

I gave him a sour look, but he was right. Cooking *did* relax me, and I needed to do something to release all my pent-up tension, anxiety, and worry. Otherwise, I was going to start screaming and smashing things.

"I really hate you sometimes," I muttered.

Finn grinned, his green eyes sparkling with mischief. "Hate to love me, you mean."

He stepped forward, lowered his arm, and drew his hand back.

I stabbed my finger at him in warning. "If you slap me on the ass like we're a couple of football players celebrating a touchdown, then I will cut you with one of my knives."

He rolled his eyes and lowered his hand. "Why do you always insist on ruining my fun?"

"Maybe because *you* always insist on acting like an overgrown child."

He sniffed. "Well, this overgrown child has work to do, and so do you. So shoo, Gin. Shoo."

Finn flapped his hands at me again, then disappeared into the den with everyone else. Somehow I resisted the urge to chuck one of my knives at him and headed into the kitchen.

When I was sure no one was going to follow me in here, I slumped up against the refrigerator, leaning my forehead on the cool metal. Liam's battered face flashed through my mind again, along with Silvio's anguished expression. They were both suffering so much because they'd believed in me, because they'd followed me in my fight against Mason.

A sob rose in my throat, but I swallowed it, not wanting my friends to hear my own pain. Hot tears pricked my eyes, and I couldn't stop them from streaking down my cheeks.

I let myself silently cry for the better part of a minute. Then I slowly straightened up, wiped the tears off my cheeks, and yanked the refrigerator door open. I couldn't do anything for Liam right now, but I could at least feed Silvio and the rest of my friends.

So I pulled some leftover grilled chicken out of the fridge, along with lettuce, sour cream, and several different kinds of shredded cheeses. Next, I grabbed some tomatoes, red onions, and limes to create a pico de gallo.

With every slice of my knife and thwack of the blade against the cutting board, I imagined filleting Mason and Emery and then squeezing the blood out of their bodies the same way I was forcing juice out of the limes. And if a few more tears rolled down my cheeks, well, they were caused by the pungent onions, rather than my own rage, guilt, and frustration. At least, that's what I told myself.

Still, the longer I cooked, the calmer I felt. The familiar, repetitive motions helped me rein in my feelings and focus on what was important right now: feeding my friends and finding a way to save Liam.

A few minutes later, I sprinkled the chicken and cheeses on some tortilla chips that I had arranged on a large platter. Then I created two more layers of chips and fixings, being extra generous with the cheese on the very top. I made two more similar platters of nachos, then slid them all into the oven to heat through and melt all that wonderful, glorious cheese.

The whole time I was cooking, I could hear my friends talking and moving around in the den. Several loud bangs rang out, along with a few muffled curses from Finn. It sounded like he was getting hangry, so I pulled the nachos out of the oven. For a finishing touch, I added the pico de gallo, lettuce, some diced avocado, and several dollops of sour cream, along with a few cilantro leaves. Then I loaded the platters onto a large tray and carried everything into the den.

"Snack time—" My words died on my lips, and I stopped short.

While I'd been in the kitchen, my friends had completely rearranged the den, shoving the couch, coffee table, and chairs off to one side. Silvio's whiteboard was still standing close to the fireplace, although it had been moved into the corner to make room for a second whiteboard, which was covered with blueprints and photos. Still more blueprints covered the walls, and several photos and documents had been taped to the mantel, hanging there like Christmas stockings.

For the second time today, I desperately hoped that something was a hallucination. I blinked a few times, but everything stayed the same. Nope, not a hallucination. "What is all of *this*?"

Finn was standing in front of the second whiteboard. He grinned at me, then swept his hand out wide, encompassing the board, as well as the rest of the den. "*This* is Operation Piggy Bank."

I groaned at the cheesy codename. "I'm not going to like this, am I?"

"Only if we don't rescue Liam and steal Mason's money right out from under his nose, both of which we are *totally* going to do," Finn chirped. "After all, we have to help Silvio get his man back. Right, Silvy?"

He held out his fist to Silvio, who closed his eyes and shook his head as if silently asking some higher power for the patience not to strangle my brother.

I definitely knew that feeling, so I stepped forward and set the tray down on the coffee table.

Finn's head snapped around, and his gaze locked on the platters of food like a heat-seeking missile streaking toward a target. "Oh, nachos! My favorite!"

Bria and Owen headed into the kitchen to get drinks, plates, napkins, and silverware for everyone. Jo-Jo, Xavier, Roslyn, and Phillip joined Finn at the coffee—nacho?— table, but Silvio remained in front of his whiteboard, his gaze flicking from one photo of the bank to the next.

I went over to him. "You okay?"

It was a stupid question to ask, but I asked it anyway, trying to let him know that I was here for him.

Silvio shrugged. "Just trying to work things out."

"Well, as much as I hate to admit it, Finn is right. No one ever figured anything out on an empty stomach. If you don't want any nachos, I still have some cinnamon rolls left over from breakfast. I know you'd rather eat sweet than spicy."

A small smile curved the corners of his lips at my gentle teasing, but it quickly vanished. "Thanks, but I'm not hungry."

"At least let me get you something to drink."

Silvio sighed, then nodded. I went back into the kitchen, fixed a glass of limeade with extra sugar, just how he liked it, and returned to the den. Silvio took the glass, but he kept staring at the whiteboard, rather than sipping the limeade.

A few more bricks of guilt piled onto the towering mountain of them already filling my chest, but I didn't want to push him anymore, so I went over to the table and put some nachos on a plate, just like everyone else had already done.

Crunchy chips, warm chicken, zesty pico de gallo, cool sour cream, melted cheese. My three-layer nachos were as delicious as ever, as was the tart limeade, although every *crack* of a chip in my mouth made me think of Emery's fists slamming into Liam's face, breaking his nose, collarbone, and ribs. My stomach churned, and I set my plate down. Like Silvio, I wasn't hungry right now.

My friends quickly polished off the nachos and limeade,

and everyone took a seat and faced the two whiteboards, ready to get down to business.

Finn stood up and rubbed his hands together like a carnival barker about to sell us a load of bunk. "Welcome to Operation Piggy Bank, a.k.a. how we're going to break into the Bellum Bank and steal Mason's money." His gaze flicked to the clock hanging on the wall, which said that it was after four. "Sometime between now and Mason's noon deadline tomorrow."

Jo-Jo frowned. "So you want to break into the bank tonight?"

Finn shot his thumb and forefinger at her. "Exactly! We steal Mason's money, then use it as leverage to get Liam back."

I shook my head. "I appreciate your optimism, but you saw the security at the bank yesterday. There's no way we could break in and empty Fletcher's vault. The Bellum Bank is an impregnable fortress. Fletcher put the stolen money in that vault so no one could get to it, but especially not Mason."

Finn waved away my concerns like he so often did. "A fortress? Maybe. But *nothing* is impregnable. First Trust was supposed to be impregnable too, remember? And Deirdre still found a way to get inside."

A shadow passed over Finn's face at the mention of his Ice bitch mother, but he quickly dialed up his smile again. "You're just cranky because you didn't eat enough nachos. Maybe you should go make some more snacks and leave the bank robbing to us professionals."

I glowered at him. "And maybe you should stop talking before I grab one of those dry-erase markers and shove it where the sun doesn't shine."

Finn's smile vanished, and he glared back at me.

"What if we do try to break into the bank?" Owen asked. "What would we be up against?"

"The bank is secure enough during the day, but Gin is right. It turns into even more of a fortress at night." Silvio walked over to his own whiteboard and gestured at some of the papers taped to the surface. "According to the blueprints I got from my contact in the city planner's office, the bank has alarms and cameras everywhere, from the main lobby, to the private offices, to the freight elevator. The only place that doesn't have any alarms or cameras is the vault level."

"What about disabling the alarms and cameras?" Jo-Jo asked.

Silvio shook his head. "Anytime the alarms and cameras go out, even if it's only for a few seconds, like with a power surge, an alert automatically gets sent to the police station. The bank also has backup generators to make sure that everything stays online all the time."

"Maybe we could deliberately trip the alarms," Bria suggested. "Then Xavier and I could show up and pretend to check things out. Everyone else could be there too, disguised as uniformed cops. Then we could all go down into the vault together, grab as much money as we can, and walk right back out through the front door."

"Even if everyone was dressed like cops, people would still realize that we had stolen from the bank, especially since so many Ashland cops already steal guns, drugs, and money from crime scenes," Xavier replied. "That would just make us stand out even more."

Roslyn stared at the boards, her eyebrows drawn together in thought. "What if we went to the bank right now? And took the money out in broad daylight?"

"Mason is sure to have people watching the bank in case we try that," I said. "Not to mention that his new best friends, Charles and Drusilla Yang, would probably call him the second we set foot inside the lobby. We can't just waltz into the bank like we did yesterday morning. That ship has sailed."

"You're looking at this all wrong. The main problem isn't getting into the bank or even down to the vault level," Phillip chimed in. "Sooner or later, Gin *will* go into the bank, either of her own volition sometime tonight or escorted by Emery Slater tomorrow at noon."

Silvio winced at the mention of the giant, while Roslyn shifted in her seat.

"Way to bring down the mood, Kincaid," Finn drawled.

Phillip ignored my brother, leaned forward, and stabbed his finger at the vault photos on Silvio's board. "The way I see it, the main problem is figuring out how to get the money out of the bank and to a secure location without Mason and Emery taking it away." He paused. "Or some other underworld boss trying to rob us. Anyone moving that much money out of the bank, night or day, is sure to be a target, even among the lower-tier criminals. Everyone will want to take a swing at a score that big."

"We could all go into the bank at once," Jo-Jo suggested. "A couple of us could cover the lobby, while the others got the Yangs to take them to the vault."

"You mean go in guns a-blazing, like an old-fashioned, strong-arm bank robbery?" Xavier nodded. "That might work. Sophia, Phillip, and I are the strongest. Between the three of us, we could carry most if not all of the cash, along with the gold bars and the bags of coins."

"And I'm strong enough to carry the painting, the jewelry, and the other valuables," Jo-Jo added.

Phillip shrugged. "Sure, that might work, but my point remains the same. How are we going to *escape* with the money afterward? No matter what goes on inside, moving the money away from the bank is still the most dangerous part."

Bria eyed him. "Why do you keep saying that?"

Phillip shrugged again. "I own a riverboat casino. Dozens of people have tried to rob me over the years. Most folks count cards and cheat at the poker and blackjack tables, but a few have tried to get below deck to the money cages, while others have lain in wait in the parking lot to hit the armored trucks that pick up the cash. And every time—*every single time*—the idiots get caught because they can't get away fast enough."

He got to his feet and stalked over to Finn's board. I hadn't noticed it before, but someone—probably Finn—had grabbed my hundred-dollar bill from the mantel and taped it to the board.

Phillip flicked the corner of the bill with his finger. "All by itself, a hundred bucks is as light as, well, a piece of paper. But even paper can get heavy, especially if you're trying to move millions of pieces, or millions of dollars, of it. Heavy things take time, manpower, and muscle to move, whether it's a backpack filled with cash or a truck brimming with bags of coins. That's how most of my would-be robbers got caught, and that's how Mason will catch us too."

Owen gave his best friend an admiring look. "Remind me to never try to rob you."

Phillip grinned and lifted his shoulders in a not-so-modest shrug. Then he glanced over at the vault photos again. "Speaking of not getting caught, how do you think Mason intends to get away with the money?"

"He's probably going to get Emery and her giants to carry it right out the front doors," I replied. "That's the smartest, easiest thing to do."

Xavier nodded. "I agree with Gin. If Emery brings, say, five or six giants with her, then they should be able to clear out the entire vault in one trip. Especially if they use some kind of hand carts." He frowned. "But Phillip is right too. Emery and the giants will still have to load the money into a vehicle and drive away with it."

"Do you think Liam will be there?" Silvio asked in a soft voice.

Silence dropped over the den. Everyone looked at Silvio, who stared fixedly at the vault photos as if they contained all the secrets of the universe. His face was calm and blank, but his right index finger tapped against the corner of his tablet, betraying his worry.

More guilt churned in my stomach, along with the few nachos I'd eaten. I didn't want to add to his concern, but I wasn't going to lie to him either. Not about something this important. "Liam will most likely be there. Mason will want to remind me of what will happen to Liam if I don't do exactly what he says."

Silvio grimaced, but he nodded, accepting my logic. I wished I could have given him better news, but there was no good news. Not in this situation.

"After Emery leaves the bank with the money, we could follow her. Force her vehicle off the road and try to rescue Liam that way," Owen suggested.

"No. Mason will be expecting that, and he'll probably have a platoon of giants guarding the money. Besides, if Emery spots a tail, she might decide to execute Liam." I sighed. "Or she might decide to just kill him anyway, no matter what Mason says. She definitely hates me enough to do that."

"Emery did try to kill you, me, and Silvio at Blue Ridge Cemetery a few weeks ago," Owen added. "She definitely wasn't following Mason's orders then."

No, Emery had her own agenda when it came to me—she simply wanted me dead more than anything else. In some ways, I admired her tenacity and willingness to do whatever it took to get her revenge, even face down my uncle's deadly wrath. But Emery's burning hatred of me also made the giant a dangerous wild card. She probably wouldn't wait until the money was out of the bank before she made her move against me, and it wouldn't surprise me if she tried to kill me as soon as I opened the vault.

Always expect the bad guys to do the worst, most inconvenient thing possible, Fletcher's voice whispered in my mind. Truer words have never been spoken, especially when it came to Emery Slater.

"So if we can't break into the bank and steal the money tonight, and we can't follow Emery when she takes the money out of the bank tomorrow, then what *can* we do?" Silvio growled. "How can we save Liam?"

His words boomed through the den, and everyone fell silent again. Silvio reached up and scrubbed his hand through his gray hair, making it stand up in a dozen different directions. He quickly smoothed it back down with a sharp, angry motion.

"Well?" he demanded, his voice much louder and harsher than normal. "Does anyone have any ideas?"

We all looked at one another, but no one had any answers to his questions, and Liam was running out of time for us to figure things out.

⁂ 15 ⁂

We spent the next two hours brainstorming, looking at the bank from every possible angle, but no one came up with any brilliant solutions to rescue Liam, prevent Emery from emptying the vault, or stop Mason from getting the money.

By this point, it was after seven o'clock, and we all needed a break, both from our pointless plotting and from each other. So Bria, Finn, Xavier, Roslyn, Phillip, and Jo-Jo left to head back to their respective homes for the night, while Silvio, Owen, and I stayed at Fletcher's house.

We all vowed to keep in touch and let everyone else know if anyone had a breakthrough, but they were hollow promises. If we had any hope of saving Liam, then I was going to have to do exactly what Mason said and let Emery remove every last penny from Fletcher's vault.

As soon as the others left, Silvio announced that he was going to bed and stalked out of the den without a backward glance. I watched him go, a fresh new wave of guilt sloshing around in my stomach.

"Silvio knows this isn't your fault, Gin," Owen said, seeing my pained expression. "He's not blaming you for what's happening to Liam."

"He doesn't have to," I muttered. "Because I'm blaming myself plenty."

Owen gave me a sympathetic look and squeezed my hand. He helped me carry the dirty dishes into the kitchen and offered to wash them, but I needed some quiet time to think, so I told him I would do it. Owen nodded and headed upstairs to take a shower, as well as call Eva and see how her spring-break trip was going. He wanted to double-check and make sure that his sister and her friends were safe.

I washed and dried the dishes, then wandered back into the den. I moved from one whiteboard to the other and back again, studying the blueprints, photos, and documents, but no new brilliant ideas popped into my mind, and I ended up sprawled across the couch, hoping that staring at my problems from a different angle—literally—would jostle something loose in my mind.

I didn't feel particularly tired, but as soon as my head touched the pillow, all my guilt, stress, and worry finally caught up with me, and I dozed off, slipping into another dream, another memory...

"I told you this was an easy job, Gin," Fletcher chirped in a bright, happy voice.

I really wished he would stop saying that, especially since I still had doubts that the job was actually over, but once again, I didn't voice my concerns, mainly because it had been smooth sailing so far.

Two hours ago, we had left the Gere mansion and gone to Fletcher's house to drop off the cash and other loot we'd stolen. Now we were hiding in the woods outside Blanche Langley's house.

Fletcher had propped the silver-framed Reverie in Gray *painting next to the front door a few minutes ago. I'd waited until he had slipped into the woods, and then I'd rung the doorbell and run away like a teenager pulling a Halloween prank. Blanche's face had lit up like a Christmas tree when she'd opened the door and spotted the painting.*

For the last fifteen minutes, Fletcher and I had been watching Blanche and Benji, her grandson, through the big picture windows in the living room. Blanche and Benji had been hugging and crying ever since they'd brought the painting inside, and Benji was currently on a stepladder, hanging the picture back in its usual spot above the fireplace.

It was a truly heartwarming scene, the kind that made all the long hours I spent training and the danger I put myself in as the Spider worthwhile. But I still couldn't shake the feeling that the job wasn't finished yet and that, sooner or later, Ethan Gere would come for the valuable painting—and his revenge.

"Easy-peasy," Fletcher crowed. "Right, Gin?"

"Right," I replied, my voice fainter and far less cheerful than his, although he didn't seem to notice my lack of enthusiasm.

Fletcher checked his watch. "It's still early. We should celebrate. How about some hot chocolate from the Cake Walk? My treat. Then maybe we can head over to Jo-Jo's salon for movie night."

Normally, I would never turn down hot chocolate from the Cake Walk, but my inner voice wouldn't stop nagging at me. The old man had taught me to trust my instincts, and I was going to do that now, even if they went against his.

"Thanks, but I need to go home and finish writing a paper for my Southern fantasy literature class. Rain check?"

Fletcher frowned, as though he could hear the lie in my

voice, but his expression brightened into another smile. "Sure. I have something to take care of at home too. See you tomorrow at the Pork Pit?"

I smiled back at him, grateful he wasn't going to press the issue. "Always."

Fletcher winked at me, then slid his hands into his pockets, started whistling, and walked away, heading toward his van, which he'd parked on the opposite side of the woods. My car was there too, and we both got into our vehicles and waved good-bye. Fletcher cranked his engine and drove away. He turned left at the end of the block, as though he were going home, while I turned right, as though I were doing the same.

But instead of returning to my downtown apartment, I whipped a U-turn and parked my car in the same spot as before. Ten minutes later, I was back in the woods, watching Blanche's house again, along with the rest of the neighborhood.

It was after ten o'clock now, and most folks were holed up in their homes for the evening, if not already snug in their beds. The March night was bitterly cold, and a few hard, tiny flakes of snow gusted through the air, further encouraging people to stay inside where it was warm and cozy.

I pulled my black toboggan a little farther down on my head and stamped my feet, trying to warm them up. I was probably being a paranoid idiot, freezing my ass off in the cold quiet, waiting for something to happen. But I just couldn't shake the feeling that Ethan Gere would realize that the whole point of robbing and killing his brother, Ivan, had been to hide the fact that we had returned the Reverie in Gray *painting to its rightful owner—*

A pair of headlights appeared in the distance. That was nothing unusual, since several houses were spaced along this winding country road, but the person was driving very,

very slowly, as though they didn't know where they were going—or were searching for a particular house.

The closer the vehicle got to Blanche's house, the more it slowed down. Finally, about a quarter of a mile away, the car's headlights snapped off, even though the vehicle was still cruising along the road. No one in their right mind would turn off their lights on this dark, snowy night—unless they didn't want anyone to see what they were doing.

I eased forward a little closer to the edge of the woods. The one good thing about the snow was that it brightened the landscape enough for me to clearly see the car, despite its lack of headlights.

The car kept coming closer...and closer...and closer...

Until it drove right on by Blanche's house.

I frowned, but the vehicle kept going, still creeping along at that slow, steady pace. Maybe I was wrong. Maybe that wasn't Ethan Gere looking for payback for his brother's death—

The car stopped.

The vehicle rounded a curve in the road, then cruised over to the side of the pavement and parked. My eyes narrowed, and that nagging voice muttered in my mind again. What was the driver doing? Were they having engine trouble?

The door popped open, and a dwarf climbed out of the driver's seat. I recognized him as one of the enforcers who worked for the Gere brothers. The passenger's-side door opened, and a second dwarf scrambled out of the car and hurried to open one of the back doors for a third dwarf: Ethan Gere.

Like the other two dwarves, Ethan Gere was roughly five feet tall, but he was much more heavily muscled, and his navy suit jacket strained to cover his broad shoulders. In addition to popping pills and snorting powders, Ethan also liked to take steroids to further enhance his physique.

I bit back a curse. I'd really, really, really *been hoping that I was wrong, but now that the dwarves were here, I couldn't let them get near Blanche's house. So I palmed a knife and eased out of the woods.*

The three dwarves went around to the back of the car, and one of them popped the trunk.

"How do you want to do this, Ethan?" the driver asked, his voice floating through the air. "You want a crowbar? A sledgehammer? Or how about one of the bone saws? We're going to have to cut up the bodies anyway, right?"

Bone saw? *I grimaced but kept moving at my quick, steady pace, scurrying from one bush and shadow to another. I was approaching the car from the direction of its hood, so I couldn't see everything the dwarves were doing back behind the raised trunk lid, but it didn't much matter. They weren't getting past me.*

"Why pick just one when we can use all three? Giovanni, take the crowbar to pop open the front door. Rico, use the sledgehammer to bash whoever gets in your way. I'll take the bone saw." Ethan Gere's low, gravelly voice drifted over to me. "I want to look into the old lady's eyes as I chop her and her grandson into teeny, tiny little bits. Nobody kills my brother and gets away with it. Nobody.*"*

I bit back another curse. Ethan obviously hadn't bought Fletcher's ruse to make the assassination look like a common robbery—

Crunch.

My boot had cracked some loose glass that was littering the pavement. I immediately froze.

"What was that?" Ethan's voice drifted over to me again.

I bit back yet another curse, then ducked down and hurried forward, careful not to step on any more glass. Then I plastered myself up against the front bumper of the car.

Footsteps sounded, growing louder and closer. I tightened my grip on my knife and waited. If I was lucky, maybe I could take the first dwarf by surprise and stab him before he realized I was here. Then I'd worry about taking out the other two men.

The footsteps grew louder and closer still, and I ducked down a little more, trying to make myself as small and invisible as possible—

Ethan Gere appeared on the driver's side of the car. Up close, he was even more muscled than I'd realized, as though he was an action figure that had somehow been stuffed into a suit. His blond hair was slicked back from his ruddy forehead, and his eyes were as black as lumps of coal in his sharp, angular face. His nose was a bright red, which probably had more to do with all the things he snorted up it, rather than the cold.

Ethan stopped and glanced up and down the road, his gaze sweeping over the snow-crusted landscape. I hunkered down a little more, hoping he wouldn't look in this direction. Ethan took another step forward, and something gleamed in his right hand: the aforementioned bone saw.

The tool glinted a dull silver, as did each and every one of the sharp, jagged teeth lining the edge. I had seen a lot of bad, bad things in my time as the Spider, but the sight of that saw—especially the dark smears of dried blood staining the metal—made me shiver.

Ethan stood there, less than five feet away from me, and started tap-tap-tapping *the flat part of the saw against his thigh. I had to grind my teeth to stop from shuddering at the awful sound.*

"Well?" one of the other dwarves asked. "See anything?"

"Nah," Ethan replied. "It must have been the wind. Let's get this done."

Ethan went back the way he'd come. One of the dwarves closed the trunk, startling me and making the car rock from side to side. Footsteps crunched in the opposite direction, and the sound of the dwarves' voices dimmed.

I drew in a breath to steady myself, then scooted forward and glanced around the side of the car. The three dwarves were walking toward Blanche's house. It was now or never, so I stood up and hurried after them.

I moved as fast as I dared, careful to make as little noise as possible. I needed to stab Ethan in the back first, since he was the most dangerous. Then I could tackle the other two dwarves. I had to kill them quickly enough that they wouldn't scream and alert Blanche and her grandson to what was going on outside their house—

Crunch.

This time, I'd stepped on a patch of ice. The sound wasn't all that loud, although it boomed in my ears like a drum beating out the fact that I was here.

The driver and the other dwarf slowed down, not sure what was going on, but Ethan glanced back over his shoulder.

"Who the fuck are you?" His gaze locked onto the knife in my hand. Understanding filled his eyes, and rage flooded his cheeks, turning them as red as his nose. "You...you killed my brother!"

"Just like I'm going to kill you!" I hissed right back at him.

I tightened my grip on my knife and charged forward. Ethan growled and lashed out with the bone saw, swinging it in a wild arc. I easily avoided the blow and lifted my blade to stab him in the chest, but he saw me coming and spun away. I growled in frustration. He was faster than I'd expected. Maybe all those steroids gave him better reflexes, along with jacking up his muscles to cartoon-character proportions.

Since I couldn't get to Ethan, I turned in the other direction, targeting Giovanni, the dwarf with the crowbar. He too swung his weapon at me in a wild arc. Giovanni wasn't nearly as fast as his boss, and I ducked the clumsy blow, moved forward, and punched my blade into his throat.

The dwarf let out a muffled, gurgling yelp. I twisted the blade in even deeper, then ripped it out, tearing through as much muscle as possible. Blood sprayed everywhere, the warmth of it quite shocking against the cold air, and the tiny drops stung my skin like hot candle wax.

I kicked one of Giovanni's knees out from under him, and he toppled to the pavement, still gurgling. His crowbar slipped from his hands, and I darted forward, bent down, and scooped it up—

Someone grabbed hold of my toboggan, along with my hair underneath, and jerked me back. Pain exploded in my scalp, and I let out an angry hiss, trying to keep the noise to a minimum. The someone yanked me back again, and I twisted to the side, tearing my hair and toboggan out of their grip.

Rico, the second dwarf, growled and reached for me again, but I slammed the crowbar against his head.

The blow probably would have killed a regular human, but the dwarf's skull was so thick and hard that it merely stunned him. Rico staggered away, but I followed him. This time, I lashed out with my knife and slashed the blade across his stomach. Again, it wasn't quite enough to kill him, but the dwarf yelped with pain and dropped one hand to his stomach, trying to stop the blood loss.

I took advantage of his distraction and slammed the crowbar against his head again. The dwarf listed from side to side like a ship caught in a storm, even more drunkenly dazed than before. I hit him with the crowbar a third time, and something finally cracked in his skull. Rico pitched to the pavement without making another sound, blood pooling under his head and stomach from the gruesome injuries.

Still clutching the crowbar in one hand and my knife in the other, I whirled around, expecting Ethan to be charging at me, but to my surprise, he was hanging back. The dwarf still had his bone saw, and he was now clutching a gun in his left hand.

I hurried forward. I needed to knock that gun away before he fired it—

Ethan pulled the trigger.

Pfft!

The gun had a suppressor, so the shot wasn't all that loud, but Ethan hit me at close range, and the bullet blasted against my stomach. It would have torn right through my guts if not for the thin silverstone vest I was wearing underneath my fleece jacket and other clothes.

My vest might have caught the bullet, but it still felt like someone had just smashed me in the belly with a fastball, and the force of the blow punched the air out of my lungs. This time, I was the one who stumbled around, trying to get my breath back.

Ethan calmly watched me wheeze like a car that was almost out of gas, then slid his gun back into the holster on his belt. "I don't know who the fuck you are, and I don't care. I'm going to use my saw on you first, then take care of the old lady and her bratty grandson."

I sucked in another breath, still desperately trying to get air back into my lungs. I raised my crowbar to take a swing at the dwarf, but he slapped it out of my hand, and the weapon clang-clang-clanged out of reach across the pavement.

I wheezed and whipped my knife up, but Ethan grabbed hold of my wrist and wrenched it backward, snapping it as easily as I could crack a potato chip in two.

My knife slipped from my fingers, and this time, I couldn't stop myself from screaming, although Ethan clamped his hand over my mouth, muffling my cries.

"Don't start screaming just yet," he cooed, his voice high and childish, as though he was talking to a beloved pet. "We haven't even gotten to the best part."

He drew his hand away from my mouth, then punched me in the face. White stars exploded in my eyes, and I felt myself falling, falling, falling...

One second, I was standing in front of the dwarf. The next, I was flat on my back on the pavement. Ethan loomed over me, staring down at me with a dispassionate expression, the bone saw still clutched in his hand.

"Since your wrist's broken, we might as well go ahead and cut your hand off," he cooed again in that strange, high, childish voice. "Oh, yeah. Let's definitely *do that."*

Despite the white stars still exploding in my eyes, I dug my boots into the pavement, trying to scramble away from the dwarf, who was slowly, steadily, relentlessly advancing toward me, a malicious smile on his face...

My eyes snapped open, and I sucked in a ragged breath, as though I were still as winded as I had been during that long-ago fight. My gaze darted around the room, zipping back and forth in time to the frantic beat of my heart, and it took me a few seconds to recognize the familiar den furniture.

Safe—I was safe at home. I'd dozed off on the couch and had another vivid nightmare. I exhaled, scrubbed my hands over my face, and sat up.

According to the clock on the wall, it was almost nine o'clock. The house was quiet, and I didn't hear anyone moving around upstairs. Owen and Silvio had both probably gone to bed to rest up for tomorrow. I should have gone to bed too, but I couldn't do that. Not with Liam still in so much danger and me hours away from giving Mason everything he needed to finally destroy the Pork Pit.

So I forced myself to get up, go over to the whiteboards, and look at everything again. I ignored the blueprints, since it was too late to break into the bank, and instead stared at the photos of Fletcher's vault on Finn's board, along with the hundred-dollar bill my brother had given me yesterday.

I moved from one side of the board to the other and back again, staring at everything in turn, but nothing jumped out at me. I moved over to Silvio's board, but it was also a dead end. Frustrated, I spun away from both boards, not sure what I should do next, and a couple of metallic gleams caught my eye.

My mother's and sister's silverstone rune pendants—the snowflake and the ivy vine—were glimmering in their usual spots on the mantel. I started to go over and fill the pendants with more of my Ice magic, but I stopped and sighed. What was the point? I couldn't kill Mason with my Ice and Stone magic, nor could I murder him with my knives.

My gaze zipped over to Fletcher's letter and zoomed in on the familiar phrase: *fight smarter*. The words were a stark, mocking, black-and-white reminder that I hadn't done anything *smart* lately—and that Liam and Silvio were suffering because of my pride, arrogance, and stupidity.

I sighed again and had started to turn away from the mantel when another glimmer caught my eye: the penny that had been part of my spider rune in the vault.

Thanks to my dreams, I remembered Fletcher arranging those wads of cash into my spider rune when we'd killed Ivan Gere, but I still didn't know why he'd done something similar in his own vault. Was Fletcher telling me that the vault contained all the loot he'd ever stolen from bad guys? Or was it yet another clue that was supposed to lead me somewhere else? To something else?

I sighed for a third time, knowing that I probably wasn't going to puzzle out Fletcher's meaning tonight. But I still needed to figure out some way to save Liam, so I forced myself to turn back to the whiteboards. I was at the end of Finn's board, and I reached out and idly rubbed the end of the hundred-dollar bill between my fingers.

All by itself, a hundred bucks is as light as, well, a piece of paper, Phillip Kincaid's voice whispered in my mind. He'd said that when we had all been in the den earlier, although I wasn't sure why I'd thought of it now.

I frowned and glanced down at the bill that I was still rubbing between my fingers. It was a fresh, crisp hundred, the kind that had probably never been touched before, but something about it felt...*wrong*. So I bent down and took a closer look at the bill, examining everything from the graphics to the color of the paper to the serial number—

A laugh burst out of my lips.

I quickly clapped my hand over my mouth, not wanting to wake Silvio and Owen if they were in fact sleeping, but merry, muffled giggles kept spewing out of my lips.

After several seconds, I forced myself to swallow my laughter, lean forward, and take another, even closer look at the hundred-dollar bill. I saw the exact same thing as before, which made even more giggles rise in my throat, although I forced myself to swallow them again.

Staring at the bill made me curious about the penny, so I grabbed it off the mantel and held it up to the light. The penny was also suspiciously shiny, as though it had never been touched before either. For the third time, I had to swallow my laughter.

Still clutching the penny, I whirled back around to the two whiteboards. I stared at the vault photos yet again, my gaze lingering on the ones of the replica *Reverie in Gray* painting. But this time, I saw the images with new eyes—and the view changed *everything*.

Phillip had been right. One way or another, I was going into the Bellum Bank and down to Fletcher's vault tomorrow. But Phillip had been wrong too. I might have to open the vault for Emery, but that didn't mean I had to let her remove all the money.

I stood there, rubbing the penny between my thumb and index finger and working out everything in my mind. There were a whole lot of variables, and dozens of things could go wrong, but at least now I had a plan, one that just might save Liam *and* keep Mason from getting the money.

There was only one catch: I was going to need an enemy's help to pull it off.

I studied the boards a minute longer, then grabbed some documents from the mantel—the memo and attached papers that I'd swiped from the Carpenter Consulting conference room. I scanned the contents again, also seeing them with new eyes. When I was satisfied that I had everything I needed, I tucked the papers into my pocket, along with the penny for luck, and left the den.

It was time to get started on the *real* Operation Piggy Bank.

❀ 16 ❀

I shrugged into a black fleece jacket, stuffed my dark brown hair underneath a black toboggan, and grabbed a duffel bag of supplies that I kept hidden inside the cold fireplace. Then I scribbled out a note to Owen and Silvio, telling them what I was doing.

Oh, sure, I could have woken Owen and Silvio and asked them to come with me. Maybe I should have done that. But my plan was still so nebulous, still so tenuous, still so much of a long shot that I didn't want to get their hopes up if it didn't work out. Plus, there was a fifty-fifty chance the person I was going to see would immediately try to kill me, rather than hear me out. I didn't want to risk Owen's and Silvio's lives too, should my late-night errand end in a Fire fight. So I placed my note in the center of the now-empty coffee table, where the guys should see it if they got up and started looking for me, then left Fletcher's house.

It didn't take me long to drive my car over to the appropriate Northtown neighborhood, park in a secluded spot, and make the rest of the journey on foot.

Twenty minutes and roughly a mile later, I reached my destination and hunkered down at the edge of the woods to get the lay of the land.

The dense woods gave way to a wide, grassy yard that stretched out for a couple hundred feet before rolling up to a modest gray stone mansion. Outdoor floodlights burned along the back of the structure, clearly illuminating a large pool, a hot tub, and a stone patio filled with glass tables and white wicker chairs. I eyed the mansion, but I didn't see anyone moving inside past the windows, so I turned my attention to my more immediate, pressing problem.

The guards.

Two giants were patrolling the perimeter, their separate routes almost equidistant from each other, in both space and time. I studied the guards' routes, as well as their body language. The men weren't completely ignoring their surroundings, but they had the slow, ambling walks of folks who had done this same exact thing for days, weeks, months, maybe years on end. Nothing had ever happened on their watches, and they didn't expect anything to drag them out of their rut. Which was probably why the two men were checking their phones far more than they were scanning the dark woods where I was lurking.

I waited until the first giant strolled by my position, then left the trees and darted over to the nearest ornamental bush. That giant didn't so much as glance back over his shoulder, despite the soft swish of my boots through the grass. I looked to my right, but the second guard wasn't in sight yet, so I scurried forward and dropped down behind another bush. Then I held my position until the second giant strolled by, as oblivious to my presence as the first man had been.

Forget diamonds. Landscaping and cell phones were this assassin's best friends.

I did that same thing over and over again, using the gaps between the distracted guards to creep closer and closer to the mansion. It took me the better part of ten minutes, but I eventually made it past the pool and the hot tub and over to the back of the house.

I gently tried one of the patio doors that led into the mansion, but it was locked. One of the guards was about to stroll back into sight, so I hurried over to the nearby pool house, which had a low roof. I hopped up into one of the lounge chairs, stepped onto a glass table, and grabbed hold of the side of the roof.

The soft scuff of footsteps sounded, and one of the giants rounded the corner of the mansion. I sucked in a breath and pulled myself up, wincing at the scrape of my boots against the wall. The second I was on the roof, I rolled over, lying flat and still. My heart thumped in my ears, and I strained to listen past the roaring noise, wondering if the guard had seen me—

"I don't know why we have to patrol tonight," the giant grumbled, his voice floating over to me. "I'm freezing my ass off out here."

"Wouldn't you be nervous if Gin Blanco was sniffing around?" a second male voice replied, although the sound was a bit tinny.

I peeked over the edge of the roof. One of the giants was standing right below me on the patio, holding his phone up to his mouth.

That man snorted. "Please. Gin Blanco is not *nearly* as smart, tough, and sneaky as everyone claims she is. Besides, she's just one person. There's no way she could get past you and me, plus all the guards out front."

I rolled my eyes. I could have killed this guy half a dozen times already, and he would have been dead before he even looked up from his phone.

"You want to bet your life on that?" the second voice sounded through the phone again. "Because I don't. Now, come on. We're falling behind."

The first giant sighed out his displeasure, but he lowered his phone and continued on his route.

I waited until he had wandered away, then stood up, studying the distance between the pool-house roof and the slightly higher first-story roof of the mansion. Then I drew in a deep breath, took off in a dead sprint, and flung myself forward.

For a moment, I hung in midair, but my momentum carried me up and out just far enough for me to latch onto the mansion's roof. I swung back and forth for a few seconds, then used that extra bit of momentum to throw my body up and hook one of my legs onto the roof. From there, it was easy enough to drag my second leg up onto the roof, along with the rest of my body. I rolled away from the edge and rested flat on my back, getting my breath back. Then I got up onto my hands and knees and carefully, quietly crawled up the sloped roof to the second story.

This time, I reached out and tried a window, which slid up. Of course it did. Few people bothered to properly secure the upper levels of their homes and businesses.

Landscaping, phones, and now second-story windows. Yep, those were definitely my best friends.

I slipped inside the window, shut it behind me, and palmed a knife. For the most part, the mansion was quiet, although a faint, steady tapping sounded in the distance. I tilted my head to the side, listening. That sounded like... someone typing on a keyboard.

My target was still awake. Excellent. I didn't want to startle them any more than necessary, something that was hard to avoid if you had to rouse someone from a dead sleep.

I followed the sound of the typing to the end of the hallway. A door was cracked open, and I peered in through the gap. A home office lay on the other side, and I could just see the top of my target's head sticking up from behind the large monitor on their desk.

I glanced back down the hallway and listened again. From what I knew of them, my target lived alone. No one else seemed to be moving through the mansion, and I didn't hear any murmured conversations or heavy footsteps that would indicate guards were stationed inside. So I reached out and politely rapped my knuckles on the door.

"What is it?" A voice floated out through the opening to me.

I took that as an invitation to come on in. The door creaked as I pushed it open, making me wince, but I moved forward anyway and scanned the room. Bookcases along one wall, a fireplace along another wall, some couches and chairs scattered around, a large wooden desk squatting in the center of it all. The office was like any other except for one thing: the photos.

Framed pictures lined the bookshelves as well as the fireplace mantel, and still more photos adorned the walls. Many of the images showed my target, along with what I assumed were various family members, given their resemblances to one another. My target was smiling in many of the photos, and they looked far happier in the casual images than I had ever seen them look in real life. Good to know that family was important to them, especially since I needed their help to save Liam and the rest of mine.

I pulled my gaze away from the photos and checked the rest of the office, but it was empty. Excellent. I wanted our conversation to be completely private. Otherwise, my plan would fall apart before I'd even had a chance to tell my target about it.

Still clutching my knife, I strode forward and stopped in front of the desk.

"I told you not to bother me unless it was an emergency." The person behind the desk kept right on typing, completely focused on their monitor.

"Oh, it's an emergency all right," I drawled.

The typing abruptly stopped, and silence dropped over the office. I didn't move or speak, and neither did my target. Then the leather chair creaked, and the person behind the monitor slowly leaned to one side and peered around the screen at me.

Black hair, dark brown eyes, pretty features. She looked the same as she had at the Bellum Bank yesterday, right down to her money-green pantsuit.

"Hello, Drusilla," I drawled. "So nice to see you again."

Drusilla Yang blinked a few times, as if she wasn't sure whether I was really here or just a figment of her imagination. I could understand the notion, given how my own dreams and memories so often bled into reality. Then her gaze dropped to the knife in my hand, and her lips pressed together into a tight, thin line. Definitely not a dream. Then again, most people would consider a late-night visit from the Spider to be the start of their worst nightmare.

Her hand crept over toward the landline phone on the right side of her desk.

I waggled my knife at her. "If it's okay with you, I'd prefer to have a private conversation."

Her hand stopped, but instead of fear, anger flared in Drusilla's eyes, along with her Fire magic. Given how cold it had been outside, the heat blasting off her actually felt good for a change.

"What are you doing here?"

I gestured at one of the chairs in front of her desk. "May I sit?"

"No," she snapped. "You may not."

I shrugged, then moved to the side, so that I could see behind the desk and be able to stop Drusilla if she did lunge for the phone—or worse, try to burn me with her Fire magic. I leaned against the wall, careful not to disturb the framed photos hanging there, and crossed my arms over my chest, my knife still clearly visible in my right hand.

Drusilla studied me for several seconds. "Come to kill me?" she asked, breaking the tense silence.

"Nope."

Her eyes narrowed. "I don't believe you."

"If I wanted you dead, I would have snuck in through that window behind you and stabbed you in the back before you even realized I was here. I'm guessing that window is open, just like the other one I came through."

Drusilla glanced over her shoulder, indicating that I had guessed right.

"Now that we've established I didn't come here to kill you, maybe we can get down to business."

She snorted. "Business? What *business*? First, you show up at my family's bank out of the blue yesterday morning and threaten my father. Then, yesterday afternoon, you try to stab a man to death right in front of me. And now, tonight, you break into my home. I'm starting to think you have some weird vendetta against my family."

"Not at all. My vendetta is squarely against my own family. Mason Mitchell, to be exact. He's my uncle."

Surprise flickered across her face.

"Ah, so Uncle Mason didn't fill you in on our familial

connection. I bet there are lots of things he didn't tell you and your father."

I knew that for a fact, since I had one of those things in my pocket, although I wasn't going to mention it unless I absolutely had to.

"What *did* dear Uncle Mason say about why I attacked him?"

Drusilla shrugged. "That you were extremely upset at the thought of losing your barbecue restaurant and that you had tried to kill him more than once, despite the generous relocation package he had offered you."

"Well, the parts about losing my restaurant and trying to kill him multiple times are certainly true, but he never offered me any relocation package—just death threats."

Drusilla's eyebrows drew together in confusion. "All the business owners will be offered a relocation package, along with the people living in the apartment buildings. My father insisted on those terms before he gave Mason the project loan."

Well, it was good to know Charles Yang wasn't completely heartless and that he wanted to help the people the Mitchell Mile would displace. But apparently, I knew Mason a lot better than the Yangs did. There wouldn't be any relocation packages. No, my uncle would send Emery and his men to threaten, intimidate, hurt, and kill people until everyone signed over their homes and businesses to him.

But I hadn't come here to debate the project's ethics—or lack thereof. It was creeping up on eleven o'clock, which meant that I had roughly thirteen hours to put my plan into motion, and I needed to get Drusilla Yang on board right now.

"Forget about Mason for the time being. I have something else to discuss with you."

Drusilla leaned back in her chair, still wary, although her posture was a little less stiff than before. "And what would that be?"

"I want you to help me rob your bank."

For several long seconds, Drusilla sat absolutely still and silent in her chair. She blinked a few times, as if replaying my words in her mind. Then the strangest thing happened. Her lips twitched upward into a smile, and she laughed.

And laughed…and laughed…

And laughed some more…

Loud, merry chuckles erupted out of her lips, the force of them making the Fire elemental clutch her ribs and double over in her chair. Oddly enough, her laughter sounded eerily similar to my own hysterical giggles when I had first figured out Fletcher's message to me.

Drusilla finally quit laughing. She straightened up and wiped the tears out of the corners of her eyes. "You're even crazier than I thought. Why would *I* ever help *you* rob *my* bank?"

I opened my mouth to answer, but she cut me off.

"Forget about me helping you. *Nobody* can rob the Bellum Bank. My family and I have made sure of that. Plenty of people have tried over the years, and none has succeeded." She gave me a look that was almost pitying. "You won't be any different, Blanco, no matter what you threaten to do to me or my father or the rest of our family. I'm not going to help you, so you might as well kill me and get it over with."

I shook my head in exasperation. People really needed to start *listening* to me and quit jumping to conclusions just because I was an assassin with an unhealthy fondness for knives. "Like I said before, I'm not going to kill you."

I drew in a deep breath, steadying my nerves and steeling

my heart. This next part was always the hardest for me to say, to admit out loud, especially to someone who was largely a stranger. But I had done it with Liam Carter a few weeks ago when I'd asked him to spy on Mason, and now I had to take a chance that Drusilla Yang would help me too. Otherwise, Liam was dead.

"I'm in trouble, and I need your help."

Drusilla blinked again, although her surprise quickly melted into a deep frown. "Why would the Spider ever need *my* help? I'm not in the business of hurting people." She paused. "Unless I have to for the bank."

"This isn't about killing someone—it's about saving a friend."

I drew in another breath and told her everything. Well, mostly everything. There wasn't time to tell her the whole sad, convoluted story, so I hit the highlights. Evil uncle. Secret Circle society. Liam held hostage. Stolen money in the vault. My plan to fix everything.

By the time I finished, Drusilla was looking more thoughtful than angry. "I'm sorry about your friend. Truly, I am. Plus, I know Liam. He's a stand-up guy."

"But?"

"But those are *your* problems, not *my* problems," she replied. "You know my reputation, my father's reputation, the bank's reputation. We have a code of absolute neutrality, and we don't get involved in disputes among our clients, no matter the stakes."

"Not even if the stakes are your own people?" I shot right back at her.

"What do you mean?"

"You have guards stationed on the vault level, and you yourself have to actually open the vault. Emery Slater isn't going to let anyone stand in her way of getting that money. I fully expect her to try to kill me the second the vault is open."

"I hate to point out the obvious, but again, Emery wanting to murder you is *your* problem," Drusilla said. "It doesn't have anything to do with me or the bank."

I shook my head again. "You're missing my point. Emery doesn't care about you, or your employees, or your bank's no-violence rules. If you're anywhere near that vault when it's open, then she will do her best to kill you. Trust me on that."

Drusilla lifted her hand, and elemental Fire erupted on her fingertips, burning bright and hot. "If Emery tries anything, then she will be in for a very rude awakening."

I admired Drusilla's confidence in her magic, as well as in her bank's defenses, even if it was inconveniencing me right now. So I tried another tactic. "But why take the risk? Why risk your people at all?"

Once again, she frowned at me. "What do you mean?"

I told her what I had in mind, how I thought I could keep everyone at the bank safe.

As soon as I finished, Drusilla immediately started shaking her head. "No—no way. That goes against every single one of our security, safety, and privacy protocols. My father and the board of directors would have my head if they found out I ever even *considered* such a scheme, as would our clients. I can't risk the bank, and everything my father, my family, has built."

"Not even to save lives?"

She shook her head again. "No. Not even to do that."

Frustration boiled up in my heart, but I forced myself to stay calm. I still had one more card left to play. I hesitated, wondering if I should throw it down, but Liam's life was on the line, and I was out of options. Plus, I would never be able to face Silvio if I didn't keep my promise to do everything in my power to rescue Liam.

"What about to save your family's legacy?"

Wariness filled Drusilla's face. "What do you mean?"

I reached into my pocket. Drusilla tensed, and elemental Fire flared up on her fingertips again, but she didn't toss her magic at me. Well, at least we were making some progress.

I pulled out the memo I'd found yesterday, eased forward, and set it and the attached papers down on Drusilla's desk.

"What is that?" she asked, suspicious once again.

"Ambitions."

Drusilla eyed me for a second, clearly wondering at my cryptic tone, but then she snuffed out the Fire on her fingertips, picked up the papers, and started reading.

"This...this is a memo about the Mitchell Mile." She frowned. "I've *never* seen this before. Where did you get this?"

"I found it in the conference room at Carpenter Consulting," I replied. "As you can see, it's all about phase two of the Mitchell Mile."

Her eyebrows furrowed together. "Phase two? I don't know anything about a phase two."

"I think that's the idea. Look at the artist's mock-up."

Drusilla flipped over to the other sheets. It took her a few seconds to realize what she was looking at, but once she did, horror quickly dawned on her face—the same sort of horror I had felt when I'd first seen the diorama of Mason's dream project and realized that the Pork Pit was gone.

Only this time, the Bellum Bank was the building that had been wiped off the map.

"I don't understand," Drusilla muttered, a sick look on her face. "Why would Mason do this to us? My father is loaning him the money for his project!"

"If there is one thing you should know about my uncle, it's that Mason *always* has his own plans. Phase one is just the beginning. He's already started working on phase two, and it wouldn't surprise me if he's already dreaming up phase three. Mason won't be satisfied until he's remade all of Ashland—and is profiting from every square inch of the city."

Drusilla stared at the sheet for a few more seconds, then looked up at me. Her eyes narrowed, and I could almost see the calculations going on in her mind as she weighed following the rules versus the enormous risks I was asking her to take.

Anger sparked in her gaze again, and her hand crumpled the papers. More Fire flashed on her fingertips, scorching the sheets, although she tossed them down onto the desk before they fully ignited.

Drusilla glared at the smoldering papers, then raised her eyes to mine. "What, exactly, do you want from me?"

I grinned. "Just a few small things. My friends and I will do most of the heavy lifting."

Drusilla kept staring at me, suspicion filling her face.

My grin widened. "Here's what we're going to do."

✿ 17 ✿

I hashed out my plan with Drusilla. It didn't take long, since my friends and I were going to assume most of the risks, just like I'd told her. When we finished, I wished her good night and headed for the office door.

"Oh, Ms. Blanco," Drusilla called out.

I stopped and looked over my shoulder. "Yeah?"

A ball of Fire popped into her hand. The flicker of the flames matched the hot sparks of magic dancing in her eyes. "If you *ever* break into my home again, I will roast you like a marshmallow over a campfire until there's nothing left of you but burned sugar. Are we clear?"

I grinned. Despite her threat, I was starting to like Drusilla Yang. "Absolutely."

I tipped my head to her, then left the office. I went back out the second-story window, climbed down to the pool-house roof, and crossed the lawn. By the time I reached the woods, the entire mansion was blazing with light, and the two giants who had been patrolling the backyard had vanished. Drusilla had probably summoned her guards to take them to task for failing to stop me from sneaking inside. I grinned again and headed into the woods.

Forty-five minutes later, I parked my car in the driveway at Fletcher's house. I reached out with my Stone magic and did my usual checks, but Emery Slater and her goons weren't lurking in the woods, and Mason hadn't sent anyone else to spy on me. So I got out of my car, unlocked the front door, and slipped inside the house.

I crept down the hallway to the den, careful not to step on any creaky floorboards. The lights were off, and I didn't hear anyone moving around. Owen and Silvio were probably still asleep—

A dull gleam of silver caught my eye, and a shadow detached itself from the wall and rushed toward me.

Acting on instinct, I spun away from the figure, who jerked to a stop and whirled right back around. Before I could react or call out a warning, the figure surged toward me, drew their arm back, and then snapped it forward with brutal force, like I was a tennis ball they were hitting back over a net.

Thunk.

Something cracked into my left shoulder, hard enough to make me stumble back into the wall. "Ouch! That hurt!"

The figure jerked to a stop right before they were going to hit me again. "Gin?" a hesitant voice called out.

I sighed, staggered down the hall, and flipped on the lights. Silvio stood near the kitchen doorway, a metal meat mallet clutched in his hand. His tablet glowed in the middle of a nest of photos and documents on the kitchen table, while steam curled up from a blue mug.

I gingerly touched my shoulder. It hadn't swollen up— yet—but I was definitely going to have a bruise. "You whacked me with my own meat mallet?"

Silvio grimaced and lowered the kitchen tool to his side. "Sorry. I thought you were an intruder."

I kept rubbing my shoulder, trying to massage away some of the throbbing pain. "I suppose I should be grateful you didn't clock me upside the head with your tablet."

He sniffed. "Please. That would only be a last resort."

"In other words, you would much rather bust up my kitchen utensil than your precious electronics."

"Guilty as charged." He put the mallet back in its proper place on the counter, then went over to the kitchen table.

I eyed the photos and papers strewn across the surface. "Couldn't sleep?"

"Just going over everything again." Silvio sighed and scrubbed his hand through his hair. "And again, and again, and *again*, although I don't see anything different from the dozen other times I've looked. *Nothing* in these photos and papers will help us break into the bank tonight, or save Liam tomorrow, or keep Mason from getting Fletcher's money."

"Oh, I wouldn't say that." I dug into my pocket and drew out the penny Finn had snitched from the vault. "Fletcher left me everything I need to derail Mason's project."

I admired the coin for a moment before flipping it over to Silvio, who easily caught it.

He set the penny down on the table without even glancing at it, annoyance filling his face. "This is no time to be cheerful, Gin. We are mere hours away from handing every last dollar, watch, and necklace in that vault over to Mason."

Silvio paused, as if having a hard time voicing his next thought. "And who knows what might be happening to Liam right now? How Emery might be hurting him?" The vampire's voice dropped to a low, ragged whisper, and fear pinched his face. "*Torturing* him?"

A few more bricks of guilt landed on that ever-growing

mountain in my chest, but I went over and put my hand on my friend's shoulder, trying to comfort him.

"I know you're worried about Liam. I am too. But we can't do anything for him tonight. The best way for us to help Liam is to prepare for tomorrow—and be ready to give Mason exactly what he wants."

Silvio frowned. "What do you mean? We should be trying to figure out some way to rescue Liam *and* keep Mason from getting the money. Otherwise, the Pork Pit is doomed, and a good chunk of downtown Ashland along with it."

I shook my head. "This was *never* about the money. Not for me. Do I want to give Mason one single cent from Fletcher's vault? No, of course not. But as soon as I saw Liam outside the Pork Pit, my priorities shifted. This isn't a bank heist or a game of keep-away anymore—it's a rescue mission."

"I appreciate the sentiment, Gin," Silvio replied. "Truly, I do."

"But?"

He threw his hands up into the air. "But *how* are we going to save Liam? We don't even know if Mason and Emery are going to bring him to the bank. Even if they do, Emery or one of her men could still kill him."

"Mason won't pass up the opportunity to dangle Liam's life over my head again," I said. "Liam will be somewhere near the bank, and Mason won't let any of his men kill Liam. At least, not until he sees Emery walking out of the bank with the money. That still gives us a chance to rescue Liam in the meantime."

Silvio continued staring at me, fear and worry creasing deep lines in his face. "But we went over *everything*. There's no good, safe way to stop Emery from taking the money."

"Then we let her and Mason have the fucking money. I

care about Liam much more than I ever cared about the money." I hesitated. "And I know that you care about him too."

Silvio didn't respond, but his lips pressed together into a tight line. The anguish and longing flickering in his eyes made my heart wrench, but I reached out and squeezed his shoulder.

"I'm going to tell you the same thing I told Lorelei about Hugh Tucker, that it's okay to like Liam. He likes you too, and he's proven that he's a good guy."

Silvio sighed. "I know. But that still doesn't make it any easier for me to trust him. I've been burned too many times in the past."

"So have I. But then Owen came along, and I let him in. And if I hadn't done that, I would have missed out on something wonderful. I don't want you to miss out on something wonderful too. Just think about it. Okay?"

Silvio nodded, and the barest hint of a smile flashed across his face. "You know, you're pretty good at giving pep talks."

I gave him a not-at-all-modest shrug. "It's one of my many hidden talents."

His eyes narrowed. "Wait. Why are you suddenly so cheerful?" His gray gaze flicked over my fleece jacket. "And where have you been?"

I grinned and slung my arm around his shoulders. "Coming up with a new plan for Operation Piggy Bank— one that is going to get us everything we want."

Silvio wouldn't let me leave the kitchen until I told him my plan.

He blinked several times, as if trying to wrap his mind around my words. "You know this is crazy, right?"

"It's only crazy if it doesn't work," I replied. "Now, come on. We have a lot to do."

We both trooped into the den. I grabbed my phone and started calling people, starting with Bria and Finn, while Silvio did the same on his own phone, contacting Jo-Jo and Sophia first. It wasn't quite midnight yet, so most of our friends were still awake. Then again, it was hard to sleep with everything that was going on.

I told everyone that I had a plan and asked them to meet me here at Fletcher's house early in the morning. I also asked them to bring the various supplies we would need to pull off my crazy idea.

Once the calls were finished, there was nothing else for us to do, so Silvio went to bed. I did the same, sliding in next to Owen, who mumbled in his sleep and spooned against my back. I snuggled closer to him, so grateful to be warm and safe with my love.

Liam's bruised, battered face flashed through my mind again. No matter what happened to me tomorrow, or to the money, I was going to do everything—*everything*—in my power to save my friend. I reaffirmed that silent promise, let it sink deep down into my heart, then forced myself to relax and go to sleep.

The next morning, I got up early, went into the kitchen, and started cooking. We had a long day ahead of us, and I wanted everyone to be well fed. So I whipped up some blueberry pancakes, scrambled eggs, applewood smoked bacon, a fresh fruit salad, and a hash-brown casserole filled with sharp cheddar cheese and topped with crumbled bacon bits and sliced green onions.

Owen and Silvio came downstairs to help me put the finishing touches on the meal, and I had just placed the last platter of pancakes on the kitchen table when everyone else started arriving.

Bria and Finn, Jo-Jo and Sophia, Xavier and Roslyn, Phillip. They all headed into the den, along with two other folks I'd invited to my early-morning soiree: Lorelei Parker and Hugh Tucker.

The vampire looked much better than the last time I had seen him at Jo-Jo's salon two days ago. His skin had finally lost its pale, waxen, sickly sheen, and he wasn't leaning on his cane nearly as heavily as before.

"Why, Tuck," I drawled. "You're looking almost human again."

His black eyes narrowed. "And you're looking smug. That doesn't bode well for Mason and Emery."

I grinned. "No, it does not."

"So what, exactly, is this grand plan of yours?" Phillip asked.

"Everyone grab some food, and I'll explain everything."

My friends loaded up their plates with breakfast vittles, then crammed into the den. For several minutes, the only sounds were the scraping of knives and forks on plates and murmurs of appreciation.

I dug into my own food. Light-as-air pancakes bursting with loads of blueberries. The honey-lime dressing coating the strawberries, kiwis, and other fruits. The hash-brown casserole oozing with cheese. Mmm-mmm-mmm. I quickly polished off one plate of food and helped myself to another.

Between bites, I outlined my plan to my friends, using the photos and blueprints on Silvio's and Finn's whiteboards to show everyone exactly what I had in mind.

I told them *almost* everything.

There was one small, tiny part of my plan that I was holding back from everyone, even Silvio. A few lumps of guilt lodged in my throat that I wasn't being completely, one-hundred-percent honest, but I needed my friends to react a certain way, and I just wouldn't get that much-needed reaction if they knew everything that I did. But I wasn't going to keep them in the dark forever. I'd written an email revealing everything and arranged to have it sent to Silvio this afternoon, just in case I didn't make it out of the bank alive.

I finished outlining what I wanted everyone to do. Stunned silence dropped over the den, and in an instant, they all forgot about their food. Instead, my friends kept looking back and forth between me and the photos on the boards.

Finn piped up first, the way he always did. "In theory, it *could* work."

I could hear the doubt in his voice. "Or?"

A worried look creased his face. "Or you could get yourself killed, along with everyone else."

"I know, and that's why I asked you all to come here." I drew in a breath and slowly let it out, steeling myself for my confession. "This is all *my* fault. I'm the one who opened this can of worms back when I first decided to investigate the Circle. And ever since then, I've just kept opening up one can of worms after another, despite all the attacks and traps and everything else that's happened. I've put you all in danger time and time again, and for that I am truly, truly sorry."

I looked at everyone in turn, even Tucker, then stared at Silvio. "If I had just stayed away from the Bellum Bank, from Fletcher's vault, then maybe Mason wouldn't have realized that I knew where his money was. Maybe Emery wouldn't have hurt Liam, and maybe Mason wouldn't be threatening us again. I am so, so sorry for all of that."

Once again, silence dropped over the den. I kept staring at Silvio. Grief darkened my friend's eyes, but he nodded, accepting my apology. Some of the waves of worry sloshing around in my stomach settled down, and I nodded back at him.

Bria shook her head, making her blond hair fly around her face. "This is *not* your fault, Gin. Even if you hadn't gone to the bank, Mason would have still come after us again. We all know that."

The rest of my friends murmured their agreement, and even Tucker joined in with the reassuring chorus.

I focused on my former nemesis. "What do you think? Will my plan work?"

Tucker studied the photos on the whiteboards. "As Finnegan already pointed out, it *could* work. As soon as you show up at the bank, Mason will be singularly focused on getting his money out of the vault. He won't be paying attention to anything else. But you still have to deal with Emery. She absolutely despises you, and she'll probably try to kill you at some point, no matter what her orders are from Mason."

I grinned. "Oh, I'm counting on that."

Still, my grin faded as I looked around at my friends. Mason had already hurt Liam, and I didn't want to put anyone else in danger, but I simply couldn't pull this off without their help. Still, it was their choice to make, not mine.

I drew in another breath, then slowly let it out. "You all know how dangerous this is. If even the smallest, tiniest thing goes wrong, we could all end up dead. So if anyone wants out, if anyone wants to walk away, I completely understand. Liam getting caught was *my* fault, *my* mistake. If I could rescue him and fix this by myself, then I would—but I can't. So I'm asking you all to help me."

For the third time, silence dropped over the den, and no one moved or spoke. My heart squeezed tight with worry.

Owen got to his feet and walked over to me, his violet gaze locking with my gray one. "You know that I'm with you, Gin—always and forever."

Hot tears stung my eyes, and I reached out and squeezed his hand. "Always and forever," I whispered back to him.

Owen grinned and threaded his fingers through mine.

"I'm in," Finn said.

"Me too," Bria replied.

In an instant, everyone was talking at once, saying that of course they would help me, of course we were going to save Liam, and of course we were all in this together. More hot tears stung my eyes, and my heart squeezed tight again, this time with love and gratitude. The fact that my friends were willing to risk themselves and to trust in my crazy plan—to trust in *me*—was far more precious than any treasure in Fletcher's vault and meant more to me than they would ever, ever know.

My friends' voices died down, and everyone looked at me again. It took me a few seconds to blink the tears out of my eyes and clear the emotion out of my throat.

"And what about you, Tuck?" I asked.

All eyes turned to the vampire, who was the only one who hadn't spoken up. He shrugged. "I'll admit to having some mild curiosity about how your little drama will play out."

In other words, Tucker wouldn't help me, but he wouldn't hinder me either. Instead, he would watch and wait for an opportunity to twist things around to his advantage. His response was more or less what I'd expected, so I ignored him and turned back to my friends.

Owen. Bria. Finn. Jo-Jo. Sophia. Xavier. Roslyn. Phillip. Lorelei. They all looked back at me, and the trust in their faces filled my heart with love and gratitude yet again.

A grin spread across my face. "Operation Piggy Bank is a go."

* 18 *

We reviewed the plan several times, then everyone geared up and left to get into position. Owen was the last one to leave, and the two of us ended up on the front porch.

Owen took my hands in his, gently stroking his thumbs over my skin. "Everything is going to be okay, Gin," he rumbled. "Your plan will work. I believe in it, in *you*, and so does everyone else."

More of those annoying tears stung my eyes, but once again I blinked them away, then leaned forward and pressed my lips to his. Owen's arms snaked around my waist, and he drew me closer. I reached up and tangled my fingers in his hair, then opened my lips, deepening the kiss. Owen growled low in his throat, his tongue stroking against my own. Warmth flooded my veins, but it was nothing compared to the fire blazing in my heart for him.

All too soon, though, the kiss ended, and we broke apart, both of us breathing hard.

Owen leaned his forehead against mine. "See you soon," he whispered.

"Count on it," I whispered back.

We both drew back. Owen winked and gave me a jaunty salute. He stepped off the porch, got into his car, and left. I waited until his car had disappeared down the driveway, then went back inside the house.

Silvio was standing in front of the whiteboards in the den, his tablet in his hand and his gaze flicking from one photo to another.

"You ready to go?" I asked.

He whirled away from the boards, a guilty look on his face, as though I'd caught him doing something he shouldn't.

I arched an eyebrow at him. "Double-checking my work?"

Silvio grimaced. "Is it that obvious?"

"Yes, but it doesn't bother me. I would be doing the same thing if Mason had Owen instead of Liam."

I walked over to stand beside my assistant. My gaze also moved over the photos and blueprints, but I wasn't really seeing them. Instead, Liam's bruised face flashed through my mind for the hundredth time. Doubt snaked through me, along with worry for him. "I still don't know if this is going to work."

"Me neither," Silvio murmured. "But this *is* our best chance to save Liam."

"Do you really believe that?"

He nodded, his gray gaze steady on mine. "I do." Silvio hesitated, then reached up and gave me a firm pat on the shoulder. "Whatever happens, you kept your promise, Gin. You found a way to save Liam. Now it's up to the rest of us to execute your plan."

At this moment, Silvio's confidence and belief meant more to me than anyone else's—because he and especially Liam had the most to lose if things went sideways.

I pushed aside my own lingering doubts. It was time to act now—for better or worse. "Let's go rescue Liam."

Silvio drove the two of us downtown and parked in the same garage down the street from the Bellum Bank that we had used for all our adventures so far this week. We got out of his van, went over to the railing, and peered down at the street below.

It was right at eleven thirty, and everything was proceeding as normal on this cold, clear March day. People were streaming out of the surrounding office buildings to eat or do errands on their lunch breaks, while cars and trucks were cruising along the streets. I eyed the Bellum Bank in the distance, but folks were trudging up and down the steps and entering and exiting the building like usual.

The only things out of place were several bright orange traffic cones that had been set out on the street outside the bank. The cones blocked off a large space directly in front of the bank entrance, but I didn't see any construction workers milling around. Odd but not particularly sinister.

"Any sign of Mason or Emery yet?" I asked.

Silvio swiped through several screens on his tablet. "I don't see them on the traffic cameras, but they could already be holed up in one of the nearby buildings. Several giants are loitering on the sidewalks, though."

So Mason's goons were already here, although the man himself probably wouldn't show up until the last possible second, just to screw with my head. Good. So far, things were going exactly how I'd expected.

"Is everyone in position?"

Silvio pulled out his phone and scrolled through several text messages. "Everyone is ready."

"All right. Time for me to show myself."

Silvio reached out and squeezed my arm. I flashed him a smile, then went down the stairs and exited the parking garage.

As soon as I stepped out onto the sidewalk, a couple of giants wearing black suits snapped to attention at the far end of the block. I squared my shoulders, lifted my chin, and walked straight toward them.

"Beautiful day for a bank heist," I drawled.

The two giants gave me flat looks, but they didn't step forward and hassle me. I ignored them, waited for the light to change, and crossed the street. As I walked along, I spotted several more pairs of giants lingering in doorways and loitering at food carts. I smiled and waved at them all, but the men and women merely glared at me in return.

I made my way over to the park in the center of the roundabout. A couple more giants were standing by an ice-cream cart, pretending to check their phones. I smiled and waved at them too, then walked over and stopped in front of the bronze plaque at the base of the statue of Marisol Patton.

The statue looked just the same as when I had walked by it two days ago—Marisol clutching a bucket in one hand, with her other fist raised high in the air. In a way, I found it weirdly appropriate that I was standing in her shadow. Marisol had saved Ashland from burning to the ground way back when, and now I was trying to save the Pork Pit from utter destruction.

Out of the corner of my eye, I spotted a black SUV creeping up the street. The vehicle pulled over to the roundabout curb and stopped, and a giant leaped out and opened the back passenger's-side door.

Mason Mitchell slithered out into the bright, sunny day.

He was wearing a navy overcoat and a matching suit. The noon sun bounced off his dark brown hair, even as it cast his face in shadow. Mason strode forward, but the giant stayed by the SUV. My uncle wasn't bringing any guards with him. Overconfident fool. I might not be able to kill him, but if everything went according to my plan, I was going to wound him in ways he couldn't possibly imagine.

Mason stopped beside me. He read the plaque, then stared up at Marisol's triumphant figure. "I've always hated this statue."

"Why?" I asked, wondering what he could possibly have against a woman from the early 1900s.

"What did Marisol Patton do that was so grand? She saved a few hovels and shacks from a fire. Big deal. She should have just let them burn so that the city could start over, build something bigger and better. Instead, people erected a statue of her, right in the middle of prime downtown real estate." His lips curled back in disgust. "What a waste of space."

I wanted to snap back that he was the only thing here that was a waste of space, but I reined in my temper. "Where's Liam?"

"Money first, traitor second," Mason said.

"No. I want to see Liam. Right now. Or you won't get one single penny out of that vault."

Mason turned toward me. Anger flared in his gray eyes, and a wave of Stone magic rippled off him and sank into the statue, causing Marisol to sway precariously on her perch.

I bared my teeth at him. "Go ahead. Drop that statue on my head. Flatten me like a pancake. But you still won't get a penny out of that vault, because I'm the only one who knows the code. Not even your new buddies the Yangs can open the vault without the code. At least, not without going to a whole lot of trouble."

I was lying, of course. Finn knew the vault code, as did Owen, Bria, and Silvio, but Mason didn't need to know that. Besides, the angrier my uncle was, the more mistakes he might make.

"Show me Liam. Right now," I repeated. "Or the deal is off."

"You walk away, and your traitor dies," Mason hissed. "And we both know you're far too weak to let that happen."

He was right. I would do just about anything to prevent Liam's death, so bluffing was my only option. "Well, if you don't want your money back, then it can sit in Fletcher's vault collecting dust for a few more years."

More anger flared in Mason's eyes, and the statue swayed on its perch again, like it was made of melting scoops of ice cream that were about to topple out of their cone, instead of slabs of solid stone. I crossed my arms over my chest and stared at my uncle, silently daring him to kill me.

Several seconds ticked by. Suddenly, the magic vanished from Mason's gaze, and the statue solidified and snapped back into place.

Mason shot me another angry glare, then turned and waved his hand. The giant standing by the SUV at the curb spoke into his phone. He flashed Mason a thumbs-up, and my uncle faced me again.

"You want to see your traitor? There he is." He gestured at one of the buildings across the street.

At first, I didn't see what he was pointing at, but then a glass door opened on the fifth floor, and two giants stepped out onto a balcony. Liam was hanging limply between the two men, although one of them gave him a vicious shake, prompting my friend to slowly raise his head.

Black eyes, broken nose, battered body, rumpled suit. Liam didn't look any better than he had when I'd seen him outside the Pork Pit yesterday, but he didn't look any worse either. I let out a quiet sigh of relief that Emery hadn't tortured him further.

Still, Liam's location was a problem. I'd been hoping that Mason would keep my friend down here on the street, maybe tucked away in another SUV, but my uncle was literally dangling Liam over my head, like a juicy steak that had been hoisted up into a tree to keep a black bear from eating it.

Frustration filled me, but I couldn't help Liam. No, right now, all I could do was go into the bank, follow through with my plan, and rely on my friends to play their parts.

Mason looked down his nose at me. "You've seen Mr. Carter. Now, let me repeat my warning from yesterday. If you try anything funny—anything at all—then my men will toss Liam off that balcony." A cold smile curved his lips. "Part of me hopes that you do try something. It would be so much fun to watch Liam splatter all over the sidewalk."

It was a good thing he'd told me not to bring my knives. Because in that moment, I would have happily given in to my rage, palmed a blade, and tried to cut his throat with it, even though I knew how useless it would be.

"Fine," I muttered through gritted teeth. "I'll behave. Now, let's get this over with."

Mason gave me another cold smile. "As you wish."

Once again, he gestured at the giant by the SUV, who murmured something into his phone. The giant flashed Mason another thumbs-up.

Instead of heading toward the bank, my uncle took a seat on one of the black wrought-iron benches. Then he made a dismissive, shooing motion with his hand. "Go ahead, Genevieve. Your chariot awaits."

I had no idea what he was talking about, but I had no choice but to walk around the statue, head through the far side of the park, and cross the street. I'd just made it to the bottom of the bank steps when a large moving truck rumbled up to the curb and parked in the empty space created by those orange traffic cones I'd noticed earlier. Definitely not a chariot—more like a getaway vehicle.

The passenger's-side door opened, and Emery Slater hopped down. The giant had shed her usual pantsuit in favor of a black leather jacket over a red turtleneck sweater, black cargo pants, and boots. Despite the jacket, I spotted the gun she was wearing on her hip. Looked like Emery wasn't going to rely solely on her giant strength to try to kill me. Smart.

The driver, a male giant, remained in his seat, but Emery went around to the back of the vehicle. She rolled up the panel, and half a dozen giants wearing heavy-duty gray coveralls and black boots hopped out of the truck.

The giants reached inside the truck and pulled out three large, deep carts, like the kind a hotel might use to store dirty laundry. Six giants and three carts were more than enough to remove every last dollar from Fletcher's vault. Emery had certainly come prepared.

Then again, so had I.

The giants set the carts on the sidewalk. Emery looked over the men and the carts, then nodded, as if satisfied.

All around us, people kept moving along the sidewalk, while vehicles kept cruising along the street. No one batted an eye at the moving truck, the giants, or the carts. Most people were so wrapped up in their phones that they didn't even glance in this direction. The few folks who did shoot us curious looks ducked their heads and hurried on. No one wanted to mess with seven giants, especially Emery, who was glaring at me like she wanted to rip me limb from limb with her bare hands.

Emery stepped forward so that she was standing right in front of me, then started massaging her knuckles, which *pop-pop-popped* like firecrackers.

I tipped my head back and peered up into her face. "Are you going to glare at me all day, or are we going to get your boss's money?"

Emery's hands stilled, although rage flared in her eyes, making them burn a bright hazel, and her mouth pinched into a thin, angry line. For a moment, I thought she was going to punch me, but then her face twisted into a sneer, and she swept her hand out to the side in an overly dramatic gesture.

"After you, Blanco," she purred.

I eyed the giant, knowing that she was going to try to kill me the first chance she got, but I had no choice but to turn my back to her and trudge up the steps to the Bellum Bank.

✿ 19 ✿

A giant wearing a black security uniform, a brimmed hat, and aviator sunglasses was guarding the entrance. The giant, who had shaggy black hair, a black mustache, and ebony skin, glanced at me and Emery, then eyed the men carrying the laundry carts up the steps. But the guard didn't say anything, and he didn't move from his position, so I walked past him, pushed through one of the glass doors, and stepped into the lobby.

Gray marble floor and walls, brass chandeliers hanging overhead, wooden desks scattered here and there, the enormous eagle clutching arrows in its talons carved into the back wall. The Bellum Bank looked exactly the same as it had the last time I'd been in here two days ago, right down to the guards dressed in black uniforms and brimmed hats who were lining the lobby. The guards were a mix of men and women of varying shapes, sizes, and ages, but they all stood at attention, watching everyone who moved through the lobby.

"Quit dawdling," Emery growled behind me.

I did as commanded and headed toward one of the tellers who was encased in bulletproof glass at the counter along the back wall. She was quite pretty, with long black hair and toffee skin, and square black glasses covered her toffee eyes.

The woman gave me a polite smile. "May I help you?"

"I'm here to access my vault."

Her gaze flicked to Emery and the six giants who were lurking behind me, but her smile never wavered. "One moment, please."

She picked up the phone by her elbow and spoke into the receiver in a low voice. A few seconds later, she replaced the phone and gave me another polite smile. "Ms. Yang will be with you shortly."

The teller had barely finished speaking before the door set into the back wall buzzed open, and Drusilla Yang appeared. The Fire elemental was wearing another one of her power pantsuits, cool white today, along with crimson lipstick and heels, and the silverstone skeleton key dangled from the long chain around her neck like usual. She probably slept with the key tucked under her pillow, just like I did with one of my knives.

Drusilla stopped in front of me. "Ms. Blanco, so lovely to see you again. My father told me to expect you and your...friends."

I held back a derisive snort. Of course, Mason would have called Charles Yang to pave Emery's way into the bank. I just hoped Drusilla kept her word—and held up her end of our bargain.

Drusilla's dark brown gaze cut to Emery, then to the six male giants clustered around the three empty laundry carts. "Making a withdrawal?"

"Something like that," I muttered.

Drusilla tipped her head. "Very well. Follow me."

She turned and strode toward the open door in the back wall. Emery sneered at me and dramatically swept her hand out to the side again, indicating that I should go first. Once again, I had no choice but to move forward.

A uniformed guard with short red hair, rosy skin, blue eyes, and silver glasses held the door open for Drusilla and me, along with the rest of my dangerous entourage. The female guard didn't bat an eye at the odd procession of people or the loud, annoying rattles of the three laundry carts. Neither did anyone else in the lobby. I doubted it was the strangest thing they had ever seen.

I just hoped this didn't turn out to be the bloodiest day they had ever seen.

But all I could do now was let my scheme play out, so I stepped through the door, moving deeper into the bank—and the tangled web of danger I had created for myself.

Drusilla led us through the corridors, just like she had when Finn and I had been here two days ago. I glanced into the glass-fronted offices set into the walls, but they were all deserted. Good. The fewer people here, the better it would be for everyone.

No one spoke, and the only sound was the giants' heavy footsteps, punctuated by the incessant squeaks of the cart wheels rolling across the floor. As I followed Drusilla, I kept my head turned slightly to the side, staring at the reflections of Emery and the other giants in the smooth marble walls. So far, everyone was behaving themselves, although all bets would be off as soon as I opened the vault.

Drusilla led us to the freight elevator and used her skeleton key to summon it. No guards were stationed here today, although several security cameras were trained on the area. The seconds dragged by in tense silence, and the bright, cheery *ding!* of the car arriving sounded as loud as a gunshot.

It was a tight fit, but we all squeezed inside the space, along with the laundry carts. Drusilla turned her key again and punched the button for the vault level, and the elevator drifted down, down, down.

No one spoke, although Emery crossed her arms over her chest and glared at me. I ignored her and focused on the six male giants. None of them had any elemental magic, which was good, but they all looked exceptionally tough, strong, and muscled, even for giants, which was bad. Since I'd been forced to leave my knives at home, I would have to blast the men with my Ice and Stone magic if they tried to kill me.

Or, rather, *when* they tried to kill me.

The elevator floated to a stop, and the metal grate rattled back.

Drusilla stepped out of the elevator, and yet again, I had no choice but to follow her, with Emery and the other giants trailing along behind me.

Two guards wearing black uniforms and brimmed hats pulled down low on their foreheads were stationed outside the elevator. Both guards were tall, muscled men with dark brown hair, silver glasses, and tan skin, although neither one of them was a giant. Drusilla flashed her silverstone key at them, then strode off down the corridor.

Once again, we walked in silence. With every mirror we passed and every corner we turned, more and more tension bubbled up inside my body, simmering in my veins like molten lava, but I shoved the emotion away, along with my worry.

The time for feelings was over, and I needed to focus on making sure Emery got exactly what she wanted—and that all the innocent people got out of the bank alive.

Finally, Drusilla reached Fletcher's vault at the end of the corridor. She inserted her skeleton key into the lock, then turned it. Three clicks sounded.

Drusilla removed her key, let it fall back down against her chest, and stepped aside. "If that's all you need, I'll be on my way."

She turned to go, but Emery blocked her path.

"Why don't you stick around?" Emery said. "I'd hate for Blanco to do something stupid, like try to renege on the deal she made with Mason."

Drusilla shook her head. "I don't get involved in disputes between clients. You know that. Besides, my father and Mason came to an agreement. I was to let you bring Ms. Blanco down here to access her vault. Nothing more, nothing less."

Drusilla started to step around the giant, but Emery moved to the side, once again blocking the other woman's path.

The giant's lips drew back into a razor-sharp smile. "I do know that—and I don't care. You're not going anywhere."

Magic flared in Drusilla's eyes, and an invisible wave of heat blasted off her, warming the chilly air. "If you do this, then you—and especially Mason—are making an enemy out of the Bellum Bank." The Fire elemental's voice was ice-cold, despite the hot magic surging off her body. "Perhaps you want to reconsider."

Emery laughed, her low, sinister chuckles bouncing off the walls. "Please. Mason has been secretly running most of the crime in this town for years from the shadows. What do you think is going to happen when he steps out into the light with his shiny new development project? He'll have even *more* power. And it's all thanks to your family's bank. The deal is done, and your father is giving Mason all the money he needs to take complete control of Ashland. Too bad you're going to wind up as collateral damage."

Drusilla's lips pinched together, but she didn't respond to the giant. She didn't look at me either. If she had, I would have said *I told you so*, as childish as that would have been.

Emery looked at me. "Open the vault, Blanco. Or my men will start shooting."

One of the male giants drew a gun from the pocket of his coveralls and aimed it at Drusilla's chest. The Fire elemental stiffened, but she didn't say anything.

"Don't make me ask you again," Emery warned. "I doubt Drusilla wants to get blood all over her pretty white suit."

I didn't have a choice, so I stepped over to the keypad and entered the *Pork Pit* code. Three more clicks sounded, and the mirrored door popped open.

Emery gestured at me. "Open the door. And no tricks."

I took hold of the edge of the door and swung it open. The door easily creaked back, revealing the same sight as the last time I had been down here with Finn: shelves crammed full of money, watches, necklaces, and other valuables.

"Now, *this* is what I'm talking about," Emery said, a note of reverent awe in her voice. She stared into the vault a moment longer, then waved her hand at me. "Go inside. I want to make sure you haven't booby-trapped anything."

I rolled my eyes, but I stepped inside the vault. I turned around and stopped, holding my hands out wide. "Satisfied?"

Emery shook her head. "Nope, not even close. Walk around the vault. Pick up some of the money and put it back down."

And people thought I was paranoid. Still, Emery was right to be cautious. If I'd had more time, I would have *totally* rigged up some booby traps. Why, nothing would have given me greater pleasure than to torch Mason's cash with some incendiary devices. But I hadn't had the chance to do that, so I strode from one side of the vault to the other, picking up some of the shrink-wrapped bricks of fifties and hundreds and setting them back down again, along with a few rolls of the smaller bills. I even hoisted a couple of the gold bars into the air and pressed them up over my head like dumbbells before returning them to the shelves.

I ended up behind the table in the middle of the room, where the *Reverie in Gray* painting was propped up against those bags of coins. My gaze dropped to the tabletop, where Fletcher had spelled out *Gin* with all those coins, my spider rune dotting the *i* in my name.

My heart twinged with equal parts pride and worry, and I patted my jeans pocket, feeling the penny Finn had taken out of the center of my spider rune. I'd brought it along for luck, and I had a feeling I was going to need every cent of good fortune that I could get.

"I would do some cartwheels, but I suck at them, and there's not enough room in here to do them anyway," I drawled.

"Watch her," Emery ordered the giant with the gun. "If she so much as twitches, then shoot her in the head."

The man nodded and aimed his weapon at me. Emery stepped inside the vault, glancing at the money and trinkets on the shelves. Finally, she looked over at the table where I was still standing. Her gaze roamed over the *Reverie in Gray* painting before landing on the coins that spelled out my name.

She snorted. "What's this? Some sort of lame-ass art project?"

I shrugged. "Apparently, Fletcher had a lot of time on his hands, sitting in here counting your boss's money."

A cruel grin spread across Emery's face, and she leaned down and swiped her forearm across the table, sending all the *Gin* coins flying through the air. I couldn't stop myself from flinching. The coins *tink-tink-tinked* all around the vault, many of them rolling underneath the shelves before rattling to a stop.

"Oops," Emery purred.

Rage roared through me that she had ruined Fletcher's message, but that male giant still had his gun pointed at my chest, so I had no choice but to stand there and stew in my own anger.

Emery bent down and peered at the painting. "I don't see what the big deal is about this, but Mason says it's worth a few million bucks." She straightened up and waved her hand at her men. "Grab it, along with everything else. You two, watch Blanco and Yang. Move. Now."

The first giant kept his gun aimed at me, while a second man pulled out a gun and trained his weapon on Drusilla. The other four men hurried into the vault. I started to step back out of their way, but Emery waggled her finger at me.

"Uh-uh. You stay put, Blanco." She grinned as though a particularly evil idea had just popped into her mind, then reached over and shoved one of the bags of coins off the table.

The bag hit the floor with a dull *thud*, then tipped over, spilling pennies everywhere in a shower of bright copper.

Emery's grin widened. "Now, Blanco, you're going to pick up all those pennies and stuff them back into that bag. Every last one."

Spiteful, petty bitch. My hands itched with the urge to shove pennies down her throat until she choked on them, but the giants were still pointing their guns at Drusilla and me, so I dropped to my knees and dutifully scooped the pennies back into the bag.

Under Emery's watchful eyes, the four male giants went through the vault like human vacuum cleaners sucking up every last bit of loot in their path. They attacked the wall filled with the shrink-wrapped bricks of fifties and hundreds first and loaded them into one cart, along with the painting.

Next, they moved over to the wall of tens and twenties and put the rolled bills in a second cart, along with all the loose ones, fives, and tens. For the finishing touch, all the watches, necklaces, and other trinkets got dumped into the third and final cart, along with the gold bars and the bags of coins.

It didn't take long, no more than thirty minutes. When the giants had cleared out the vault, Emery crooked her finger at me, and I stepped back out into the mirrored hallway.

Drusilla was still out here as well, although she had remained silent this whole time. She must have known there was no use trying to reason with Emery. I made sure to keep my distance from the Fire elemental. I didn't know what Emery had planned for me, but I didn't want Drusilla to get caught in the crossfire.

Emery stared out over the carts full of money and valuables, a greedy look filling her face. The other six giants were also staring at the money with covetous expressions.

"You could keep some of this for yourselves," I said. "Mason's not here. He doesn't know exactly how much cash is in the vault. You could skim some off the top, and he would never know the difference."

Emery's blond eyebrows shot up. "Trying to bribe me into betraying my boss, Blanco?"

I shrugged. "Just pointing out an obvious fact. Mason doesn't strike me as the kind of man who pays his employees particularly well. Especially not for the danger that you and your men put yourselves in by coming here with me."

A couple of the male giants nodded, and agreement flickered across Emery's face before she could hide it. She kept staring at the carts full of money, clearly tempted.

Drusilla cleared her throat and stepped forward. "There are dozens of other vaults down here. I know the codes to many of them. I could open them for you."

Emery glanced at the other woman. "Trying to bribe me not to kill you?"

Drusilla shrugged much the same way that I had. "Just trying to negotiate the best outcome for everyone."

Emery snorted. "A businesswoman to the bitter end, eh? I can respect that." Her face hardened. "But it's not going to save you."

She waved her hand, and the two giants with guns stepped forward.

"You see, this isn't just about Mason getting his money. He also wants to make sure that Gin isn't a problem anymore. And what better way to do that than by having the Spider tragically assassinate the banker who was only trying to help her?"

I cursed. "You're going to make it look like *I* killed Drusilla. You're going to frame me for her murder, so that Charles Yang and the rest of his family come after me."

It was a smart plan, and I was a bit envious I hadn't thought of it myself.

A cruel grin twisted Emery's lips, and a cold light sparked in her eyes. "Well, that's Mason's plan. He told me to lock you in the vault and let the Yangs deal with you. But *I* think it would be so much better if Drusilla managed to kill you before she succumbed to her own injuries."

Emery pulled the gun out of the holster on her belt and

aimed it at me. Another grin split her face. "Good-bye, Blanco."

Her finger curled back on the trigger, and I reached for my Stone magic, ready to harden my skin to protect myself—

"Ms. Yang?" A voice boomed down the hallway. "Are you okay?"

Startled, Emery whirled around, as did the other six giants. I used their distraction to inch closer to the laundry carts, creeping up on the one filled with the bags of coins. Drusilla eyed me, clearly wondering what I was doing, but she didn't move.

Footsteps sounded, and the two security guards who'd been stationed by the elevator appeared at the far end of the hallway.

"Ms. Yang?" one of the guards called out again.

Emery glanced over her shoulder. "Tell him that everything is fine," she hissed.

Drusilla waved her hand at the guards. "I'm okay. Just helping the clients move a few last things out of their vault. You two can return to your posts."

But her words didn't reassure the guards. Instead of turning around, they kept moving in this direction. The man in front frowned, his gaze sweeping from Emery with her gun to Drusilla and back again.

"Ms. Yang?" he asked. "What's going on?"

Drusilla smiled at him, but it was a tense expression. "Everything's fine. Go back to your station. I'll be along shortly."

But instead of doing what she asked, the guard kept creeping forward, eyeing Emery and the other giants with suspicion.

"Ms. Yang, you should come with me," the guard said. "We can help these folks move their money."

"I'm fine," Drusilla repeated, although it was obvious that no one believed her, especially not her own men.

The two guards slowed, and their hands drifted down to the guns on their belts.

"Oh, fuck this," Emery muttered. She waved her hand at the other giants. "Kill them all! Now!"

✳ 20 ✳

mery whirled around and aimed her gun at Drusilla. I grabbed hold of my Stone magic, hardening my skin, and darted in front of the other woman.

Crack!

Emery fired, and the bullet slammed into my chest. It would have killed me if I hadn't been using my Stone magic to protect myself. Even then, it still hurt, as though the giant had sucker-punched me in the middle of my sternum. I gasped, trying to suck air back down into my lungs.

Crack! Crack! Crack!

Emery kept firing at me. Each bullet drove me back, and I rammed into Drusilla, making her stagger into one of the mirrored vault doors on the opposite side of the corridor. One of my boots slipped, and I had to use the wall to catch myself. Drusilla bounced off the mirror, then spun around and sprinted toward the two guards, who had drawn their own weapons.

For a moment, the only sound was the rapid *snap-snap-snap-snap* of Drusilla's heels on the floor, but then Emery cursed and raised her gun again.

"What are you waiting for?" she yelled. "Shoot them, you idiots!"

Even though Drusilla was running away, trying to escape, Emery still fired at her, as did the two male giants who'd drawn their guns.

Crack!

Crack! Crack!

Crack! Crack! Crack!

Shot after shot rang out, and bullets zipped every which way down the corridor, cracking into the marble walls. Some of the bullets slammed into the mirrored vault doors. The glass shattered on impact, although the stone underneath remained whole and intact.

Drusilla reached the two guards, then whirled around, elemental Fire exploding on her fingertips. She reared back her hand to throw her magic, but Emery took more careful aim and fired another shot.

Crack!

This bullet punched into Drusilla's chest, and she screamed and crumpled to the floor. The Fire snuffed out on her fingertips, and she didn't move after that.

"No!" one of the guards yelled.

He started to bend down to help her, but—*crack!*— another shot from Emery sent him tumbling to the floor as well.

Crack! Crack! Crack!

A hail of gunfire from the other two giants dropped the second guard, who screamed, pitched forward, and sprawled on the floor on top of Drusilla and the first guard. My heart squeezed tight, but I couldn't do anything to help them— except kill Emery and her men.

I sucked down another breath and pushed away from the wall, heading straight toward my enemies.

Emery must have seen me move out of the corner of her eye, because she swung around in my direction. "Kill Blanco!"

She pulled the trigger, but her gun clicked empty. Emery cursed and stopped to reload, as did the other two giants with guns. The other four men stayed by the carts, as though they didn't know whether to wade into the fight or not.

I darted forward and grabbed a bag of pennies off the top of one of the laundry carts. The bag was much heavier than I expected it to be, but I latched onto it with both hands, hefted it up and back like a baseball bat, and swung it at Emery as hard as I could.

Tink-tink-tink.

Several pennies flew out of the top of the open bag and bounced off the walls, but the main solid mass of coins slammed straight into Emery's face, causing her to grunt with pain. I'd put so much force behind the blow that the momentum ripped the bag clean out of my hands, but that was okay, because the whole thing exploded all over Emery.

Tink-tink-tink.

Tink-tink-tink.

Tink-tink-tink.

For a moment, the giant looked like some sort of mythological goddess, with pennies cascading down all around her like bright copper teardrops. She growled, shook off the coins like a dog slinging water off its coat, and waded through the carpet of pennies toward me. I snarled, used my magic to make a long, jagged Ice dagger, and stepped toward her—

One of the male giants grabbed her shoulder. "Forget Blanco! We have to get the money out of here! Before more guards trap us down here!"

Emery glared at me, clearly wanting to finish what we'd started, but she jerked her head at the other giants. "Get the carts to the elevator!"

The six men hurried to do as she commanded. I tightened my grip on my Ice dagger and charged forward, wanting to end her right here and now.

Emery gave me a cool look, then snapped up her gun and pulled the trigger.

Crack!

Another bullet punched into my chest. I was still holding on to my Stone magic, so the bullet bounced harmlessly off my body, just like the others had, but the hard blow still tossed me sideways. My hand slammed into the wall, shattering my Ice dagger into cold chunks. Even worse, my boots slipped on the thousands of pennies littering the floor, my feet flew out from under me, and I landed hard on my ass on top of the coins. I cursed and struggled to get to my feet, but my boots kept sliding every which way, on the coins and on the slick marble underneath.

"Move! Move! Move!" Emery yelled, backpedaling the whole time.

The giants pushed the carts to the end of the hallway, careened around the corner, and disappeared from view. Emery followed them. The giants' heavy, thudding footsteps quickly grew faint and dim, as did the annoying squeaking of the laundry carts' wheels.

Still cursing, I finally managed to crawl out of the field of pennies, lurch to my feet, and stagger down the hallway.

Drusilla and the two guards were lying on the floor where they'd fallen, and bright red stains dotted the Fire elemental's white pantsuit. I didn't have time to check their vitals, so I skirted around them and started running, moving from one hallway to the next.

I rushed around the corner and sprinted into the corridor that led to the freight elevator—

Crack!

Another bullet from Emery's gun blasted against my chest. I was still protecting myself with my Stone magic, so this bullet rattled away like the other ones had, but it did slow me down. I growled in frustration and charged forward again.

But I was too late.

The six giants had already shoved the three carts into the elevator, and Emery took hold of the grate and slammed it shut right in my face.

I grabbed hold of the bars, rattling the metal, but I couldn't budge the grate.

Emery grinned at me. "Have fun explaining this to Charles Yang, especially how you murdered his daughter. Maybe he'll do you a favor and kill you quickly with his Fire magic. I hope not, though."

She sneered at me a moment longer, then used the barrel of her gun to stab the elevator button. Emery snapped up the weapon and gave me a mocking salute with it as the elevator rose, whisking away her, the giants, and the carts.

I slammed my hand on the grate a few times, even though I knew it was pointless. Anger and frustration pounded through me, but I forced myself to rein in my emotions and think. By the time the elevator returned, Emery and the giants would be long gone with the money—but the elevator wasn't the only way out of here.

I whirled around, my gaze darting over to the emergency door set into the wall, the one I had noticed when Finn and I had first come down here. I sprinted over to the door and twisted the knob, but it was locked, so I blasted the knob with my Ice magic, then cracked away the cold crystals. The knob shattered in my hand, and I wrenched the door open and hurried through to the other side.

I charged up the emergency stairs, taking the steps two at a time. The vault level was several floors underground, and I was huffing and puffing by the time I reached the top of the stairs. As much as I wanted to put my shoulder down and barrel through the door to the other side, I didn't know where it opened up in the bank, so I forced myself to twist the knob and carefully crack the door open instead.

For once, luck was on my side, and the door led into the main lobby, although I didn't remember seeing it before. It must be designed to blend in with the rest of the wall or perhaps hidden behind a mirror, like so many things seemed to be around here.

I glanced out into the lobby, but everything was the same as before. People coming and going, other folks sitting at the desks with bankers helping them, tellers working behind the bulletproof glass, guards lining the walls.

My heart plummeted. Had I been too slow? Had Emery and the giants already left—

Squeak-squeak-squeak.

A familiar sound caught my ear, and I looked to my right. The elevator must have taken longer than I'd thought, because Emery was just now striding into the lobby, with three of the male giants flanking her and three more pushing the carts.

"Move!" Emery barked out. "Or get run over!"

Everyone scrambled away from the giants and the loud, rattling carts. A few folks shot covetous looks at all the money whizzing by them, but the cold, flat expression on Emery's face, as well as the tense, watchful looks of the other giants, kept them from trying anything. Money was no good if you weren't alive to spend it.

Emery and the giants were busy staring at the people in front of them, so I slipped out from behind the emergency door, darted over to an empty desk, and hunkered down behind it. Then I peered around the side of the wood.

People were still moving out of Emery's path, and she was about halfway across the lobby. I needed to act now if I had any chance of stopping the giants before they got outside. Because once the money was gone, so was any leverage I had to stop Mason from ordering his men to throw Liam off that balcony.

Of course, I was hoping Silvio and my other friends had already found a way to rescue Liam, but I couldn't take the chance that they hadn't, and I needed to do everything in my power to buy them some more time.

So I scurried over to another desk and crouched down behind it. The people loitering in the lobby had forced Emery and the giants to slow down, so I was able to draw even with them. But I still needed to do something to further delay them, so I leaned forward, placed my hand on the floor, and reached for my Ice magic. Cold crystals shot out from my palm and snaked across the floor, their subtle silvery sheen the only clue that they were creeping toward the giants.

I fed even more of my Ice magic into the stream of crystals surging across the floor. Instead of targeting Emery and the three giants flanking her, I concentrated on the three men at the back of the pack, with their carts full of loot.

The first giant reached my elemental Ice field. He pushed the cart in front of him and trudged along behind it. Disappointment and frustration surged through me. Apparently, I hadn't created enough Ice to make him slip and fall—

The giant's feet flew out from under him, and the cart skittered out of his reach. He landed flat on his back on the floor, his head snapping against the marble with a loud, audible *crack*.

Emery whirled around. "What was that?"

I surged up from behind the desk and raced across the lobby. The first giant was still down on the floor, dazed and confused, so I reached for my Ice magic and flung a spray of daggers out at him. Several of the daggers punched into the giant's throat, and he started choking to death on his own blood.

I leaped over the dying man and charged at the giant manning the second cart. His eyes widened, and he released the cart and fumbled for the gun in his coveralls pocket. I put my shoulder down and rammed into the second man, knocking him even farther away from the cart.

That giant reached out and latched onto me, and the two of us went down in a heap in the middle of the lobby. He snarled and tried to raise his gun to shoot me, but I ripped the weapon out of his hand, then shoved the barrel up against his stomach and pulled the trigger three times.

Crack! Crack! Crack!

The giant screamed and flopped back down onto the ground. He grabbed my arm, ripping the gun out of my grasp and sending it sliding across the floor. I didn't have time to chase after the weapon, so I scrambled to my feet and charged toward the third man, who was still standing behind his cart.

This giant already had his gun out, and he aimed his weapon and pulled the trigger.

Crack!

The bullet blasted against my stomach, momentarily knocking the wind out of me, despite my Stone-hardened skin.

"Get the carts, and get out of here!" Emery screamed. "I'll take care of Blanco!"

I sucked down a breath and kept going, ramming my shoulder into the third man, who lost his grip on his gun and staggered away. Then I whirled back around to face Emery, who was storming toward me, a murderous expression on her face.

By this point, the customers were yelling and screaming, trying to figure out how they could stay out of the line of fire. Most people hunkered down behind the desks and chairs, while a few made a beeline for the glass doors. Several of the guards along the walls moved forward, yelling at me, Emery, and everyone else to stop, although the crowd of panicked people kept pushing them back and rendering them useless.

Emery shoved a man out of her way, sending him crashing down to the floor. She stepped over him, her angry gaze focused on me and her hands clenched into tight fists. I didn't have my knives, so I lurched over and grabbed a letter opener off one of the desks, along with a mug emblazoned with the Bellum Bank's eagle symbol.

Emery put her head down, stretched her arms out wide, and lunged forward like a linebacker trying to tackle a quarterback. I spun to the side, away from her angry, reckless charge, and lashed out with the letter opener. But it was a dull, pitiful little blade, and it didn't even cut through her clothes, much less break her skin. Cursing, I tossed the letter opener aside, still gripping the mug in my other hand.

Emery snarled, whirled around, and charged at me again. The giant swung her fists in vicious arcs, trying to land a one-two combo that probably would have shattered my ribs, but I avoided her blows and stepped in even closer to her body. I couldn't hurt her with my own fists, so I decided to improvise.

Before Emery could try to punch me again, I smashed the mug into her nose, much like I had the bag of pennies outside the vault. The ceramic mug shattered on impact, and I snapped up my other hand and blasted the bitch with my Ice magic, turning all those sharp shards into cold daggers that I sent shooting straight into her face.

Emery screamed and clawed at her skin, trying to dislodge the icy shards, which stuck out of her cheeks, nose, and chin like oddly shaped porcupine quills. Blood trickled down her face, spattering onto her clothes.

I reached for my Ice magic again and created a long, jagged knife. Then I lifted my weapon, determined to punch it into her neck, eye, or anything else soft and squishy that I could reach.

Emery must have sensed me coming, because she lashed out again. This time, she got lucky, and one of her fists clipped my right shoulder, sending me spinning away. Despite my Stone-hardened skin, pain exploded in the joint and rippled all the way down my arm. My fingers went numb, and I lost my grip on my Ice dagger, which hit the floor and shattered into a dozen pieces.

Since I couldn't feel my right arm, I formed another Ice dagger with my left hand. I wasn't as strong and accurate with my left hand, but I'd make it work. I'd clutch the dagger between my teeth, my toes even, if that meant finally killing her.

Instead of coming at me again, Emery backpedaled. I started toward her, but she reached out, grabbed one of the desks, and yanked it forward, shoving it between us. The people who'd been hiding behind the desk screamed and scrambled back on their hands and knees, trying to get out of the way of the wild melee.

I pulled up short, trying to stop, but I was moving too fast and was too committed to my charge, and my legs rammed straight into the side of the desk. Emery stretched out one of her long arms, grabbed a fistful of my hair, and slammed my head down onto the desk.

The move took me by surprise, and I didn't have time to grab hold of my Stone magic to harden my skin again. Pain spiked through my skull, while white stars exploded in my eyes. My feet flew out from under me, and I slid off the side of the desk and flopped down onto the floor.

"Let's go!" Emery screamed.

The remaining four giants rushed over, grabbed the carts, and steered the containers over to the doors at the front of the lobby. It took the giants a couple of tries, since they were all trying to leave at once, but they rammed the carts through the doors, breaking the glass, and disappeared outside.

I blinked away the last of the stars in my eyes, scrambled to my feet, and chased after them. I ran as fast as I could, even though I had a sick, sinking feeling that I was going to be too late. I took hold of my Stone magic again, then shoved through the ruined doors and charged outside—

Crack! Crack! Crack!

Bullets punched into my chest, one after another, once again sending me staggering backward. I hit the broken doors and bounced off. It took me a few seconds to regain my balance, shake off my daze, and focus on what was in front of me.

The four giants had already maneuvered the laundry carts down the steps and across the sidewalk and were picking up the containers and shoving them into the back of the moving truck one after another.

A few folks strolling along the sidewalk stopped and stared at the giants, as if wondering what all the commotion was about. But a couple of cold glares from the giants had those people turning around and scurrying away from the obvious danger.

Emery was standing on the sidewalk beside the truck, her gun clutched in her hand again. She gave me an evil grin and pulled the trigger. I tensed, not sure if I had enough Stone magic left to protect myself—

Click.

Click-click.

Click.

Emery cursed and lowered her empty gun. For a moment, I thought she might cross the sidewalk, charge up the steps, and attack me again, but a shout cut through the air, drawing her attention.

"We're loaded up! Let's go! Let's go!" One of the giants was hanging out of the back of the moving truck, waving and yelling.

Emery hesitated, clearly torn between trying to kill me and getting while the getting was good. She gave me another murderous glare, then hurried over, yanked open the passenger's-side door, and climbed up into the truck. She slammed the door shut, then leaned out the window.

"Kill the traitor!" she screamed.

It took me a second to realize that she wasn't screaming at whoever might be in earshot but that she was yelling the order into the phone in her hand. My heart leaped up into my throat, and I looked past the truck at the building down the street.

The two giants were still standing on the fifth-floor balcony, with Liam hanging limply between them. I watched in horror as one of the giants nodded, lowered his phone from his ear, and slid it into his pocket. He said something to the other man, who also nodded. Together, they dragged Liam forward, getting ready to toss him off the balcony.

My gaze snapped back to Emery, who gave me a mocking salute. The driver hit the gas, and the moving truck zoomed away from the curb.

I'd lost the money, and now I was going to lose Liam too.

✲ 21 ✲

I ignored the moving truck barreling down the street. I'd told Silvio this wasn't about the money, and I'd meant it. Unfortunately, I had no idea how to save Liam from plummeting to his death. I stood there, paralyzed on the bank steps, knowing that I was too far away to do anything but watch helplessly while the man, the friend, whom I'd sent into this horrible danger cracked against the sidewalk like an egg.

Liam must have finally realized what was happening, because he started struggling. But he was too weak and injured to fight back, and the two giants easily maneuvered him over to the edge of the balcony and the death that was waiting on the sidewalk five stories below—

Crack!

Crack!

Two shots rang out. The first giant's head snapped back, as did the second giant's head, and the two men dropped like bricks, dead from the bullets that had just punched into their skulls.

My gaze zoomed back and forth, finally landing on a figure standing next to the railing on the top of the parking garage.

Finn patted his rifle and waved at me.

I waved back at him. Then I looked over at the balcony again.

Liam was clutching the railing, obviously using it to hold himself upright. The doors flew open behind him, and Silvio ran out onto the balcony. He went over to Liam, gingerly reaching out for the other man.

Liam staggered forward into Silvio's arms, hugging him tight. Silvio hesitated, then hugged Liam back just as tightly. The two of them stood locked together, swaying back and forth, as if they couldn't believe that they were both still alive and holding each other.

Liam was safe. Relief flooded my heart, and a tight knot of tension loosened in my chest.

Silvio drew back and gestured at someone else. A few seconds later, Jo-Jo stepped out onto the balcony. Together, they helped Liam limp inside the building.

More relief surged through me. Not only was Liam still alive, but Jo-Jo could repair all the damage that had been done to him. As for his memories of the beating and the trauma he'd suffered at Emery's hands, well, all I could do was hope the experience wouldn't haunt him too badly—and that he could someday forgive me for everything he'd endured.

My gaze zoomed over to the park in the middle of the roundabout in front of the bank. People strolling along the paths, other folks standing in line at the ice-cream cart, the statue of Marisol Patton looming above it all. Everything was the same as when I'd gone into the bank, with one noticeable exception.

Mason was gone.

I bit back a curse. Of course he was gone. No doubt my uncle had skedaddled the second the giants had rushed out of the bank with the money. Mason had probably seen no need to stick around, since he thought he'd gotten everything he'd wanted.

I couldn't do anything about Mason right now, so I pushed him out of my mind. I still had a whole host of other problems to deal with, starting with everything that had happened inside the bank. So I squared my shoulders, pushed through the broken glass doors, and stepped back inside the building.

Now that Emery and the giants were gone and the danger had departed, everyone inside the lobby was slowly getting to their feet. My gaze swept from one person to another, but it didn't look like anyone had been seriously injured, except for the two giants I'd killed.

A third wave of relief surged through me, loosening several more tight knots of tension in my chest. I had been so, so worried about collateral damage, but it looked like my plan had worked, and that had been kept to a minimum. Still, the chaos of the fight had taken its toll. Chairs had been smashed to pieces, desks had been flipped over onto their sides, and everything from scissors to rubber bands to water bottles littered the floor.

I was still studying the damage when several sets of footsteps scuffed behind me.

"Well, that was certainly far more dramatic than I expected it to be," a feminine voice drawled.

A grin tugged at my lips, and I turned around to find Drusilla Yang standing in front of me.

✳

Drusilla's black hair was mussed, and her white pantsuit was rumpled and ruined, thanks to the bright red stains dotting her jacket, but she too was in one piece. So were the two guards flanking her, the men who had been down on the vault level during the fight with Emery and the giants.

"Well, I'm glad I could give you a chance to flex your acting muscles," I drawled. "You can certainly scream with the best of them. The rest of your death scene was pretty good too."

Drusilla unbuttoned her jacket, revealing the thin silverstone vest she was wearing underneath. Several red dye packs, like the kind banks used to mark money, were taped to the front of her vest, which had caught the bullet Emery had fired at her, the one that had supposedly killed her.

Drusilla rubbed her index finger over the bullet sticking out of the vest. A shudder rippled through her body, and she dropped her hand and raised her gaze to mine. "You were right about Emery. I'm sorry I doubted you."

"Any other criminal in Ashland probably would have followed your no-violence rules, but Emery isn't just any other criminal. Neither is Mason."

Drusilla nodded. "We certainly agree on that now."

Beside her, one of the guards crossed his arms over his chest, staring me down. "And what about us?" he rumbled. "Because the way I remember it, we were outside the vault too, getting shot at by Emery and her crew."

The guard reached up and removed his black brimmed hat, along with his brown wig and silver glasses, revealing his true self—blond hair, blue eyes, and familiar features. Phillip Kincaid grinned at me. "We totally rocked those death scenes. Right, buddy?"

He turned to the other guard, who also removed his hat, brown wig, and silver glasses.

Owen grinned at his best friend. "Oh, yeah. We absolutely *killed* them."

The two of them laughed at his bad joke, then bumped fists.

Drusilla rolled her eyes. "Ugh. Please spare us the bromance."

"Bromances are awesome." Phillip winked at her and held out his fist. "Come on, get in on the action."

While he tried to convince her to join in the fist-bump fun, Owen stepped forward and focused on me. "You okay, Gin?"

"A few bumps and bruises. I've had worse."

Owen's gaze dropped to my chest, and he grimaced at the numerous bullet holes in my fleece jacket and T-shirt. Unlike him, Phillip, and Drusilla, I hadn't worn a silverstone vest to protect myself. I hadn't wanted Emery to be any more suspicious of me.

The giant who'd been standing guard outside the bank walked over to us, along with another guard, the much shorter woman who'd opened the door in the back of the lobby. The giant removed his aviator sunglasses, along with his hat and black wig, and peeled the fake black mustache off his upper lip. The woman also took off her hat, removed her red wig and silver glasses, and shook out her own shaggy blond hair.

Xavier and Bria looked me over the same way Owen had, making sure that I was okay.

"How are you two?" I asked.

Xavier shrugged. "I stayed outside and kept an eye on things, just like you asked, but the driver stayed in the truck the whole time, looking back and forth between the bank and his phone."

"What about Mason? What did he do?"

Xavier shrugged again. "He sat on that bench for a long

time. Eventually, he looked at his phone, like he'd gotten a text, and then left the park, climbed back into his SUV, and vanished. Emery must have sent him a message, saying she had the money." He glanced over at Bria. "A few seconds later, Bria texted me that Emery was in the lobby, so I slipped inside in case a fight broke out, which it did."

"Doesn't it always when Gin is around?" someone added in a teasing tone.

Another person joined our group, removing her wig and glasses and revealing her true features—Roslyn. She was the teller I'd spoken to, the one who had called Drusilla to the lobby.

"You're right," I replied. "Fights usually do break out when I'm around, which is why I'm so grateful that you and everyone else agreed to pretend to be bank employees."

Roslyn grinned, her eyes sparkling in her face. "Are you kidding? It was fun. Reminded me of some theater classes I took in college. I think Lorelei enjoyed it too."

Roslyn waved at another woman dressed like a bank teller, who grinned and returned the gesture. Lorelei waved at me too, then glanced down at Hugh Tucker, who was sitting in a chair. Lorelei had been stationed at one of the lobby desks, along with Tucker, who'd played the part of a bank customer, although he hadn't hit the floor like everyone else when the fight had broken out.

I glanced over the rest of the folks in the lobby, all of whom actually were real bank employees Drusilla had asked to take part in a robbery exercise. That was the story we'd come up with to explain what we were doing, although Drusilla had warned her people that the supposed bank robbers would be using live ammunition.

I had wanted all the volunteers to know exactly what they were getting themselves into, and I had already arranged with Drusilla to compensate them handsomely for their time and especially the danger they had experienced.

One of the bank doors opened, and Finn strolled into the lobby and walked over to me. He stopped and slapped his hands on his hips. "So while I was outside, making two tough shots and saving Liam, you all were just standing around in here."

Drusilla snorted. "Hardly."

He ignored her and kept right on crowing. "Yep, I took care of the bad guys just like I always do. They don't call me Dead-Eye Lane for nothing."

I rolled my eyes. "No one has called you that. *Ever.*"

He grinned. "Well, consider it a new trend."

"How's Liam?" I asked.

Finn shrugged. "He's okay, all things considered. Emery beat him pretty badly, but Silvio, Sophia, and Jo-Jo are taking him to the salon to be healed. He should be okay."

A final knot of tension in my chest loosened. We had all made it through this alive, which had been my main and most important goal.

"So..." Owen said. "Do you think Emery bought it?"

"That she and her men killed Drusilla and got away with the money?" I mentally reviewed everything that had happened. "I think so. Between us and the regular bank employees, we put on a pretty good show. We didn't give Emery a reason *not* to believe it. Besides, most of the time, people see what they *want* to see—or at least what they are *expecting* to see."

I gestured at Xavier. "Like a giant guard standing outside the bank like usual."

Next, I gestured at Phillip and Owen. "And two more guards stationed on the vault level."

Finally, I gestured at Drusilla. "And someone falling to the floor, seemingly dead, after being shot."

Phillip glanced down at the hat, brown wig, and glasses still in his hands. "When you told us your plan this morning, I didn't think it was going to work, especially not on such short notice. I thought for sure that Emery would recognize Owen and me, but she didn't even glance at us." He paused. "At least, not until she started shooting."

"That's because she was completely focused on breaking into the vault and getting away with the money," I replied. "Emery didn't even consider that it might all be an act staged solely for her benefit."

"Well, it wasn't all an act," Roslyn replied. "She did manage to escape with the money."

Finn let out a long, loud, exaggerated sigh. "Yes, the money. Don't remind me. All of that beautiful, beautiful money. All gone." He let out another loud, overly dramatic sigh and stuck his lower lip out in an exaggerated pout.

I laughed.

And laughed.

And laughed some more.

My hearty chuckles echoed from one side of the lobby to the other and back again, and several people started eyeing me, wondering what was going on. I laughed so long, loud, and hard that my ribs ached, and tears gathered in the corners of my eyes.

Xavier frowned. "What's so funny, Gin?"

"Oh, yes," Finn drawled, his eyes narrowing with suspicion. "Please, tell us what is so freaking *amusing* about Emery Slater getting away with millions of dollars."

I finally managed to stop laughing and wipe the tears out of my eyes, although I couldn't keep the smug smile off my face. "Emery didn't get away with millions of dollars of cash, jewelry, or anything else. Why, there's probably only a couple hundred thousand dollars in those carts—total."

"But we all saw the money in the carts," Bria protested. "All those bricks of shrink-wrapped fifties and hundreds. And the gold bars. And the jewelry. And everything else that was in the vault."

"You all saw exactly what I wanted you to see, what *Fletcher* wanted you to see."

Finn stabbed his finger at me. "Okay, Gin. Stop talking in riddles, and tell us what you mean."

I reached into my jeans pocket, pulled out a hundred-dollar bill, and handed it to him. "This is the bill you gave me from that brick of money you opened the first time we went into Fletcher's vault."

"Yeah? So what?" Finn said.

"So look at the serial number. Read it out loud."

He frowned, but he glanced down at the bill. "F8KE…" His eyes widened, and his gaze snapped up to mine. "*Fake*? As in, this bill is *fake*?"

I shot my thumb and forefinger at him. "Got it in one, Bro. Emery didn't get away with the money. All she stole was a bunch of worthless paper."

✲ 22 ✲

My words stunned my friends, rendering them completely, utterly silent. They all blinked and blinked, trying to wrap their minds around my revelation.

Finn rubbed the bill between his fingers. "You know, I didn't pay any attention to it before, but the paper feels… *wrong*." He kept rubbing the bill between his fingers, then held it up to the light. "Oh, yeah. Now I see it. The ink is wrong too, along with the serial number. This is a good fake, but it's still a fake."

Drusilla stalked over and snatched the bill out of Finn's hands. She too rubbed it between her fingers and held it up to the light, examining it with a critical eye. "He's right. This is definitely counterfeit."

Finn reached over and took the bill back. He was never one to let cash out of his sight, even if it was funny money.

Phillip looked at me, his blue eyes narrowing in thought. "So you're telling us that *all* the money in the vault was fake? Every last bill?"

"Well, I didn't get a chance to look at very much of it,

thanks to Emery, but no, I don't think that *all* the money was fake. Just most of it."

"But what about the gold bars?" Xavier asked.

"Those were fake too. I didn't realize it until I picked them up, but the bars weren't quite heavy and dense enough to be real gold. My guess is that Fletcher spray-painted some bricks to make them look like gold."

"And the jewelry?" Bria asked.

"Usually, gemstones constantly murmur about their own beauty, which any Stone elemental can hear, but none of the sapphires, rubies, or emeralds in the rings, bracelets, or necklaces made a peep. They were made of glass and crystals, instead of real jewels."

"So Fletcher put all that fake stuff in the vault to make whoever opened it think they had found a treasure trove." Owen shook his head. "That's crazy—and brilliant."

"*Crazy and brilliant* perfectly sums up Fletcher Lane," I said, a fond tone in my voice. At times like these, I really missed the old man and his sly, mischievous ways.

"But…if everything Emery took is fake, then where did Fletcher put the *real* money he stole from Mason?" Phillip asked. "Is it in an account?"

Everyone looked at Drusilla, who shook her head. "No. I double-checked the records last night. The vault was the only thing Fletcher Lane ever opened at my family's bank."

"Maybe Fletcher spent all of Mason's money?" Bria suggested.

"On what?" Finn said. "Dad didn't care about driving fancy cars or owning big houses or buying expensive wines. As far as I know, all his income came from the Pork Pit, along with the assassin jobs he booked for himself and Gin. Don't get me wrong. Dad made a lot of money, but he never bought big-ticket items or gambled or did anything else to spend millions of dollars. That just wasn't him."

No, it wasn't. Fletcher might have charged a lot for his services as the Tin Man, and even more for mine as the Spider, but he had also done far more pro bono jobs. The old man had simply never cared much about money. As long as the restaurant had been successful enough to put food in our bellies, clothes on our backs, and a roof over our heads, he had been happy.

Oh, sure, every once in a while, the old man would splurge on a new set of silverstone knives for me, or a Fiona Fine suit for Finn, or even a new book for himself. But he'd never spent close to the fifty million dollars he'd stolen from Mason.

Owen eyed me. "Gin figured it out."

"Figured what out?" Xavier rumbled.

A slow, knowing smile spread across Owen's face. "Gin has been saying all along that something was wrong with the money. That there didn't seem like there was enough of it. So she figured it out. She figured out what Fletcher did with the *real* money."

I grinned back at him. "Well done, Grayson. Very well done."

"So where is it?" Finn demanded.

My grin widened. "Follow me, and I'll show you."

Drusilla made sure her employees were okay, then used her silverstone key to open the appropriate doors and summon the elevator. A few minutes later, my friends and I were back down on the vault level.

Finn, Bria, Owen, Phillip, Xavier, and Roslyn all peered into Fletcher's emptied-out vault, as did Drusilla. Lorelei and Hugh Tucker had also come down here for my big reveal.

Finn shook his head. "I don't get it. Did you find a letter or some other clue from Dad about where he hid Mason's money?"

I stepped into the vault and gestured at the empty table. "The *Reverie in Gray* painting was the first clue. It was part of an assassin job that Fletcher and I did years ago, so I knew it was fake. But I just couldn't figure out *why* he would leave a fake painting in a vault, a place where you are supposed to store valuable items."

I pointed at the empty shelves. "But then I saw the serial number on that hundred-dollar bill, and I realized that the money was fake too—that just about *everything* in the vault was fake."

"But that still didn't help you find the *real* money," Lorelei pointed out.

"I didn't have to find anything. Fletcher spelled it out for me, as plain as day. I was just so busy looking at the forest of valuables that I didn't see the real treasure in the trees. Or in this case..."

My voice trailed off, and I reached into my jeans pocket and dug out the penny Finn had taken from the vault the first time we'd come in here. I flipped it over to my brother, much the same way he had flipped it over to me that day.

"Penny for your thoughts?" I drawled.

Finn held the coin up to the light, examining it the same way he had studied the fake hundred-dollar bill. "Wait a second." His green eyes brightened, and a hushed, reverent tone crept into his voice. "This is a 1954 Patton penny."

Bria frowned. "What on earth is a Patton penny?"

"Back in the nineteen fifties, there used to be a mint in Ashland," Drusilla replied. "Right in this very building, as a matter of fact. The mint wasn't operational for very long, but it made several coins, mostly pennies, all stamped with an image of Marisol Patton, like the statue that sits outside the bank. Only a few of the pennies are still in existence, which makes them highly sought after."

I gestured at the penny Finn was still holding. "I looked it up online last night. A Patton penny similar to that one sold for more than two million dollars at auction last year to a private coin collector."

Phillip let out a low whistle, and everyone looked both startled and impressed. Finn's fingers curled around the penny like he never wanted to let it go.

"But that's just one penny," Xavier said.

"Oh, no," Finn whispered, staring at me. "There were *more* pennies in the vault. Other coins too. Dad used them to spell out Gin's name and draw her spider rune on the table."

I rapped my knuckles on the empty tabletop. "That's right. He might as well have left me a treasure map that said *X marks the spot*."

"But Emery took all the coins," Roslyn pointed out. "I saw the bags in one of the laundry carts."

"Oh, Emery got away with bags of pennies—*regular* pennies. But she didn't bother taking any of *these*."

I dropped to my knees, reached under the closest shelf, and pulled out six more pennies. Then I crawled around the rest of the vault, scooping up several nickels, dimes, and quarters, along with a couple of fifty-cent pieces and dollar coins.

I got to my feet and arranged the coins on the table, spelling out *Gin* again and forming a crude spider rune over the *i*. Some of the coins glimmered brightly, as though they had been freshly minted, while others looked dull and worn.

"The coins were sitting here just like this when Emery

made me open the vault, but she sneered at me and shoved all the coins off the table. Emery thought she was insulting me, hurting me, when really, she was only hurting herself and Mason."

"But how could you possibly know Emery would do that to the coins?" Drusilla asked.

I shrugged. "I didn't. If she hadn't shoved the coins off the table, I would have found some way to grab as many of them as possible. Either way, I would have made sure that *I* had the coins, not Emery."

"So you let Emery take the fake money and valuables out of the vault, then chased her through the lobby to make her think you were truly desperate to recover everything, all the while knowing that the real valuables were still down here." Grudging respect rippled through Tucker's voice. "Well done, Genevieve. Truly."

I tipped my head, accepting his praise.

Everyone gathered around the table, staring down at the treasure I had spelled out.

"I'm going to have to start collecting coins," Finn said in a dreamy voice, still clutching the Patton penny. "Starting with these."

He stretched his hand out to grab some of the coins, but I slapped it away. "As much as I would like to share these with you, with all of you, I can't do that."

"Why not?" Phillip asked.

I sighed. "Because it won't be long before Mason realizes his mistake. Once he—or whomever he gets to handle the money—starts counting it, they'll figure out that most of it is fake, along with the gold bars and the jewelry and everything else. Once that happens, Mason will come after us again. He'll want the money *and* revenge for us fooling him. No matter how careful we are, it won't be long before Mason finds a way to kidnap one of us. Then he'll use that person for leverage to make me hand these coins over to him."

They all fell silent, turning that horrible possibility over in their minds. One by one, agreement filled their faces. Except for Tucker, they had all been at Mallory and Mosley's wedding reception when Emery had kidnapped me, and they had all witnessed Emery and her men shoot up the bank today, a place that was supposed to be a safe, neutral location for everyone in Ashland, criminals and common citizens alike.

"As long as I have these coins, I'll be a target—and so will everyone I care about, everyone *we* care about." I looked from one person to another. "I know that you all don't want to put anyone in danger any more than I do."

Several seconds ticked by in silence. Then Phillip spoke up. "So what do you want us to do? How are you going to keep Mason from getting his hands on the coins?"

His questions were the same ones I had been asking myself for weeks now, ever since I had first learned about the money. As the days had gone by, I'd come up with one plan after another to keep the money—and especially my friends— safe from Mason. And one by one, I'd discarded all those plans because they simply wouldn't work.

"There's only one way to make absolutely sure that Mason *never* gets his hands on one single cent of this money. Do you trust me?"

Owen. Bria. Xavier. Roslyn. Phillip. Lorelei. They all nodded at me. Even Drusilla nodded, after a few seconds of contemplation. Tucker remained neutral and aloof, as always.

"I have a plan to take care of everything once and for all, but I'm going to need everyone's help—one last time."

Finn sighed. "I'm not going to like this, am I?"

"Nope. Not one little bit."

My brother sighed again, a little louder and deeper than before, but he too nodded. His approval was the one I'd wanted—needed—the most. I never would have even found the vault without Finn's help. In a way, the coins were just as much his as they were mine, and Fletcher had left them in here for us to discover together. I felt like everything—the vault, the fake painting, the coins—was Fletcher's legacy to both of us.

And now I was going to use the coins and everything the old man had taught me to make sure that Fletcher's legacy lived on and to honor Tristan, Eira, Annabella, and everyone else whom Mason Mitchell, Emery Slater, Mab Monroe, and the rest of the Circle had ever hurt.

A few days ago, I'd wondered if everything I'd suffered, all the bad guys I'd faced down, all the pain, heartache, and trauma I'd endured had been worth it. Well, now I knew the answer to that question was a resounding *yes*. And perhaps even more important, I finally had a way to change Ashland—for the better.

I grinned at my friends. "Here's what we're going to do."

✲ 23 ✲

We all squeezed into the freight elevator and went back up to the lobby.

Bria and Xavier stripped off their guard uniforms, revealing their regular clothes underneath, along with their gold badges. Then the two of them went outside to deal with a couple of uniformed officers who had come to investigate the ruckus.

Bria and Xavier were sticking to our story and were going to pass off the commotion as a security drill gone wrong. I doubted anyone would actually believe them, but Drusilla had assured me that she and her father paid out enough bribes to make the cops look the other way, especially since no one had been seriously injured and everyone inside the bank had been either one of my friends or part of her staff.

Lorelei said her good-byes and left the bank to take Tucker back to the shipping container so he could rest, while Phillip helped Roslyn pack up all the wigs, glasses, and uniforms she had supplied from her stash of props and costumes at Northern Aggression.

That left me, Owen, and Finn in the bank with Drusilla,

who escorted us to her office, where she had a coin expert standing by, as per one of my many requests to her last night.

I pried the 1954 Patton penny out of Finn's grasp and handed all the coins over to the expert, who examined them with white-gloved hands and critical eyes. The longer he looked at the coins, the more excited he got, and soon he was swooning over what a magnificent collection Fletcher had assembled.

Even better, the coins were worth much more than I had expected. Even after the expert subtracted his appraisal fee and Drusilla took her cut for helping us, along with the hefty bonuses we'd agreed to give her staff members for participating in the robbery, I still had more money left than I had ever dreamed of.

When Drusilla told me the final total, I sank back in my chair, simply stunned. Beside me, Owen and Finn both had similarly incredulous expressions on their faces.

"I never thought I would say this, but I agree with Finn," Owen said. "I don't think I like your plan anymore, Gin."

"Forget the plan," Finn chimed in. "Let's take all that money and buy our own tropical island somewhere. And a ski chalet. And a volcano. And whatever other real estate we can get our hands on."

Drusilla frowned. "What would you do with a volcano?"

"Build the ultimate secret bad-guy lair," Finn replied, a dreamy note in his voice again.

I rolled my eyes. "Forget about a volcano. This is the only way to stop Mason from using the money against us. If he ever got his hands on this much cash, he could do whatever he wanted in Ashland, and we wouldn't be able to stop him. Trust me. This is for the best."

Even more than that, I thought Fletcher would have wholeheartedly approved of my plan. He'd set things up so that

Mason would have an extremely hard time getting his hands on the cash, and now I was going to make sure my uncle never got to spend one single penny of the Circle's blood money.

Owen nodded his agreement, but Finn slumped in his chair and crossed his arms over his chest, pouting again.

I arched an eyebrow at my brother. "Come on, Finn. You know this is the right move. Even more important, it's the right thing to do, not just for us but for everyone in Ashland."

"It might be the right move, but you know how much this *pains* me," he grumbled, shooting a wistful look at the coins spread out across Drusilla's desk. "How much this *hurts* deep, deep down in my greedy little heart."

I clapped him on the shoulder. "And that's why it's going to be so *good* for you. Really give that greedy little heart of yours a workout."

"More like a heart attack," Finn muttered.

I ignored his griping and focused on Drusilla again. "What do you think? Can you help me with this?"

"I'll have to see how much cash reserves we have on hand, but I'm sure we can come to some arrangement." A thin smile curved her lips, and a cold light sparked in her eyes. "Besides, I want to be there when you take down Mason and Emery."

I grinned back at her. "Oh, we can definitely arrange that."

Two hours later, I walked out the front door of the Bellum Bank pulling two large wheeled suitcases along behind me. Owen and Finn were flanking me, each rolling his own suit-case, and Roslyn and Phillip were behind them, with two more suitcases.

By this point, the uniformed cops had left, and people and

vehicles were moving normally on the sidewalks and streets again. A glazier was already setting up outside the bank, getting ready to fix the glass doors that Emery and the other giants had broken in their rush to escape.

Bria and Xavier were loitering near a funnel-cake food cart at the corner, and the two of them came over as we maneuvered our suitcases down the steps.

"The coast is clear," Bria said. "No sign of Mason, Emery, or any other bad guys."

"Good. Let's get out of here."

My friends and I rolled our suitcases to the parking garage, which had become our unofficial base of operations this week. Sophia was waiting for us on the first level, leaning against the side of the Pork Pit food truck, which I'd asked her to drive over here.

We all stopped, and Finn eyed the suitcases with a hungry expression. "Can I just look at it all? Just for a few seconds?"

"No," I said. "We don't have time for that. Besides, wouldn't looking at it just make it that much harder to give up?"

He sighed. "Fine. Crush my dreams, the way you always do."

"Gin Blanco, crusher of dreams." I grinned. "That has a nice ring to it."

Finn sighed again, but he grabbed a suitcase and hoisted it into the back of the food truck. Together, we formed an assembly line, and a few minutes later, all the suitcases were stacked in the truck.

Bria and Xavier got into my sister's sedan, which she had stashed in the garage earlier, while Finn, Owen, Phillip, and Roslyn climbed into the back of the Pork Pit truck and sat down on top of the suitcases. Sophia got into the driver's seat, while I slid into the passenger's seat.

"Everyone got their lists ready?" I asked.

Finn, Owen, Phillip, and Roslyn pulled out their phones, while Sophia grabbed a couple of pieces of paper off the dashboard and handed them to me.

"My list," she rasped. "Jo-Jo's too."

I nodded. "Good. Then let's get started."

Sophia cranked the engine, then steered the food truck out of the garage. Bria and Xavier followed us in her sedan.

While Sophia drove, I kept an eye out, fully expecting Emery and her goons to come barreling after us in a swarm of black SUVs, but everything remained quiet, and we were able to do exactly what everyone wanted to do with the money.

Our journey took longer than I expected, and it was after seven by the time Sophia finally parked the food truck in front of Jo-Jo's house. Bria parked her car behind us, and we all trooped inside. The others stepped into the kitchen to grab some drinks, but I headed into the salon.

Liam was lying in one of the salon chairs, his eyes closed, as though he was taking a nap. Jo-Jo had healed him, and no trace of the ugly beating remained on his face. He'd also taken a shower and changed clothes, and he looked like he was just another customer waiting for Jo-Jo to cut his hair or give him a facial.

I let out a quiet sigh of relief that Liam was whole again. His body, anyway. I just hoped the damage to his psyche would also heal in time.

Silvio was perched in the chair next to Liam, swiping through screens on his tablet, while Jo-Jo was sitting on the floor, petting Rosco, who had flopped over onto his back so that the dwarf could rub his tummy.

Silvio and Jo-Jo looked up at the sound of my footsteps, and Liam cracked his eyes open.

I went over to him. "How are you feeling?"

He sat up. "Better, now that Jo-Jo healed me. I can actually breathe through my nose again since she put it back into place."

Liam smiled, but his blue eyes still looked tired. It would take his mind some time to catch up with the rest of his body and realize that he wasn't at death's door anymore.

"I'm sorry—so very, very sorry. You getting hurt was my fault. What Emery did to you..." I had to stop and clear my throat. "I'm sorry. For all of it."

Liam waved his hand. "No apology needed, Gin. I knew the risks. This wasn't the first time I've gotten injured on a job. Emery just made it hurt a little bit more than most. But you and me? We're good. We always have been."

He flashed me a smile, then held out his fist. I returned his smile and bumped my own fist against his. My guilt lingered, though, just as it always did.

"So what happened?" I asked, pulling up a stool and sitting down beside him.

Liam shrugged. "I got sloppy. I should have attacked you the second I saw you on the sidewalk, but I didn't, and Mason noticed my hesitation. He still had some doubts about me, and that was more than enough for him to order Emery to start beating some answers out of me. I didn't talk, but she was happy to keep hitting me."

"I should rip her throat open with my fangs for hurting you," Silvio growled.

Liam flashed him a smile. "Have I ever mentioned how charming it is when you go all full-fledged vampire?"

A pink blush stained Silvio's cheeks, but his lips twitched upward into an answering smile. "No, but perhaps you can tell me later."

I blinked. Was Silvio actually...*flirting* with Liam? Well, well, well. Looked like my assistant was finally willing to take a chance on a new romance. I was so happy for him—and so happy that Liam was still alive for the two of them to take that chance together.

"I hate to interrupt, but we still have some unfinished business." I looked at Liam again. "You helped plan the security for the gala Mason is throwing to celebrate his development project, right?"

"Yeah..." Liam's eyes narrowed. "Please tell me that you're not thinking of going to that event tomorrow night. Emery is no fool. She's sure to have changed up the security by now, along with bringing in extra men, especially since you were able to rescue me. There's no way you'll be able to sneak into the party."

"Oh, I don't plan to sneak in anywhere. I'm going to walk right in through the front door and tackle Mason head-on. He's spent most of his life skulking around in the shadows. Well, I think it's high time we dragged his ass out into the light for all of Ashland to see."

Silvio eyed me. "What are you planning to do, Gin?"

"For starters? Expose my uncle for the sadistic, murderous, coldhearted bastard he truly is to everyone who is anyone in Ashland." I paused, my heart brimming with venom. "And then I'm going to kill him."

✼ 24 ✼

Liam told us about the security plan he had set up for Mason's fancy shindig, as well as the changes he would make if he were in Emery's shoes and wondering if I was going to crash the party. Based on Liam's intel and suggestions, my friends and I hashed out a plan of attack for tomorrow night. No one particularly liked my plan, especially since it meant me confronting Mason, but that was nothing new.

Besides, Mason was my blood, my problem, my nightmare, and I wanted to be the one to finally end him.

By the time we finished our plotting, it was creeping up on midnight. Jo-Jo wanted to keep an eye on Liam, who agreed to stay at the salon with her, Sophia, and Silvio. Everyone else went back to their own homes, except for Finn and Bria, who decided to bunk with me and Owen at Fletcher's house.

Once we got home and I made sure no one was lurking around, everyone took a shower and got cleaned up. Then Finn and Bria headed into his old bedroom, while Owen and I went into my room and climbed into bed together.

I was still amped up from everything that had happened,

although the adrenaline quickly wore off, and I started to dream, to remember...

Ethan Gere dropped to his knees beside me. With one hand, he latched onto my broken wrist. With his other hand, he raised the bone saw high, carefully aiming it like it was a gun he was about to fire.

The dwarf sneered down at me. "This is going to hurt—a lot. Feel free to scream, though. I'd love for the old woman and her grandson to come rushing outside and see what I have in store for them."

He brought the saw down. The instant before the tool hit my wrist, I reached for my Stone magic and used it to harden my skin—

Scrape.

Scrape-scrape.

Scrape.

The saw dragged along my wrist, but the sharp teeth couldn't break through the protective shell of my power.

"Stone magic? Really?" Ethan sneered again. "How long do you think that will last? I can saw at you all night long. You'll run out of power sooner or later, and then you'll start bleeding."

He was right. I only had so much Stone magic, and it wouldn't be long before I exhausted it, especially since my broken wrist was throbbing and my head was still aching from where he'd punched me. So I reached for my Ice magic. Even though it was my weaker power, I still managed to make an Ice dagger. I snapped it up, but Ethan saw the motion, and he used his bone saw to block and then shatter the frozen blade.

"Ice magic too, huh?" he said. "Well, aren't you just full of surprises? It's too bad you killed my brother. We could have used someone like you in our organization."

I ignored his taunt, made another Ice knife, and tried to stab him again, but he knocked it away just like he had the first one.

Ethan shook his head. "You should stop wasting your magic. All you're doing is making it easier for me to kill you."

I growled with frustration. He was right, but I couldn't do anything with the dwarf kneeling beside me and me flat on my back. I had to get out from under him if I had any chance of winning this battle.

So this time, instead of trying to kill him, I grabbed hold of the jagged edge of the bone saw. I was using my Stone magic to protect myself, but the razor-sharp edges of the saw still dug into my hand, like needles about to prick my skin. It wouldn't be long before my magic ran out and the teeth sank into my flesh. When that happened, Ethan would take his time cutting me up into little pieces.

I needed to end the fight—now.

Ethan sneered down at me yet again. "If that's how you want to play it, fine with me."

He wrapped both hands around the handle and surged forward, putting his heavy body weight behind his effort to shove the saw into my skin. I didn't know if the dwarf had enough strength to physically force the tool past my Stone magic, but I didn't want to find out.

Desperate, I released the saw, reached up, and clawed at his face with my hand, despite the pain shooting out through my body.

Ethan laughed and ignored the weak, clumsy blow. I couldn't hurt him with my fingernails, so I curled my hand into a tight fist and reached for my Ice magic, gathering up the cold force deep inside me. Then, when I had a firm grip on my power, I lifted my hand, spread my fingers out wide, and blasted the bastard with as much magic as I could muster.

Truth be told, it was a weak burst of power, since my Ice magic was limited by the silverstone spider-rune scar branded into my palm. But I still managed to summon up several long, sharp needles of Ice, all of which sank deep into Ethan's face.

That *finally got the dwarf's attention, and he yelped and jerked back like a wounded animal. One of his feet slid out from under him, and he listed to the side. I grabbed the edge of the bone saw, jerked it out of his grasp, and then rammed it up and into his throat as hard as I could.*

The metal handle punched straight into Ethan's neck. While he was coughing and sputtering, I snaked my foot up between us and kicked the bastard away from me. He toppled over onto the pavement, still coughing and trying to suck down some air, and the bone saw clattered to the ground between us.

I rolled away from the dwarf, getting back up onto my knees. Ethan swiped out at me, but I avoided the blow. Then I grabbed the knife from the small of my back, lifted the blade high, and threw myself down and forward, aiming for the dwarf's throat.

Bull's-eye.

I drove the blade into Ethan's neck, forcing him down onto his back. He let out a loud, strangled cry and slammed his fists into my face, chest, and every other part of me that he could reach. I grunted at the hard, heavy, bone-bruising blows, but I tightened my grip on my knife and kept twisting and twisting it, slowly sawing through his muscles and driving the blade deeper and deeper into his neck.

Ethan let out another strangled cry, but more and more blood gushed out of his throat, and his arms slowly dropped to the ground. His head lolled to the side, and his eyes became fixed and still.

He was dead.

I finally loosened my grip on the knife. I should have gotten to my feet. Should have looked around and made sure no one had heard the fight, clicked on their porch lights, and peered out their windows. But my broken wrist was throbbing, my head was aching, and my whole body was trembling with shock, adrenaline, and exhaustion, and it was all I could do to slide off the dwarf's body and flop over onto my back.

I didn't know how long I lay there, staring dully up at the night sky, before footsteps crunched on the pavement, and a shadow fell over me, blotting out the night sky.

I blinked up at the figure looming over me. "Fletcher?"

The old man dropped to a knee beside me. "Gin! Are you okay?"

He put his hand behind my back and helped me sit up.

"Yeah, I'm okay. Just a little beat up." I held up my left arm. "And my wrist is broken."

Fletcher reached down and gently hoisted me onto my feet. My head spun around, but the pain was better than lying dead on the pavement like Ethan.

I glanced down at the dwarf, who seemed to be staring right at me. I shuddered, turned away from him, and focused on Fletcher. "What are you doing here?"

"I took care of my other business, then swung by your apartment building to make sure you had gotten home safely. I got worried when I didn't see your car in the lot, so I came back to look for you. What are you doing here?" He gestured down at Ethan and the other two dwarves. "Other than killing people."

"I thought that Ethan might try to take the Reverie in Gray *painting away from Blanche, and I wanted to be here to stop him."*

Fletcher frowned. *"Why didn't you tell me you were so worried about that?"*

"I did, but you brushed me off. Remember? You said Ethan wasn't as dangerous as his brother."

"And I was wrong," Fletcher said. *"Dead wrong. And you almost died because of my mistake. I'm sorry, Gin. So sorry."*

I shrugged. "It's not your fault. I came out here by myself. I knew the risks."

"I know, but I should have listened to you," Fletcher replied. *"I was just so certain I was right and that Ethan wasn't a threat. I should have been more careful. I should have protected Blanche and Benji better—and you too."*

Guilt tightened his face, and I reached out and squeezed his shoulder with my good hand. "It's okay," I repeated.

Fletcher smiled, but the expression didn't quite reach his green eyes. "Well, it's a mistake I won't make again." He stopped and cleared his throat, as if he were having trouble getting his next words out. *"I want you to know how very proud I am of you, Gin."*

This time, I frowned. "For what? Almost getting killed?"

Fletcher shook his head. "No. For trusting your instincts, for trusting yourself, *even when I doubted you, even when I dismissed your concerns. You* taught *me* an important lesson *tonight—to always trust in yourself, in your own skills, smarts, and abilities, no matter what anyone else says or how hard they doubt you. That unshakable belief you have in yourself is the best, deepest, most reliable strength you can* ever *have, more so than any Ice or Stone magic or even the sharpest knife."*

His words reached into my chest and squeezed my heart tight, and I had to blink back the tears stinging my eyes. Still, there was a tone in his voice I had never heard before.

Something that sounded a bit sad and wistful but happy and proud at the same time.

"Belief in yourself is all well and good, but what are you really saying?" I asked.

Fletcher stared at me, his gaze steady on mine, his face completely serious. "I'm saying that I don't have anything left to teach you, Gin. You are so much more than I ever was, and you can be so much more still. Never forget that, and always remember how very much I love you, and especially how proud I am that I got to train the Spider."

By this point, tears were streaming down my face, and emotion was clogging my throat. Somehow, I forced out the most important words. "Well, you've been a terrific teacher. I never would have made it this far without you. I owe you so much, and I love you too."

Fletcher nodded, a couple of tears streaking down his own wrinkled cheeks. "Now that we've confessed our feelings, let me call Sophia to dispose of the bodies, then we'll go over to Jo-Jo's so she can heal you. Maybe she'll even make us some hot chocolate since we didn't get to the Cake Walk. Okay?"

I smiled at him through the tears still streaming down my face. "Sounds like a plan to me."

Fletcher returned my smile with one of his own, then leaned forward and hugged me tight, careful of my injuries. I wrapped my one good arm around the old man's waist and hugged him back just as tightly, wanting this one perfect moment to last for as long as possible…

My eyes fluttered open. I stared up at the ceiling, but I wasn't seeing the blank space. I was still lost in the remnants of my dream. For an instant, I could still feel Fletcher hugging me, could still hear him saying how proud he was of me and how much he loved me.

I lay quiet and still in bed, reveling in the memory, letting it sink even deeper down into my heart, where it would always stay.

Then, when I was sure that I would always remember it, I threw back the covers to face the day—and get ready for my final confrontation with Mason fucking Mitchell.

The clock on the nightstand said that it was after ten o'clock. Bria, Finn, and Owen were still sleeping, so I put on some clothes, went downstairs to the kitchen, and rustled around in the refrigerator and cabinets, seeing what I might be able to whip up for lunch.

After all, it might be the last meal I ever had, and I wanted it to be *spectacular*.

So I dredged some chicken in buttermilk and then in flour seasoned with a pinch of salt and loads of black pepper. That first loud sizzle of the chicken landing in a skillet full of hot oil inspired me, and I started humming as I prepared the rest of my potentially last meal.

In addition to fried chicken, I also whipped up some buttermilk biscuits and gravy, along with white cheddar mac and cheese, buttery mashed potatoes, cinnamon apples, and a green salad filled with cherry tomatoes, cucumbers, red onions, and carrots. I set out some of Jo-Jo's homemade strawberry and blackberry preserves to slather onto the biscuits and made a honey-mustard dressing for the salad and to serve as a dipping sauce for the fried chicken. For the finishing touch, I whipped up some blackberry lemonade.

With every cut of a knife and stir of a spoon, I felt a little calmer and more certain about what I had to do. I had already thwarted Mason's plans for the Pork Pit, and tonight I was going to expose him for the sadistic bastard he truly was. Oh, Mason might still end up killing me, but by the time I was done with him, no one in Ashland would touch him with a ten-foot pole, no matter if I was alive or dead. If that was my only victory against my uncle, then it was still a good one.

Eventually, my clattering woke the others, and Owen wandered into the kitchen.

"It all smells amazing," he rumbled, leaning down to kiss my cheek.

I grinned, then shooed him away with a wooden spoon. "Go set the table in the dining room."

"Yes, ma'am," he said.

Bria and Finn came downstairs as well, and the four of us gathered around the table for my potential last supper.

Silvio and Liam were still at Jo-Jo's house, as was Sophia, but Silvio had called me earlier to say they were fine and that everything was quiet. I'd also checked in with Xavier, Roslyn, Phillip, and Lorelei, but they were all fine too.

It didn't seem as though Mason had discovered my ruse yet. Then again, he was probably too busy getting ready for his grand gala to suspect how thoroughly I had snookered him.

He'd realize his mistake soon enough, though—I'd make sure of that.

Owen, Bria, Finn, and I dug into our food. The fried chicken was crispy and crunchy on the outside and moist and tender on the inside, while the biscuits were as light and fluffy as clouds melting in my mouth. The creamy mac and cheese and buttery mashed potatoes added plenty of richness to the meal, while the salad offered lots of crunch, along with the bright, sweet tang of the honey-mustard dressing.

Everything was perfect, and I quickly cleaned my plate and went back for seconds and thirds, as did everyone else.

"I think this is one of the best meals you've ever made," Bria said.

"I do try." I grinned and held out my glass of lemonade, and she grinned back and clinked her glass against mine.

But all too soon, we finished eating. Finn needed to deal with some things at First Trust, and Owen wanted to check in with his office as well, so the two of them grabbed their phones and stepped out onto the front porch to make some calls. Bria and I ended up in the den.

My sister walked over to the mantel and grabbed the sapphire paperweight, hefting it in her hand. "What are you going to do with this?"

"I don't know. I'd like to find some way to use it against Mason, but so far, I haven't come up with any brilliant ideas."

Bria set the paperweight down, then stared at the two silverstone pendants that were draped over Eira's and Annabella's snowflake and ivy-vine rune drawings. Bria stroked the matching rings stamped with our mother's and sister's runes that she wore on her finger.

"I wish we didn't have to confront Mason tonight," Bria confessed. "I wish that none of this had ever happened and that Mom and Dad and Annabella were still alive and here with us."

Her words perfectly mirrored my own feelings, even as they wrenched my heart. When I was younger, especially when I was living on the streets, I used to imagine what my life would have been like if Mab Monroe hadn't attacked our family.

I would daydream about the parties and school dances and football games I would have attended like a normal teenager. The birthdays and Christmases and Mother's Days I would have celebrated with Eira, Annabella, and Bria. The shopping trips and family dinners and vacations we would have taken as a family. Even now, I still got a bit wistful imagining all those happy, little, ordinary moments that would have made up the life of Genevieve Snow.

It would have been a good life. I was certain of that. But I wasn't so certain it would have been the right life for *me*.

Despite my grumbling about facing down one bad guy after another the past few years, I had to admit that part of me thrived on the action, the danger, the life-and-death battles. They all pushed me to *do* more, to *be* more, just like Fletcher had said. To stand up for people who needed help. To protect my friends and family. To love truly and fiercely.

Oh, yes. Genevieve Snow would have been happy, but Gin Blanco was a *warrior*.

I went over and put my arm around Bria's shoulder. "I wish Mom and Dad and Annabella were still alive too, and I'll always miss them."

"But?" she asked.

I let out a breath. "But they're gone, and we're still here, and the best thing we can do is make sure that Mason never hurts another family like he hurt ours."

Bria nodded, then slipped her arm around my waist and leaned her head against mine. We stood there, staring at the drawings and pendants, for the better part of two minutes, soaking up all of the love, comfort, and strength we could from each other.

"I want you to have something." I pulled away from Bria, grabbed our mother's snowflake pendant, and held it out to my sister.

Bria shook her head. "No. I can't take that. I won't."

"But—"

Bria shook her head again and gave me a fierce stare. "*No.* The snowflake is bigger, which means it contains more Ice magic. You're the one who's going up against Mason, so you'll need every drop of Ice power you can get." She paused, then continued in a softer voice. "Besides, you're the head of our family, Gin. Our mother's pendant belongs to you now."

She reached out, gently took the chain from my hands, and dropped it down over my head. The snowflake pendant came to rest against my chest, right above my own spider-rune pendant, both of them eerily similar and yet distinctly different at the same time.

Hot tears stung my eyes. "Thank you," I whispered.

Tears shimmered in Bria's eyes too. "You're welcome."

I turned back to the mantel and grabbed Annabella's pendant. Then, before Bria could protest, I dropped the chain down over her head. "I'm not taking no for an answer this time. You're going to be right there with me tonight, and you're going to need all the Ice magic you can get too."

I smiled. "Besides, it looks good on you."

And it truly did. Annabella's ivy-vine pendant was a perfect complement to Bria's own primrose rune, and it almost looked like the two necklaces were one.

More tears shimmered in Bria's eyes, and she lurched forward and hugged me. Words failed me, so I hugged her back just as tightly, trying to show her how much I loved her.

"For our family," she whispered in my ear.

"And for us too," I whispered back.

We stood there, hugging and holding on to each other tight, both of us committed to one thing: finally getting our revenge on Mason for all the terrible things he'd done to our family.

❋ 25 ❋

Owen and Finn finished their calls, and the four of us got dressed. Given the formal occasion, the guys donned classic black tuxedos, while Bria and I opted for fashionable, feminine, but functional pantsuits and boots—blue for her, black for me. No way was I going to try to fight Mason in a gown and heels.

Bria was wearing our sister's ivy-vine pendant, while I was sporting my mother's snowflake. I hoped the extra Ice magic in the runes would be enough to help us kill Mason, but only time would tell. I also slid the sapphire paperweight into my pants pocket, although I still hadn't figured out a way to weaponize its Stone magic against Mason.

When we were ready, we headed over to Jo-Jo's house. Several cars were parked in the driveway, and everyone else had already arrived.

Jo-Jo. Sophia. Silvio. Liam. Xavier. Roslyn. Phillip. Lorelei. Tucker. They were all in the salon, dressed in formal attire, and I squeezed in there too, along with Owen, Finn, and Bria.

Everyone stopped talking and looked at me, their faces pinched with worry.

"Y'all need to lose the long faces," I drawled. "We're going to a grand gala, not a funeral."

"It might very well *be* your funeral, Gin," Finn snapped. "You don't have to confront Mason. I can set up a sniper's perch in the woods and take him out with my rifle. I've done it before."

Liam shook his head. "That won't work. Emery had already planned for several guards to patrol the woods, and she's sure to have increased that number. Her men would find you before you even got a chance to take a shot at Mason. As much as I don't like Gin's plan, her idea to go in through the front door is our best option, if only because it's the last thing Emery or Mason will expect."

Finn sniffed his disbelief, but he didn't argue anymore.

"Well, Finnegan certainly got one thing right," Tucker piped up. "No one else has ever been quite this suicidal with Mason before, not even Fletcher."

The vampire was sitting by himself in the corner. He was once again clutching his cane, although I got the sense he was doing it more out of habit, rather than actually needing it. His color was also much better today, and his face had started to fill back out.

"Aw, Tuck, it almost sounds like you're worried about me. How sweet."

"Worried? About you?" He snorted. "Hardly. That would be the height of foolishness, especially given how reckless you are. No, I'm merely concerned for my own safety."

"Shocking no one," Bria muttered.

I ignored her snide words and looked at the vampire. "You don't have to come."

Tucker blinked, as did the rest of my friends. "What?"

"You don't have to come to the gala. You held up your end of our deal. You told me what Mason was planning to do to the Pork Pit, which gave me a chance to stop him. That's all I wanted. So go. Leave if you want to. I won't stop you, and neither will anyone else."

Bria shot me a sour look, but I shrugged. We couldn't keep Tucker hidden away forever. Besides, I needed to focus all my energy tonight on killing Mason, not worrying about the vampire slipping away.

Tucker looked at me, then at my sister. He glanced around at everyone else. Finally, his gaze landed on Lorelei. Once again, that hunger sparked in his black eyes. Lorelei stared right back at him, an unreadable expression on her own face.

Tucker got to his feet and leaned on his cane. "Very well. Since you no longer require my services, I will take my leave of the lot of you." He stabbed his finger at me. "But don't say I didn't warn you, Gin. Walking into Mason's party is a suicide mission, and you're only going to get yourself killed, along with the rest of your friends."

"Then I guess this is good-bye. Because I am *done* letting Mason terrorize people, especially the people I care about."

Tucker sighed and shook his head, as though he thought I was the grandest sort of fool. Then he turned around to leave the salon. He stopped and stared at Lorelei again, but her face remained blank, and she didn't say anything. Tucker stared at her a moment longer, then walked right on past her, his cane tapping on the floor as he made his way down the hallway. The front door opened and then shut, and I didn't hear anything after that.

"What is he going to do?" Bria asked. "Walk all the way back to town?"

"Believe me, he is more than stubborn enough to do that," Lorelei muttered.

"Well, he's gone now," I replied. "And we still have a lot of work to do."

A shadow passed over Lorelei's face, but she nodded, as did everyone else.

"All right," I said. "Let's go over the plan again..."

We reviewed everything one final time, then went outside. There was no sign of Tucker, but that wasn't surprising. He always seemed to scuttle off and disappear like a cockroach whenever there was fighting to be done.

"I'm sorry that Tucker didn't stay," I said in a low voice to Lorelei.

She shrugged, trying to pretend his desertion didn't matter to her, although I could see how much it did. "Tucker made his choice. If he couldn't stand with you after everything that's happened, then there's no hope for him."

"To be fair, he did save me from Mason. I would have died in the Circle cemetery, if not for Tucker."

Lorelei shrugged again. "And then he walked away tonight, after you healed him and protected him instead of just letting him die in the cemetery. He made his choice, and I've made mine. I'm with you, Gin. Until the end."

"Thank you," I whispered, and squeezed her hand.

Lorelei squeezed back, then got into her car.

I slid into the front passenger's seat of Owen's vehicle. He cranked the engine, and we left Jo-Jo's house.

I glanced in the side mirror, watching the white structure grow smaller and smaller before we coasted down the hill and it vanished from view. Bittersweet melancholy washed through me. I wondered if this would be the last time I ever saw the house, if this had been the last hour I would ever spend with my friends, my family.

No, I told myself sternly. I couldn't think like that. Otherwise, Mason had already won.

I had stolen his money, swiped it right out from under Emery's nose, and I was going to do the same thing to Mason again tonight—yank the rug out from under him and then kill the bastard when he was down on his knees.

I was looking forward to it.

Owen cruised along the curvy mountain roads, with the rest of my friends following in their own vehicles. It didn't take us long to reach our destination. Owen steered his car into a long line of vehicles crawling toward an open iron gate. A couple of giant guards holding clipboards were standing by the entrance, and they gestured for Owen to stop and roll down his window, which he did.

One of the giants bent down and looked into the car. He didn't recognize Owen, but his eyes widened in shock at the sight of me.

I gave him a dazzling smile. "Be a dear, and tell my uncle Mason that his favorite niece is here. I'm sure he's expecting me. After all, he gave me an invitation himself."

I waggled the fancy engraved invitation, then passed it over to the giant. His eyes widened again, looking from me to the paper and back again.

"Um…wait here," the giant muttered, quickly stepping away from the car as though he thought I was going to lunge past Owen, whip out a knife, and stab him in the eye.

As tempting as that thought was, Owen looked far too handsome in his tuxedo for me to ruin it with the giant's blood.

The giant conferred with his colleague, who jabbered something into a cell phone. The second giant jerked the phone away from his ear and stared at it in surprise, as though he wasn't sure if he'd heard the person on the other end correctly. But the second giant waved his hand, telling Owen to drive through the open gate.

"Here we go," Owen said.

"Into the lion's den yet again," I replied.

He reached over, grabbed my hand, and pressed a kiss to my palm, right in the center of my spider-rune scar. "There's no place I'd rather be."

"And no one I'd rather be with," I murmured back.

I leaned over and kissed him. Owen cupped my cheek and leaned into the kiss, his mouth opening and his tongue stroking against mine. I drew in a breath, letting his rich, metallic scent sink deep into my lungs and imprinting his touch on my body, my mind, my heart—

A horn honked behind us. Finn, getting impatient. Owen and I broke apart. We stared into each other's eyes, and I squeezed his hand before leaning back in my seat.

Owen steered up the driveway, and the Mitchell mansion loomed into view. The last time I had been here, Mason had almost killed me in the Circle family cemetery in the nearby woods. If I had my way, Mason would be the one bleeding out tonight.

The Mitchell mansion was five stories of gleaming white stone, with massive columns that stretched from the ground up to the top level. Each floor featured a wide wraparound porch, all of which had been adorned with tiny white twinkle lights that glowed like fireflies in the cold, dark night. It would have been a beautiful scene if I didn't know how much ugliness lurked inside, and especially if I couldn't hear each and every stone of the mansion murmuring about Mason's power. I had to grind my teeth to block out the smug chorus.

Valets rushed to and fro, parking people's vehicles, while a couple of giant guards flanked the entrance. Owen and I got out of his car, with Finn and Bria behind us. The rest of my friends also exited their vehicles.

Phillip, Xavier, Roslyn, Lorelei, Silvio, Liam, Jo-Jo, Sophia. Everyone looked at me, their features and bodies tense. I nodded back at them, trying to hide my own worry. We were officially in enemy territory now, and there was no turning back.

Owen held out his arm, which I took, then led me up the front steps. The guards eyed us, but they didn't stop us from entering. Of course not. Mason thought he'd won, and he wanted to lord his supposed triumph over me. Why, he probably would have been disappointed if I hadn't shown up. Arrogant fool.

Still arm in arm, Owen and I entered the mansion, with our friends following us. In addition to being the ancestral home of the Mitchell family, the mansion also served as the headquarters for the Ashland Historical Association, and a little piece of history was stuffed into every single nook and cranny—including the *Reverie in Gray* painting.

I spotted it hanging above a fireplace in one of the exhibit rooms filled with antique furniture, old-timey photos, and vintage tools. The sight of it made me grin. No doubt Mason had ordered it to be displayed because he thought it was the real deal, which meant he hadn't discovered that the painting—and everything else he'd stolen—was fake. Excellent. I wanted to be the one to break that particular bad news to my uncle.

I pointed out the painting to Owen. "Remind me to come back for that."

He nodded, and we walked on.

More guards were spread throughout the first floor, and it seemed there were almost as many giants in the structure as there were historic antiques, artifacts, and photos.

I stopped counting after the first dozen guards. Liam had been right. Emery had dramatically increased security for the gala. But I didn't care about killing the giants—only ending Mason.

Owen escorted me to the back of the mansion, where we stepped through a pair of open glass doors and out onto an enormous white stone terrace. The last time I had been here, the area had been a bit plain, adorned with only a few planters of winter flowers, but tonight it had been transformed into a wonderland for Mason's swanky soiree.

White twinkle lights had been strung up along the porches on the back side of the mansion, while blue lights outlined the windows and doors, looking like neon spiders squatting in the center of a massive electrified web. Still more strands of white and blue twinkle lights had been strung up over the terrace itself, providing a cheery glow that brightened the entire yard, as well as the woods in the distance.

My gaze flicked over the terrace. Buffet tables, champagne towers, fresh-cut flowers, a parquet dance floor, a string quartet. All the usual party accoutrements were present, with one notable addition: the diorama of the new, improved downtown Ashland.

The diorama stood in the center of the terrace, smack-dab in the middle of the gala, looking even larger than when I had seen it in the Carpenter Consulting office a few days ago. White banners with bright blue words that screamed out *The Mitchell Mile—The future is now!* were draped along the bottom of the diorama like sashes on a pageant queen, while clusters of white and blue balloons shaped like skyscrapers were attached to the corners of the table, gently bobbing up and down in the chilly winter breeze gusting through the backyard.

All put together, it was a lovely scene. Mason had really gone all out for his moment of triumph.

I was *so* going to enjoy ruining his night.

A few feet away from the diorama, a large video screen had been set up, along with a wooden podium and several rows of chairs. I glanced over my shoulder at Silvio, who nodded at me, then slipped into the crowd.

And then there was the man of the hour.

Mason was standing close to the diorama, wearing a black tuxedo and shaking hands with the mayor. The police chief, the city planner, and several other bigwigs were clustered around my uncle, sipping champagne and nodding at whatever lame-ass story he was telling. Well, I had my own story to tell tonight, an epic tale of love, loss, revenge, and survival that was years in the making, and something that no one here would ever forget.

Mason caught sight of me. Instead of looking concerned, a smug smirk stretched across his face, and his gray eyes actually fucking *twinkled*, as if he were thoroughly pleased to see me. He murmured something to the bigwigs, then grabbed a couple of glasses of champagne off the tray of a passing waiter and strode over to me.

But Mason wasn't the only one who had noticed me— so had Emery. The giant was dressed in a glittering gold pantsuit with matching ballet flats. She quickly moved to flank Mason, but she didn't seem bothered by my presence, and a sneer twisted her red lips. All around the terrace, more and more giants snapped to attention at the sight of me. None of them was reaching for a gun yet, but it was only a matter of time.

Mason stopped right in front of me, that smug smirk stretching even wider across his face. "Hello, Gin," he purred. "I wasn't sure if you were going to show up to my little party, but I'm so glad you could make it. Especially given all that nastiness at the Bellum Bank yesterday."

I tamped down my anger. "*Nastiness*? Is that what we're spinning it as now? Let's call it what it truly was—*attempted murder*."

Mason shrugged. "Why, I heard that it was a training exercise gone wrong. Some sort of security snafu at the bank. Nothing of consequence."

He didn't say anything about Drusilla supposedly being killed by Emery. Then again, that too was nothing of consequence. No, Mason Mitchell didn't care about anything other than himself and this monstrosity he was trying to build.

Mason held out a glass of champagne to me. "Don't be a sore loser, Gin. It's not a good look on you."

I wanted to slap that glass out of his hand, but I settled for arching an eyebrow at him instead. "Who says I've lost?"

A merry chuckle tumbled out of his lips and splattered all over me like acid. "Please don't tell me that you came here with some grand delusion of stopping me. This gala is just a formality. First thing tomorrow morning, I'll have a crane parked on the street outside the Pork Pit, and I'll be there to pull the lever to release the wrecking ball. I think I'll destroy the sign over the front door first. I've always thought a pig holding a platter of food was so very gauche. Why, destroying it will be a public service."

I snorted. "The only public service you could ever do would be to drop dead from natural causes."

A thin smile curved his lips. "Well, unfortunately for you, I am in excellent health. And thanks to Emery, I plan to stay that way for many years to come."

Emery preened at his praise. For the first time, well, *ever*, I felt sorry for her. The giant didn't seem to realize that she was just a piece of gum stuck to the bottom of Mason's shoe and that he would scrape her off and throw her away the second she was no longer useful.

Mason peered down his nose at me. "And don't you even *think* about making a scene and ruining things for me, Gin. That's not why I invited you and your friends here."

"Why did you invite us? To gloat?"

He smiled. "Of course. And to show you, once and for all, that your continued struggles are useless. You might be the Spider, but you've been stuck in *my* web this whole time. Be grateful you got to hold on to the Pork Pit this long. Because if it had been up to me, I would have leveled it long ago."

I stepped even closer to him, letting him see the chill in my own wintry gray eyes. "But it wasn't up to you, was it? Fletcher made sure of that. And now, so have I."

He must have finally heard the conviction in my voice, because he frowned. "What do you mean—"

"Sir?" One of the guards came up to Mason. "It's time for your speech and the video presentation."

Mason kept staring at me. This time, I was the one who smiled at him.

"Go on, Uncle. I wouldn't want you to miss giving your big speech."

He kept eyeing me, more and more suspicion creasing his face. He jerked his head at Emery. "Watch her. Make sure she doesn't interfere."

He shoved the two champagne glasses into Emery's hands, sloshing the liquid all over her gold jacket, and stalked over to the podium. Emery shot him an annoyed glare, then shoved the glasses at the giant who had come over to them. That man grabbed the glasses, splashing what was left of the champagne all over his own jacket.

"What are you up to, Blanco?" Emery hissed. "What did you do?"

I gave her the same razor-thin smile I had given my uncle. "You'll find out soon enough. And don't worry. I wouldn't *dream* of interrupting Mason's speech. Why, I wouldn't miss it for the world."

Emery kept staring at me with equal parts hate and suspicion, but I threaded my arm through Owen's again, turned my back to her, and strolled away.

I hadn't been lying. I wasn't going anywhere, and I wasn't going to interrupt.

Not when Mason's downfall was about to begin.

✳ 26 ✳

ason stepped behind the podium. The string quartet stopped playing, a hush fell over the crowd, and everyone faced him.

He *tap-tap-tapped* on the microphone, then leaned forward and spoke into it. "Is this thing on?"

Several people laughed politely at his cliché joke. I did not, but that was okay. I was going to have the last laugh before all was said and done.

Mason beamed at the crowd. "Thank you all so much for coming tonight, especially on such short notice. But I was just so excited about my project that I didn't want to wait any longer to announce it…"

He started droning on about how the Mitchell Mile project would revitalize the downtown area, how much money and tourism it would bring in, and all the other usual empty promises and platitudes you would expect to hear at this sort of event.

Mostly, though, Mason talked about how this had been *his* vision, his cherished *dream*, from the very beginning, from when he was a child growing up in Ashland. I snorted.

Bullshit. Oh, Mason might have dreamed this up, but only as a way to legitimize himself and the Circle—and get back at Fletcher for stealing his money all those years ago. Then again, I supposed that the thirst for revenge was a powerful motivator. It certainly had been one in my own life.

After about ten long, excruciating minutes, Mason wound down his self-congratulatory talk, picked up a remote, and pointed it at the film screen standing nearby. "I know you've all been admiring the diorama, but my architects have also come up with some graphics so that you can really see what the downtown area will look like when the Mitchell Mile is completed."

He clicked the remote a couple of times, and a few photos popped up on the screen, showing the new, supposedly improved downtown area. Mason clicked the button again, and the screen went dark.

I glanced over at Silvio, who grinned and flashed me a thumbs-up. I winked back at him, and Silvio slipped deeper into the crowd, as did the rest of my friends. Owen remained by my side, though. He'd insisted on it.

Mason clicked the button again. "Sorry, folks, but I think we're having some technical difficulties—"

Suddenly, a bright light appeared on the film screen, so bright that some people had to shield their eyes against the glare, but not me. I didn't want to miss a single second of this.

The light faded away, and an image of Fletcher's vault at the Bellum Bank appeared. In addition to asking Drusilla to participate in my fake heist, I'd also gotten her to install some security cameras on the vault level, just so I could drive a few more nails into Mason's coffin.

Drusilla's voice sounded in the chilly night air. "If you do this, then you—and especially Mason—are making an enemy out of the Bellum Bank. Perhaps you want to reconsider…"

From there, the confrontation outside the vault played out exactly as it had in real life, albeit with some clever editing, thanks to Silvio. But everyone clearly saw Emery Slater shoot Drusilla, and the other giants take down Owen and Phillip as the two fake security guards. Surprised gasps rippled through the crowd. Suddenly, everyone was staring at Emery, who shifted on her feet, uncomfortable at the intense scrutiny.

Mason stared at the screen, his face blank with shock. For perhaps the first time, I had completely surprised my uncle. I grinned. This was just the beginning.

I took advantage of the relative quiet to stride forward so that I was standing at the front of the crowd, in full view of everyone. Once again, Owen came with me, remaining right by my side, supporting me the way he always did.

"Problems, Uncle?" I called out in a loud, mocking voice. "Or are you just upset that everyone is finally seeing you for the murdering, backstabbing bastard you truly are?"

Mason shot me an angry glare and made a slashing motion with his hand. One of the giants scrambled over and pulled the plug—literally—on the film screen. It went blank and black again, but the damage had already been done, and people kept whispering and glancing from Emery to Mason and back again.

"I'm afraid there's been some misunderstanding," Mason said.

"Misunderstanding?" I drawled, my voice even louder and more mocking than before. "There's no *misunderstanding*. You told the head of your security team to shoot Drusilla Yang and her guards and blame their murders on me. To get me in trouble with Charles Yang and out of the way so that you could move forward with your pet project to destroy the Pork Pit and the rest of downtown Ashland."

Mason's lips pinched tight with anger, but his face quickly smoothed out into a somber, regretful expression. "I'm not sure what this video shows, but if Ms. Slater hurt anyone, then she did it of her own free will and volition and certainly not on *my* orders."

I glanced over at Emery, whose face had turned beet red. Rage glinted in her hazel eyes, and her fingers were twitching like she wanted to charge forward, wrap her hands around Mason's neck, and squeeze him until his head popped like a balloon. Malicious glee filled my heart. He had thrown her under the proverbial bus even quicker than I'd expected.

Emery noticed me smirking at her. She glared at me for a moment before directing her ire at Mason again.

My uncle opened his mouth, as if to shove the giant a little further under that bus, but I cut him off.

"Oh, please," I called out. "You're Mason Mitchell. You're the head of the Circle, a secret society that's responsible for a large portion of the crime and corruption in Ashland. Emery doesn't even look at people sideways unless you tell her to."

He shook his head, denying my accusation. "Ladies and gentlemen, I'm so sorry for this interruption. Please forgive Ms. Blanco. Her restaurant is in the heart of the downtown development zone, and I'm afraid she hasn't been very happy about my plans to improve the city for the good of us all."

I gestured at the blank film screen. "Not when those plans involve murdering innocent people just so you can get your way."

Mason shrugged, as though the evidence everyone had just seen meant nothing. "Who's to say that video is even real? Maybe it's all some elaborate stunt you set up to try to incriminate me."

"And how would I do that? Much less get your head of security to go along with such a complicated, grandiose scheme?"

Mason opened his mouth, but no words came out. He didn't have an answer for that.

I had my uncle on the defensive, and now it was time to truly cut his legs out from under him. Owen squeezed my hand, knowing what was coming next. I squeezed back, then stepped into the open space in front of the podium, addressing the crowd gathered in front of me, which included the richest, most important, powerful, and dangerous people in Ashland.

I recognized dozens of faces, either by reputation or from my own dealings with them. They all stared back at me with a mixture of curiosity and wariness. The last time I'd done something so public was the night I'd challenged Madeline Monroe to an elemental duel when she tried to take control of the underworld. I wasn't going to challenge Mason to a duel, though. I wouldn't win. Besides, exposing him was more important right now.

"Most of you know me as Gin Blanco," I said in a loud, clear, strong voice. "That's the name I go by today, but it's not my birth name. My real name is Genevieve Snow. My mother was Eira Snow, and she was a member of the Circle too."

More surprised whispers and murmurs rippled through the crowd. I glanced to my left. Mason's eyes glittered like chips of gray ice in his face, but he made no move to stop me. He probably thought my confession was useless. Maybe it was, given all the bad, bad things so many other people here had done, but I was armed tonight with far more than just words.

"Some of you might remember my mother. Some of you might remember that Eira Snow was killed in an accidental fire, along with her oldest daughter, Annabella. I supposedly died in that fire too, along with my baby sister, Bria."

I nodded to Bria, who returned the gesture. "But Bria and I didn't die, and there was nothing accidental about the fire that destroyed our home. Mab Monroe set the blaze. Mab killed my mother with her Fire magic, and she did so on Mason's orders."

Once again, Mason did nothing to stop me, so I pressed on.

"Not only is Mason the head of the Circle, but he's also my uncle. The twin brother to my father, Tristan Mitchell." I paused, staring out over the crowd. "Mason tortured my father to death with his Stone magic right here at the Mitchell family mansion, and a few weeks ago, he tried to kill me here too."

Mason waved his hand, dismissing my accusations. "You have no proof of any of this," he called out. "But you're right about one thing. All these people definitely know *you*, Gin. They know you're the Spider, an assassin, a cold-blooded killer."

"You're absolutely right. I am all of those things, and I've never pretended to be anything different." I stabbed my finger at him. "Unlike you, putting on this ridiculous dog-and-pony show and swooping in like you want to save Ashland. You don't want to *save* anything. All you want to do is line your own pockets, and you don't care whom you have to kill in order to make it happen."

"Then how does that make us any different?" Mason sneered at me. "The strong thrive, and the weak suffer. That's simply the law of nature."

I shook my head. "Maybe that's your law, but it's not *mine*. You asked how we were different. Well, for starters, I don't make deals with people and then try to kill them."

I paused. "Isn't that right, Drusilla?"

"Ms. Blanco is entirely correct on that point." A familiar feminine voice floated through the air.

Drusilla Yang strode forward to the front of the crowd, arm in arm with Charles. The Fire elemental looked stunning in a long red evening gown, while her father was quite distinguished in his tuxedo. More surprised murmurs rippled through the crowd.

Drusilla looked at Emery. "What's that old saying? Oh, yes. The reports of my death were greatly exaggerated."

The giant's eyes bulged, and she shot a nervous glance over at Mason, who gave her an icy glare in return. Not only had Emery failed to frame me for Drusilla's murder, but she'd also bungled actually killing Drusilla. That was two strikes against the giant. One more, and Mason might just go ahead and murder Emery himself.

Drusilla looked out over the crowd, much the same way I had done. "The video you saw was real. Every single second of it. Emery Slater and her men tried to kill me in the Bellum Bank, despite my family's no-violence policy—a policy that many of you have benefited from over the years, just as you've benefited from doing business with the Bellum Bank."

She gestured at me. "Gin Blanco saved my life and protected me and everyone who works at my bank from Emery Slater and her men. I am in her debt. And if there is one thing you should know about me and my family, it's that we always honor our debts."

Drusilla glanced at her father, who stepped forward.

Charles Yang stared at Mason. "The Bellum Bank will not be loaning you any money for your development project, and we will no longer do business with you or any of your associates. Effective immediately."

More shocked gasps rippled through the crowd, louder than before, and the mayor, the police chief, and the city planner actually clutched their stomachs, as though they were going to be physically ill. Yeah, the thought of losing all the hefty bribes Mason had promised them for pushing the project through was probably enough to make even the most greedy official panic.

"You can't do that," Mason said in a low, angry voice. "We have a signed contract."

"We did—until you tried to murder my daughter," Charles replied in an icy tone. "In my own bank, no less."

"I'll take you to court," Mason threatened.

Charles gave an unconcerned shrug. "Go ahead. From what Ms. Blanco has told my daughter, I have a lot more money and far more lawyers at my disposal than you do."

Mason's mouth opened, but no words came out. Once again, he didn't have an answer.

Charles tipped his head at me. I returned the gesture. He held his arm out to Drusilla, who took it, then looked out over the crowd again.

"We're leaving," Charles said. "And anyone who wants to continue to do business with the Bellum Bank will do the same."

Drusilla shot me a worried look, but I nodded, telling her that it was okay. I wanted people to leave. My fight with Mason could only end one way now, and I didn't want anyone else, not even Ashland's greedy criminals, to get hurt in the crossfire.

Charles and Drusilla left the terrace and stepped back inside the mansion, vanishing from sight.

Several seconds passed in eerie, utter silence. Then, in ones and twos and threes, other people began to follow the Yangs.

Folks set down their champagne glasses and plates of half-eaten hors d'oeuvres and beat a hasty retreat off the terrace. The guests, the waiters, the members of the string quartet. Everyone left, including the mayor, the police chief, and the city planner, who all skedaddled away as fast as possible, not even bothering to glance back at Mason.

The mass exodus didn't take long, and a few minutes later, the only folks left on the terrace were me and my friends, along with Emery and the giants. And Mason, of course. He was still standing behind the podium, a bewildered look on his face, as if he couldn't quite figure out how everything had gone so very wrong so very quickly.

Mason focused on me again, and his face hardened. "You think you've won? Please. Your little theatrics don't matter," he hissed. "Not one damn bit. I still have Fletcher's money, *my* money. That's more than enough to start my development. And once I break ground on it, everything else will fall into place, and everyone else will fall back into line."

"Or what? You'll torture and kill them like you did my parents?" I shook my head. "It's too late for that, Uncle. Look around. The thing that made you so successful for so long was that no one knew you even existed. Well, you outed yourself in a major way tonight. There's no putting that genie back into the bottle. You can't operate the Circle from the shadows anymore and expect people not to notice or know that you're the one threatening them."

I gestured at Emery. "And she can't operate from the shadows anymore either."

Mason shrugged. "I can find someone else to take care of things for me. I always do."

Emery jerked back in surprise, as if it had never occurred to her that she was as disposable to him as everyone else was. Mason didn't seem to notice Emery's consternation, but her eyes slowly narrowed, and I could almost see the wheels turning in the giant's mind as she thought of the best way to extricate herself from this situation.

"You haven't won anything, Gin." Mason sneered at me again. "Money fixes *everything*, especially in Ashland. It always has. Once I throw enough of it around, people will forget all about your little tirade. No one wants to risk losing out on an opportunity like this. I have every last penny that Fletcher stole from me. That money is going to speak volumes for me and drown out your pitiful mewling here tonight."

I couldn't help myself. I laughed.

And laughed. And laughed some more.

Mason frowned. So did all the giants, except for Emery, who was subtly sidling to the left, as though she wanted to leave the terrace the same way everyone else had.

"What's so damn funny?" Mason growled.

I spewed out a few more laughs, then wiped the tears out of the corners of my eyes. "You haven't put it together yet, have you? You should have started thinking about it the second you saw Drusilla."

"Thinking about what?" He ground out the words.

I smiled at him. "That if Drusilla's death was fake, then maybe the money was fake too."

Mason's eyes widened, all the color drained from his face, and he actually swayed on his feet, as though I had knocked the ground right out from under him. "But...but I *saw* the money. The jewelry, the shrink-wrapped bundles of cash, even those stupid bags of coins. I have them all in a secure location."

I shook my head and clucked my tongue in mock sympathy. "Oh, Uncle. All you have are some pretty costume necklaces, piles of worthless paper, and a few thousand dollars in loose change. That's not going to be nearly enough to fund your downtown destruction project."

"I don't believe you," he snapped.

I reached into my pocket. Emery tensed, as did the rest of the giants, but they didn't reach for their weapons. Not yet. I drew out the fake hundred Finn had given me in the vault the day this whole thing had started. "Here. See for yourself."

Mason flapped his hand, and one of the giants crept forward, snatched the money out of my hand, and scurried over to my uncle. Mason grabbed the bill and held it up to the light.

"Check the serial number," I called out in a helpful voice.

"F8KE..." Mason's voice trailed off, and he crumpled the bill into a tight ball and threw it back at me. "Fletcher fucking Lane."

I picked up the bill, smoothed it out, and tucked it back into my pocket. Oh, how I wished the old man were here to see this. It was just the kind of sly, sneaky, dastardly, devastating revenge he would appreciate, and I was so happy I was the one finally dishing it out to our enemy.

Mason stewed for several seconds, but then his eyes slowly narrowed to slits. "Well, if I don't have the money, then that means *you* have it. That's why you're here chattering at me. That's why you think you've won."

He shook his head. "How many times do I have to tell you, Gin? You haven't won anything."

"How do you figure?"

He huffed. "Please. We both know that all I have to do is threaten Bria or one of your precious friends, and you'll be begging to turn the money over to me."

"Yesterday you would have been absolutely right about that—but not today."

"Why not?"

I grinned again. "Because I don't have the money anymore."

Mason blinked a few times, looking even more puzzled. "What?"

Once again, my smug smile must have convinced him that I was telling the truth, because his face paled again, and a faint sheen of sweat popped out on his forehead.

"What did you do with the money?" he demanded. "Tell me. Right now."

My grin widened, and I told him the last strand of my plan. "I gave it all away."

✳ 27 ✳

ilence dropped over the terrace. No one moved or spoke, although I could once again hear the mansion's stones. Their shocked whispers chimed out like cymbals clanging together in my mind. The stones were so attuned to my uncle's emotions that they were already reflecting back his sick, stunned disbelief.

"You...gave...the...money...away?" Mason slowly, clearly enunciated each word, as if he was trying to speak some foreign language and wasn't quite sure he was saying the right thing to communicate his thought.

"Every...last...penny."

Mason kept staring at me, more and more horror filling his face. Even Emery stopped her subtle exit from the terrace to stare at me, her mouth gaping in surprise. The giant guards looked back and forth at each other, shifting on their feet. I wondered if Mason had promised them a bonus for their work here tonight. Well, if he had, they were never going to collect it.

"You know as well as I do how clever Fletcher was," I said. "All those gold bars. All those shrink-wrapped bricks of cash. All those necklaces and rings and watches. They were all just for show. The *real* money was in the rare coins Fletcher had laid out on the table, the ones that spelled out my name. The ones that Emery threw onto the floor because she thought they were just regular pennies and dimes and quarters."

I looked at the giant. "Thanks for that—and for clearing out the vault. You and your men made it *so* much easier for me to go back and retrieve all those rare coins."

Mason glared at Emery, who grimaced. He glowered at her for a few more seconds, then swung his angry gaze back to me.

"*The money*," he hissed. "What did you do with the money?"

"I told you. I gave it all away."

He shook his head like he had water in his ears and just couldn't understand what I was saying. "No, I don't believe you. No one in their right mind just *gives away* fifty million dollars."

"Well, according to Finn, I'm hardly ever in my right mind," I drawled.

"Truer words, never spoken," my brother chirped.

I ignored his cheery voice and kept staring at Mason. "I knew this would happen, that you would focus on the money. After all, it's one of the few things you actually care about, that you actually *need*. I also knew that as long as I had the money, my friends would be targets. You've already kidnapped Bria and Lorelei, and you let Emery beat Liam to within an inch of his life. I couldn't bear for you to hurt anyone else, so I decided to do the one thing you would never expect, the one thing no one could ever undo. I gave all the money away."

Mason threw his hands out wide. "How? How did you give that much money away? You couldn't have gotten rid of it all since yesterday."

"Drusilla Yang helped me. I gave her Fletcher's coins, and she gave me a whole lot of cold, hard cash in return," I replied. "After the battle at the bank yesterday, my friends and I loaded several suitcases stuffed with money into the Pork Pit food truck. And then we drove around town, visiting our favorite charities and making donation after donation after donation. Ten thousand dollars here. Twenty-five thousand dollars there. Fifty, a hundred thousand. You'd be surprised how quickly it adds up. Why, we hit just about every library, soup kitchen, homeless shelter, food bank, and animal shelter in the greater Ashland area."

I glanced over at Silvio. "Are we still trending online?"

My assistant glanced down at his phone. "Yep. Hashtag AshlandStrong, Hashtag PorkPitPalooza, and Hashtag TheSpiderForever are all still trending. The local news outlets are starting to pick up the story too."

I grinned. "Excellent. I've really been wanting my own hashtags."

"So you gave the money away. So what?" Mason growled. "I might not be able to get those coins from the Yangs, but I can certainly send Emery and my men to retrieve the cash you foolishly squandered on all those charities. Maybe not all of it but enough for me to start my project."

"I thought you might try something like that, so I made a special stop yesterday and gave a slightly larger donation to one organization in particular." I waved my hand at Silvio. "If you will be so kind as to share the good news."

Silvio cleared his throat, looked at his phone again, and started reading. "*The Ashland Historical Association is pleased to announce it has received a five-million-dollar donation to preserve and restore several downtown buildings, including the one that houses the Pork Pit barbecue restaurant. That building was constructed in the early nineteen hundreds and is considered a historic landmark.*"

Mason reared back in surprise. "You gave a donation to the historical association? *My* historical association?"

"One and the same," I replied. "And I have you to thank for the idea. When you had Emery bring Bria, Lorelei, and me here a few weeks ago, you droned on and on and *on* about how the historical association had preserved the Mitchell family mansion. So I decided to see if it would do the same thing for the Pork Pit. And guess what? The historical association director was more than happy to accommodate my request when I strolled into her house yesterday afternoon and dropped a big bag of cash on her kitchen table."

I paused and tapped my index finger on my lips, as though a thought had just occurred to me. "I guess you're right. Money *is* all that matters in Ashland. And I absolutely *adore* the irony of using your own money to screw you over six ways from Sunday."

Mason fell silent, although he kept staring at me. His eyebrows creased in thought, and I could almost see the wheels frantically spinning around and around in his mind as he tried to figure some way out of this. But I had made sure there was no escape for him—not this time.

"When I found your missing black ledger, I also came across a letter that Fletcher had written to me. He told me that I didn't have to be stronger in my magic to beat you, just smarter. He was absolutely right about that. And now all the strands of Fletcher's plan—and mine too—have finally fallen into place, and *you're* the one who's trapped in *my* web, Uncle. The only question is how much you're going to squirm before I kill you."

I palmed a knife, welcoming the feel of the spider rune stamped into the hilt pressing against the larger, matching scar embedded in my palm. This might be the last time I ever wielded my knife, and I was going to embrace every single second of it.

"Oh, you've certainly been clever, Gin, but I can still kill you. Now that my money is gone, there's no reason to let you live a second longer." Mason waved his hand again. "Emery. Dispose of her. Now."

But instead of charging at me or ordering her men to do the same, the giant sighed and shook her head. "No. It's over. Blanco is right. She's won. Without the Yangs' loan or your missing money, we can't do *anything*, including paying the bribes you promised to the city officials. We should leave now and get out of town while we still can. It won't be long before Charles Yang or some other underworld boss comes back here with a squad of men to kill us, loot the mansion, and steal whatever they can get their hands on."

"For once, Emery and I are in complete agreement," I said. "Charles is extremely upset that you tried to murder his daughter. Why, it wouldn't surprise me if he returned with his whole family so that the Yangs can use their Fire magic to burn you alive inside your own mansion—just like Mab burned my mother inside our home. Wouldn't that be some poetic justice?"

Mason's gaze flicked up to the mansion looming over us all. Once again, the stones muttered, reflecting his mood, which was turning darker, angrier, and more murderous by the second. I watched him closely, not wanting to be taken off guard, even as I reached for my Ice magic, getting ready to block whatever attack he made.

"Emery," Mason growled. "Kill her. Now."

The giant shook her head again. "No. I've been in this situation before, so I know exactly how it ends. You might be the most powerful elemental around, Mason, but Blanco has outsmarted you, and she'll find some way to kill you, just like she killed Madeline and Uncle Elliot. I'm not going to be another one of her victims."

"Aw, Ems, you flatter me," I drawled.

Emery shot me an angry glare, then whirled around to walk away.

Liam stepped forward, blocking her exit. "You're not going anywhere. I still owe you for rearranging my face, along with my ribs."

Emery's hands clenched into fists, and she sneered down her nose at him. "I might not be stupid enough to take on Blanco, but I already beat you once. I can do it again, traitor."

"Seems like *you're* the traitor," Liam countered. "You're the one who's turning tail and running away from her boss."

"I don't work for people who can't afford to pay me. And thanks to Blanco, Mason is broke. So as far as I'm concerned, any deal I made with him is off." Emery raised her hands and cracked her knuckles one after another. "But I'll be more than happy to teach you one final lesson before I leave."

Liam's jaw clenched, and his own hands clenched into fists. "Bring it on."

I glanced around the terrace at the rest of the giants, who all looked completely shell-shocked. Then again, most bullies usually did whenever you got the better of them. "If I were you fellas, I'd be hightailing it out of here."

The giants glanced back and forth between me, Mason, and Emery. Most of them stood their ground, but a few hurried across the terrace and slipped inside the mansion, leaving like all the guests had done earlier.

I stepped forward, staring at Mason. "I'll give you the chance you never gave my father. Surrender now, and I won't kill you."

He laughed. "Please. You would never let me live."

"Of course not. I want you to turn me down. I want you to attack me."

He rolled his eyes. "But?"

"But I imagine that Tristan would have wanted me to at least give you, his brother, my uncle, the option to surrender. Tristan might have tried to take control of the Circle away from you, but only because he wanted to do things differently, only because he wanted to help people, rather than use and abuse them. But you couldn't stand that, you couldn't stand not being in control, so you murdered him in the most vicious, brutal way possible."

I shook my head. "It takes a real cold-blooded bastard to torture and murder his own twin brother. You think I'm a killer? You have me beat all to pieces, Uncle."

A thin smile curved his lips. "Well, according to you, Gin, I have nothing left to lose, so I should take everything away from you as well. If Emery won't kill you, then I'm more than happy to do it myself."

And that was all the warning I had before magic flared in Mason's eyes, and he snapped up his hands and threw his Stone magic at me.

Even though I had been expecting the attack, even though I had reached for my own power to protect myself, the invisible wave of Mason's Stone magic still slammed square into my chest, knocking me back five feet. My boots skidded on the terrace, and I had to windmill my arms, but I managed to hang on to my balance, along with my knife.

I growled and charged at Mason, but one of the giants stepped in front of me, blocking my path. Last mistake he ever made. I lunged forward and buried my knife in his chest.

The giant screamed and swung at me, but I ducked his clumsy blow and ripped the blade out of his body. Then I shoved him aside, my gaze zooming back over to Mason.

He watched me stalk toward him, an amused smile on his face. "Oh, Gin," he purred. "You're never going to learn that you can't beat me."

He flicked his fingers, and more Stone magic surged off him. This time, he aimed lower, and his power pulsed through the terrace, making the flagstones rise up like a tidal wave about to crash down on top of my head. I lifted my free hand, but instead of using my own Stone power to block his, I sent out a blast of Ice magic instead.

The second my cold crystals touched the flagstones, they stopped in midair and clattered back down to the ground, many of them shattering to pieces. White dust puffed up like powdered sugar and swirled in the chilly air between Mason and me, as well as gusting across the rest of the terrace.

"You're wrong," I called out. "I've learned a great deal since our last fight. I don't have to beat you with my Stone magic. I can just kill you with my Ice magic instead."

Mason blinked in surprise, but his mouth quickly flattened into a hard, thin, angry line. This time, he grabbed hold of the jagged chunks of flagstones and threw them at me, but once again, I blasted the shrapnel with my Ice power, and the flagstones dropped harmlessly to the ground before they ever even touched me.

Mason's eyes narrowed, and he waved his hand again. But this time, he didn't use his magic. Instead, he bellowed at the remaining giants. "Kill her! Now!"

The giants hesitated, looking back and forth between my uncle and me. None of them wanted to end up with my knife in their chest—or, perhaps worse, be crushed and frozen in the elemental crossfire between Mason and me.

"Emery!" Mason yelled. "Do your damn job. Kill her!"

My gaze cut over to Emery, who was standing at the edge of the terrace. She too was glancing back and forth between Mason and me, and warring emotions flickered across her face like matches lighting up one after another. Her hatred of me versus her anger at my uncle for tossing her aside. Her burning desire for revenge against me versus her disgust at him for falling for my tricks.

After a few seconds, Emery's face hardened with a decision. "Next time, Blanco," she snarled.

I couldn't fault the giant for her sense of self-preservation. If there was anything I admired about Emery, it was that she was a survivor, just like I was.

The giant whipped around, probably to run into the woods, but once again, Liam was there to block her path.

"Like I said before," he called out, "we have unfinished business."

"Fine by me," she growled. "Going through you will be more fun anyway."

Emery lowered her head and charged at him, while Liam raised his fists.

And that was all I saw before I noticed a giant sneaking up on me out of the corner of my eye. I raised my knife and turned in that direction—

"Argh!" the giant screamed, then toppled to the ground, a long, jagged Ice dagger sticking out of his back.

Bria stood behind him, an Ice dagger glinting in her other hand. It matched the gleam of the silverstone primrose and ivy-vine pendants around her neck. In that moment, she looked so much like our mother and Annabella that it made my heart ache, but I shoved the emotion aside. The only thing that mattered right now was finally, finally killing Mason.

The giant's scream rang out like a bell announcing the start of a winner-take-all prizefight. The remaining guards charged at my friends, and within seconds, the entire backyard was a battle zone.

Liam and Emery were snarling, grunting, and exchanging blow after blow, while Silvio was sinking his fangs into any giant who came near him. Finn was shooting and pistol-whipping enemies, standing back-to-back with Owen, who was doing the same thing. Sophia and Jo-Jo were also standing back-to-back, the younger Goth dwarf punching the giants while her older sister battered them with her Air magic.

Roslyn was also punching enemies, then shoving them toward Xavier, so that he could pummel them with his fists. Phillip was using his combination of giant and dwarven strength to attack the guards, while Lorelei was using her metal magic to rip the men's guns out of their hands, as well as blasting them in the face with her Ice power.

Chairs splintered, tables flipped over, and champagne glasses shattered, the quick, staccato *tink-tink-tinks* sounding like wind chimes scattered in the middle of the louder *crack-crack-cracks* of gunfire and the resulting shrieks and screams. Despite the noise and chaos, my friends steadily waded through the giants' ranks, taking down one enemy after another.

Bria stepped up beside me. She held out her hand, and I took it, feeling the same Ice magic flowing through her skin that was zipping through my own body. Our mother's magic, one of her many legacies to us. The thing we were going to use to finally end Mason.

I looked into my sister's eyes, seeing the determination blazing there and adding it to my own. Then, together, we faced Mason.

"You know what I see when I look at the two of you?"

He sneered at us. "Two little girls who are just as scared now as they were the night their mother died. It's too bad Mab isn't here. I would let her roast you with her Fire magic, like she should have done all those years ago, if she hadn't been so clumsy as to leave the two of you alive."

Bria jerked forward, as though she wanted to charge at Mason, but I gripped her hand even more tightly, anchoring her to me. He was the strongest, most dangerous enemy either of us had ever faced, and we needed to be at our cold, level best to beat him. Even now, I still wasn't sure if we could win, but we'd both agreed to try, and I had never felt closer to my sister than I did at this moment, holding her hand just like I used to when we were children.

Bria let out a ragged breath, but she stopped and squeezed my hand.

All around us, the battle continued, but my sister and I stood in an odd little bubble of space, staring at our uncle, the man who had caused us and so many other people so much pain, misery, and suffering.

"What?" Mason called out. "No threats? No taunting? No crowing about how you're going to kill me? No bragging about finally avenging your dead parents?"

Bria and I both remained silent. I'd already said everything I needed to say to him, and it seemed as though she had as well.

"Very well. I'll kill you both and finally be *finished* with things," he said, a bitter note seeping into his voice. "I'll finally be finished with Tristan, Eira, their betrayal, everything."

In that moment, Mason almost sounded...*haunted*. As if what he'd done to his brother and sister-in-law had dogged him the same way it had dogged me all these years. Oh, I doubted that Mason felt even the smallest shred of remorse for killing my father and then ordering my mother's murder, but doing those things hadn't gotten him the control he craved. Not really.

Instead, Mason's cruel actions had set off a long, long chain of events, things he probably never dreamed would happen, much less come back around to bite him on the ass. Like Fletcher stealing his money, or me finding that money and using it against him, or Bria and me standing before him right now, both of us strong, powerful, and determined.

Even if the worst happened, and Mason killed us, he could *never* escape what he'd done to Tristan and Eira. My parents had defied him to the very, bitter end, just as Bria and I were doing right now, just as people would *always* stand up for what was right.

Mason kept staring at us, but Bria and I both remained quiet. "Fine," he growled. "Die in your silence."

He growled again, then raised both his hands and unleashed his magic.

My uncle grabbed even more stones than before. The shattered flagstones, the benches lining the terrace, even some garden planters sitting out in the yard. One by one, he picked them all up, hoisting them into the air until they floated around his head like a mobile over a baby's crib.

And then he threw them all at us.

Bria sucked in a breath, and her hand clenched around mine. I squeezed back, letting her know that I was right here with her and that we were going to get through this together.

"Don't bother trying to destroy the stones!" I yelled. "Just coat them with your Ice magic! He can't use them against us if he can't feel the stones with his power!"

Bria nodded, her face grim, her blue gaze locked on the stones flying toward us.

Together, we snapped up our hands and sent out wave after wave after wave of Ice magic, as though we were blasting a blizzard over the backyard. One by one, the combined bluish-white crystals of our power covered the stones, benches, and planters, and they all dropped out of the air like dead flies.

But Mason reached for even more magic, and more stones, benches, and planters started flying through the air. Bria and I kept swatting them away with our Ice magic, but every time we got rid of most of them, still more rose to take their place.

"There are too many of them!" Bria yelled. "How much magic does he have?"

And that was the problem with my plan—that had *always* been the problem with my plan.

Mason had more raw magic than any other elemental I'd ever encountered, even Mab Monroe. Even with Bria's help and the additional Ice power in our mother's and sister's silverstone pendants, it was painfully apparent that we were going to run out of magic long before Mason did. And then he could use all the resulting stone shrapnel to torture and kill us just like he had done to our father.

Still, we had to try to beat him—or, rather, *I* had to try to beat him.

After all, this was my plan, so I should be the one to suffer the consequences of its failure, not Bria and the rest of my friends.

"Cover me!" I yelled.

"Gin! What are you doing?" Bria yelled back.

I didn't answer her. I didn't have the energy for it. No, right now, my sole focus was on getting to Mason. I might not be able to cut him with my knife, but I could certainly get him to aim his magic solely at me. Our only hope was for me to distract him, to make his magic waver, to make him lose his grip on his Stone power, so that his body would be momentarily vulnerable.

One bloody second—that was all I needed to finally gut the bastard.

Or maybe Bria could blast him with her Ice magic. Or Finn could shoot him in the head. Or someone else could use my uncle's distraction to kill him. It didn't much matter who struck the fatal blow, as long as he died.

But even if none of that worked, I still had to try.

So I charged at my uncle. Mason waved his hand again, sending more stones shooting out at me. Well, at least he wasn't targeting Bria anymore. So I bobbed and weaved and ducked and did my best to dodge the flying chunks of stone, but pieces of shrapnel filled the air like swarms of bees, and I couldn't avoid them all.

A fist-sized stone slammed into my left thigh. A dagger-like shard cut my right forearm. Another shard sliced across my left shoulder. Bruises and blood bloomed on my body like spring flowers, but I kept going, my gaze still focused on Mason.

His eyes narrowed, an evil grin split his lips, and he waved his hand yet again. I flinched, expecting another vicious attack, but this time, his magic sailed right on by me.

My head snapped around, and I looked back just in time to see his power slam into Bria and toss her through the air. My sister hit the ground hard, and she didn't move after that.

"Bria!" I screamed.

She still didn't move, but Finn rushed over and dropped to a knee beside her, a gun in his hand and a worried look on his face.

Mason took advantage of my distraction to send another round of rocks zooming out at me. I jerked to the side, but I was too slow, and one of the shards sliced along my right cheek, drawing blood.

I hissed with pain and started toward him again, but he

threw another round of magic at me, forcing me to stop and dig my heels into the ground to keep from being knocked off my feet like Bria had been.

"Enough of this," Mason snarled. "You want to see what true power looks like, Gin? Well, here it is."

This time, he lifted both his hands high overhead, and more magic poured off him than before—more magic than I had ever felt from anyone ever before.

I tensed, knowing I couldn't possibly hold back that much raw force, but once again, Mason sent his power shooting out at something else instead.

Crack!

Crack! Crack!

Crack! Crack! Crack!

My head snapped up, and my eyes widened in horror. My uncle wasn't targeting me anymore. No, he was attacking the mansion looming over all our heads.

Mason was going to use his magic to destroy the Mitchell family mansion—and bury us all in the rubble.

28

Out of all the things that could have happened, I hadn't expected this.

Oh, coming here had definitely been a risk but a necessary one to expose Mason as the murderous fraud he truly was. And really, there was no place in Ashland where I could face him that was completely, utterly devoid of stone. With as much raw power as he had, my uncle could pry boulders out of the ground if he wanted to. But I'd never thought he would destroy his beloved mansion. Not after he'd crowed to Bria, Lorelei, and me about how proud he was of the structure and how very much it meant to him.

Then again, he had collapsed the ceiling of the pavilion containing my father's tomb and had dropped it on me like a ton of proverbial bricks. I should have expected him to do whatever was necessary to crush me, even if that meant destroying something he loved.

Instead of charging toward Mason again, I stopped and waved my hands at my friends.

"Move! Move! Move!" I screamed. "Get away from the mansion!"

By this point, most of the giants were dead. Liam was still battling Emery, but he slammed his fist into her stomach, knocking her down to the ground. Silvio ripped his fangs out of another giant's throat and shoved that man away. Then he and Liam raced toward the woods in the distance.

Owen ran over and helped Finn scoop up Bria and carry her to relative safety as well. Sophia, Jo-Jo, Roslyn, Xavier, Phillip. They all managed to get out of the shadow of the mansion and make it to the edge of the woods.

Everyone except for Lorelei.

She blasted another giant in the face with her Ice magic. She turned to run, but the giant reached out and grabbed her arm, yanking her back toward him. Lorelei blasted him in the face with her magic again, making the man howl and stagger away, but it was too late.

Above her head, part of the wraparound porch cracked away from the side of the mansion. Lorelei staggered forward, throwing her arm up over her head to try to protect herself, but she wasn't going to be able to get out of the way in time—

An instant before the first chunk of stone would have hit her, a black blur moved behind Lorelei, and she was suddenly yanked forward several feet and thrown down onto the grass.

Thud.

The porch railing hit the ground less than two feet away from Lorelei's boots and broke apart, sending more white dust surging up into the air. I coughed and waved my hand in front of my face, trying to see what was happening.

The dust cleared, showing a familiar figure kneeling on the ground beside Lorelei—Hugh Tucker.

I didn't know where the vampire had come from, but he had used his amazing speed to push Lorelei out of the path of the falling stone.

Crack!

Another piece of the porch broke off the mansion and zipped through the air, heading straight toward the vampire.

"Tucker!" I screamed. "Watch out!"

His head snapped up. He saw the enormous stone zooming toward him, but he must have still been weak, because he just gazed up at it with a weary expression, instead of trying to get out of the way.

Beside him, Lorelei scrambled to stand up, grabbed his arm, and yanked him to his feet. "Run, you idiot!" she yelled.

Then she shoved her shoulder under Tucker's and half dragged, half carried him toward the edge of the yard as fast as she could.

Thud.

The stone landed roughly a foot behind them and shattered on impact. The resulting shrapnel punched into their backs and legs and tossed Lorelei and Tucker both down onto the grass again.

I tightened my grip on my knife and whirled back around to Mason. Maybe I could still get to him. Maybe I could still distract him long enough to shove my blade in his cold, black, dead heart.

Even as I took a step forward, I realized that I was too late—again.

Mason raised his hands, and more and more pieces of the wraparound porches cracked off the side of the mansion. The second floor, the third floor, the fourth, the fifth. One after another, the stone porches, railings, and more ripped off the side of the mansion, like my uncle was tearing building blocks off a dollhouse.

I grimaced and braced myself, expecting him to immediately throw the debris at me and my friends and bury us in boulders, but he didn't. Instead, Mason stood there in the

center of the ruined terrace, with these huge, jagged chunks
of stone floating all around his head, as though he were a
juggler who'd somehow managed to suspend his balls in
midair.

Horror, fear, and dread spread through me, burning like
venom in my veins. At the edge of the yard, my friends
watched in stunned silence, horror creeping across their own
faces. None of them, not even Jo-Jo in the more than two
hundred years she'd been alive, had ever seen anything like
this—and neither had I.

Still, despite the horror, fear, and dread pounding through
my body, I forced myself to look around, to see if there was
anything—*anything*—on the ruined terrace or farther out in
the yard that would help me. But there was nothing. Just
shrapnel and churned grass and other busted, broken,
battered things.

I was still clutching my knife, but even if I could get close
to Mason, the silverstone blade wouldn't so much as scratch
the surface of his skin. Not when he was so effortlessly holding
on to so much raw magic.

Fight smarter, Fletcher's voice whispered in my mind,
just as it had been doing ever since I'd read his letter to me.

I had been smarter than Mason by stealing and then
giving away all his money, so how could I beat him now?
What was the last strand that I needed to weave into my web
of death?

Desperate, I tapped the blade of my knife on my leg, as if
that motion would help me figure out how to save us all from
certain death—

Thump. Thump. Thump.

My knife hit something buried deep inside my pocket.
Something that I'd forgotten about. But as soon as I remembered it, I thought of one last, crazy, desperate plan.

I looked over at Finn. "Get everyone out of here! Now!"

My brother opened his mouth to protest. So did Owen, who started forward to help me. Sophia grabbed his arm and used her dwarven strength to drag him back to the edge of the yard and hold him in place.

"Gin!" Owen yelled, still trying to get to me. "Gin!"

His loud, hoarse cries shredded my heart, but I forced myself to turn away from him and face Mason again, thinking about distances and angles. I'd only have one shot at this, and I had to make it count—or I would die right here in the yard so close to where my father had.

So instead of retreating, I eased forward, slowly approaching my uncle, for the very last time.

"What do you say, Gin?" Mason called out. "Finally ready to admit defeat and die?"

Instead of answering him, I tightened my grip on my knife and kept slowly moving forward. The blade wouldn't help me in this situation, but I had one more thing that just might.

I kept going until I was about twenty feet away from Mason. Then I stopped, staring up at the enormous pieces of stone suspended in the air above his head. He had been holding them up for more than a minute now, and he wasn't even sweating or breathing hard. Despite the chaotic battle in the backyard, his dark brown hair was still perfectly in place, and his black tuxedo was still immaculate.

It was one of the most impressive things I had ever seen. I couldn't have managed it. I didn't know any other elemental who could have managed it either.

Then again, I didn't need to be stronger than Mason to kill him, just smarter.

And I was certainly that, thanks to Fletcher.

So I switched my knife to my left hand, then reached into my pocket and pulled out the third and final thing I had taken off the mantel at Fletcher's house earlier today: the sapphire paperweight Mason had given to Mab Monroe so many years ago.

I held the paperweight up where he could see it.

Mason frowned. "What are you doing with that old relic?"

"It was one of Mab's things that I bought at the auction at the Eaton Estate a couple of months ago." I stared down at the gleaming blue facets. "For the longest time, I couldn't figure out why Mab had it. Then, when I found out that you were the head of the Circle, I realized why she had kept it. As a visual reminder that you were stronger than her and that you could reach out and kill her anytime you wanted to with your Stone magic, no matter how useful Mab was to you or how many people she murdered for you."

"Of course, that's why I gave it to her," Mason replied. "Mab thought her Fire magic made her special, and she was always too ambitious for her own good. She needed reminding, quite often, that *she* worked for *me*, not the other way around."

I eased a few steps closer to him. "You did a good job setting up Mab as your front person, letting everyone believe that she was the most powerful person in Ashland, when it was really you. That was perhaps the cleverest thing you could have done, to make her a target for me and all the other underworld bosses for all those years, instead of putting yourself in the line of fire, so to speak."

Mason's eyebrows creased together in confusion. "What does it matter now? Mab is dead, and all that's left of her is that little trinket you're holding. It's not going to save you, Gin. Not from me and my magic."

I grinned. "That's where you're wrong, Uncle. It's *exactly* the thing that's going to help me kill you."

He frowned. "What do you mean—"

Before he could finish asking his question, I threw the sapphire paperweight, aiming directly for the center of his chest.

Bull's-eye.

Of course, it was just a paperweight, not even the size of a baseball, and it didn't do the slightest bit of damage, given his Stone-hardened skin. No, all the sapphire did was drop harmlessly to the ground right in front of him.

Mason glanced down at the sapphire, which was glinting in the white, powdery dust at his feet. Then he looked up, a chuckle spewing out of his lips. "Really? This was your big plan? Throw a chunk of rock at me?"

My grin widened. "Nah. *This* is my big plan."

I snapped up my free hand. Mason flinched, probably thinking I was going to throw my Ice magic at him again, but that wasn't my plan. Not at all. Instead, this time, I reached for my Stone power.

Oh, he still had more magic than I did, still had more raw power than I would ever have. But I was smarter than he would ever be, and my brains were about to be the death of him.

Instead of using my power on Mason, I focused it on the paperweight sitting oh-so-harmlessly at his feet. I blasted the sapphire with every single shred of Stone magic I had. Normally, my power wouldn't have any great effect on Mason, since he could just block it with his own magic.

And that was precisely why I'd decided to use the bastard's own power against him.

Even now, all these years later, a fair amount of Mason's Stone magic still coated the sapphire. I hammered at the small blue stone, adding my magic to what Mason had put on the sapphire so long ago.

And then I shattered it.

The sapphire exploded like a grenade at Mason's feet. He screamed and staggered back, trying to get away from the blast. Of course, given its small size, the sapphire didn't do all that much damage, but it spat shards up into Mason's face and finally made him do the one thing I'd been hoping he would do all along.

He lost his grip on his magic.

All those huge chunks of stone, all those heavy, heavy pieces of the porches that he'd ripped off the side of the mansion wobbled in the air above him. They dipped precariously, but Mason's head snapped up, and he used his magic to shove them all upright again.

He took another step back, but he wasn't watching where he was going, and his wing tip slipped on one of the many rock piles he'd created. Mason skidded to the side, and the stones above his head dipped precariously for a second time.

He went down on one knee, now visibly sweating from the effort of trying to keep all those stones upright. His hands and arms started shaking, and his skin also reverted back to its normal soft, vulnerable texture.

Mason looked at me, his gray eyes wide and the veins in his neck standing out from the strain of trying to keep his monstrous creation floating in the air above his head.

I cupped my hand around my ear, as though I was straining to hear him. "What?" I called out. "No threats? No taunting? No crowing about how you're going to kill me? No bragging about how you murdered my father just a short distance away from here?"

Mason snarled and tried to rise to his feet, but he couldn't do that without completely losing his grip on his magic. Desperate, he tried to shove the stones away from himself and throw them at me, but he couldn't do that either.

With every second that passed, the stones got a little

lower and closer to Mason's head. As much fun as it was to watch him sweat and suffer, I didn't want him to wriggle out of my trap, so I reached down and grabbed a snowball-sized chunk of one of the flagstones he had thrown at me earlier.

I didn't have any Stone magic left, but that was okay. Instead, I coated the rock with my Ice magic, then stared Mason in his gray eyes, the ones that were so similar to mine, right down to the power gleaming in them like snow swirling around in a globe.

"Good-bye, Uncle."

I threw the rock. This time, I aimed not for him but rather for the largest piece of balcony he was holding—the one hovering right above his head.

Bull's-eye.

My little Ice-coated rock smacked into the much larger balcony boulder. I wasn't quite sure what happened next— if that one small, jarring motion broke Mason's concentration, or if perhaps the tiny bit of Ice covering my rock further weakened his grip—but the boulder dipped precariously for the third time.

"No!" Mason screamed. "No! No! No!"

And then all the stones dropped at once.

One moment, Mason was staring up in abject terror at the rocks hovering over his head.

The next instant, he was gone, buried under the rubble.

Crack-crack-crack.

The rocks shattered one after another as they plummeted to the ground. Enormous plumes of dust rose up, clouding the entire area like an eerie white fog, and the stones *clap-clap-clapped* together, sounding strangely like applause to my ears. As if my father and all the other ghosts and haints who haunted these grounds were enthusiastically celebrating Mason's downfall.

I waited for the rocks and dust to settle. Then, still clutching my knife, I cautiously crept forward. I thought I'd killed Mason, but I wasn't taking any chances. He might have had enough Stone magic left to protect himself.

So I eased forward, stopping at the edge of the rubble and waiting for the worst of the dust to dissipate. When it finally did, I was greeted with a most welcome sight.

Mason lying flat on his back, half buried underneath the rubble.

I walked over and went down on one knee beside him, my gaze moving over his body—what I could see of it, anyway.

His legs were completely hidden under the mountain of rubble, and blood cut a swath across his stomach, like a line of red paint demarcating him from the stone. More blood trickled out of the side of his mouth, an odd, dark crimson streak slashing through the white dust that now coated him from head to toe.

In addition to the shattered stones, the main building from the diorama was also lying close to his head like a discarded toy, although it was as crushed and broken as my uncle was now.

Mason looked up at me. No magic burned in his gray eyes now, only pain—all the pain and fear and helplessness and desperation I had longed to see in his gaze. All the same pain and fear and helplessness and desperation he had made me feel over the past few weeks every time I thought about all the horrible ways he could torture my friends, my family.

Mason's mouth opened and closed, and more blood dripped down the side of his face.

Plop-plop-plop-plop.

Perhaps it was my imagination, but I thought I could hear each and every drop staining the stones, each one as soft as a bell tolling for the dead. One peal for each person who should have been here to witness this but wasn't. Tristan. Eira. Annabella. Fletcher.

"Help…me…" Mason rasped.

"Never," I replied.

And then I leaned down and cut his throat, just to be sure.

✷ 29 ✷

I kneeled there and watched my uncle bleed out. It didn't take long. A minute, two tops.

Even after his eyes were fixed and still and I knew that he was dead, I kept kneeling there, staring down at his body. Adrenaline and shock crashed through me, and my knife hand trembled, along with the rest of my body. Part of me couldn't believe the fight was finished, that he was actually gone, that I had actually managed to *kill* him.

The other part of me felt...so many things. Relief that it was over. Anger that I couldn't have made his death more painful, that I couldn't have inflicted some of the torture on him that he had inflicted on me and my father. Sadness that Fletcher, my parents, and Annabella weren't here.

All those emotions and dozens of others roiled and raged inside me, as though someone had tugged on my web of death and had set all the resulting strands to vibrating and swaying deep inside me.

Footsteps scuffed behind me, and a hand landed gently on my shoulder. "Gin? Are you okay?"

I looked up to find Owen standing beside me. More emotions flowed through me. Relief that he was okay. Gratitude that he had stood with me. But most of all, love— so much love for him and myself and this crazy, tumultuous life we were building together.

I surged to my feet and wrapped my arms around him, hugging him tighter than I had ever hugged him before. Owen wrapped one arm around my waist and tangled his other hand in my dust-covered hair.

"I've got you, Gin," he whispered, holding me against his firm, solid chest. "I've got you."

I shuddered out a breath and let myself relax into him for several long, quiet seconds, soaking up all the love, care, concern, and affection that flowed between us. Then, when my trembling had subsided and I was steady again, I drew back, cupped his face in my hands, and kissed him. It was a sweet, gentle kiss, careful of the injuries we had both sustained, but I packed it with everything I was feeling, especially the joy.

The kiss ended, and I drew back, staring into Owen's beautiful violet eyes.

"I love you." I rasped out the words through the dust and emotion still clogging my throat.

"I love you too," he whispered back.

I rested my forehead on his, drinking up his presence for a moment longer, then stepped back and looked out over the backyard.

Surprisingly, the damage wasn't as bad as I'd expected. The worst of the destruction was limited to the terrace, but the mansion itself was still standing, although large chunks of it were missing, and I could see the antiques and other artifacts in the rooms inside, as though I were peering at the furniture through the open side of a dollhouse.

Finn stepped up beside me and let out a low whistle. "The historical association people are *not* going to be happy about this."

"Then it's a good thing Gin gave them that big donation yesterday," Bria said, limping up beside him.

I scanned my sister, but other than a knot on her head, she seemed okay. I reached out and hugged her too, along with Finn.

One by one, the rest of my friends stepped forward. Jo-Jo. Sophia. Phillip. Xavier. Roslyn. Silvio. Liam. Lorelei. Even Tucker had stuck around, although he was limping, and his face looked pale, sweaty, and sickly again.

A low groan of pain caught my ear, and I glanced to my left. The other giants had all been killed, but Emery Slater was still alive. Her left arm was pinned underneath some rubble, but the hate-filled glare she gave me indicated that she wasn't even close to being dead.

"What do you want to do about her?" Phillip asked.

"Let's let Liam decide," I said. "He's the one she tortured."

Liam went over and stared down at the giant. He looked at her for the better part of a minute, then shook his head. "Maybe I'm crazy for saying this, but can you two arrest her for trying to kill Drusilla Yang?"

Bria and Xavier glanced at each other, then both nodded.

"Absolutely," Xavier rumbled.

"This isn't over!" Emery hissed, her face contorting with pain.

Liam glared down at her. "It *is* over, and if you ever come at me again, I *will* kill you. Understood?"

Emery kept glaring at him, but her arm was pinned, and she couldn't move, much less try to attack any of us.

"What do you want to do about Mason, darling?" Jo-Jo asked in a soft voice.

"Want me to dig him out of the rubble and dispose of his body?" Sophia offered.

I stared down at my uncle. All those emotions coursed through me again, and I knew that they would for quite some time. But in the end, I shook my head.

"No. Mason loved this place and all the secrets and power it represented. I might feel differently in a few days, but for tonight, let's leave the bastard here. Let this be his tomb for now."

I glanced at my uncle a second longer, then threaded my arm through Owen's and walked away, leaving the mansion behind, along with Mason fucking Mitchell.

We went around to the front of the mansion. All the guests and guards had vanished, and our cars were the only ones left. Since we had the place to ourselves, Jo-Jo healed everyone's injuries on the spot. There were lots of cuts, scrapes, and bruises, and Bria had a concussion from where Mason had blasted her with his power, but we were all more or less in one piece, something I was extremely grateful for.

Xavier pulled out his phone to call in the rest of the po-po. He wanted to make sure that Emery was pulled out from under the rubble and arrested. Roslyn stayed with him, and they both promised to update me as things progressed here.

"Hey," Finn said. "Where's Tucker?"

Everyone glanced around, but the vampire had vanished. Of course he had. I glanced over at Lorelei, who was staring off into the woods like she could see something the rest of us couldn't. Tucker might be gone for now, but I had a feeling he would be back sooner rather than later.

Since the cops were on their way, I ducked back into the

mansion just long enough to grab the fake *Reverie in Gray* painting, which had been untouched by all the fighting. Then we headed over to the salon. Me, Owen, Bria, Finn, Jo-Jo, Sophia, Liam, Silvio, Phillip, Lorelei.

Jo-Jo announced she was going to make hot chocolate for everyone, along with some chicory coffee for Finn, so my friends all trooped into the kitchen.

"You coming?" Owen asked.

"In a minute," I said. "There's something I need to do first."

He nodded and headed into the kitchen with everyone else. I walked down the hallway, stepped outside, and sat down on the front-porch steps. I scooted over to the side and traced my fingers over the spider rune Fletcher had carved into the wood of the top step so long ago.

"I wish you could have been there tonight," I whispered. "You would have loved being in the thick of the fight again."

Of course, the old man was gone, so he didn't answer me, but to my surprise, the wind picked up, howling around the house, tangling my hair, and kissing my cheeks. The gust didn't last long, only a few seconds, but it still made me smile and peer up at the starry night sky. I was going to take it as a sign that Fletcher was watching over me, even from the great beyond.

Behind me, the front door creaked open. Footsteps sounded, and Bria walked over and sat down on the step beside me. She handed me a mug of hot chocolate, then clinked her own mug against mine. We sat there, sipping our hot chocolate in companionable, sisterly silence.

After a couple of minutes, Bria set her empty mug down and glanced over at me. "You seem...lighter."

"I feel lighter."

And I truly did. I had been so concerned about Mason these past few weeks that I hadn't realized what a toll it had taken on me until right now. The boulder of worry that had been pressing down on my heart for so long had vanished, and equal parts relief, happiness, and exhaustion swept through my body. I felt like I could sleep for a week. Maybe I would, now that Mason was gone.

"Maybe it's wrong, but I feel lighter too, knowing that bastard is finally dead," Bria said.

The venom in her voice took me by surprise. "You're not usually as vicious as I am."

She shrugged. "Plenty of bad guys have hurt us before, but this was different. It was *always* different."

I nodded. "Because it was personal. Because Mason took our parents and Annabella away from us."

"Yes," Bria rasped, her voice thick with emotion. "He robbed us of our childhood. He robbed us of being a family with Mom and Dad and Annabella, of all those years we could have been happy together."

I nodded again. "Yes, Mason did do that. He and Mab and Tucker and everyone else who was part of the Circle. Even Fletcher, in some ways."

Bria eyed me. "But?"

I swept my hand out wide. "But Mason also gave us the opportunity to have all of *this*, to find this new family we've created for ourselves. You, me, Finn, Owen, and everyone else. None of this might have ever happened if it hadn't been for Mason. I'll always miss what we lost, what we could have had. But moving forward, I'm going to try to dwell less on the past and focus more on all the good things that we *do* have."

I started to add that I was also going to do whatever it took to protect all those good things, including her, but I held my tongue. I didn't have to say the words. That love, that promise, that need to protect beat just as fiercely in Bria's heart as it did in mine.

A wry smile curved my sister's face, and she bumped her shoulder against mine. "Well, if I'm not usually so vicious, then you're not usually this hopeful."

I laughed. "Maybe I'm getting soft in my old age."

She smiled again. "Maybe." Then her expression turned serious and wistful again. "I miss Mom and Annabella."

"Me too," I whispered back. "But we still have each other, and we always will."

"Promise?" Bria asked, her voice shaking, just a bit.

I wrapped my arm around my sister and hugged her tight. "Promise."

* 30 *

T he next few days passed in a blur of activity, meetings, and more.

Finn was right. The historical association folks were most definitely *not* happy about all the destruction at the Mitchell mansion, but Finn kept reminding them about my generous donation, so the members eventually moved on to the tasks of clearing away the rubble, seeing how badly the artifacts inside had been damaged, and the like. According to Finn, the historical association was hoping to reopen the mansion sometime during the summer. I didn't particularly care what happened to the property. With any luck, I would never set foot on the grounds ever again.

Emery Slater was carted off to jail for the attempted murder of Drusilla Yang. The giant had quickly lawyered up and was offering to trade information on Mason's many misdeeds for a lighter sentence. Either way, Emery would probably be locked up for quite some time, so I put her out of my mind, the same way I had Jonah McAllister, Mab's former lawyer, who was also awaiting trial on murder and other charges, thanks to me.

The final bit of business concerned Mason. His body had been removed from the mansion rubble, and Dr. Ryan Colson, my friend and the coroner, had asked what I wanted done with the remains. I thought about letting Mason's body go unclaimed at the morgue, so that the city would eventually cremate him, but in the end, I arranged for my uncle to be buried in the Circle family cemetery. I didn't go visit his grave, though. I didn't need to.

Mason would haunt me enough as it was.

A week after the fight at the mansion, I was in the Pork Pit, slinging barbecue like usual. It was after two o'clock, so the lunch rush had died down, and I was using the lull to sit behind the cash register and reread *Where the Red Fern Grows*, which had been one of Fletcher's favorite books. Mine too.

Silvio cleared his throat and slid off his stool. "Since things are a bit slow, I'm going to head over to the Cake Walk for my coffee date with Liam."

"Coffee date?" I arched an eyebrow. "I thought you considered those to be dirty words."

"Admittedly, my last coffee date over the holidays didn't go so well, but I'm much more hopeful about this one with Liam."

I grinned. "I'm so happy for you both."

Silvio grinned back at me. "Me too." Then he stabbed his finger at me. "But I'll be back in time for the late-afternoon briefing. I'm still collecting info from my contacts about how the underworld is reacting now that they know about Mason and the Circle."

The underworld was still buzzing about all the revelations I'd dropped during the mansion gala. I didn't know how much unrest the news would cause or if anything would truly happen, since Mason was dead and his downtown development project along with him. But I hoped things would be quiet—at least for a little while.

If nothing else, after my uncle's death, the remaining members of the Circle had scattered, and I was now the official, unopposed queen of the Ashland underworld. I still wasn't sure how I felt about that, but now that the job was mine, I was going to tackle it head-on, with my knives out and my magic ready, just like I did everything else.

"So don't get any bright ideas about sneaking off early, going home, and reading the rest of that book," Silvio continued. "We still have a lot of work to do."

"No breaks for me. Got it." I raised my hand and snapped off a mock salute to him. "Sir! Yes, sir!"

Silvio gave me a sour look, but his lips twitched up into a smile as he packed up his electronics, grabbed his briefcase, and put on his gray overcoat, scarf, and fedora. My trusty assistant was actually whistling as he opened the front door and headed off to his coffee date with Liam.

I went back to my book. A few minutes later, the bell over the front door chimed again, indicating that I had a new customer.

Hugh Tucker strolled into the restaurant.

The vampire looked much better than when I had last seen him the night of the mansion fight. His color had returned to normal, and his face had filled out to its previous shape. He was still using a cane, although he didn't seem to be leaning on it at all. He was definitely on the mend, which was something else I wasn't sure how I felt about.

Tucker hesitated, but he came over and sat down on a stool close to the cash register. His gaze flicked over to the wall near the cash register where the *Reverie in Gray* painting was now hanging.

"That's new," Tucker murmured.

"What can I say?" I drawled. "I felt like classing my gin joint up a little bit."

"With a fake painting?"

I shrugged. "Fake or not, its beauty remains the same."

So did its—and Fletcher's—message to me, although I didn't tell Tucker that.

I marked my place in my book with a credit-card receipt, then set it aside. "What can I get you?"

He shook his head. "I didn't come here to eat."

"Well, that's too bad, because you're going to eat anyway. So, what can I get you?"

Tucker rolled his eyes, but he ordered a barbecue chicken sandwich, along with some mashed potatoes, mac and cheese, and coleslaw. Sophia was in the back, doing inventory with the rest of the waitstaff, so I fixed Tucker's food and slid the plates across the counter to him, along with a glass of blackberry iced tea.

The vampire dug into his meal. I picked up my book and read a few more pages while he wolfed down his food. For dessert, I gave him a generous piece of the chocolate-cherry cake I'd baked this morning, topped with vanilla-bean ice cream and warm, homemade chocolate and cherry sauces. He wolfed that down too.

Finally, when he was done, Tucker pushed his plates away and looked at me, his face serious. "I came here to apologize, Gin."

"For what?"

He sighed. "Everything."

The vampire didn't say anything else, and I didn't ask him for an explanation. In some ways, Hugh Tucker was just as much of a villain as Mason had ever been. But in the end, the vampire had saved my life, and Lorelei's life, and he had chosen to help me find out what Mason was planning to do to the Pork Pit before it was too late.

I'd meant what I'd said to Bria on Jo-Jo's porch the other night. I wanted to focus on all the good things in my life, instead of dwelling on everything that had been taken away from me in the past. Oh, I might have finally killed Mason, but that hadn't brought back Mom, Dad, and Annabella. Nothing could ever do that, and I would always miss my family. But when Fletcher had willed me the Pork Pit, he'd also left me a letter, one that had urged me to *live in the daylight.*

Back then, I'd thought he'd meant I should give up being an assassin, and I had tried that—for a while. But over the past few days, I'd realized that Fletcher had just wanted me to find whatever made me happy—and being the Spider made me happy, despite all the bad guys, blood, and battles.

Daylight might not be for me, but the shadows, the gray, most definitely were. I'd hung the *Reverie in Gray* painting on the Pork Pit wall so I would never forget that—or everything that Fletcher had taught me about trusting my instincts and believing in myself.

And like it or not, part of letting go, moving on, and living in my version of daylight meant forgiving Tucker for the part he'd played in Mason's schemes and all the hurt he'd caused me. Or at least agreeing to live and let live when it came to the vampire.

"Thank you," I finally replied to him, and meant it. "And I want to apologize too."

He frowned. "For what?"

I shrugged. "Locking you in a shipping container for a couple of weeks. Cursing your very existence. Trying to kill you multiple times. You know. The usual. Finn calls it the Spider special."

A brief smile flitted across his face, and he nodded, accepting my apology as well.

"So what will you do now?" I asked.

Tucker shrugged. "I have absolutely no idea. This is the first time in…well, years, that I haven't been beholden to Mason. I've spent my entire adult life working for him or someone else in the Circle, and this is the first time I've ever been truly *free*. Not just of Mason but of my family's legacy within the Circle too. All the mistakes my father made and all the things I had to do in order to try to atone for them." He paused. "Although now, I suppose, I have my own mistakes and sins to atone for."

I could certainly relate to that. "You could always stick around Ashland."

He snorted. "And do what? Work for one of the underworld bosses? They're all idiots. No, thank you."

"They're not *all* idiots. Lorelei is most definitely not an idiot."

Tucker's eyes narrowed. "You should stick to killing people, Gin, instead of playing matchmaker."

"And methinks the vampire doth protest too much," I drawled.

He shifted on his stool, but he didn't respond. Interest flickered across his face, though, and that hunger once again sparked in his black eyes.

"Well, regardless of however you decide to occupy your time and enjoy your newfound freedom, I hope that you'll stick around Ashland," I repeated. "You are welcome here anytime."

Tucker frowned. "Do you really mean that?"

Another part of my letting go of the past was letting go of old grudges, like the one I'd nurtured against Tucker for so long for loving my mother but not saving her from Mab Monroe.

My gaze drifted over to the spot on the floor where I'd found Fletcher's body after a client had double-crossed us and beaten and tortured him to death. I hadn't been able to save Fletcher from being murdered after that botched assassin job any more than Tucker had been able to help my mother escape Mab's and Mason's wrath.

I needed to let go of my guilt and stop beating myself up for all my past mistakes, just like I needed to quit blaming the vampire for something that hadn't been his fault.

"Yes," I replied. "I truly mean it."

He nodded at me again. "I might take you up on that someday, Gin."

"I hope you will."

I held out my hand. Tucker reached across the counter, and we shook on it, marking a new beginning between the two of us.

Tucker paid for his meal and left. He stood outside the front door of the restaurant, as if he wasn't certain which way to go, but he eventually turned to the right, into the rays of sunlight dappling the sidewalk. I chose to think of it as an omen of better things to come for him.

I was doing that a lot lately, seeing omens in everything. Maybe I was truly getting soft and sentimental in my old age.

People strolled by on the sidewalk outside, while cars zipped up and down the street. Just another typical weekday afternoon in Ashland.

But the sun was shining brightly, and today looked and felt more like spring than winter. It wouldn't be long before the chill completely faded from the air and the summer heat started boiling up, and I would be here through it all. Cooking food, hanging out with my friends, dealing with the underworld bosses, and just waiting for the next round of trouble to stroll through my door.

But this was the life I had built, the one I had *chosen* for myself, and I wouldn't have had it any other way.

So I returned to my book with a smile on my face, my knives tucked up my sleeves, and more peace in my heart than I'd felt in a long, long time.

My name is Gin, and I kill people.

Always and forever.

✿ GIN BLANCO WILL RETURN...SOMEDAY. ✿

I started writing **Spider's Bite**, the first book in my **Elemental Assassin** series, around 2007, and the book was published in January 2010. Now, here I am, many years removed from that first glimmer of an idea, with **Last Strand**, book nineteen.

It has been a wild and crazy ride, with plenty of ups and downs, although I'm very happy that there have been far more ups. I never expected the series to go on this long, but I'm so very grateful it has. I also appreciate all the nice comments, emails, letters, and more that I have received about Gin and the gang over the years. Knowing that folks are reading and enjoying my books truly is a dream come true, and I'm so happy that Gin and her friends have struck a chord with so many readers.

Last Strand will be the final book in the series—for a while. As of right now, my plan is to write stories about some of the secondary characters and give them the same sort of adventures that Gin has had. But I do hope to write more stories about Gin someday.

But whatever happens in my life and my writing career, please know that Gin Blanco is always in my heart, as is your kindness in embracing her and the world of Ashland.

Thank you all so much for reading.

Jennifer Estep
New York Times bestselling author

About the Author

Jennifer Estep is a *New York Times*, *USA Today*, and internationally bestselling author who prowls the streets of her imagination in search of her next fantasy idea.

In addition to her **Elemental Assassin** series, Jennifer is also the author of the **Crown of Shards**, **Gargoyle Queen**, **Section 47**, and other fantasy series. She has written more than forty books, along with numerous novellas and stories.

In her spare time, Jennifer enjoys hanging out with friends and family, doing yoga, and reading fantasy and romance books. She also watches way too much TV and loves all things related to superheroes.

For more information on Jennifer and her books, visit her website at **www.JenniferEstep.com** or follow her on Facebook, Goodreads, BookBub, Amazon, Instagram, and Twitter. You can also sign up for her newsletter on her website.

Happy reading, everyone! ☺

Other Books by Jennifer Estep

THE CROWN OF SHARDS SERIES
Kill the Queen
Protect the Prince
Crush the King

THE GARGOYLE QUEEN SERIES
Capture the Crown

THE SECTION 47 SERIES
A Sense of Danger

THE BLACK BLADE SERIES
Cold Burn of Magic
Dark Heart of Magic
Bright Blaze of Magic

THE BIGTIME SERIES
Karma Girl
Hot Mama
Jinx
A Karma Girl Christmas (holiday story)
Nightingale
Fandemic

THE MYTHOS ACADEMY SPINOFF SERIES
FEATURING RORY FORSETI

Spartan Heart
Spartan Promise
Spartan Destiny

THE MYTHOS ACADEMY SERIES
FEATURING GWEN FROST

Books
Touch of Frost
Kiss of Frost
Dark Frost
Crimson Frost
Midnight Frost
Killer Frost

E-novellas and short stories
First Frost
Halloween Frost
Spartan Frost

CPSIA information can be obtained
at www.ICGtesting.com
Printed in the USA
FSHW011508050321
79222FS